DEVIL'S ADVOCATE

John Humphrys

HUTCHINSON
LONDON

First published in the United Kingdom in 1999 by Hutchinson

The Random House Group Limited
20 Vauxhall Bridge Road, London SW1V 2SA

Random House Australia (Pty) Limited
20 Alfred Street, Milsons Point, Sydney,
New South Wales 2061, Australia

Random House New Zealand Limited
18 Poland Road, Glenfield, Auckland 10, New Zealand

Random House South Africa (Pty) Limited
Endulini, 5A Jubilee Road, Parktown 2193, South Africa

The Random House Group Limited Reg. No. 954009
www.randomhouse.co.uk

A CIP catalogue record for this book is available
from the British Library

Papers used by Random House Group Limited are natural,
recyclable products made from wood grown in sustainable forests.
The manufacturing processes conform to the environmental
regulations of the country of origin

ISBN 0 09 180048 X

Typeset by MATS, Southend-on-Sea, Essex
Printed and bound in Great Britain by
Mackays of Chatham PLC, Chatham, Kent

for

Catherine, Christopher
and Val

Contents

Introduction

THE TROUBLE WITH journalism is that so few of us who have spent a lifetime at it can claim any lasting achievement. Engineers have their bridges, midwives their babies, teachers their snotty-nosed little troublemakers who ended up in the Cabinet thanks to them instead of in jail. The grandest of all journalists, the weekly columnists in the broadsheet newspapers who tell us what to think, may claim that they have influenced events and at least no one can prove otherwise. The most we daily hacks can claim is that we have tried to chronicle events and sometimes might even have got it right. The news camel train passes in the night and the dogs seldom even bother to bark.

By and large we have a good time while we are doing it. There may occasionally be danger, though no more than a frisson for most of us. I experienced just enough to satisfy myself that I prefer the risks of a live interview with an angry politician in a cosy studio to those of a live round from an assault rifle in a foreign war or a land mine buried in a dirt road. There are many hours of boredom, waiting for the conference to finish or the aeroplane to take you to a destination where you are not welcome and where the only decent hotel in town has run out of ice. But most of it is great fun and I have yet to meet a moderately successful reporter who would willingly swap his job for another. I certainly have no complaints, though my grandchildren yet to be born may curse the scrap book of my memory with which I shall bore them.

Curiously the memories that stay brightest are the details rather than the substance of the great events I have reported over the years. I remember only vaguely the speech Richard Nixon made in the White House on the morning he became the only president of America to resign in disgrace, but much more sharply, as I wandered the corridors, the sight of one of his daughters weeping alone in a side room. The celebration party after Nelson Mandela became the first black president of South Africa made less of an impression on me than a conversation I had the day before with a very old black woman as she waited to vote for the first time in her life. She patted the round belly of a heavily pregnant young woman standing next to her and said: 'My vote is so that this child will always have the dignity we never knew.'

In most respects it is much easier to report what is happening abroad than at home. I blush at the number of times I have stood in the capital of some foreign country in crisis and, having flown in no more than a few hours ago, delivered to the camera the immortal lines: 'The feeling here is . . .' A more honest way of putting it would have been: 'As the taxi driver told me on the way in from the airport . . .' You cannot get away with that when you are reporting on your own turf. The people about whom you are reporting will know just as well as you what 'the feeling' is.

Those taxi rides from airport to capital city took half an hour or so; my own career as a journalist began back in 1958. Perhaps it is about time I made my penance for so many snap judgements over the years by trying to extend my usual deadline from twenty-four hours to forty years. I want to look at the route we in Britain have been following since I made my first, nervous entry into a newsroom as a spotty fifteen-year-old and ask whether it is what we would have chosen all those years ago.

I want to explore a range of doubts and worries of my own and those of the thousands of listeners and viewers who have written to me over the years and see whether there is anything that links our many concerns. For more years than I care to remember I have made my living by arguing. The difference this time is that I shall be arguing from my own viewpoint, instead of playing my usual role of devil's advocate.

I believe we should all argue much more about many of the things that we have come to take for granted or accepted with resignation or even indifference because some powerful group or vested interest has foisted them upon us, or because we have simply not stopped to think.

I am not suggesting for a moment that an argument is not already in progress. For some people I suspect there is already too much of it in the columns of the newspapers and on programmes such as my own on Radio 4. But the problem is that we in the media get bored very quickly. Our excuse is that you, the reader or the listener, have a short attention span and do not want to see the same story covered day after day. In truth it is we who get bored, so we are endlessly seeking something new. Fair enough, that's what the news business is all about. But it means that no sooner has one issue been raised and more or less briefly aired than we are onto something else.

We are the children of our times, affected by the climate in which we live and the dominant culture. But climates change, and so does culture. If we do not look carefully at the climate in which we are living today, there is little hope that we can change it in the future – assuming that is what we want to do. So I begin with my own personal, impressionistic account of the climate as I have seen it change and what it might be doing to us.

If you have no worries, no reservations, about what has been happening and where we are heading in the future, then fine. You might as well stop reading at this point. But if you want to join in the argument I hope you will read on.

Section One

The shoulder-shrugging society

Chapter 1

The victim culture

ON A CRISP October morning in 1966 I was the new boy in the newsroom of HTV in Cardiff, the rawest of recruits in the television business. I was about to start on my second cup of coffee when the news editor handed me a piece of copy from the Press Association news agency. It reported that there had been a tip slide at Aberfan in the Merthyr Valley. There was nothing particularly unusual in that; it often happened. The waste tips above the old collieries were notoriously unstable and shamefully neglected; they were slipping and sliding all the time. Sometimes they took the odd miner's cottage with them; usually they just made a great mess of the road and the land beneath. This time it seemed it might be a little more than that. I knew the little village of Aberfan well from my years on the *Merthyr Express*. My closest friend on the *Express* lived there and I often stayed with him after we'd drunk too much beer in his local. So I knew that there was a primary school below the tip and we all knew that at that time in the morning it would have been full of children.

There was nothing in the PA report to suggest that anything very serious had happened at that stage. Even so, nothing else of any news value was going on in South Wales that morning, so the news editor thought I might as well drive up the valley to take a look. It was only twenty-five miles away and if I thought the story was big enough to merit sending a film crew I could always phone in and ask for one. I knew long before I got to Aberfan that this was more than the usual tip slide. The steep sides of the Welsh valleys are lined with cottages, little terraced homes of drab grey squatting defensively against the hillside. You could tell which were the miners' cottages – almost all of them in those days – because that was the day of the week when they had their small piles of coal dumped outside. Cheap coal was one of the few perks of being a miner. Normally the women would have been busy shovelling it up and carrying it through the cottage to dump in the coal house at the back. This morning they were standing at their doors looking worried, peering up the valley in the direction in which I was driving. They knew something bad had happened and so, by now, did I. None of us could begin to imagine how bad.

Two hours earlier – just after 9.15 – a group of workmen had been sent to the top of the big tip that loomed above Aberfan, grey-black and ugly. There had been some worrying signs that it was sinking more than usual. A deep depression had formed within the tip like the crater in a volcano. As the men watched, the waste rose into the depression, formed itself into a lethal tidal wave of slurry and roared down the hillside, gathering speed and height until it was thirty feet high and destroying everything in its path. From that moment the name of Aberfan has been synonymous with tragedy beyond comprehension. It crushed part of the school and some tiny terraced houses alongside like a ton of concrete dropping on a matchbox. And what that foul mixture of black waste did not flatten, it filled ... classrooms choked with the stuff until the building was covered and the school became a tomb.

The moment the news reached them, hundreds of miners had abandoned the coal face at the colliery which had created that monstrous tip and raced to the surface. And there they were, their faces still black – save for the streaks of white from the sweat and the tears – as they dug and prayed and wept. Many of them were digging for their own children. Every so often someone would scream out for silence and we would stand frozen. Was that the cry of a child we had heard coming from deep below us? Sometimes it was. And some were saved. I saw a great burly policeman, his helmet comically lopsided, carrying a little girl in his arms, her legs dangling down, her shoes missing. She was a skinny little thing, no more than nine years old. Thank God, she was alive. The men dug all day and all night and all the next day. They dug until there were no more faint cries, no more hope, but still they kept going. They were digging now for bodies.

I watched through the hours and days that followed as the tiny coffins mounted up in the little chapel. There is nothing so poignant as the sight of a child's coffin. By the end of it there were 116 of them. One hundred and sixteen dead children and twenty-eight adults.

When the rescuers finally left they went home to weep, to mourn their dead; to nights of sleepless hours reliving the nightmare; to cherish the children still alive and, later, to shout their anger at the criminal stupidity of the officials and politicians who had allowed it to happen. Never was anger more justified. The National Coal Board, who owned the mines and the tips, had tried to claim that the tragedy was an act of God. It was not; it was an act of negligence by man. The politician responsible for the NCB, Lord Robens, had even gone on television to say that the cause of the disaster was a natural spring which had been pouring its water into the centre of the tip and produced the 'water bomb' that finally exploded with such devastating results. The spring, said Robens, would have been 'completely unknown'. Untrue. Not only was it known, its presence was marked on local maps and the older miners knew exactly what the danger was. They had been saying so for years, and they had been ignored.

Twenty-three years later another disaster happened. This time ninety-six people were killed, the life crushed out of them at a football stadium. This was Hillsborough, a tragedy that was ultimately to change the face of football in this country. Just as at Aberfan, it was a tragedy that need not have happened. At Aberfan warnings about the condition of the coal tip had gone unheeded; at Hillsborough warnings about the press of people and the need to open another gate had gone unheeded. At both Aberfan and Hillsborough many people – including police officers – worked heroically to save those who could be saved. They saw some terrible things. But then the two sad stories begin to diverge.

At Aberfan the police did what they had to do and when they could do no more they tried as best they could to carry on with their lives. If they were traumatised by what they had seen, they did not say so, at least not publicly – the word trauma was not much used in those days. Many of those policeman would have fought in the last war, their fathers in the war before. They had seen such things in Northern France as we, three generations later, cannot begin to imagine, and perhaps they had been inoculated against horror. I had an uncle who was gassed in the trenches. He survived, and if he suffered long-term damage from the trauma he endured there he never showed it to us, but physically he never recovered. For the rest of his life he could not lie down to sleep for fear that his useless lungs would fill with liquid. He was remarkably uncomplaining. 'We did what we had to do and that was that,' was all he would say. He and many of his comrades had plenty of complaints to make about what happened to them *after* the war, but when they were in the trenches they were doing their duty.

The police officers at Hillsborough were doing their duty too. Whether they were more or less traumatised than the men in the trenches or their colleagues at Aberfan is a moot point, but their reaction was different. Some of them went to court to argue that they had been negligently exposed to trauma and had suffered as a result. Millions of pounds were awarded in compensation and the ruling was upheld by the appeal court. Two years later the law lords overturned the ruling. That did not stop other police officers at yet another tragedy. When Thomas Hamilton went crazy in an infant school in Dunblane he shot dead sixteen children and a teacher. Once again the police were called in to deal with the harrowing aftermath. Three years later two of the policewomen involved filed a claim for compensation for their trauma. They wanted

£400,000 each. In an interview the morning after the claim was filed the father of one of the dead children said: 'I don't think anyone ever thought it would come to this.' The officers said they had not received adequate counselling to enable them to cope with it.

More and more professional people are making claims for compensation because they have apparently been traumatised by events they had been trained specifically to cope with. A policeman saw his colleague shoot a burglar. He sued for 'psychiatric distress'. A paramedic in Glamorgan sued his health authority for 'psychiatric injuries' incurred in the course of his work tending to victims of road accidents. A young doctor was awarded £465,000 because she had been pricked by a needle and was afraid it might have been contaminated. It wasn't, but she got the money anyway; apparently she had not received adequate counselling for her fears. A deputy head was given a small fortune because he had been persistently bullied by the head.

My uncle would have been surprised at all that. He might have been even more surprised at the notion of soldiers in Bosnia seeking compensation for the atrocities they witnessed. His view would have been simple enough. If you sign up as a policeman, or a soldier, or a paramedic, shouldn't you *expect* that you're going to encounter some fairly nasty things? And shouldn't we require you to expect it? Isn't it part of the responsibility that goes with the job? By definition, compensation is paid only for something people should not have to expect to undergo: salaries are what we pay for the expected. So what the compensation settlements among professionals suggest is that our society no longer believes that policemen should expect to have to handle situations where people get crushed to death, nor that soldiers should expect to see carnage, nor paramedics the effects of road accidents, nor should deputy headteachers of primary schools expect to need to stand up for themselves against over-assertive bosses. I await with some trepidation the first case of a reporter suing the BBC or his newspaper for sending him to cover a war or a disaster that exposes him to nightmarish scenes.

It seems that as a society we have become much readier to see ourselves as victims. The evidence is there in the enormous increase in personal litigation in recent years as people seek compensation for things that have happened to them. Mark Boleat, a former director general of the Association of British Insurers, put it like this: 'Over the past ten years, there has been a huge growth in what might be called the "compensation culture". There is the expectation that, if anything goes wrong, then somebody is to blame and will provide compensation. People are now more inclined to seek compensation, aided by a media which encourages them to do so and by a legal system which now has this effect, and organisations are more likely to pay compensation, perhaps feeling it is the lesser of a number of evils.'

Personal injury claims made against local authorities are growing at an extraordinary rate. There were eight times as many in 1998 as there had been ten years ago. That's an awful lot of uneven pavements for people to trip over. In the NHS they now have to deal with about 20,000 claims for compensation every year. That costs the taxpayer about £250million. In the same period the insurance premiums that GPs pay to protect them from being taken to law by their patients grew five-fold. In the United States the biggest single expense a doctor has is the cost of his insurance policy. The effect can be grotesque. It means, for instance, that a woman is likely to have her baby by caesarean section rather than naturally because there is less likelihood that the child will be damaged that way, even if there is not the slightest clinical need for a caesarean. We are, it seems, heading down the same road.

Many – perhaps most – of the claims for compensation behind all this litigation will have been wholly justifiable. Some people really are to blame for things they do to others, and compensation is often the only sort of restitution that can be made. But the explosion in the number of claims being made cannot be explained in terms of more people doing more terrible things to others. What can explain it is a shift in our attitudes.

Language, as ever, gives the tell-tale signs about how our attitudes are changing – in this case, how ready we are becoming to see ourselves as victims. You hear it on the news and you read it in the papers all the time. People don't get injured in road accidents any more, they become victims of road accidents. They don't 'have' cancer, they are cancer victims. A football player is the victim of a bad call by a referee. And if he breaks his leg he doesn't just break it, he suffers it.

On the face of it the difference may not seem important but, slight and subtle as the change may be, the implications of it are profound in what they say about our changing attitudes: being a victim is not the same thing as having unfortunate things happen to you. In the first place, the very word 'victim' suggests you are helpless, unable to do anything for yourself, dependent on others for getting you out of the terrible situation you're in. It implies that the responsibility is not yours. But even more, being a victim requires you to be a victim *of* something: it is not the same as thinking that chance has dealt you a bit of bad luck which you'll just have to make the best of. If you are a victim it is because someone or something is to *blame* for the predicament you find yourself in. It is our readiness to blame anyone or anything outside us that is the surest sign of our growing addiction to victim status. 'Ah, I see,' a droll friend of mine said, when I was talking to him about all this, 'so you blame the blame culture.'

But it is true that things we used to hold ourselves responsible for, we now blame on others. When tourists start to sue holiday firms because they get a dose of the runs in the Dominican Republic, it is not because holiday makers have only just started falling sick in the Dominican Republic; it is because people used to expect to fall sick in the Dominican Republic, but now they think someone else is to blame for not having warned them that they might.

I remember hearing on the radio a glorious example of people *anticipating* the chance to see themselves as victims. The *Daily Mail* had been promoting itself with a contest in which the big prize was a seaside cottage, right on the beach. The *Guardian* had done a bit of enterprising and laudably mischief-making journalism and discovered that the cottage had been damaged in a hurricane some years before, and who knew what might happen in the future. The idyllic dream cottage, the *Guardian* suggested with tongue in cheek, might not look so idyllic when it was being battered by storms. The programme may or may not have seen the joke, but in any case there followed an earnest interview with the man from the Advertising Standards Authority. What were the rights of the person who won the cottage if it subsequently got damaged by high waves?

What? Here's a cottage slap bang on the beach and the new owner, who's just won it for free, needs to have an assurance that it will be protected from the unpredictability of the weather?

Getting away from it all, by the sea or in the country, seems to bring out the victim in people. A couple who made their fortune and decided that country life was what they wanted bought a pile and prepared to settle down in rural bliss. The trouble was that there was a farm next door and farms, it seems, can spoil the countryside. They took the farmer to court complaining that he was making the lane they shared too muddy. In the course of the case (which the judge had the sense to throw out), the offended wife remarked how unfortunate it was that cows made a noise.

Or take the case of the lawyer from London who bought a house next to a pub in a Norfolk village for his family to live in at weekends. He discovered that cooking smells and kitchen noise wafted over from the pub and he sued the village charity, which exists to help poorer people in the village but happens to own the pub, for £85,000 as compensation for lowering the value of his house.

What is interesting about these cases is how people turn themselves into victims when their expectations of creating a feel-good life collide with ordinary reality.

I would ordinarily be the last person in the world to defend the cigarette companies. They spent years denying that smoking caused the most appalling illnesses even when they knew it did. They deliberately covered up the evidence. They went on promoting their lethal products long after the link with cancer had been proved beyond doubt. They try to defend their indefensible advertising by insisting that all they're doing is protecting their own brands from competing brands and no, of *course* they don't want young people to start smoking. They make vast profits by selling things that help people die horrible deaths, and when sales start to dry up in countries where the truth has finally seeped through, they switch their attention to third world countries and push their foul products even more vigorously there instead. They are, in a word, loathsome. But, yes, there is a 'but'.

How in the name of common sense can anyone who has continued smoking for the last ten, fifteen, twenty years complain that they did not know what it was doing to them? And yet they do. Tobacco companies are being sued because these people say they have become their 'victims'. They are not victims; they are idiots. By all means sue the tobacco companies for covering up information or deliberately misleading us, but to claim that you are a victim when you knowingly embark on a course of self-destruction is to abuse the word and to devalue the suffering of genuine victims. If we choose to smoke it is our fault. Not, however, when we have a victim culture.

Seeing ourselves as victims means we stop seeing ourselves as responsible. But it has another effect. If we get in the habit of thinking we are victims and suing for the slightest misfortune that befalls us, those who might be in the legal firing line will want to protect themselves against the litigator. The best way to do that is to prevent us from doing anything that might involve risk. In other words our sense of responsibility gets whittled away because we are treated as children and not allowed to decide for ourselves

That was what Jack Cunningham did when he was the agriculture minister and banned the sale of beef on the bone. The scientists told him the risk from eating a T-bone steak was approximately the same as the risk of being hijacked on the M1 by Elvis Presley, but you never know ... so he banned it. I suggested to him more than once that if he really took that view then the government should ban smoking. Well, he said, we can't do that but we do put warning notices on cigarette packets. So put warning notices in butchers' shops, I said. Don't be silly, he said.

For the life of me, I still can't see why he could not have done so if the government really thought there was a risk involved and were not doing it for purely political reasons to appease our friends on the Continent. In any sensible society people assess risk for themselves and take decisions accordingly. A risk-free society is not sensible nor, ultimately, workable. The real problem is that we are not allowed to use words such as 'sensible' or 'common sense' now that we are all consumers in a risk-free compensation culture.

Now there's a word: 'consumers'. Why have we stopped being people and become 'consumers'? It is, when you think about it, a preposterous word since there is nobody, anywhere, who does not consume. It implies that 'consumers' are special sorts of beings in a way that mere 'people' are not. When we were people we did things such as buying and drinking fresh 'green' milk that had not been pasteurised out of existence, and eating bacteria-ridden cheese that tasted of cheese, blissfully unaware of the terrifying risks we were running. Now that we are 'consumers' we must be allowed to run no risks because, if something bad were to happen, we would turn into victims. Then we might sue, or even demand the scalp of a politician. Much better, think those in authority, to ban things and treat us as children who are not sufficiently mature to assess risk for ourselves.

Even if we were more likely to pick up a bug by eating real cheese made with unpasteurised milk than by eating the taste-free, cellophane-wrapped candle wax masquerading as cheese that's piled high in the supermarket chill cabinet there would be no argument for stopping us exercising our choice. But we are not. Green milk is no more likely than pasteurised milk to carry nasty things like E-coli and lysteria. They are killed off by the acidity of the maturing cheese. But at least give us the choice. I happen to prefer the infinitely small possibility of a stomach ache every fifty years to the other possibility of something hideous happening to my insides because of all the chemicals used to produce the processed rubbish. If others choose otherwise, that's fine. And let us try to put this sort of thing in perspective. From the number of prosecutions involving small cheese-makers you might think the stuff is one of the great killers of our time, but the data produced by the Communicable Disease Surveillance Centre suggests otherwise. Most food-born illnesses come from eating chicken and eggs that have not been properly cooked. They account for a third. Drinking water accounts for 2.7 per cent. Cheese accounts for a massive 0.1 per cent. *All* cheese.

Before the war there were 15,000 small cheese-makers in this country. Now there are 300 and falling. Social change and postwar economics have undoubtedly played their part, but petty bureaucracy has accelerated the decline.

My mother, and I suppose yours too, used to say things like 'a little bit of dirt never hurt anyone'. She probably couldn't have explained why, at least not in a way that would have satisfied today's experts, but everyone knew what it meant. Now we must never be exposed to any risks, to any little bits of dirt. In pubs we can't even have our own glasses refilled. We must have a clean one every time whether we wish it or not. We are well on our way to becoming entirely antiseptic and, remarkably enough, the experts are discovering that our mothers were right all those years ago. Children today are much more likely to suffer from a whole variety of allergic reactions and go down with all sorts of bugs because they have no resistance. And why do they have no resistance? Because their protected little bodies have never had the chance to build it up.

The last time it snowed in London I walked past my local primary school at lunchtime and was surprised that the school yard was not full of small children throwing snowballs at each other and trying to stuff it down each other's necks the way kids do. One of their mothers told me why. The school had kept the tots in just in case anyone got hurt. Similarly when the yo-yo was rediscovered in the late nineties one school after another banned them, lest a small nose was whacked. No yo-yo, no risk.

*

I cannot believe that most of us want to live in a sterile, antiseptic, no-risk, tooth-fairy, compensation-for-everything environment and yet every day we travel a little further down that road. The journalist Christopher Booker has made a successful career for himself cataloguing the absurdities of the regulators and the bureaucrats who are driving endless small companies out of business with their pettifogging and usually unnecessary regulations, and who are preventing things happening that have gone on happily for centuries. You might, I suppose, argue that businesses must have rules, but what of the rest of us? Why should our lives be regulated by the official worriers? Here's an example.

In Gloucestershire they had been rolling cheeses – big, fat Double Gloucester cheeses – down a hill for as long as anyone could remember. You have to be pretty crazy to do it. The hill is almost vertical and by the time the cheeses get to the bottom they're going at quite a lick. Get bashed by one of them and you know it. But still they did it. The young men hared after the cheeses down the hill, twisted their ankles, occasionally broke a leg or an arm, and lots of people risked the runaway cheeses by standing at the bottom and cheering them on. Completely pointless, totally eccentric, but they wanted to do it and if they took the odd knock so what? It was their tradition and their choice. Until 1998, that is, when the organisers were formally warned that next time anyone was injured they might be held liable for compensation. They said: 'But it's their *choice*. They're doing it because they want to do it.' The police said: 'Maybe, but that defence will never stand up in court.'

Then the organisers got a letter from the county council land agent asking for assurances about public safety. 'They particularly asked us to give them an assurance that the Health and Safety Executive had been involved in the planning of the event – which of course they haven't,' said Damien Whitworth. 'How could they ever be happy about an event like this?' And that was that. In 1998, for the first time for centuries, nobody got bruised by a Double Gloucester rolling down Witcombe Hill because they called it off. The following year the cheese roll was on again, but this time with protective fences around the hill in case anyone got whacked by a runaway cheese. Next year, no doubt, the cheeses will have to be made from foam rubber.

Do not be surprised if, one of these fine days, you wake up to find that trousers and tights have been banned. In 1999 the Department of Trade and Industry reported that carelessly pulling on a pair of trousers causes 4,400 accidents a year and putting on socks and tights another 6,585. The number of accidents involving tea cosies has, you will be relieved to hear, begun to fall. And no, I am not making this up.

In the summer of 1999 the Royal Geographical Society convened a special meeting because it was worried about the way we are over-protecting our children. Expedition leaders, teachers and parents are so afraid of accidents that they are abandoning field trips and expeditions. The fault lies with 'risk assessment, blame culture and cautious licensing authorities'. As David Hempleman-Adams said: 'We are becoming a society of softies. It is a crazy reflection of our times that we are surrounding our children in cotton wool . . . they will not be able to cope with risk when they encounter it as adults.' We may not want our kiddies to spend their lives walking across the North Pole or skiing down Everest, but if nothing is ever risked, nothing is ever achieved.

Short of actually banning things, the best you can do is issue warnings. But in the United States these have reached a new level of madness. 'This product is hot when heated.' Gosh. 'It is inadvisable to carry out open-heart surgery on your husband whilst driving this motor vehicle on the highway.' 'Warning! Do not insert small child in microwave oven and activate appliance.' I parody, but not very much. You can see why they do this sort of thing. If they don't, and somebody really is daft enough to put a cup of hot coffee between her bare legs while driving a car and, worse, sues for scalding herself when the laws of physics take their toll, then what can anyone do?

We in the media are partly to blame for the hysteria. We are endlessly finding a 'consumer crisis' where none exists, creating a panic and then, when the whole scare turns out to have been unjustified, forgetting all about it. The trouble is, a good scare story rather loses its impact if the headline reads: 'MICROWAVE OVENS COULD CAUSE CANCER,' and the sub-head reads 'BUT PROBABLY DON'T.' And it's not only the newspapers at fault. Anyone who has ever worked as a researcher on a badly edited investigative programme on television knows the routine: find a scare, however thinly supported, try to make sure children are involved and, if possible, the odd death, and dig up some academic – it doesn't matter how quirky his colleagues may think him – to give 'respectability' to the case. Then you're off. Before you know it some obscure backbench MP will be on the news gravely warning that unless something is done about killer zippers on anoraks we shall all be at risk and I'll be wanting to know from the relevant minister on *Today* when we can expect legislation. The minister cannot tell me to stop being silly just in case some idiot really does manage to hurt himself with a wayward zipper. Then our indignation would know no bounds.

The truth is that most of us see ourselves as reasonably sensible and responsible individuals who accept the need for a framework of laws and regulations to protect our basic rights and health but reckon we can look after ourselves pretty well otherwise. If we are grown-ups we also accept that many things we do inevitably involve a small element of risk. That's part of living. But if, increasingly, we are portrayed as potential victims who must be guarded against the tiniest vicissitude, that is how we will ultimately see ourselves. Victims.

Blaming somebody else is only part of the story of our growing addiction to victimhood. Sometimes there is nobody there to blame so then we have to find something else to excuse us from facing up to our own responsibilities. And the victim culture provides us with opportunities. Far and away the richest source is health. If you can discover that there is something wrong with you, you are absolved from all responsibilities. So we have become obsessed with our health. Polls show us that health is the thing that concerns us most. Two thirds of us worry about our health more than anything else. Objectively there is no reason at all why we should be so neurotic. We are healthier than any previous generation, our life expectancy continues to grow, and there is more care available than ever there was. But worrying about health serves a psychological function: it allows us to imagine ourselves as potential victims of bad health.

Professor Arthur Barsky, an American psychologist and authority on attitudes to health, puts it this way: 'Health seems to be one of those things where you can get caught in a kind of cycle in which the more preoccupied you get with health the less satisfied you are with your health.' It's the old business that if you keep a medical dictionary in the house you soon discover you've got all the diseases.

This notion that our preoccupation with health has persuaded us that we are victims of bad health is borne out by the figures. The percentage of the population who reported to a national survey that they have some long-standing illness went up from around 20 per cent in 1973 to over 30 per cent a generation later. The proportion who say they've had an illness that has restricted their activity in the last two weeks has almost doubled over the last twenty years. These extraordinary rises cannot be explained just by the ageing of the population, since the proportions have grown in all age groups.

What's going on is that we're finding more things with which to be ill. Sir Miles Irving, Professor of Surgery at Manchester, says: 'If one looks back maybe thirty, forty, fifty years then people had other ways of coping with illness. And in fact many things that were regarded then as merely discomfiture have now been turned into illness.' Another way of putting it is that people have been turned into victims. Things they used to cope with and take responsibility for become things beyond the reach of their responsibility. They become illnesses. The world is awash with new syndromes and disorders, all kitted out with alarming technical names that carry with them the authority of science. It always used to amuse me when I lived in the United States that nobody ever had a cold; they always had flu. They never had a sore throat; they had a 'strep' throat. It's happening here. And now, the more complicated you can make it, the better.

There's nothing quite like a string of Latin nouns you can't possibly remember to reassure you that you're the victim of something really nasty.

If victimhood requires the creation of the thing that's tormenting you, it also requires you to feel helpless and dependent. And that, as Roy Porter, Professor of the Social History of Medicine at the Wellcome Institute, says, is what happens. 'It seems to me that in the present climate of fear and maybe panic we are taking aspects of human life that are normal, risky activities and turning them into medical conditions in a way that is far from obviously helpful. And the danger is that the more you medicalise approaches to that you create new sorts of dependencies without any guarantee at all that the medical profession can genuinely help people who are suffering from, as it were, the regular course of life. And under those circumstances the fear is that you will end up with a situation where people cannot look after themselves.' What is happening is that we are expecting doctors not only to tell us we are suffering from some identifiable illness or other, but also to put it right. Because one of the things about being a victim is that even if you can't blame someone for the condition you're in, you can hold them responsible for getting you out of it.

Doctors, therefore, are becoming the new priests, the people who will save us. The number of prescriptions issued for every GP consultation has doubled in the last twenty years, and the reason is not so much that there are now more treatments (though there are), but because patients demand something to take. They expect the doctor to be able to 'do something' and, harassed and over-stretched as he's likely to be, he succumbs to the demand for the prescription to get them out of the surgery. The medical profession, and the wider science community, are in part responsible for making us like that. It's not just that the great successes of medicine – surgery and the magic bullets of antibiotics – have demonstrated that we can be cured, sometimes spectacularly, it's that scientists and medics among them cultivate the idea that their expertise has got it all sorted and that all we need do is behave and do as we're told.

The next time a scientist writes a book about how science is on the verge of having a Grand Theory of Everything, he should be hung out of the window by his fingernails not only for misleading us, but for encouraging us to believe that science has the answer to all our problems and that we can simply lie back and follow the instructions. Genetics is the most recent example of triumphalism in science. News reports give the impression that a genetic cause can be assigned to virtually anything, and while the more sensible scientists will make clear that that's not quite true, the idea that genes are to blame for all our defects is the ultimate spur to seeing ourselves as victims. We are the victims of our genes.

The cult of the expert persuades us that we don't need to take responsibility for ourselves because there's somebody else who will. If it's not a conventional doctor with a stethoscope and a fat prescription pad, increasingly it is likely to be some sort of New Age therapist, or maybe a counsellor, or somebody who offers a different kind of treatment. I have become a relatively recent convert to complementary medicine. Note that I do not say 'alternative' medicine; it complements and is not an alternative to conventional medicine. I used to think its practitioners were a bit like fortune tellers in a fairground, except that they have a white coat and a couch instead of a scarf and a crystal ball. Then my former wife was diagnosed with terminal cancer and I saw the other side of it.

She was given two choices: die within a couple of months without chemotherapy, or survive a little longer with chemotherapy and suffer the side effects. She chose to do neither. She refused the chemotherapy and opted for 'complementary' therapies: reflexology, aromatherapy sessions, that sort of thing. She knew she would not be cured – she was a fiercely practical ex-nurse and knew precisely what was wrong with her – but she wanted to die with some dignity and with the minimum of drugs. She lived for another seven months, during which she had some good times, was able to come to terms with her life and death, and was comforted enormously by the different complementary therapies. My arrogant and stupid assumption that the only good medicine is that which comes out of a pharmaceutical laboratory was comprehensively blown apart. My daughter Catherine, who had given up her job with Children in Need to be with her throughout it all, was so impressed that she retrained as a therapist and now has her own practice.

I do not believe my ex-wife saw herself as a victim, any more than the journalist John Diamond does. His cancer was caused by smoking and he has written brilliantly and movingly about every stage in the hideous process of the disease. There was not a word about how cigarettes were 'to blame'. He acknowledged throughout that it had been his choice to smoke the filthy things. It takes courage not to see yourself as a victim and to go against the whole climate that we live in, particularly when in some ways that climate has been brought about because people genuinely want to help those in difficulty. But it is wrong to make misfortune, even fatal misfortune, synonymous with victimhood when often it is not.

What's true of our attitudes to personal health is also true in the public arena. Whenever something nasty happens in a school these days – the killing of a teacher or the death of a child – we immediately cast a victim interpretation over the whole scene. Teams of counsellors are flown in and the impression is created that the entire school are victims needing help. The truth is probably not so stark. There will inevitably be one or two who find it difficult to come to terms with what has happened and they may need help, but the notion that 'teams of counsellors' are needed is surely nonsense. One of Britain's leading child psychiatrists – Professor Richard Harrington, who heads the department of child and adolescent psychiatry at Royal Manchester Children's Hospital – certainly thinks so.

Professor Harrington wrote in the Royal Society of Medicine's journal that counselling techniques were based on the notion that bereaved children must go through a 'grief process', but there is no evidence to support it. He believes that children are resilient in the face of death and encouraging them to 'confront' their grief can be positively harmful. Wise words, you might think, but the counselling industry is with us to stay.

I almost wept when I read how the American government reacted after some evil people blew up their embassy in Nairobi in 1998 and killed and maimed hundreds of people, mostly Kenyans. Inevitably, they flew in teams of counsellors. A Washington official pointed out, with breathtaking condescension, that 'these people' had no tradition of counselling and no 'resources' to help them come to terms with the tragedy. Did it not occur to the numskull that they might very well help each other to 'come to terms' with the tragedy, just as generations before them had dealt with the reality of life and death, and that sending in foreigners with no knowledge or awareness of *their* traditions would be about as much use as a cat flap on a submarine. I'll bet they would have preferred a few million US dollars to help the children who were orphaned or the people with their legs blown off.

Chapter 2

Shame and fame

IT WAS A hot afternoon in mid summer and I was opening the windows of my house in what the estate agents call a 'highly sought-after' London street. That means that it was once middle class, then went down in the world when housing associations bought some of the properties, and is now trying to be middle class again. What I saw shocked me. A pretty young girl was leaving the house opposite wearing the teenager's nineties uniform of T-shirt and jeans but, on the front of the T-shirt in large thick letters, were the words 'Fuck You'. Many of the teenagers in my street – noisy but otherwise perfectly normal and pleasant kids – seem to have difficulty forming a sentence without at least one four-letter word, and it occurred to me with hindsight that I was not so much shocked by the girl wearing the wretched T-shirt as by my own reaction. It was perfectly obvious why she was wearing it: for the same reason that when I was a teenager we wore ridiculous hair cuts or skin-tight trousers. We wanted the grown-ups to be outraged. That's what teenagers do.

What really dismayed me, I suppose, was that so many grown-ups can no longer be bothered to be even mildly outraged. We have passed through the so-called permissive society and moved into the 'why bother?' society with scarcely a jolt. Why bother to make a fuss about the offensive T-shirt or swearing youngsters or the lout with his boots on the train seat or even the grown-up lout bellowing into his blasted mobile phone three inches from your ear? It will make no difference and anyway standards have changed, haven't they? Well perhaps. What really matters is that attitudes have changed.

Let's go back, for a moment, to the beginning of the permissive society. Sexual intercourse may not really have begun in 1963, but it was a darned sight less problematic after the pill had arrived. No more furtively sneaking down Caroline Street, the nearest thing to a red-light district in the centre of Cardiff, where you could buy questionable magazines (no top shelves in respectable newsagents then) and condoms without the unimaginable embarrassment of asking the nylon-overalled and stern-faced woman behind the counter at Boots. Now it was up to the girls, and the boys were suitably appreciative. That's what it was mostly about: a *sexually* permissive society.

In many other ways the sixties were the opposite of permissive. There were so many things a confident younger generation thought should not be permitted and they did their damnedest to rail against them. They marched against the bomb and against Vietnam and against sexual and racial discrimination. They sat in on their campuses and made a general nuisance of themselves. They dropped out so that they could grow their hair long and live in communes and smoke pot and talk a great deal about righting all the wrongs of the world. And they thoroughly enjoyed the fact that the sexual revolution had arrived.

If most adults were shocked by it all, that was the whole point. They were meant to be. They were probably a bit jealous too. 'Kids today! Don't know they're bloody born.'

And they had a point. People of my parents' generation, who'd survived the horrors of war and the degradation of depression without the cushion of a welfare state, were entitled to look at these feather-bedded youngsters enjoying sexual liberation and a buoyant economy with jobs for all and shake their heads. But many secretly approved. Most wanted their children to have what they could only have dreamed of and the wise ones understood that long hair and silly caftans were a very small price to pay.

The girl with the T-shirt represented something quite different and I watched as a grey-haired woman, old enough to be her grandmother, passed her by, pulling her shopping basket on wheels behind her. She looked at the T-shirt and then looked away quickly. She was shocked, no doubt, but resigned too. There was something in her expression that said, 'How did this happen?' I suspect if the old lady had summoned the energy and the will to speak to the girl she might have said something like, 'Have you no shame?' But she said nothing. Which was probably sensible. Who knows how a youngster with 'Fuck You' on her T-shirt might have reacted to an interfering old biddy? The way the woman looked away and bit her lip conveyed the sense that you can't say anything these days. For that brief moment in a sunny London street, that tiny tableau of teenage girl and puzzled old lady seemed to me say a great deal. Our attitudes have changed. Where we might once have raised our eyebrows and reacted, we now avert our gaze.

It's a funny thing, this business of shame. It seemed to be part and parcel of life when I was growing up. If you did something that was wrong you might or might not have been punished, but you were certainly made to feel ashamed about it. That was part of the punishment. In a small and fairly tightly knit community a lot of people would get to hear about it, so it was difficult to hide, which is what shame made you want to do. The great thing about reading the *News of the World* in those days was not just the titillation but the thrill of imagining how those benighted souls caught *in flagrante* managed to cope with the shame of it all. Nowadays if it's shocking enough the culprit will get offered his own chat show on television.

So shame is not what it used to be. Increasingly we don't seem to care what other people think of us, and we don't seem to care that other people don't care. Good riddance to shame, some people will say, and they have a point. You don't have to go back to witch-burning in the seventeenth century to see what terrible harm and suffering can be caused in close communities with strong beliefs and no tolerance. The worst joke in the Welsh valleys when I was a boy was the old one about two old biddies gossiping on the street corner. One of them says to the other, 'I see that young Megan's getting married then.' 'Dew! There's a snob!?' says the other, 'I didn't even know she was pregnant.' It got a laugh only because the reality was precisely the opposite.

I knew a bright and extremely attractive young woman who disappeared from Cardiff just after she had qualified as a nurse, told no one where she was going and did not come back again until almost a year later. It wasn't until I was very much older that she told me she had gone off to have a baby. He was adopted at birth and she never saw him again. The nurse's father – a businessman who took his position in the local community very seriously indeed – had pressured her into it. He could not accept the shame of an unmarried mother for a daughter.

Many years after that, when I bought my farm in West Wales, one of my first visitors was a local farmer who stood in the muddy yard looking very embarrassed but clearly determined to say something of great import.

'I hope we can be good neighbours,' he said, 'but I will understand if you do not wish to be friendly with me.'

'Why on earth shouldn't we?' I asked him. It was hard to know which of us was the more embarrassed.

'Because I am living with a woman who is not my wife, and there are many in the village who will not accept that.'

It turned out that he had been a deacon of the local chapel and was now ostracised by many of his former fellow worshippers. What a contrast between communities. I wanted to tell him that in my London street he would have been in the majority and that many, if not most, of my younger friends got married only when babies started arriving on the scene.

I cannot believe that many of us would choose to return to the days when shame dominated our society at all levels, when homosexual men and women were branded as dangerous misfits or worse, when single parents and their children were stigmatised, when the word 'bastard' was used in its literal sense. We wince at what happens in a country like Japan where shame is felt so intensely that you can never admit failure, never own up to having made a mistake. There are businessmen in Japan who get up in the morning, put on their suits, go off into the business world, meet their old contacts, tell them they've changed companies and hand out new business cards. But the cards are a fake. The phone number puts you through to a fake secretary, paid to say the boss is out and to take the message. The call-back is never made because the truth is that the man has lost his job and is too ashamed to admit it. Shame can be a terribly destructive force.

But it is one thing to deplore the stigma attached to behaviour that we might no longer consider shameful; it is quite another to chuck out the notion of shame altogether. We still use the word shame, we might even still mean it, but less and less does it have any purchase. 'BRITAIN'S SHAME', said the headlines about the football hooligans at the 1998 World Cup in France. No doubt many people felt the thuggery at Marseilles was indeed shameful, possibly for England, certainly for those involved. But that isn't how the yobs themselves seemed to take it. Quite the opposite. They revelled in it.

Shame was supposed to make you want to hide your face; they wanted to get theirs on as many front pages and television screens as possible, and they did. Front page pictures in not only the tabloids but the broadsheets, action shots on every television bulletin of the boot or the bottle going in. Follow-up pieces about their lives back home, what their girlfriends were like, what their mates at the pub thought of them. Some of the older hands, those who'd won their battle honours in the past by fearlessly terrorising other fans or intimidating local people, acted as consultants and pundits for journalists anxious to get an insight into what passes for their minds. Thugs they might be; mugs they are not. After all, there's good money in it. Some have written books celebrating the art of soccer violence. It has all helped them to become somebody. One of them told the *Daily Mail*, 'Make no mistake, I loved it. I feel no need to justify what I did, because I'm not ashamed of it. Being part of any such movement means you don't give a fuck what anyone outside thinks of you. We felt we could take on the world.' Another told the *Guardian*, 'To be truthful, you like people talking about you.' Forget shame; here comes fame.

A few years ago I was asked to present a series on BBC1 called *Family Matters*. The essential ingredient was ordinary people talking frankly about the different problems we face in bringing up our children. Some of the programmes dealt with pretty sensitive subjects, and I wondered how on earth the producers and researchers would find the people they needed to appear in front of millions of viewers and talk about such intimate matters. I remembered how I hated having to do what broadcasters call 'vox pops', standing in the street and trying to get people to talk in front of a camera. Every time someone pushed past, refusing to say a word, I felt personally rejected. Humiliated even. And it happened all the time. People were shy, and who could blame them? So much more difficult, I thought, to persuade them to travel all the way to a London television studio and, with cameras bearing down on them and lights blazing onto their sweaty faces, to answer revealing questions about their intimate family lives. I imagined the poor researchers scouring the land to find their victims and employing the skills of a double-glazing salesman to talk them into it. How naïve I was. All it takes is a modest little advert in a national newspaper, and you sit back and wait for the phones to ring. The extraordinary thing is, it doesn't matter how outrageous the requirement. 'Are you a wife-swapping transvestite with a weakness for group sex in public lavatories and would you like to face the most embarrassing questions imaginable in front of a jeering crowd of morons?' The answer is always yes, yes and yes again.

Perhaps all that proves is that there are some deeply strange people in this world. There is nothing new in exhibitionism, after all. But how to explain the apparently normal folk who will willingly talk about their intimate relationships, well aware that it may cause them personal embarrassment and their loved ones great pain? We used to laugh at our American cousins for being so desperate to get on the box that they'd sell their granny. We have joined them. Now there seems to be a need to tell the world, 'Look at me, look at how weak and sad and imperfect I am' or 'Look at him, look at how badly he has treated me.' The world – the studio audience and the millions of viewers beyond – becomes the court to which they appeal, their partner the accused. Self-justification is usually the message: you are either the victim, or you're making a claim of absolute right to pursue your own selfish interest. That's why it always seems so shameless, because it literally is. Self-justification is the antithesis of shame, and self-justification before millions is shamelessness with knobs on. But it certainly gets you your Andy Warhol fifteen minutes of fame. Or more.

I suppose people like me should tread carefully on this delicate subject of fame. After all, one of the easiest ways of getting to be famous is to read the news on the box. We broadcasting hacks like to think that we are pretty serious people doing pretty serious jobs: fearless defenders of the truth, champions of the democratic process, exposers of wrongdoing shining a light into the darkest of dark corners. But most of us don't half enjoy the bit of fame that can go with it. Show me a television journalist who says, 'Me become a presenter? I'm a reporter and that's the really worthwhile job' and I'll show you a reporter who's never been *asked* to become a presenter. Show me a presenter who says, 'Fame? It's all a load of nonsense and *so* boring. I *hate* being recognised in public!' and I'll show you a presenter who's lying through his (or her) capped and shiny teeth. It's always good fun to be in a restaurant with a couple of other presenters when someone comes along and asks for an autograph . . . but only asks one of them. The others pretend not to mind, might even make a joke of it. If the one who has been asked is really malicious (which, of course, he is) he will say to the autograph hunter with phoney surprise, 'But surely you want *his* autograph, too, don't you?' and then sit back and smile sympathetically while it becomes deliciously clear that the hapless hunter hasn't the first idea who the other one is.

The perfect illustration, I thought, of turning what ought to be a matter of shame into its very opposite was the young woman who was – like so many pretty young women with blonde hair, a decent cleavage, long legs and awe-inspiring ambition – trying to 'break into' the celebrity circuit. She was doing reasonably well, getting her name in lots of gossip columns, being seen at the right parties (I've always wondered what a 'wrong' party is) but not getting the big break-through that would bring an offer of her own chat show on some obscure satellite or cable television channel. She fell to musing about one of her more successful competitors in the would-be celebrity stakes, a young lady called Sheryl.

'Of course,' she told the *Sunday Times*: '*She* was struggling too until she got her big break.'

And the 'big break' in question? Being beaten up by the man who was then her husband, a certain Mr Paul Gascoigne. Ah, how enviable in this strange world to be assaulted by a man with a very famous name. After that, it seems, you've got it made.

Derek Draper, you will recall, was a young Labour lobbyist who was at the centre of an exposé by the *Observer* in 1998. He was not accused of doing anything wrong but he was extensively quoted in terms which were acutely embarrassing, not only to him but to his friends and to the party. It was a classic case of shaming, in that he exposed himself (he never denied the quotes) as an arrogant, boastful, big-mouthed, cynical and shameless individual on the make, whose main interest, as he put it, was in 'stuffing £250 an hour into my bank account'. It was the sort of exposure which, in a society that still had a sense of shame, would make you want to crawl under the nearest stone.

He was fired from his column on the *Express*, because it was alleged that he'd had his words vetted by Peter Mandelson (he did deny that) and was suspended from his directorship of the lobbying company, from which he eventually resigned. But shameful notoriety did not mean oblivion. It meant an opportunity for celebrity. Draper became far better known than he'd ever been before, and he'd barely lost his job on the *Express* before he was snatched up as a newspaper columnist and as a regular presenter on a radio talk show. The very thing which was supposed to have shamed him became what the marketing people would call his 'unique selling proposition'. He was billed as the 'Big Mouth'. He lost that job only when he called in to Talk Radio from a Continental brothel.

You can see how our changing attitudes to shame and celebrity are reflected in our political scandals. In the early sixties the Tory Cabinet Minister John Profumo was exposed for having had an affair with a prostitute, Christine Keeler. Thirty years later another Tory Cabinet Minister, David Mellor, was also caught by the prying lenses of the Sunday tabloids. He was having an affair not with a prostitute, but with an actress who possessed (so the tabloids told us) a particular skill at sucking toes. Both ministers were eventually forced to resign. There the similarity between the two stories ends.

Mr Profumo did what was expected of those who are shamed: he disappeared into obscurity, devoted the rest of his life to unpublicised charitable work in the East End of London, for which he was ultimately honoured. Mr Mellor took a different route. He had fought like a tiger to hold onto his job. He had bought the services of the country's most famous public relations company to try to help him save his skin. He staged a display of family togetherness for the photographers with wife, kiddies and even his in-laws outside the family home, for all the world as though the affair had been a momentary aberration and the marriage was as solid as a rock. It was not and everyone knew it. The stunt did not work and Mellor had to go. It might even have contributed to his leaving. People who may have been prepared to forgive infidelity appeared less willing to forgive exploitation. After Mellor resigned he set about building another successful career in the most high profile trade of them all: broadcasting. He barely went into quarantine before he started popping up on radio and television again, as a pundit and programme presenter, and later took on a public role as the head of the government's football taskforce.

You could argue that Profumo's sins (which included lying to Parliament) were greater than Mellor's. You could take the line that it was wasteful that Profumo – like Mellor, an able man – should have been lost to public life. Both may be true. My interest is simply in what the two cases say about what has happened to our attitudes to shame.

Freud thought that shame is what we feel when we fail to live up to the standards that we imagine our fathers have set for us. For fathers read the wider community to which we belong. Or sort of belong. The point about the gradual erosion of our sense of shame is that the wider community no longer offers us the sort of belonging where we can recognise the values, the standards, that we might try to live up to. That community has been taken over by something that has been referred to in many ways: the 'me' society, the culture of narcissism, the society of rampant individualism. What the girl with the 'Fuck You' T-shirt, the football hooligans who get themselves on the front of the tabloids and the Derek Drapers are doing is cocking a snook at the very notion that there is anything which we might collectively want to value, or even revere, and feel shame if we fail to live up to. The old lady's averted eyes and the media's avid collaboration with the hooligans are the mark of their success. The result is the erosion of what could be called the public sphere – the world we share with each other – and within which we might hope for some values to be held in common. They are replaced by apathy and passivity.

Staying for the moment in my part of London, let's walk down the street and to the corner of the next block, where you will find a building, much smarter than most, darkened windows and fake marble, and a couple of extremely large gentlemen standing outside with reflecting sunglasses, oddly shaped noses and muscled bodies bulging out of dinner jackets. This is what they are pleased to describe as a table-dancing establishment. To you and me, a strip club. Now think of strip clubs in London and you think of Soho. A seedy character stands at the entrance of a paint-peeling basement leering at you to come in for a minute to ogle lots of lovely, lovely girls and then charges you £150 for a chat with an ageing hooker and a glass of fizzy, coloured water. Or so I am told. My personal experience is limited. But I *have* been to this 'table-dancing establishment'. It was all in the line of duty – I was commissioned to write an article on it for the *Evening Standard* – and I was surprised.

This, as I wrote at the time, is a high class joint. All stripped pine floors and modern décor, reasonably priced booze and a menu that won't break the bank either.

And the girls? Well, they are ... yes ... lovely. Lisa was delightful. Early twenties, a slim blue-eyed blonde, perfect teeth and hair, articulate and bright and demure in an elegant dress that came up to her throat and down to her ankles. If she came home with your son one evening you would congratulate him on his taste. We talked about why she did it. Money, of course. The deal is that she pays the owners £50 a night and keeps everything she makes. In other clubs she had made as much as £850 in one night. Two to three hundred pounds would be reasonable.

The next time I saw her she was busy, and a little less demure. For the £10 note stuck in her garter she was gyrating and stripping in front of a group of young men. The £10 buys one dance, which lasts as long as one record. In that time she strips naked.

Now there *are* rules. Alan Whitehead, part owner and manager, was very anxious to tell me about his code of conduct that had been agreed with Hammersmith police. 'Thirty-two pages, took me two years to get it right.' And every girl has to sign the 'code'. For instance: 'Table dancers must be at least three feet away from the guest's chair.' Well, perhaps they had left their tape measures at home, but while I was there they leaned on the 'client's' shoulders, waggled their breasts in his face, and if they'd been any closer they'd have had to get married.

'Lewd and lascivious behaviour' is frowned upon, said another rule. Is it not 'lewd and lascivious' for two naked girls to caress each other and simulate oral sex for the gratification of voyeurs? My granny might have thought so. Mr Whitehead, apparently, did not.

But why should anyone care about it? It was all being done by consenting adults and no one was getting hurt, except financially. The group of lads on a stag night were having a great time – especially when the girls stripped the groom and filled his underpants with ice cubes.

I'm not so sure about the sad, silent characters alone in the quieter corners who sat, mesmerised, shelling out one tenner after another for three minutes with their own personal dancers. But again, if they could afford it, so what?

So nothing, I suppose, so long as we are all perfectly happy that these 'establishments' should spring up all over the place. The businessman behind Alan Whitehead, who set the whole thing up, told me he was planning many more. He did not want me to use his name. 'Call me a consultant. Alan's the front man.' The 'consultant' expected the number of table-dancing clubs to double every year.

A few months after that conversation I received a glossy brochure in the post inviting me to invest in a company called Garden Inns plc. The picture on the front cover offered a hint that we weren't talking about herbaceous borders and manicured lawns here. It was a silhouette of a naked woman. Garden Inns intended to set up a chain of table-dancing clubs and there are other companies doing the same. Half a dozen more clubs have opened in various parts of London, and about two dozen in other towns and cities. The 'key points' to attract potential investors were: 'Men admire beauty. Men can't take their eyes off beautiful women. Table dancing clubs take phenomenal money.' No doubt. And here was the other big attraction: Garden Inns qualifies under the Enterprise Investment Scheme, which means considerable tax advantages are to be had.

I can see it now, the next Chancellor of the Exchequer delivering his budget speech: '. . . and this is the government that has made it possible through our far-sighted investment incentives for the citizens of this great country to ogle naked women the length and breadth of the land!' There will be much waving of order papers and slurred shouts of 'Yur Yur!' before the honourable members adjourn to the Lobby Lap-Dancing Club for a quick flash or two before the next vote.

Total nudity, Whitehead had earnestly assured me, was a

positively good thing. If you had only topless dancers the frustrated 'clients' would be encouraged to 'go underground'. Not that there's any *real* sex or prostitution allowed. Of course not. The code says so.

But might not that change, too, I asked him? After all, the boundaries are being pushed further and further out every year.

'Well, I'm not going to stop it am I? If we don't do it, someone else will.'

After I had written about the club I wondered what the reaction from my neighbours would be. A few were outraged; most seemed resigned. Someone got up a petition and sent it off to the council. The council 'reviewed' the club's licence and after endless months of hearings and solemn deliberations the rules were slightly amended. This was the big concession: 'When performances are given other than on the designated stage the performer shall retain a non-transparent garment which covers the genitalia and anus at all times.'

In years to come when I dandle my grandchildren on my knee and they ask what my finest hour was as a campaigning journalist I shall be able, proudly, to say: 'I made the Hammersmith lap dancers keep their knickers on.'

But I might as well not have bothered. As I write, another 'club' is being opened in another residential area of London. So effective was my diatribe against them in the *Standard* that they selectively filched bits of what I wrote to use in their publicity material, implying that I approve of their sordid activities.

The other interesting reaction was from colleagues and friends who know me well and had not suspected I was a prude. Neither had I. No doubt they thought this was the reaction of a middle-aged man, resenting what he had missed in his youth. A flash of knee was pretty damned sexy in the fifties and the ultimate in eroticism was a dog-eared copy of *Health and Efficiency*. Now we have naked girls doing things just down the street that we didn't know were even possible. And it is wrong. There is all the difference in the world between a seedy club in a seedy part of Soho and a smart 'establishment' right on the edge of a residential neighbourhood. Whitehead and his 'consultant' thought it the ideal location. Instead of the young man calling into his local for a quick pint or glass of wine on his way home from work, he would drop in for an hour or so of lap dancing. Eventually it would just become accepted; a perfectly natural thing to do . . . and why not? Why not indeed.

It may or may not harm the girls who stuff the £10 notes into their garters. It may or may not harm the sad loners who watch them perform . . . with or without knickers. I have absolutely no doubt that it harms the community. In Soho, fine, if that's what people want. But what is wrong is that such places should spring up in communities that are struggling to maintain some common public world for themselves, some place to which they can feel they belong and in which some standards and values implicitly prevail. Some place where the old lady does not feel an exile in her own community.

We are losing our sense of what shame is because we are losing the sense of belonging to a community. It is the community that produces the values necessary for us to feel shame or its opposite. Instead what we are preoccupied with is something quite different: feeling good about ourselves.

Chapter 3

Feelgood

THE BBC HAS a deeply ambivalent approach towards those of us who present its programmes. It wants us to be 'personalities' with minds and attitudes of our own because it dimly perceives that that is what the audience wants. Viewers and listeners do not like blandness except, apparently, when it comes to certain game-show or Lottery hosts. But let our attitudes surface for a moment and it runs like hell for the nearest bunker.

My old colleague Brian Redhead was perhaps the greatest radio broadcaster of his generation. At his peak nobody could touch him. I sat alongside him in my early years on *Today* in the dingy studio on the fourth floor of Broadcasting House admiring, envying and being irritated in equal measure by this extraordinary man.

He had all the obvious qualifications: what pretentious people like to call a well-stocked mind; laser-swift reactions; a brilliant memory; an ease with words and a love of the English language. Above all he had the ability to talk to an audience as though there were no microphone between him and them. He engaged in conversation with them and did not speak *at* them. He also had a very, very short fuse and a deep and unshakeable conviction that he was right on every subject under the sun.

Anyone who disagreed with him was a 'prat'. Most members of BBC management were, by definition, prats. There was a great deal of innocent pleasure to be had watching various bosses trying to cope with this mercurial mix of brilliance and ego, knowing that the audience loved him and fearing those moments when he would go off the rails and cause problems. It was almost (not quite, but almost) possible to feel sorry for the bosses on occasions.

Towards the end of his life, when diabetes and a bad hip contributed to making his fuse even shorter, Brian frequently threatened physical violence. Sometimes he even delivered it. There was a celebrated occasion when he was on an aeroplane returning from a trip to Russia and punched a *Guardian* journalist on the nose over some real or imagined slight. He frequently threatened to 'slap' producers who failed to do things as he believed they should be done. I once had to intervene to stop him physically assaulting the then editor over some affront to the Redhead dignity. He and I almost had a fist fight in the studio live on air one morning because he had criticised one of my interviews (his fellow presenters were prats just as often as the bosses) and I had responded with a fairly mild criticism of something he had done. I always wondered if the listeners noticed a certain chill in the air for the rest of that programme. I don't suppose they did; they tend to assume that fellow presenters are friends off the air as well as on, and that is seldom the case. It was always assumed that Brian Redhead and John Timpson, a great partnership on air, were close friends. They were not.

Brian was brilliant and dangerous and entirely unpredictable which was, of course, precisely why the listeners loved him and why the bosses feared him. It was why some politicians feared him too. They never quite knew what he would say next. Politicians like to know the general direction from which an interviewer is likely to come at them. Most of us are, I suspect, generally predictable. Brian was, to put it at its mildest, idiosyncratic. That, I suspect, was why Margaret Thatcher refused to be interviewed by him once she was safely ensconced in Number Ten. That, and the general Tory belief that he was a Labour supporter. The truth is that he had no political ideology. Like many intelligent men he had a ragbag of convictions which satisfied him intellectually and spiritually but which, when you put them together, could not be neatly labelled. That said, he did not like most of the things the Thatcher government was getting up to. I remember his introduction to an interview with a Conservative minister which included the typically Redhead phrase: 'In the old days it was the Oxford–Cambridge boat race that divided the nation. Now we leave it to the government.' You could hear the sound of management teeth grinding together from every bosses' office in Broadcasting House.

He had a point though. Thatcher's great talent, if talent it be, was to make it impossible for anyone to remain neutral about politics. We all had a view of what she was and what she had achieved. One of those views was that Thatcherism had been responsible for destroying something we still valued – that sense of community and society in which people were not selfish but looked out for each other. Hadn't she said there was no such thing as society? We seized on the remark, completely misinterpreting it in order to support the allegation that it was she who was turning Britain into a truly selfish nation. Its ultimate expression was all those awful yuppies in the City, with their red braces, overstuffed bank accounts, open-topped Porsches, mouthing into mobile phones while they cracked open another bottle of bubbly. They were Thatcher's children, and all this selfishness was really all her fault. When we got rid of her at the beginning of the nineties we told ourselves it was all going to be different and the nineties would return us to the era of caring which she had destroyed. It was complete hogwash. The eighties were not an aberration at all. They were just a rather startling and vivid intensification of a pattern that had been in train for some time – and which would continue in the nineties.

No one has put the point more crisply than that shrewd commentator George Walden. I first met Walden on an aeroplane to China when he was a very senior civil servant in the Foreign Office, travelling the world with the Foreign

Secretary and whispering sound diplomatic advice in his ear. Then he became a politician himself, a Conservative MP, and almost immediately hated it even though he was promoted quickly to the bottom rung of the ministerial ladder. Walden is living proof that natural politicians are born, not made. They have to nurse their constituencies, treat people who are sometimes very stupid as though they are not, attend the bring-and-buy fundraising events at the weekends and appear to be enjoying it all. Walden loathed it, could not pretend otherwise, and so he packed it all in. Politics' loss was journalism's gain.

'The eighties were nicely summed up for me,' he wrote in the *New Statesman*, 'when, parking my car one day in 1989, I put my last pound coins into the wrong meter. In seconds a white Merc had eased noiselessly into the pre-paid space. Out jumped a weasel-faced individual sporting a pony tail, who moved with the lightness of a fox. The man was all animal – a pop star, I assumed. Toting a plastic bag full of pounds – you see the class of person – he loped up to the meter, grinned at his luck, and closed his bag. I explained what had happened. I asked if he could change a fiver. Weasel-features looked at me pityingly before pronouncing these era-defining words: "Get real. This is the metropolis, sunshine." Then he locked his coins in his Merc and buggered off.'

Today, wrote Walden, the Merc driver would be a changed man. He would be 'boyish, with Jarvis Cocker hair and iguana eyes, looking as vulnerable as anyone with a Mercedes can, he would have sighed in commiseration and said, "I feel your pain, sunshine." Then locked his coins in his Merc and buggered off.'

So we are just as selfish as we have ever been and maybe more so. There seems to be plenty of evidence of the more mundane kind: the queue jumpers in the supermarkets; the double-parkers who clog up the traffic for everyone; the road hogs who sit in the fast lane on a motorway or drive in the bus lanes; the commuters who squeeze onto the tube without waiting for people to get off first; the youngsters who drive the other passengers mad with the squeaky noises coming from their Walkman headsets; the businessmen who show off by bawling into their mobile phones. It's all rather petty stuff, and anyway it misses the point.

That sort of thing happened less forty years ago because we lived a different sort of life, with no supermarkets or Walkmans or mobile phones (oh blessed days), and fewer cars and less crowded commuting. I'm interested not so much in our selfishness as our growing self-absorption.

Under Thatcherism, so it was claimed, it was wimpish to show your feelings. Under Blairism it is compulsory. But here's the curious thing: it is possible to insist 'I feel your pain' and at the same time remain totally self-absorbed. More than possible, it seems to be required. You must *show* that you care for others, even as you remain totally preoccupied with yourself.

Blair is no more the cause of this than Thatcher was of the selfishness culture. What's interesting about those cultures is not that they are opposites but that they are the same. The climate that has grown up over the last forty years or so encourages us to focus our feeling not on other people but on ourselves. That has not necessarily made us more selfish, but it has certainly made us more self-absorbed. 'How are you feeling?' used to be a question we asked only of those who were ill. Now, 'How do you feel?' is a question the climate invites us constantly to ask about ourselves. How do we feel about ourselves? Are we feeling good, or are we feeling bad?

Feeling good seems to be the central goal of modern life. The message is that feeling good about ourselves is the mark of success, of having made it. *Hello!* magazine is the ultimate showcase: endless pictures of celebrities feeling good about themselves, relaxed, at home, wallowing in comfort, surrounded by a loving family and always with the soft focus hint of a completely fulfilling sex life. The not so subtle subtext is that they are the models for what our lives should be. Fair enough, celebrity envy has been around for a very long time, but there does seem to have been a clear change of attitude. For most of us in previous generations life was a struggle and feeling good was just a lull in the storm, an exception to be thankful for, rather than the goal in life. The goal was to keep your head above water, to improve your lot if you could. That meant the focus was outside you. The real goal was overcoming what was out there, not looking inward, self-absorbed, constantly taking the measure of how good you felt.

Some people have linked this turning inwards, this self-absorption with our inner well-being, with something that marks a big change over the last forty years: the growth of the therapy culture. Christopher Lasch, the American social critic, has written that 'the contemporary climate is thera-peutic, not religious. People today hunger not for personal salvation, let alone for the restoration of an earlier golden age, but for the feeling, the momentary illusion, of personal well-being, health and psychic security.' A generation ago the only therapists most of us knew were the sort who appeared in Woody Allen movies. Their patients were invariably Cali-fornians or New Yorkers with too much money and time on their hands and too little sense. They talked about 'my therapist' in the way that rich American women talked about 'my gynaecologist'. They sniffed white powder through rolled-up hundred-dollar bills and divided their time more or less equally between their divorce lawyers, the latest most fashionable restaurant, their mistress and their shrink. Their great obsession was how they felt.

You remember the sort: the guy who walks out on his wife and four kids to go off with a bit of totty and weeps to his therapist, 'I feel so bad'. The joke is that he wants us to feel that it is *he* who needs help. And of course if feeling bad is the worst thing in the world, then he does. All that matters is that he should be able to feel less bad, never mind his res-ponsibilities, and that's what the therapist is there to sort out. Such is the caricature of therapists. They exist to make us feel good about ourselves. But it's only partly a caricature. It is true that there are many people who cannot function properly because they have such bad feelings about themselves – even when they haven't done something reprehensible such as dump their wife and children. But some therapists think we should all be in therapy.

My neighbour Gina struggled for several years to qualify as

a psycho-dynamic counsellor at the same time as she was bringing up two terrific children. She is a warm and wonderful woman, the perfect neighbour and a good friend: funny, intelligent, kind and sympathetic. And we argue endlessly about her work.

Like many therapists, she believes that our lives can be enriched and many of our problems solved and relationships improved if only we can get in touch with our inner selves. But if you are not actually depressed and are able to function perfectly well, what is so valuable about getting a therapist to make you feel even better about yourself? Why should feeling good inside be such a goal? For people who can get on perfectly well, *not* feeling good about yourself can often be productive. It can be the stimulus that spurs you on. I suspect that the most creative people do not spend their lives feeling good about themselves. Would it be better for the world at large if they lay on a therapist's couch, got to feel good about themselves and lost the need to write? Their lives might well be happier, but the world would lose some wonderful books or music or paintings. Beethoven was apparently a pretty miserable sod most of the time – he had a lot to be miserable about – but if that's what led to him writing the late quartets I'm all for a bit of inner angst. It might not be as desirable as it sounds to prescribe happiness as the ultimate goal for everyone.

I have a personal interest in some of this because my trade involves a lot of arguing and it's very difficult to argue with people who are seriously into this kind of thing. It reaches its ultimate expression in the more well heeled parts of California. Because so many of them are in therapy and trying so hard to find the inner peace and happiness they hanker after they want to avoid what you or I might consider a most enjoyable argument and what they would call 'conflict'. So they have invented that intensely irritating technique of answering everything you say to them with the calming, nodded 'Okay', spoken with that ridiculous upward inflection. It makes you want to scream: 'No it's bloody well NOT okay you smug, self-centred, self-absorbed, self-indulgent prat!' But there's no point. They just smile even more indulgently and recommend a good therapist to help you cope with your anger.

Not that therapy is the main reason so many of us are becoming obsessed with feeling good about ourselves. There is a more obvious suspect to put in the dock. It defines our era and is so pervasive that it's virtually impossible to get away from it: consumerism.

Consumerism is all about feeling good. It holds that buying things should be our goal in life, that buying things will make us feel good. One link between consumerism and feelgood is the way advertising has changed.

Some say the cynic's first rule of journalism is 'First simplify, then exaggerate.' I think that works even better when it is applied to advertising. In its early days advertising concentrated on telling us what we needed to know about whatever it was we might be thinking of buying, and then exaggerating. The advertising revolution changed all that. Now it seems almost obligatory for advertising to make us identify the product being plugged with all the things we associate with feeling good. It makes us think that buying things leads to fulfilment in life, ceaselessly represented by images of freedom, youth, beauty and sexual satisfaction. Especially sexual satisfaction. Buy this car and your only problem will be how to keep a naked Claudia Schiffer out of it. Use this shampoo and beautiful women (naked again) will want to wrap themselves around you every time you wash your hair. Eat this ice cream, but make sure you take your clothes off before you start because you wouldn't want that lovely young woman (still naked) to dribble the stuff all down your nice clean shirt, would you? There was a time when it was only tyre manufacturers who used naked women to sell things; you'd see them on calendars on oily garage office walls. Now sex, youth and freedom, the hallmarks of feelgood, are branded onto virtually everything.

Consumerism goes a stage further than simply telling us that feeling good should be our goal in life. It says feeling good is easily available. It should be, and can easily be, the norm in our lives, our daily expectation. Don't put it off, buy now, get instant gratification and feel good straight away. That's the basic message of consumerism: take the waiting out of wanting. It's reflected in the economics of consumerism: instant credit means no one need bother to save up first before enjoying the feelgood of buying something. You can just borrow and get the feeling straight away. If times are hard and it doesn't seem too clever to add to the amount you're in debt, well, just wait a bit; the good times will come again, the feelgood factor will return. That notion, the return of the feelgood factor, carried with it something not far short of the promise of the Second Coming when it was endlessly parroted by politicians during the recession of the early nineties. It reveals a lot about the essentially passive nature of feelgood in our culture: it's something you wait for, not something you might have any hand in trying to create. The essence of the new consumer creed is precisely the opposite of how it used to be.

The modern feelgood notion is a confidence trick. Feeling good cannot be a norm, not least because we're told you can't possibly feel good unless you are young. And if you can't actually *be* young then it is necessary to look and feel young. Whatever happened to the notion of growing old gracefully? We are endlessly told that feeling good is associated with everything that's wonderful about youth – good looks before the lines carve into your face, your hair drops out and the pot belly emerges; sexual freedom before you settle down and the libido declines – and that if we do the right things we don't have to worry about all that ghastly stuff happening to us. Our culture tries to tuck away the untidy and inconvenient reality that it will all end one of these days, so death stops being seen as an inevitable part of life that needs integrating within it, but as something phobic to be resisted. Death is the ultimate enemy of feelgood.

Happily there is a group of people who worry about us not feeling good all the time. They wear white coats and work in laboratories and they are the new masters of the universe who will make everything come out right in the end. They are the boffins who work for the big drug companies, many of whom peddle their products as lifestyle drugs while pretending that they're intended only for those with a medical condition. They tell us that each can be justified on strict medical grounds, and so they can: Viagra for men who have severe problems in maintaining an erection; Seroxat for those who suffer so severely from social phobia or social anxiety disorder that they can scarcely bear to leave the house; and Xenical for the clinically obese. But look a little more closely at some of those.

The moment that news of Viagra broke it was immediately seized upon as the 'love pill'. Shares in the company that developed it rose with the speed of a satisfied customer. The more the company protested with an apparently straight face that no, honestly, this drug was not intended for perfectly healthy men (and women) who wanted an even better sex life, the more everyone believed precisely that. And why not? Viagra was the proof we needed that the natural process of ageing need not apply to us. We were treated to endless television programmes about elderly folk who, in another age, might have been accepting with resignation or even relief that all good things come to an end but who instead were boasting about swinging from the chandeliers and leaping from the top of wardrobes as they performed like stallions at stud. Soon another company produced its own version of Viagra and before very much longer we shall be buying the stuff over the counter.

As Viagra became the love pill, so Seroxat became the 'shyness pill'. You might think that the one thing this country does not need is a pill to cure shyness. Quite the reverse. As Ian Jack has written, confident speech and confident appearance matters more now than at any time in history. The great new industries – the media, advertising, public relations, cold-call selling, conferences – depend on it. He has a point. Like most of my colleagues in the broadcasting business I have made a bob or two in the past from what is known as 'media training'. It is a commonplace that all politicians go through the grisly process and there might be some value for them. You can't have a politician who shudders and shakes and stutters and stammers his way through a television or radio interview . . . or seizes up altogether, though I can think of one or two who'd have benefited if they had. Better, as President Lincoln is believed to have said, 'to remain silent and be thought a fool than to speak out and remove all doubt.'

What always astonished me in my 'media training' days (never with politicians: you think I'm mad?) was how many companies sent all manner of employees for the treatment. It is perfectly understandable that the chief executive or his spokesman might want some coaching in facing up to thugs like Paxman or me, but they frequently sent along junior managers so far down the totem pole of power that the only way they'd have ever appeared on the box was if they'd been caught setting fire to the chairman's trousers. There seems to be the assumption today that we must all be fluent and articulate, persuasive and polished even if we have nothing to say and no need to say it.

My father was a great craftsman who restored and polished furniture and if you ever asked him about his skill he would say he was still learning. Even when he was eighty. Today he would be required to talk about it and 'promote himself'. As Ian Jack says, 'After the age of workers by hand and brain comes our age: the Age of the Workers by Tongue.' So what a wonderful market there is for Seroxat. Pop a pill and you'll be up there on the stage or at the dinner table with the best of them, chatting away and dazzling all with your confidence. Except, of course, that that is not what it is meant for. So the drug company says. When Jack went to a press conference to launch the pill the company was at great pains to insist that it was not a 'lifestyle' drug. And yet, when a professor involved in the launch tried to prove its worth he used the story of a woman who had told him how nervous she was when she had to make a presentation. Her mouth dried up and her sentences were scrambled when she stood on the platform. Could the drug help her? Yes indeed it could.

Xenical, the daddy of them all, got much less publicity than Viagra for entirely obvious reasons – nothing, but nothing, can compete with sex in the publicity stakes – but Xenical's potential is far greater. One of the biggest medical problems of the late twentieth century in a rich country like Britain is obesity. If we are too fat we are prone to all sorts of horrible diseases. Some obese people have a genuine medical problem and need help. The vast majority are overweight because they eat too much of the wrong things, especially fatty food. The way to lose weight is to eat less. If you have any doubt at all about that obvious statement, look across the Atlantic at the United States. As they became richer and ate more, so they became fatter. Might there be a link? They now send obese schoolchildren on special courses where they do things like try to 'boost their self esteem'.

Boost their self esteem? If they ate fewer chips and burgers they would be less fat and that, presumably, would do the trick. Ah, but that requires discipline, and their parents taking responsibility. Since their parents are probably doing the same thing it is unlikely salvation will lie in that direction. Now – hallelujah and praise the Lord! – we have Xenical. Pop a pill or two and if you eat a greasy burger the fat is not absorbed. Once again we have the drug company telling us this is not a lifestyle drug. It is for those who are clinically obese. Of course, of course. No doubt the company will fight like tigers to stop the pill being sold to those who want to buy it (or have the NHS buy it) so that they may continue their gluttony without piling on the calories.

How strange, then, that only a few weeks after the drug was released I received in the post a glossy leaflet headlined 'Attention All Slimmers!' and offering me the new wonder drug for a very reasonable £110 for one month's supply or, even better, £295 for three months. Plus post and packaging, of course. How could I refuse? This, as the leaflet pointed out in its subtle way, was 'The new slimming breakthrough for the millennium ... available to you now!!' We already have the love pill and the shyness pill. Now we have the greed pill too.

Within months of Xenical hitting the market the world rejoiced at yet another wonder drug ... son of Xenical. This one is called Cellasene. The clinical trials were carried out in Australia and the women of that great country were apparently fighting amongst themselves to get at it once its miraculous existence had been revealed on television. This one not only allows you eat and stay slim; it attacks that scourge of womankind: cellulite. 'My son called me jelly legs,' said one satisfied customer, 'but no longer.' Stand by for many more such wonders of modern medicine. I confidently predict a miracle cure for double chins, beer bellies and big noses. Soon we shall all look like super models without having to take any responsibility for ourselves at all.

Feelgood culture makes us passive and erodes the sense of responsibility we should have for ourselves. Self-absorption in feeling good distracts us from recognising that many of the things we might want to happen, or we might want to prevent, have their causes in us, and that it's up to us to take responsibility. And feelgood, of course, is the flipside of the victim culture. It undermines our sense of responsibility for ourselves and encourages us to view disappointment, adversity and feeling bad as opportunities to see ourselves as victims. We must blame others rather than try to put things right ourselves. That can be really corrosive. For many people, all that the hyped expectations produce is anxiety, deep unhappiness and depression.

Chapter 4

Sentimentality

WHEN I WAS a child a small boy was killed in an accident near my home. His parents did what we all did when there was a bereavement in the family. They drew the blinds in the room facing the street and withdrew into their grief. Wilfred Owen recalls this universal practice in the line 'And each slow dusk a drawing down of blinds' in his incomparable poem 'Anthem for Doomed Youth' – and every contemporary reader would have known what he meant. Today, instead of Owen's 'tenderness of silent minds', a 'shrine' would be created at the place he was killed, a mound of flowers placed there by neighbours and neighbours' children to be filmed and photographed by the local media as proof that a victim was being mourned.

Similarly, it is not so very long ago that the only thing most of us ever wore in our button holes was a carnation at a wedding and a poppy. We wear the poppy, I like to think, as a mark of respect for those who died, not because we see those brave men as 'victims'. But now many of us wear ribbons the year round, apparently to 'identify with the victims' of whatever affliction it may be. Sometimes they are enamel brooches, to mark the permanence of our feeling.

One of the hazards of writing about the sentimentalising of

victims is that people think either that you believe all feeling and emotion should be suppressed and we should get back to the stiff upper lip, or they think you believe all expressions of emotion are bogus and displayed for effect. Or both. I don't happen to think either of those things. Celts like me tend to let it all hang out and leave it to our Norman conquerors to put the case for bottling it all up. But it must be genuine feeling, and too much of our display of feeling and caring for victims seems, rather, to be shallow.

Why, then, are we becoming so sentimental? For some people the answer may be cynical calculation. In a climate in which there is such a premium on displayed emotion, it's good to be seen to emote. When the Hollywood actress turns up in Africa, dressed down and without make-up to be photographed holding the baby dying of starvation, she may well be performing a valuable service, bringing publicity to a worthy cause. But you don't need much cynicism to see that there may be benefits in the photo-shoot for her. Yet her motivation may not be that different from many other people's, even though they may not be so calculating. The opportunity to flatter our moral vanity – to tell ourselves what kind and feeling people we are – is one of the treats that sentimentalising remote victims makes available to us. It's certainly a lot easier than actually putting oneself out to help those in need closer at hand. So we are back to the climate of feelgood. It makes us feel good about ourselves to do a bit of vicarious emoting. As George Walden has put it: 'Today the feel-good factor means feeling good about feeling bad on behalf of those who are not so rich and secure as ourselves.'

Feelgood and self-absorption have emerged out of changes which have left us feeling less belonging, less attached to communities, more isolated and insular. It may be that our increased sentimentality is because we are more lonely. The columnist Francis Wheen has written of sentimentality as a cure for solitude and of its outbursts as 'anguished pleas of a lonely and atomised populace, desperate for company'. The sociologist Frank Furedi makes a similar point. Criticising what he calls 'the politics of emotion' in *LM Magazine*, he puts our sentimentality about victims down to our common sense of victimhood and to the fact that there's very little else that holds us all together. 'People identify with the cult of vulnerability because they sense a shared experience of victimhood. The common bond is that of suffering, and everybody who wears a ribbon becomes part of the same drama of victimisation. Through a collective display of emotion an otherwise fragmented society achieves a temporary moment of unity.'

He has a point. In postwar Britain, most notably in working-class areas clustered around factories or docks where the bombs had fallen night after terrifying night, the sense of community was strong, fed by the knowledge that they had survived the worst that two world wars had been able to throw at them. Shared hardship can be a strong social glue. Since then we have become increasingly insular and we have television, as much as anything, to thank for it. The more time you spend staring at the screen in the corner, the less time there is for anything outside.

In the early days, as if by compensation, the box provided its own form of social glue as we all talked to each other about what we had seen the night before. That began to disappear when the number of channels grew and then VCRs came along and we could create our own schedules, recording endless programmes that we probably never got around to watching. The digital revolution means that pretty soon there will be so many channels we might go for ever without meeting somebody who'd seen the same thing as us the night before. Except, perhaps, for the soaps. In some ways the popularity of *Coronation Street* and *Eastenders* is evidence that we still want to be part of a community, but they are a poor substitute for the real thing. Outside the soaps, the things television invites us to get emotional about pass fleetingly. We are moved, the images shift to something quite different, our feelings pass and we're engrossed in something else. So television, our new community, inevitably cheapens our emotional responses, not only because it leaves them frustrated and passive, but also because they have no time to take root. Sentimentalism is the result.

We media folk must carry the blame for most of that, the broadcasters more than the papers. 'How does it feel?' we would breathlessly ask the victim of some terrible tragedy, the camera a few inches from his face. If he had any sense he would have answered: 'How the bloody hell d'you *think* it feels! I've just lost my wife and children and my house has burned down. Now push off before I ram that microphone down your throat.' Sadly, they seldom did. Eventually the BBC sent out edicts about that sort of crass question, but it took a long time and by then the damage had been done.

The sole purpose of news reporting is to give people accurate information so that they can use it to draw their own conclusions, form their own judgements, make up their own minds. That is the case whether we are reporting on a famine in a faraway country or a punch-up in Parliament. Our job is to deliver facts but we have a terrible tendency to tell our audience and our readers how somebody is feeling about something or other when the truth is that we don't know. There is only one person who actually knows how he feels at any given moment: the person involved. If he has told us, that's fine. We can report what he said. If he hasn't – and by and large Prince Charles, for instance, tends not to confide his innermost thoughts to the latest hack he stumbles across – we ought to stick to the facts and let people make their own assumptions about how he's feeling. It's bad enough when newspapers do it; there is even less excuse for a television reporter. The whole point of showing moving pictures is that people can see for themselves. Let the audience make their own judgement.

I'm not arguing against 'human interest' reporting. Quite the reverse. When twelve thousand people died in the floods and mud after Hurricane Mitch swept across Central America in 1998 an enormous amount of coverage was devoted to one single woman who had survived. She had been swept out to sea and was picked up, alive, after three days of clinging to bits of wreckage. It was an extraordinary feat of human endurance, a powerful demonstration of the will to live, and deserved every inch of space it got. It also reduced the story of appalling destruction on an overwhelming scale to a dimension that we could grasp. The woman had lost her husband and children, all swept out to sea with her and drowned. It helped us understand the story, put it in perspective.

So it does when we report on the problems of the NHS and pick on one small child who has suffered as a result of its failings. It may be one tiny figure in a mountain of statistics, but we can relate to the plight of a single child who might have been refused desperately needed treatment in a way we cannot relate to the big picture. The politicians and the health professionals may get cross, accuse us of exploiting 'sob stories', but the criticism is valid only when we allow emotion to cloud or even obscure the coverage.

Television can corrupt genuine emotion and convert it into a cheap form of sentimentalism tinged with self-gratification. The journalist Dea Birkett wrote in the *Guardian* about watching one of those hideous 'confessional' shows in which the 'victims' try to out-do each other when they parade their sufferings. This one was about sexual abuse. When one woman claimed that she had been abused no fewer than 432 times (she counted?) the audience broke into spontaneous applause. For what? They were clearly deriving some ghoulish pleasure from wallowing in the details. You have to wonder what they were doing in the studio in the first place. The pleasure, or perhaps the thrill, they get from this stuff gives a synthetic flavour to their sympathy. For them it's an entertainment, not a tragedy, and the sympathy is skin-deep, sentimental. It would be real only if they were affected personally by the awful thing that has happened, but of course they are not. And that is what distinguishes real emotion from sentimentality.

It is impossible to write about the climate of sentimentality, and television's role in fostering it, without some reference to the icon herself: Diana. I confess that after all this time I am still deeply puzzled by the whole Diana phenomenon. Heaven knows what the historians will make of her, if indeed they try to make much at all. She had no power, led no great political parties, waged no wars and yet, some say, she had the most profound effect on our national psyche, and her death revealed a great deal about ourselves. I wonder.

On the morning of her funeral I interviewed Cardinal Basil Hume, then leader of the Roman Catholic Church in England and Wales and a man of great learning, wisdom and common sense. The night before, we had heard that Mother Teresa had died. I assumed that the Cardinal would want to talk about her. But he did not. He wanted to talk about Diana. I must have shown my surprise and he was clearly irritated with me but I found it extraordinary. Here were two women, one of them regarded by much of the world as a living saint and, in her death, certain to be canonised; the other a woman who had certainly carried out some worthy charitable work but who had broken her marriage vows – a sin, according to the lights of the Church, whatever the provocation – and whose life was mostly lived in self-indulgent luxury. And the Cardinal wanted to talk about Diana. Clearly he had spotted what I had failed – or perhaps refused – to see. Diana had a hold on the nation's emotions and sentiment that appeared, certainly at that time, to be unique.

She was the celebrity of all celebrities, embodying all the values of our times: youth, beauty, sex appeal, wealth and status. She was the central figure in the soap opera with the biggest audience of them all and, like all enduring soap heroines, her role in it endlessly evolved to suit the storyline that was required. It was she who led fashion, had all the pop star friends, the glamorous and extravagant lifestyle, the Mediterranean cruises, the millionaire lover. But over and above all that – far, far more important in our sentimental times – she was a victim. Through her eating disorders, her failed marriage and the manner of her dying, she had achieved a status that placed her way beyond rational judgement.

When she died we were all obliged to join in the grief. Shops were forced to close for the funeral even if they offered to donate the profit to the Diana fund. A council in Cornwall closed the local beach. If you wanted to watch anything other than the funeral on BBC television you were not allowed to. So much for the licence payer's right to choice. There was, as

Matthew Engel put it at the time, a degree of emotional fascism stalking the land.

'Emotional fascism' is an ugly phrase, but there had been moments in that ghastly week following the crash in Paris when it was possible to smell a tiny whiff of what it must be like to live in a state where only one view is tolerated, when intelligent people were afraid to admit that they thought the whole grieving business was being ridiculously overdone. I went to a concert in the Albert Hall the night before the funeral and the programme was changed, the Fauré Requiem replacing the symphony we had expected to hear. The conductor warned the audience beforehand not to applaud at the end of it, as a mark of respect. Later, over dinner, after looking for the nearest exit in case I had to get out quickly, I ventured that I thought that had been ridiculous. How could applauding a group of fine musicians be disrespectful to anyone? The man I was talking to, a powerful businessman seemingly afraid of no one, almost kissed me in gratitude. 'Oh God!' he said. 'I've been wanting to say something like that all week and I haven't dared.'

Now I try not to lie to the newspapers, if only because you invariably get caught out in the end. But I did when the *Telegraph* rang me, many months after the event, and wanted to talk about Diana's death. They were doing a feature on the theme of 'Where I was when I heard that Diana had died'. As it happens I can remember precisely where I was, but I lied. I said not only could I not remember, but I had absolutely no interest in trying to remember. I hung up, satisfied that they'd get lots of people to give them what they wanted and that I would not appear in what I thought was a ridiculous piece of journalism. I got my comeuppance. They printed the 'I have no interest' bit. I shuddered as I read it and waited for the sacks of vicious letters from those who had been worshipping at the Diana shrine, who did remember, and would surely see me as a desecrator. I am still waiting.

If the feelings for Diana had been anything like as profound as we were all led to believe at the time, if she had really awoken in the nation something deep and real, then surely that would have survived long after her death. The lack of reaction to my unwitting comment in the *Telegraph* was the first small sign for me that perhaps the flame she had apparently ignited was already beginning to die. There were many more signs. When a respected academic, Anthony O'Hear, wrote an essay saying that we'd got it all a bit out of proportion, he was pounced upon by the media and viciously attacked. He was accused of having said disparaging things about Diana that he hadn't said, and reviled as the ivory tower professor, out of touch with the masses. The politicians, anxious as ever to be in touch with the sentiment of the masses, joined in the attack, Tony Blair amongst them. It turned out to be they who were out of touch.

I interviewed O'Hear on the *Today* programme and expected, again, a mountain of mail demanding his head. The opposite happened. The letters ran about five to one in his favour. One after another, events held in Diana's memory failed to attract the support expected, not just in Britain but even in California where they know a star when they see one and seldom deny themselves the chance to emote in public. On the first anniversary of her death we were warned to expect another mass outpouring of grief. Again, it did not happen. Fifteen thousand people were expected to show up at a walk following the route of the funeral cortège. There were three hundred. It cost the organisers a small fortune. Eventually the politicians saw which way the wind was blowing. The lavish memorial planned by a committee under the chairmanship of Gordon Brown was scaled down. Instead of a vast £10million flower garden and statue they settled for a kiddies' playground. Not a murmur from the masses. Who, now, remembers the idea (endorsed by no less a figure than William Hague) of renaming Heathrow Airport 'Diana'?

The fact that the great emotional outburst about Diana has largely faded away, and that people can now talk reasonably sensibly about her will appear to some people as evidence that we've *not* become sentimentalised. But I think it shows the opposite. It is the very transience of public emotion as conveyed through the media – the fact that it can be so hot one moment, so cool the next – which marks its shallowness, its sentimental nature. That is not to say that some people weren't genuinely moved. Those listeners who wrote in support of O'Hear were not attacking genuine expressions of grief; rather they were standing up for proportion against sentimentality and even hysteria.

So does it matter, this sentimentalising of our view of the world? I think so. If we look at the world through the soft focus of sentimentality we get a distorted sense of reality and that affects how we behave. If we see only potential victims in the world then, when someone like Louise Woodward turns up, we can see her only in that role. Our belief in justice, in looking at evidence, at actually *thinking* about things, is pushed to the margins. When Gitta Sereny, an author with impeccable credentials as a serious journalist, published *Cries Unheard* in 1998 – a book that tried to make sense of the child killer Mary Bell – there was outrage, partly because she had paid Bell some money (although nothing like as much as was first reported), but also because the book might have upset the parents of the children Bell had killed. The sentimental, emotional approach says that nothing must be done to upset 'victims' and in this case the victims were those parents. If Sereny had been a sensationalist whose only concern was to turn a fast buck it would have been understandable. Yet, even though many people accepted that her meticulous work might possibly help us understand why a young girl turns into a child-killer, she was pilloried. Better simply to condemn the killer as 'evil' rather than try to understand what would make an eleven-year-old girl do such a terrible thing.

Even well-intentioned actions born out of sentimentality can have bad consequences. Look at what has happened when we have poured money into funds set up for victims of tragedies such as Aberfan and Dunblane. It might seem shocking to regard such generosity as sentimental, but if it is a pure reaction to feeling, without thought to how the money could conceivably be of use, then that's what it is. Disaster relief is one thing – millions of people desperately need food and shelter after a hurricane in Central America or an earthquake – but how is money supposed to help parents whose children have been killed when a slag heap has engulfed their school, or when a madman with an arsenal of guns has burst into their classroom? After Aberfan the nation opened its hearts and its wallets. We were all staggered by the amount of money that poured into the appeal fund, and deeply touched. This was a country that cared. And yet there was a nagging worry even then. What was it for? It was an enormous sum, a total of £1.75million in 1966 money when £15 a week was a very respectable wage.

The rows began almost immediately, as did the envy, resentment, bitterness and greed. First of all a large chunk of the fund was seized by the government to pay for clearing the treacherous tip. The people of Aberfan were, quite rightly, outraged. 'That's not what people gave the money for,' they said. 'Why shouldn't the government pay for clearing the tip?' That row went on for thirty years. But for Aberfan that sort of wrangling with stupid officialdom was the least of it. The real harm was done as villager turned against villager. People who had been friends all their lives came to resent those who had suddenly become rich. A village that had been united in grief was divided in envy.

At Dunblane something very similar happened. Nearly £7million was donated, but it served only to divide a largely harmonious community. Inevitably there were those who felt it was being distributed unfairly. It may be that the only people who are really helped by such sentimental giving are those who send the cash, and if you look at all the damaging effects it is hard to avoid the conclusion that sentimental giving is, in the end, self-indulgent and potentially destructive.

Sentimentality about victims is affecting our politics too, encouraging politicians to appeal to our superficial emotions rather than our capacity to follow an argument. When the Labour MP Michael Foster introduced his bill to ban fox-hunting, he stood in front of the Houses of Parliament with his supporters holding a cuddly toy fox with a benign smile on its face. The message was clear: fox-hunting victimises cuddly foxes with cute smiles. We should feel sorry for them, and leave them alone to smile and be cuddly. Now whatever you may think of hunting, foxes are not smiling, cuddly creatures. They are efficient predators; that is their role in the natural order of things. But our sentimental culture encourages us to think otherwise: we're to feel as sorry for them as we would for a persecuted child.

For politicians it has become second nature to identify with feeling, however superficial. No disaster may happen these days without a politician rushing to the scene. They can't do any good – indeed their visits often get in the way of the rescue effort – but it would be thought terrible politics, terrible image management, not to be seen to be there. It is tempting to accuse them of cynical exploitation, but they would say that the public expects it and perhaps they are right. Perhaps all they are doing is responding to the public mood.

If this affected only the PR dimension of politics it could be dismissed as part of the tackiness of the whole business, but it goes further and sometimes stretches into the area of policy making. Politicians increasingly seem to feel that our sentimental culture requires them to abdicate their re-sponsibilities to take rational decisions after cool reflection and virtually to hand over the job to prominent victims who have moved the public.

When the London headteacher Philip Lawrence was stabbed to death in front of his school while trying to break up a fight, politicians of both main parties rushed to identify with his widow. They did not want just to be seen with her, they wanted to be seen consulting her, listening to her, taking guidance on what should be done. As she would no doubt have been the first to point out, the death of the man she loved in such terrible circumstances would hardly equip her with the clearest or most objective mind. But even so there was a sense, for a week or two, that anything she might choose to advocate would immediately be rushed onto the statute book. As it happened Mrs Lawrence turned out to be an eminently sensible woman who recognised that she was not the right person to lay down the law and declined to do so.

Something rather different happened after Dunblane.

Because of their status as victims, the parents who founded the Snowdrop Campaign to get handguns banned could virtually dictate policy. The attitude of the public to the victims was such that no politician could easily argue the counter case, though a few brave ones tried. And though the founders of Snowdrop may well have been right, that is not the point. What both episodes showed is that, even in a democratic society that still lays claim to a politics of argument and debate, policy can be driven by the power of unthinking feeling and politicians simply have to tag along behind. Nowhere is that more evident than in foreign policy.

The power of television to influence world events is manifest. I reported from Washington throughout the closing stages of the Vietnam War and saw the enormous relief, disbelief almost, that the long nightmare was finally coming to an end. This had been the first true television war in history and the broadcasting networks claimed with typical immodesty that it was their coverage that eventually forced the hands of the politicians and made it impossible for them to keep pouring American riches and American blood into a hopeless conflict. There were other factors – the most powerful army the world had ever seen was fought to a standstill by a bunch of will-o'-the-wisp figures who refused to fight by the rules of conventional war – but there was something in the networks' claim. Images such as a GI setting fire to the roof of a grass hut because 'he had to destroy the village in order to save it', or pictures of GIs smoking pot through the barrels of their guns, or the never-ending succession of body bags, brought both the horror and the futility of it all into the homes of every American. Ultimately the political leaders would have had to act whether they wanted to or not but the public's reaction to the television pictures certainly contributed to the ending of the war.

It can help start wars too. Slobodan Milosevic was not the first European leader to select ethnic cleansing as his favoured tactic for turning his political ambitions into reality – God knows how many atrocities have been carried out through the ages in every corner of Europe – but he was the first to have the results of his brutality filmed at every stage, the pictures fed back to every world capital often before the tears and the blood of his victims had dried. It was inevitable that the cry would go up of 'something must be done' and inevitable that the politicians would have to respond to it.

I would not argue for a moment that the people who reacted with revulsion to the scenes from Bosnia or Croatia or Kosovo and demanded action were behaving in a purely sentimental way. There was sympathy, anger, hatred for the monster prepared to inflict such suffering, and deep desire for revenge against him and his henchmen, quite apart from fear of where it might all lead. All of them are perfectly understandable reactions for human beings faced with such savagery. The problem is that television generates these emotions but does not require the viewer to think through the consequences of taking action.

If you see a little girl being physically abused in the street you decide whether or not to intervene, knowing you may yourself get hurt by confronting the adults abusing her, but also that the little girl needs protection. You make a choice. You see on television a little girl crying beside the body of her dead father in a foreign land and you feel just as strongly that something must be done, but you are not faced with having to work out what the consequences of acting might be. Before you have started to think about it the news programme has moved on to something else. So you are left simply with the strong emotion that something must be done. Troops may be sent to war in response to public feeling, but if they start returning in body bags we see another set of emotion-generating pictures on our screens, of mothers in Glasgow and Sunderland following the funeral cortèges of their sons killed in action. Then the feeling is that something must be done about *that*. The connection between the two is lost. In short, television tends to create a morally unreal world which stimulates our feelings without requiring us to think responsibly through the consequences of the reactions they inspire.

That's why wise politicians know they should treat these

emotions with great caution. Political leaders must operate by a different set of criteria from the rest of us. If we are struck we instinctively strike back. Politicians must pause, consult, reflect and then ask themselves a series of questions. What will be the long-term consequences if I strike back? Will my response ultimately hurt more people than it helps? Am I behaving like this because I fear for my reputation if I do otherwise? They need thinking time. Even threats can be dangerous. If the bluff is called and the threat must be carried out, then what is the next step? But as events unfold or speed up there is so little time to pause and reflect, and the political pressures become immense.

As the television viewer identifies with the victims, demands that something must be done and switches channels, the cry is taken up by people like me on programmes such as *Today* and the clamour grows louder. We amplify the voices that demand action and we do so because we feel we should identify with our viewers and listeners. Arguing for caution and restraint in the face of strong emotion is very difficult for politicians to do when our political culture seems not to value the thoughtful and judicious, but rather the dynamic and powerful. And in this climate cynical politicians will see public emotion not as something to be restrained but to be exploited. If you doubt it read *All Too Human*, a book about his time at the White House by President Clinton's former press secretary George Stephanopoulos. In it he recounts a conversation with Dick Morris, one of the most efficient election-winning operators in the business. Here's the reason Morris gave in that conversation for wanting to bomb the Serbs when they were going about their nasty business in Bosnia: 'They're slaughtering the Bosnians, but so what? I want to bomb the shit out of the Serbians to look strong.'

Technology which allows you to bomb from 15,000 feet and so wage and win a war without a single casualty on your own side makes such political calculations even more tempting.

In the spring of 1999, at the beginning of the NATO bombing campaign against the Serbs over Kosovo, I interviewed a string of Cabinet Ministers and questioned the wisdom of the action, that being what I am paid to do. Morning after morning the response came: 'But, John, what would you have said if we had done nothing?' To which there is only one answer: 'That should not be your concern. I am a pipsqueak journalist. You are a government minister.' But life, as the ministers know, is not like that. Any politician who ignores the call will be accused of callousness even though the options for doing anything effective may be few or even non-existent.

However useful British soldiers in Bosnia or Kosovo may be, their presence there owes a great deal to our feelings, as we watch the box, about helping victims. We send our money to the victim funds and our boys in uniform to the troublespots. If the voters did not see the pictures there would be less pressure on the politicians to act, rightly or wrongly. Conversely, I wonder how long the trench warfare of the First World War would have lasted if television cameras had sent home pictures night after night of all those young men marching into the machine guns.

Responsibility has been redefined to include *being seen to do something*, anything, in response to transient public sentiment often generated by television images, rather than coolly assessing what are realistically the best options. History will judge whether our intervention in Kosovo turns out to have been the responsible thing to do or not. It may be that our prolonged involvement there will lead to a different sort of treatment on television, one that requires us to think harder as well as feel emotion. If that does not happen the danger remains that, as with giving money to Aberfan and Dunblane, decisions are taken primarily to satisfy our fickle moral vanity rather than to do the right thing.

Chapter 5

Children

WRITING ABOUT CHILDREN is a dangerous business since we all think we are experts; even if we haven't had our own we can observe their strange ways. If we are parents ourselves we think we know it all and can't imagine how other parents can be so hopeless. In short, we cannot avoid being judgemental. That has become a terrible insult. When politicians are being interviewed on radio or television they will wriggle and squirm and try to pull the microphone cable out of its socket while you're not looking rather than say anything that might be interpreted as judgemental. You've heard the sort of thing: 'Minister, are you really saying that just because this man is a double murderer who abandoned his entire family on the central reservation of the M1 when he came out of prison, but now wants to settle down in a stable relationship with a cannibal, he should not be allowed to foster children? Isn't that terribly judgemental?'

'Well, of course I'm not saying that one kind of relationship is necessarily better than another one. However . . .'

Fair enough if you're a politician; you need all the votes you can get. But there are, happily, many others who have looked coolly at the way society deals with children and have no problem passing judgement. Take this from the Mental

Health Foundation's 1999 report, 'The Big Picture':

> We claim to be a child-centred society, but in reality there
> is little evidence that we are. In many ways we are a
> ruthlessly adult-centred society where children are
> defined almost exclusively in terms of their impact on
> adult lives ... Our adult-centred society has tried to
> contain and limit the impact of children on adult life by
> either excluding them from much of it, blaming them for
> disturbing it or by admitting them only as designer
> accessories or treating them like pampered pets.

You may think that to be a harsh judgement, but consider one
of the biggest social changes to have taken place in society over
the past generation: our attitude to divorce. Not much more
than a generation ago people in unhappy or even violent
marriages could not divorce and start a new life without being
stigmatised, and that was plainly wrong. The new spirit of the
age encourages self-absorption and tells us we must put our
own right to feel good about ourselves above all else.
Disapproval of divorce meant there were many unhappy
homes. Acceptance of it means there are many more broken
homes. If the present trend continues, within twelve years a
majority of adults will be unmarried and it won't be long before
half of all marriages in Britain end in divorce. A generation ago
fewer than ten per cent of children were born outside marriage.
Now it is nearly four times that. The vast majority of those who
divorce have children below the age of sixteen.

Children of divorced parents are twice as likely to experience
psychological, economic and social problems in adolescence
and adulthood as are children of non-divorced parents. That is
the result of a survey by the Joseph Rowntree Foundation of
no fewer than two hundred studies into the subject. Perhaps
the same would apply to children who lost a parent for any
reason, such as an early death? No. The findings relate
specifically to divorce.

Another survey in Western Europe and the United States
shows that there has been a sharp increase in the number of

children with psychological problems in recent years. Professor Sir Michael Rutter and Professor David Smith wrote about it in their book *Psychosocial Disorders in Young People*. They concluded that those trends could not be accounted for by rising poverty or unemployment, not least because they had increased during periods of low unemployment and rising living standards as well as during periods of high unemployment. What worried them was the part played by broken homes. Other factors included the growth of an alienating youth culture and earlier engagement in sexual relationships. The Parliamentary Family and Child Protection Group found that children from broken homes are more likely to exhibit behavioural difficulties at school, to play truant and to drift into crime. Other studies have shown that a child from a broken home or born out of wedlock is much more likely to be abused than one whose natural parents are married. Home Office research on aspects of crime shows that the strongest influence on when a youngster begins to offend is his relationship with his parents.

You might say that it is no more than common sense. Or you might say that so-called experts can do anything with statistics. Or you might say that it has more to do with social class than anything else. Take a child from a nasty, rundown housing estate with a drug addict mother who was never quite sure who the father was and is more interested in finding her next fix than registering little Wayne at the local library, assuming there is one. Now compare him with young James, whose middle-class mother wouldn't know crack cocaine from talcum powder. It is reasonable to assume that James will have a better start in life than Wayne. But what if it's Wayne who comes from a stable family and James whose father has done a bunk with the nanny? Then the picture changes. In 1998 the chairman of the Headmasters' Conference – the organisation that represents independent schools of the sort James is likely to go to – talked about a survey he had carried out into the social problems facing the schools' middle-class children. You might think it would have been drugs or drink. It was marital breakdown.

We go to great lengths to dodge and weave around the

evidence that proves divorce is bad for children. For instance, it is argued that there are plenty of single mothers who do an excellent job of bringing up their children. So there are, but it does not dispose of the issue. Or it is argued that children should not be brought up by parents who are not happy together and if divorcing will make them happy apart, then that is what they should do. For the sake of the children, you understand.

I remember my own childhood. Endless sunny days when we made tree houses in the woods, fished for sticklebacks and tadpoles in the ponds and streams, staged our inventive and hilarious plays in Farmer Jones' barn, went on endless hikes and cycle rides with picnics in our backpacks and joy in our young hearts . . .

If that sounds like a fairy tale childhood, that's because it is; a load of wishful thinking. My childhood was nothing like that at all; it's what I remember from all those *Just William* books I used to read, with a bit of Enid Blyton thrown in. I wouldn't have known what a tree house was if I fell out of one and you didn't get too many barns to the acre in the back streets of Cardiff. What's more it rained an awful lot. And we got bored an awful lot. There's a limit to how many tadpoles you can catch and kidnap and how long you can watch them wiggling around in their new jam jar home.

There is an element of this fantasy that is true: contrary to another of the prevailing myths, we did not spend a great deal of time with our parents. They were too busy. Five kids and no washing machine or vacuum cleaner does not leave a mother with much spare time. One of the consequences of parents feeling so anxious about their children these days is that they are actually spending much more time with them. Jonathan Gershuny, Professor of Sociology and director of the research centre on micro-social change at the University of Essex, has put together a mass of data from 1961 to 1995 which shows that 'childcare time' has pretty much doubled among men and women in every category. Ah yes, but what *sort* of childcare time?

I may not have spent so much time with my parents, but there was one thing that we always did together: eat. Gershuny found that over the thirty-four years he studied, the family meal had virtually disappeared. It has been replaced, in the prose beloved of academics, by 'irregular and non-familial grazing of pre-cooked or fast foods'. In other words he discovered that the time devoted to eating nearly halved during that period, and when we did eat we tended not to do so as a family. In 1961 we spent ninety-five minutes a day eating; by 1995 it was down to fifty-two minutes. Gershuny describes it wonderfully as 'a retreat from the civilities of the table, but also a "masking" of food consumption which increasingly takes place simultaneously with (and is subsidiary to) some other activity such as watching television'. In other words, parents spend time with their children but don't actually communicate: all eyes are focused on the box. So what are they doing with the extra together time? The answer is: chauffeuring them around.

Modern mothers should be given blue suits and peaked caps because they spend so much time behind the wheel. Anyone who lives in a big city knows what happens during the school holidays. The traffic jams disappear. In London you can get into your car at 8.30 am with a reasonable expectation of arriving at your destination the same day. In the mid-seventies one in three primary-age children walked to school. Now it is one in nine. A research team at University College London looked at how much walking was done by 2,000 children in Camden and Islington and compared it with a generation ago. It had fallen by more than a quarter. One of the results of all this is that children are fatter than they have ever been. Researchers at Exeter University found an 'epidemic of obesity' in a study of teenagers. Now we are importing 'fat camps for kids' from the United States which charge £3,000 for a nine-week course. Something else for middle-class parents to spend their money on. Something else to worry about.

Worry is the chief reason parents get the car out to ferry their children around so much instead of letting them make their own way. A survey published by the London School of Economics in early 1999 discovered that most parents thought the place where they grew up had been 'perfectly safe'. Only one tenth thought the same for their children. A third of them allowed their children little or no time outside the home on their own because they thought it was dangerous. As recently as ten years ago, ninety per cent of children were allowed to play outside regularly. Now only twenty per cent do.

What are the parents so worried about? Traffic is one thing, though it's worth remembering that there would be a lot less of it if Mum's car stayed in the garage. In fact the fear is unfounded. Children were more likely to be killed in road accidents forty years ago than they are today.

The real worry seems to be the fear of dirty old men in grubby raincoats or, in the phrase used by Gershuny, 'the perceived growth of child abuse'. Note that he says 'perceived'. Some people believe it to be real. In 1998 the *Guardian* devoted acres of space over several days to a series of frightening reports by Nick Davies on paedophilia. He claimed the scale of it is huge: 1.1 million paedophiles in Britain. Think about that figure for a moment. For every fifty people in Britain there is one paedophile. Remove the women and children and it's down to one in eighteen. So you will almost certainly know one paedophile and probably several. If it is true it is truly terrifying. But is it? Let's look at some figures.

Nick Davies is a first rate investigative reporter. His book *Dark Heart* brilliantly described the life of some of the most deprived children in Britain, youngsters who sell their bodies to get another fix of drugs and end up diseased and corrupted and, quite often, dead. Davies talked to those children. He gave first-hand accounts of how they were living and what they were doing. You can't do that with paedophiles, not if they want to stay secret as most do. They pursue their loathsome deeds in the dark, hidden away, known only to their victims, to other paedophiles and to the police if they are eventually caught. The police figures show that about 110,000 men have had a conviction at some time for a sex offence against a child. That includes possession of child pornography which, disgusting though it is, does not necessarily involve any actual offence against a child by the convicted man himself.

Of course it is possible that there are another million who
have never been caught. Again we cannot know. We can,
though, use our own judgement, our own experience and our
own common sense. Even if we cannot be sure how many of
our friends and acquaintances may themselves be paedophiles
we can certainly ask ourselves how many children we know
have been attacked by a paedophile outside the home. That,
after all, is what we seek to protect our children against when
we try to guard their every movement.

The problem is that this is not a subject to which we apply
much rational thought. It is surrounded by hysteria and we in
the media are responsible for much of it. We give massive
coverage, reasonably enough, to those mercifully rare cases in
which truly evil men torture and even murder children. But we
give equally massive coverage to those 'Satanic rings' which are
supposed to exist and almost never do. God knows, the
children who are taken from their parents because the social
workers got it wrong have suffered terribly too, not to mention
their innocent parents. That's the trouble with hysteria. It can
produce more victims than it protects. We seldom point out
that the number of children killed every year by perverts has
remained pretty much constant for generations. The Mental
Health Foundation report says physical attacks on children
have not increased since the 1950s. As Matthew Parris put it in
The Times: 'On any reckoning of the myriad ways adults in
modern Britain hurt children and children hurt each other,
paedophilia ranks right down the scale – way behind neglect,
bullying, indifference, divorce, cruelty, bad parenting and bad
example.' But we ignore that and let the hysteria grow.

My study window at home overlooks the roof terrace next
door. A few summers back I was sitting at my typewriter
waiting for inspiration to strike and staring out of the window.
I do a lot of that, anything but look at the empty sheet of paper.
The two little girls who live next door were playing in the sand
pit. They were aged two and four. The four-year-old had
obviously persuaded her innocent little sister that sand was
some sort of rare delicacy, and was feeding it to her on her

spade. The two-year-old was puzzled because it obviously didn't taste as good as her big sister promised her but she's a determined little soul and wasn't going to give up until she'd learned to appreciate the finer points of a spadeful of sand. It was wonderfully funny, so I fetched my video camera, filmed the whole thing and went next door to give the tape to their mother. She was delighted and will no doubt torment the four-year-old with it for many happy years to come.

Then, a few weeks later, I saw a picture of my old friend Julia Somerville in the morning papers and when I read the story I shivered. Julia and her husband had been questioned by the police because of photographs taken of her child fooling around in the bath. The toddler was naked. My little neighbours had been naked too. Julia had taken her film to Boots to be developed and some nasty little sneak had told the police. What if another nasty little sneak had seen me shooting pictures on that sunny afternoon and told the police? It had not occurred to me for a tiny fraction of a second that I was doing anything remotely suspicious, any more than it had occurred to Julia's husband when he took his pictures and she sailed off to Boots with them, but we live in the new dark ages when every adult is a potential child molester. Has it really come to this, that loving parents can no longer take pictures of their children in the bath without the fear of a knock on the door and the police car parked outside the house?

It is easy to spot the ways in which the climate gradually changes. *The Times* reported that 'alarming evidence' of the abuse of schoolchildren on international exchange trips had led the Home Office to fund a full-scale study of the risks. It summarised the evidence: 'Children who are sent to stay with families in Europe have found themselves sexually assaulted, kept in cupboards, or sleeping five to a room, according to a preliminary investigation.' Naturally any responsible parent would respond to that by thinking, 'I'd never realised there were such risks in school trips abroad. Thank God someone's looking into it.' But think again. Can sleeping five to a room really be regarded as 'abuse'? Is it really a bad thing that a child should have to rough it for a couple of weeks, sharing a room with four others? Isn't it possible it might actually do them some good? That it might even be fun? And this cupboard. Who said it was a cupboard, and what exactly is meant by being 'kept' in it? Once you start to think a touch more sceptically about all this, other questions arise. What exactly was the evidence of sexual assault? It turned out that the strongest evidence the preliminary investigations could come up with was a case of 'indecent assault' (note the shift from sexual to indecent), and that had been committed by another child.

So on the basis of that we were to have a full-scale study. That means one of two things. The study may produce nothing, but the fears have already been raised, making nervous and suggestible parents reluctant to let their little darlings go on exchange trips. Or we shall end up with tighter regulations, so that in future all exchange families here and abroad will have to be much more closely vetted to make sure there aren't any dodgy uncles lurking in the shadows, no cupboards and no makeshift dormitories. The likely effect of that would be to close down the opportunities for children to go and stay with families abroad because, quite simply, ordinary decent families won't much like having inspectors prying into their affairs, asking embarrassing questions about whether there are any child abusers among them. Children will have lost one of the ways in which they can learn to grow up.

So why have we let ourselves become so wound up about child abuse? The writer A.N. Wilson thinks we seize on a few particular sins, such as paedophilia, because we are in a moral muddle and we need demons. Brian Appleyard takes a similar view: 'Our morally confused society can only conceive of absolute goodness in a child. Child abuse becomes, therefore, the only absolute evil.' The idea that we should see absolute goodness in any human being, child or not, is a sign of how distorted our moral vision has become. The trouble is that it has consequences, not just for children but for all of us.

Some say that the horror of child abuse is so great it is impossible to protect the child too much; you can't be too careful. Oh, but you can. If a man can no longer smile at a child in a park or the supermarket without a little twinge of worry lest his motives be questioned, or pick up and comfort a toddler who has fallen down and grazed her knee, we have done ourselves great damage. I suppose most of us will come to terms with it, but what of the people who work with children? Everyone agrees that the best primary schools are those with a mixture of male and female teachers, but the way things are going there will be no men left teaching the younger children. The British Educational Research Association looked into the reasons why so few men apply to teach in primary schools. Money has always been a problem – you don't get rich teaching seven-year-olds – but this is something new. Mary Thornton, a researcher at Hertfordshire University, spoke to men on teacher-training courses. 'Should they cuddle a distressed child? Should they ever be alone with children?' They spoke of the 'fear of being accused of abuse'. They were right to be worried.

Michael Emery is a decent man who cares for children and spent his life working with them. He was the deputy head of a Church of England primary school in Leeds, fifty-one years old and the father of two children of his own. He had been a teacher for thirty years, and was happy in the career he loved. Then his life fell apart. He was accused of indecently assaulting two girls, aged nine and ten. The court recognised the accusations for the nonsense they were and threw the case out. But the damage had been done ... to the school and to him. When you read what Mr Emery had to say after his acquittal it makes you want to weep.

'Teaching has been my life for thirty years but this has made me wary of children. I love children. I feed off them and it's lovely to see them smile. Sometimes you feel really proud of them, so I put my arm around them and hug them ... We are in a society now where you can't just innocently touch anybody, whether it be an adult or a child. If a child falls down you daren't put your arm around them. Is that right when they are crying?'

The answer is no, of course it is not right. Soon after the case of Mr Emery the same topic was in the news again. It was early summer and we were, remarkably enough, getting some hot sun. The Local Government Association issued guidelines to local education authorities on what to do about small children playing outside at midday. Simple enough, you would think. Tell them to wear a hat and if their necks are bare slap a bit of sun block on them. Oh no, said the advice, don't even think about that. Your actions might be misinterpreted. They were warned specifically 'not to apply sun cream' in case they were accused of sexual abuse. So if the toddlers are too young to do it for themselves, better they should get burned necks than risk some perverted teacher laying his abusive hands on them. I thought the report had been exaggerated and interviewed the leader of one of the teachers' unions. Surely he would kill the story and tell me it was some over-zealous bureaucrat who had now been shifted to less onerous duties where he was not required to think or exercise judgement. Not at all. The union leader said it was regrettable, but on balance sensible. After all, his members had to be protected.

I had many letters after that programme, mostly from teachers, mostly anonymous. It is rare to receive anonymous letters but such is the climate of fear in this area that they did not want to be identified. Too dangerous. They might be thought to be a bit dodgy themselves. One, an infant school teacher, wrote this: 'One pupil came to school in tears after the death of a beloved pet and no one could give her a cuddle of comfort. That child now sees the staff as uncaring.' Precisely.

What really matters is the damage this is doing to children. If they are told not to trust adults, then adults start behaving in ways that suggest they should not be trusted. We withdraw. We cease to engage with children. In their eyes we start to look remote, inaccessible, suspicious. We are creating a climate which is supposed to protect children and which is having precisely the opposite effect. How can children develop a proper sense of trust and a proper sense of wariness if no one is to be trusted, if all men are potential abusers? Not only are we making physical affection more difficult for children to come by, we are at risk of making them feel isolated in a world defined by danger. If we tell children to be suspicious of adults and not to trust them, that's what they will do. But you cannot live life not trusting people. You cannot be happy unless you trust people. You cannot love unless you trust. How to trust, and who, is something that has to be learned. Children who are overprotected from risk, or who live in a climate of mistrust, cannot learn.

I try to imagine a group of child experts in the pre-television age discussing the best way to bring up children. One of them suggests something like this: 'Shut 'em up in their bedrooms for several hours a day with no company except a box in the corner that pumps out moving images electronically. Some of the things they watch will be informative and educational, might even stretch their imagination from time to time. Much of it will be meretricious rubbish, often coarse and vulgar or even violent and full of crude language and sexual innuendo. You will not be able to monitor what they watch because you will not be there with them. But at least they'll be occupied and won't be out in the street getting up to mischief.' An unlikely recommendation, you would think. But now that television is into its second age let us look at what is happening.

According to the Independent Television Commission, one fifth of children aged four and under have their own television set in their bedrooms. By the time they reach the age of eight the figure rises to one third, and by the age of eleven it is more than two thirds. They spend three hours a day in front of either the television or the computer screen. A 1999 London School of Economics report entitled 'Young People, New Media' concluded that more and more children are retreating from the real world into a 'bedroom culture'. The vast majority of the parents do not like it and – here's the odd thing – neither do the children. They are resentful at not being allowed out and say they find television boring.

The Chief Rabbi, Dr Jonathan Sacks, believes it all contributes to the destruction of family life: 'They starve our children of the oxygen of togetherness ... The Walkman, computer games and the Internet we enjoy alone ... Families can only flourish on the basis of dedicated time, shared celebration and conversation.'

In 'The Big Picture', the most comprehensive study of its kind ever carried out in Britain, the Mental Health Foundation reported that one in five children is suffering from mental health problems of one kind or another and growing isolation is a big factor. It may be happening as a result of the screens in the bedroom or parents separating or the fragmentation of extended families and community responsibility for children. Add to that the reduction in the time spent outside in unsupervised travel and the increasing fear of abuse. What we are left with is a growing number of children unpractised in making and consolidating friendship, dealing with conflict, taking risks – all 'key components in the development of emotional literacy'.

There is no doubt that the climate we are creating for our children is having some curious and deeply worrying effects. By making them increasingly isolated it makes it harder for them to become mature adults. Yet, at the same time, it is pushing them into becoming grown up at an ever earlier age.

We used to say it was a sign of advancing age when the policemen started to look younger. Now it's more a case of the kiddies looking older. We can thank our better diets for that. I used to be of average height (for Welshmen, at any rate) but now, if I walk into a room of young people, I know how Alice must have felt when she drank from the bottle and shrank. Suddenly they're all giants. It must be hard for a modern mother – or father, for that matter – to talk sternly to her errant fourteen-year-old son when she has to tilt her head back as he towers above her. I don't know why we get so exercised about parents occasionally slapping their children. The way things are going the kids will be able to hit back once they're out of their nappies. It's happening already. 'Darren, go to bed! You're only eight years old and it's way past your bedtime.' 'But Mum, I hate that bed. It's only six feet long and my feet stick out of the bottom.' 'Darren, go to bed ... Darren, put me down!'

Boys used not to have their first pair of long trousers until they were thirteen or so. Now those longs would be the perfect shorts for a thirteen-year-old. That was when our voices used to start going funny and we either squeaked or growled. Now puberty for boys is common at the age of ten. At the turn of the century most girls started menstruating when they were sixteen. Now it's thirteen. A quarter of all girls have their first period when they are still in primary school.

Whatever else we may have enjoyed as children after the war there was not much justice and democracy about. Adults were always right, and children were automatically wrong. Adults took the decisions and if you didn't like it you kept your mouth shut and comforted yourself by thinking that you'd be grown up yourself one day and then you could get your own back. For the most part it was tolerable, but the occasional blatant injustice rankled. Breaking wind at the dinner table (I'm sorry for the indelicacy, but there was much more roughage eaten in those days) was always a risky business. If you did it and you got a clip, fair enough. But if your father did it and you *still* got a clip . . . well, where was the justice in that? Openly accusing your father was not an option. In that respect life was much easier after we got a dog. She could be blamed for everybody's flatulence. Now, according to the Future Foundation, modern families are more open and democratic: 'There is more discussion with children and a greater expectation of their right to participate in the family decision-making process.' Their focus groups told them that 'family negotiations within clear parameters were likened to workers' councils . . . There is an explicit wish in many cases to invert adverse relationships of their own parents' experience . . . They want children to be "mates" not to keep their distance.' Instead of being subordinates, children treat adults as 'their own kind'. Most of that seems eminently sensible, though I'm still sufficiently old-fashioned to bridle when I hear small children using the Christian name of someone old enough to be their grandmother. Incidentally, I bridle even more when television reporters patronisingly refer to old people by their Christian names. Mrs Mavis Jones becomes 'Mavis', just because she is in her eighties. Reporters who do it should be sacked on the spot and replaced by their grannies.

It surely makes sense to remember that children are still children. In the late eighties I presented an edition of *Family Matters* for BBC1 in which we looked at mothers who encouraged their little daughters to dress like grown-ups. We all know that little girls love to do it, and we have all laughed at the child who has raided her mother's bedroom and tottered around on high heels, a long skirt dragging behind her and lipstick smeared over her mock-serious face. But the little girls on my television programme were no laughing matter, nor were their mothers. Some were clearly seen as their ambitious mothers' tickets to fame and fortune: future stars of stage and screen, painted and primped and preening. Others were little fashion plate replicas of their elegant mothers. Their clothes were fashionable and immaculate; so was their make-up. Some were no more than eight or nine years old. I was deeply uneasy at the time and so, to judge by their response, were many viewers. Still, these were pretty rare exceptions were they not? You don't get many mothers encouraging their little tots to dress like little tarts. Well, not then maybe, but you do now.

For a middle-aged man like me, doing research on this subject can be a pretty dangerous business. I draw the line at wandering through Marks and Spencer closely studying little girls' dresses and skirts. One call to the *News of the World* is all it would take and you can see the headline: 'SEXY SECRETS OF JOHN'S GYMSLIP JAUNTS!' It is not necessary. The evidence of what is happening to children's fashion is all around us. Mothers tell me it is increasingly difficult to resist the pressures of a culture that is turning ten-year-olds into miniature eighteen-year-olds.

The fashion industry is partly to blame for using younger and younger girls as models. They want the fresh-faced look, the flat-chested skinny look, the innocence combined with the hint of sexual awakening. It is distinctly unnerving to spot a beautiful and sexy young face in a newspaper and then discover that its owner is a child. But our entire culture conspires in this. The teen mags and the pre-teen mags, the films and the television, the lyrics of some of the most popular songs all play their own part. It is easy to blame pop stars for encouraging their tiny fans to emulate them when they're strutting their sexy stuff, but they are only one small part of it. If Marks and Spencer sell padded bras for pre-pubescent children they do it because they know there's a market out there. There is a lot more money to be made from selling mini-adult clothes that go out of fashion as swiftly as a rock band than selling white blouses, short socks and sandals. So we have raunchy little skin-tight miniskirts for seven-year-olds and if they end up as pre-pubescent sex objects, so what?

Let us consider the teen mags. It's hardly surprising that they are not called comics any longer; they bear as much resemblance to the sort of things children used to read as *Fanny Hill* does to Enid Blyton. I used to kid myself that I was not entirely naïve about this sort of thing. I knew your typical twelve-year-old was interested in more than ponies and football; even so I blushed at some of this stuff. There should be a warning on the covers: 'UNSUITABLE FOR THE OVER-FIFTIES.' Much of the editorial content would fit perfectly well between the covers of *Penthouse*. If I needed any advice on 'HOW TO GIVE MY BLOKE A BLOW JOB HE'LL NEVER FORGET'; 'HOW TO ACHIEVE MULTIPLE ORGASMS (FOR BOTH OF YOU!!)'; the relative merits of anal sex and mutual masturbation or how to make the most of love beads (they do *what* with them?) that is where I'd turn. And why not, you may say, it's a long time since Angela Brazil provided all the thrills a girl needs and I doubt that too many boys regard Roy of the Rovers as their role model any longer. If the mags were full of moralising homilies in which the clean-cut young lads blushed when a girl smiled at them and the girls took off their knickers only after they'd put on their wedding ring, they would still be collecting dust on the shelves of WH Smith when the youngsters were collecting their bus passes.

Instead the magazines sell well and clearly the children would not buy them if they did not enjoy them. Their adult defenders say they do an important job; they inform and educate as well as entertain. Yvonne Roberts – mother and journalist – says that because they 'show the size and shape of a willy', for instance, curiosity is not such a pull and therefore, presumably, temptation is reduced. That bit intrigues me. I suspect most men know the size and the shape of women's breasts and may even have seen one or two in their time, but that does not stop them wanting to see more of them, if only to compare and contrast. Then again, perhaps a willy is less aesthetically pleasing than a breast. But these are dangerous waters.

If the teen mags fail to do the trick, the curious kiddies can turn to the box. One television programme called *Love Bites* was shown at lunchtime and dealt with how to perform foreplay. There were complaints but it was deemed to have been 'educational'.

What is clear is that children have access to more information about sex than they have ever had. The closest we got to the naughty bits in my primary school was learning about pistils and stamens in biology. Now children are, sensibly, told not only where babies come from but how to stop them coming. Condoms are handed around in sex education classes as freely as rock samples in a science class. If the advice fails and the tots become pregnant they can get the morning-after pill. So in theory, with all the advice and contraception available, we should be witnessing a sharp reduction in the number of teenage pregnancies and cases of sexually transmitted diseases. There should be many fewer unwanted pregnancies today than there were in the days when only the bravest and boldest young lads would risk the terminal embarrassment of going into a shop to buy a packet of three. The reality is the precise opposite.

By the end of the twentieth century teenage girls were having more babies, more abortions and more venereal diseases than ever before. Almost one in a hundred girls aged fifteen or younger was becoming pregnant. That is the highest rate of teenage pregnancies in the western world, except for the United States, and still rising. Most calls to the charity ChildLine from fourteen- to fifteen-year-old girls were about pregnancy. A minority of the callers were aged ten to twelve. Britain also holds the record in Europe for teenage abortions. A study in the *British Medical Journal* found that the same was true for sexual disease amongst teenagers. It was not just the worst, but getting worse still. There has been an enormous increase in the incidence of chlamydia, up by nearly a third in one year alone. It is a particularly nasty disease because there are no obvious symptoms and it can leave a woman infertile in years to come.

More than half the underage girls who became pregnant had abortions. Two who did not appeared in the *Daily Mail* after one more set of depressing statistics had been published. They were sisters, Miranda and Charlene Way, aged fifteen and sixteen. They were posing bump to bump, winsome expressions on their puppy fat faces. Both had been put on the pill by their mother when they were fourteen.

While all this has been happening there has been an even sharper rise in the availability of contraception to underage girls: Boots the Chemists opened a clinic at their store in Glasgow offering free confidential contraceptive advice and the morning-after pill to children from the age of thirteen. The doctor in charge of the experiment said it was all 'extremely exciting'. The MP Jenny Tonge has been campaigning for the morning-after pill to be available in all chemists and from all school nurses. Some school nurses recommend pupils to the neighbouring GP for the morning-after pill. The medical director of a family planning clinic in London advocates contraceptive implants for some teenagers.

Clearly it will not be too long before almost every child in the country has access to the morning-after pill. If we are to have fewer unwanted teenage pregnancies that may well be the thing to do – there is some evidence that the numbers do fall in areas where they can get it with no questions asked – but what a bleak picture all this paints. The message given to the children, when everything else is cut away, is simply this: try not to get pregnant but it doesn't really matter too much if you do because you'll be able to pop a pill in the next day or two and you'll be fine.

We can hardly blame the children themselves. Young teenagers are impressionable, and always have been. They are mightily interested in sex, and always have been. When their hormones kick in and they discover sex they assume that they are the first generation to do so. A number of things have changed, though. Martin McKee, Professor of European Public Health at the London School of Hygiene and Tropical Medicine, said in the *British Medical Journal* that one of the clues might lie in the home, in 'the amount of time families spend together'.

Something else that has changed is that we now drench the senses of children with sexual messages of one kind or another. Polly Toynbee, one of the more thoughtful voices in liberal Britain, belonged to what she describes as the sexual liberation generation. When the sexual revolution began in the late sixties, she once wrote, sex was a metaphor for revolutionary change, a weapon in a fight against staid respectability. It had wit, bite and meaning. 'We used to mock prudishness, censorship and petty lace curtain censoriousness. We said let it all hang out, let sex be free and open and natural, and then it will be just a normal part of life. The laws changed, things relaxed and everything was cool, right?'

But, a generation later, she found that everything was not 'cool' and sex did not become just a normal part of life. Now she is appalled at 'all this weary, stupid sex' which is just a 'dim little bit of dumbly respectable titillation'. We are fed 'an endless, dreary de-humanising diet of smut and innuendo and sexual imagery'.

Parents who have watched the explosion of those teen mags which, for all their educational content, are frequently little more than soft porn, will know what she means. So will anyone who watches television or glances at the advertisements in newspapers or on billboards. Sex – especially teen sex – is now used to sell everything and, as Toynbee says, we are more obsessed with it, more prurient, more lubricious than ever. Why should we expect our children to behave differently?

I have talked to many professionals in the field – practice nurses, district nurses, social workers – who are concerned that the children who most need the advice they can offer are the least likely to seek it. Some display a terrifying ignorance. One study shows that a quarter of eleven- to sixteen-year-olds believe the contraceptive pill guards against venereal diseases. I have a niece, Judith, who is the nurse practitioner with a group of GPs in a small country town in Dorset. She has two children of her own, has been a nurse for seventeen years, is broad-minded, well informed and very bright. She is one of the least prudish and censorious people I know, but she is dismayed at the way children now come into her clinic routinely demanding the pill. Not seeking advice, not wanting to discuss their problems, just demanding contraception as of right. Being the tough and sensible young woman that she is she sits them down and refuses to give them what they want until she's had a proper talk with them, but she knows in truth it's a waste of time. In the end she will give them what they came for.

Sometimes they will come back pregnant, sometimes not. She feels desperately sorry for them. 'Every message they get from society says that sex is cool so they ask for the pill and we have to prescribe it. But they're still children. Their bodies are grown-up but their minds are not mature enough to deal with this sort of pressure. How can a girl say no to her boyfriend when he knows how easy it is for her to get the pill? It's all so sad.'

Judith is right. It's sad that we have let them down and taken the easy road of treating them as small adults when what they really are is confused children. If we plaster the country with instant access clinics doling out pills as if they were chocolate drops we might gradually reduce the number of unwanted pregnancies. But it will still be sad.

You do not have to be sentimental about the golden innocence of childhood to believe that there is something special about it. We say, with a sad shake of our heads, 'Honestly, kids today, they just grow up so quickly,' as if we have no influence over it. But we do. It is we who treat them like adults, look on nervously as they are exposed to the adult world of television violence and gratuitous sex and the worst excesses of consumerism and broken families. If not us, then who?

We endlessly confront children with problems and dilemmas and worries and difficulties that they simply should not have to face. The children's charity NCH Action for Children wants all children from primary school age to read a pamphlet containing advice about how to handle their parents' divorce should it happen. Talk about having to grow up quickly. If we force children of eight and nine to confront the realities of adulthood, we should not be surprised if they start behaving as if they were adults. What is extraordinary is that we then start to treat them as though they were.

When a seven-year-old girl claimed in 1998 that she had been raped by two of her classmates in a primary school not only did her headteacher believe her, but so did the police. The boys were charged and the case got into the courts. Only after the trauma of that court case for the girl, for the boys and for their parents, was it established that nothing of the sort had happened and all that had gone on was the sort of messing about that there's always been among kids of that age. Why did she claim she'd been raped? It can only be because the idea of rape had been introduced into her world. It was part of the reality about which she could fantasise. She could put two and two together and get five; she was not knowledgeable enough to know that boys her age almost certainly could not rape her, but because she had the idea of rape in her head she was able to link it to what she and they had been up to. But why did adults believe her? Again it can only be because, in their anxiety about the dangers lurking everywhere for children in relation to sex, they lost a sense of proportion and imagined that children upon whom they'd been forcing an adult world had indeed started behaving as adults.

Why else warn children about what might happen if their parents divorce? Tell a child how to cope with a monster hidden in the wardrobe and he will believe there really is a monster in the wardrobe. It may be well intentioned but it's potentially damaging. It risks making children mistrustful of their parents and wary of their love, and making them feel isolated and exposed. They may well suffer all that if their parents do divorce. Why make them go through it if it is only a possibility?

In postwar Britain advertisers did not target children, for the perfectly good reason that children did not have much money to spend. Now they have a great deal, or at least their parents do. We've managed to persuade ourselves that if we don't buy our son the latest fashion (it's not just our daughters who care about clothes any longer) then he will 'suffer stress'. So we pay up. We spend a fortune on them, far more than we have ever done before in real terms. We submit to what is grotesquely called 'pester power'. When a 1999 survey showed that middle-class parents spent £200 a week on each child the *Daily Mail* interviewed three mothers, each with two children. None spent less than £65 a week on clothes and shoes for the two children. One spent £95 every week on average – and they were both boys. 'Charlotte,' said another mother, 'is very conscious about how she looks and regularly has a manicure and leg wax and her haircut costs almost as much as mine.' Charlotte was fourteen. 'They tend to want the best,' said her mother. Just so. Another said, 'So much of it is peer pressure. They want what all their friends have.'

As a result of all this we are producing the most materialistic little monsters in the world. A recent poll suggests that a third of British teenagers say the thing they want most out of life is to be rich. In Germany it was a quarter and in Italy many fewer again. And it seems that one of the ways they're trying to be rich is gambling. The experts tell us 145,000 children between the ages of twelve and fifteen have a serious gambling problem.

There is a paradox here. We proclaim the rights of children now in a way that society has never done before, and yet our behaviour towards them is marked by ambivalence and confusion. We want to protect them in ways we never did before, but at the same time we turn them into premature adults and give them licence to leave their childhood behind at an earlier and earlier age. We work harder to earn more money to give our children a better life, but we often deny them what they need most, and what their parents can provide best. We create the concept of 'quality time' but allow our children to spend much of their lives in isolation. We accept the notion promoted by society that self-indulgence is fine and self-restraint is, at best, mildly eccentric. It is good to be tolerant; it is bad to be judgemental.

So it's a pretty bleak picture on the face of it. Half the kids in Britain are from broken homes and so sexually sophisticated they make Bill Clinton look virginal. When they're not reading about sex or talking about it they're actually doing it, and then either getting pregnant or having abortions. All that matters to them is money, which they spend on clothes that would make a tart blush. They are more aggressive, selfish, indulged and insecure than their parents, and yet protected more than any other generation from all the horrors lurking on the other side of their front door.

Yes that is a caricature, a gross exaggeration. The truth is that most children are decent and loving; selfish and generous; hard working and lazy; happy and miserable and thoroughly mixed up. Just as children have always been. But look at the trend, at the changes that are taking place, and it is worrying. If we allow the advertising whiz-kids, the film and television programme makers, the pop stars and the teen mags to destroy what remains of the culture of old-fashioned shame and morality we should at least look at what is taking over, and ask where that might go.

What I have been trying to do in the first section of this book is look at the climate that prevails in Britain today and at how our notion of responsibility has changed over the past forty years. Increasingly we are reluctant to accept responsibility for our own actions and for the way in which society is changing. There is still a voice telling us to ask ourselves 'What responsibilities do we have?' but it is being virtually drowned out by a much stronger voice encouraging us not to bother about whether we have responsibilities, even to doubt whether responsibilities exist. The prevailing climate tells us that what life is really all about is feelgood, satisfying our desires, getting all we can, trying to make life easy for ourselves, regarding the world as something there to entertain us. So what has happened to move us from the one world to the other, from a world where there was a recognisable moral framework with its attendant demands and responsibilities to the world of today? What are the forces that are feeding this new climate? Those are the questions I shall try to address in the next section.

Section Two

Consumer populism

Chapter 6

How we got here

IT WAS A glorious sunny morning in 1930s England. The Great War had been over long enough for the worst of the memories to start fading and Hitler still seemed more manic than menacing. My mother and father had crossed the Bristol Channel for a few days away from the grime of industrial Cardiff in the rural quiet of Somerset, staying with an aunt in the small village of Wellow. They were about to sit down for their Sunday lunch when the door was knocked back on its hinges and the Vicar marched in. The aunt leapt to her feet and dropped a mini curtsey.

There was no polite 'Good morning' or 'Sorry to burst in like this' from the Vicar.

'Where were you this morning, Mary-Ellen, and why were you not in church!'

Not a question, a demand.

The aunt stumbled out some apology and explanation about her nephew and his new young wife being over from Cardiff for the weekend and it being a lovely morning and wanting to take him for a walk before he left to go home again, but the Vicar wasn't interested in any of that. Nor did he acknowledge the presence of my father and mother.

'Don't do it again!' he ordered. And he marched out.

My father – now in his late eighties – still recalls every detail of that morning in Wellow and his anger is as bright now as it was more than half a century ago. But such was the climate of deference in those days, an unquestioning attitude to authority, that nobody challenged it because it seemed the natural order of things.

A generation later my father had his own children and, though he loathed unthinking deference, he and his generation knew what was socially acceptable and what was not. He was a french polisher who hated taking orders and so had no choice but to set up his own one-man business. Once, when there was not enough money to buy food and even he could find no work, he pawned my mother's engagement ring, the only thing they owned of any value. But he got it back and swore he'd never do it again. Nor did he.

If his main supply of work dried up – polishing the panelling in the officers' quarters of the ships that called into Cardiff or Barry or Port Talbot docks to offload their cargoes of iron ore or bananas – he would send me and my older brother, Graham, out to stuff badly printed circulars advertising his services into the letter boxes of the wealthier neighbourhoods

My father was a rare craftsman – sadly a dying breed – and could transform something that had been bashed and battered, scratched and scalded and generally rendered worthless into something of real beauty. His shelves were the shelves of an alchemist – endless old aspirin bottles or tobacco tins filled with powders and potions that he would mix together until he found the perfectly matching colour for the work in hand. What he lacked was a workshop. There were no garages in those back-to-back houses so the kitchen became the workshop. One of the abiding memories of my childhood is nasty smells: a disgusting and lethal substance called oxalic acid being boiled by my father in an old tin can on the gas stove which got right into the back of your throat and seemed to hang in the air for days, or the smell of home perms. My mother was a hairdresser who refused to go out to work once she had children, so the local ladies came to the kitchen to have their hair done.

I hated all of that, but it was worse if the work did not come in. My father could not tolerate being out of work. He – and countless more like him – felt diminished if he was not working and earning for his family and he simply could not cope with it. I sometimes wonder if those economists who talk so blithely about the need for a certain level of unemployment to 'encourage labour mobility' and 'act as a rein on inflationary pressures' have ever seen at first hand what being out of work does to people, to their self-esteem and sense of worth.

Before television came we would stay out until dark, until our mothers started bawling for us to come home and go to bed. It was not just your own mother who told you what to do. A mother was a mother. She represented authority. If someone else's mother gave you a clip and you told your own mother, you were as likely as not to get another clip for good measure. Oddly enough, it was different if a man did it. I remember telling my father that I'd been walloped by a man in the next street for no good reason (though now, half a century later, I suspect there was actually a very good reason) and he exploded, dragged me around the corner to the man's house, almost bashed the door down and told him he'd flatten him if he ever laid a finger on me again. Justice tended to be more arbitrary then. It was accepted that you would be caned by teachers and cuffed by policemen or park keepers. The notion that there were other societies out there in which different rules applied simply did not occur to us. How could it?

We did what we were told by figures in authority or else we paid the price – assuming we were caught, of course, and most of the time we weren't. Apples pinched from trees in the posher neighbourhoods tasted all the sweeter. It's true about forbidden fruit; the risk of getting nabbed added to the flavour.

Of course it was wrong and we knew it. We were told endlessly what was wrong and what was right, if not by our parents then by somebody else. For those of us who went to Sunday School, the Vicar reinforced the message. There was a clear line of authority running through those tight little communities. At its peak stood the Vicar himself, the headmaster and perhaps the local GP. Interestingly, the local chemist often had considerable status. You went to him for all sorts of advice, and for getting things out of your eye. He was a surrogate doctor, counsellor and, in my family's case, he even provided shelter in his cellar during the air raids.

Perhaps my childhood community was a paradigm for the wider world. For most of our history there has been an élite, various figures of authority to whom, by and large, we paid some heed. Sometimes they were fair and just and sometimes – as with the appallingly rude Vicar – they behaved like martinets. I suspect real deference of the sort displayed by Great Aunt Mary-Ellen began its long, slow death not many years after her encounter with the Vicar; it scarcely survived the Second World War. And a good thing too. The question is whether we threw out the baby of responsibility with the bath water of deference. If we no longer have the élites telling us what our responsibilities are we have to define them for ourselves. That is altogether more difficult because we have not only rejected unthinking deference, we also question authority and the institutions in a way that we never did before.

I spend my professional life challenging authority and some people say it is people like me who are to blame for the decline of authority in general. I could paper my office with letters from retired colonels who clearly think that the nation would be a damn sight healthier if cocky smart alecks like me were given a spell in a decent regiment cleaning the lavatories and obeying orders. Perhaps they're right but I usually reply that people like me have reacted to, rather than created, a change in attitude to authority in general. I get even more letters telling me that respect has to be earned and that authority is there to be challenged.

We have been challenging it for many years now, at the highest level and the lowest. In the grandest courts of the land the Lord Chamberlain might have been exposed to ridicule over the denial of an actor's right to bare his backside on a theatre stage, or a publisher might have had to fight for the right to sell a work of real literary merit that happened to contain some fruity language. At the lowest level, how many times has the naughty little boy run away from the park keeper over grass that was NOT to be walked upon.

Richard Hoggart, one of Britain's most respected cultural critics, believes that the powers of authority, whether religious or lay, have been eroding for more than a century but the erosion has accelerated in the past fifty years or so. He thinks the watershed came roughly at the end of the last war, which means that anyone under the age of fifty would not easily appreciate the strength of that sense of 'them' and 'us'.

Few will mourn the passing of that old automatic deference. We have moved on from that world of hierarchy, in which the élite set the standards and the rest of us were expected to conform. We are better educated, more widely travelled, better informed about what's going on, so we do not need an élite to supply us with a set of standards. But then the question arises: if the 'guiding authorities' have lost their power, what has taken their place? As Hoggart says, no society can tolerate a vacuum so something must have filled it. Part of the answer – though only part of it – is the consumer society.

At about the time I was toddling off to infants' school the modern consumer society was beginning to find its feet. The middle classes were already starting to spend again after the austerity of the war years, but the working class was a long way behind. In the street where I was brought up there was only one car and that was owned not by a local family but by the man who ran the little timber yard two doors from my house and drove in from the posh suburbs. We kids admired it and tried the doors occasionally when the owner wasn't looking just in case he'd forgotten to lock it (he never did) but I can't remember that we ever envied it. Nor, I'm sure, did my parents. It simply wasn't achievable and so the question of envy did not arise. Not most of the time, at any rate.

Rationing was still a fact of life for my early school years and, although I can't remember ever going hungry, there was never enough of the things we really wanted. We did not miss exotic fruit such as bananas because many of us had never seen one, but chocolate was another matter. And meat. I hated the fat little kid who lived opposite me because his father was a butcher. Having a butcher for a father in those days was a bit like the nineties equivalent of having a Spice Girl for a mother. Not quite so glamorous, perhaps, but infinitely more desirable. The fat kid would walk out of his house ostentatiously chewing on a lamb bone and deliberately drop it, only half eaten, in the gutter. It required enormous powers of self-restraint not to pick it up and finish it off when his back was turned. You couldn't do that, of course, because that's exactly what he wanted you to do. Far better – and almost as satisfying – to punch him on the nose instead. I hear he's a chef these days. May his mousses never set.

It took a number of changes to move the consumer society into top gear and set it roaring away. The first thing that had to happen was to connect those two vital links in the consumer chain: supply and demand. Once the factories around the world stopped having to produce as many tanks and fighters and shells and bombs, they could start producing all sorts of other things that we didn't know we wanted until we realised we could have them: cars and vacuum cleaners, telephones and fridges and, of course, television sets. What's more, it was increasingly possible to afford them, both because the emerging new technology and mass production was delivering them more cheaply and because we were almost all in work.

So as soon as that supply–demand link was properly established, the idea began to take root that we are all essentially consumers, with ever-increasing needs and appetites that have to be satisfied *now*.

For the first time we had an economy that could supply it all on a mass scale, and a mass media telling us what we wanted. Not that we needed much persuading. It was to be a while yet before commercial television arrived, but we did not have to be subjected to the hard sell of television advertisements for our expectations to be aroused. What we saw on our tiny black-and-white screens encased in their vast mahogany cabinets was another way of life, and that did the trick. There was no gritty real-life soap opera in those days, no *Eastenders* or Albert Square. What the BBC offered us was the middle class, or at least an idealised version of the middle class, blue in tooth and claw. For the first time we were invited into the middle-class living-room, saw the antimacassars and the fitted carpet and the perfect little middle-class family sitting around the perfect little middle-class dining table. The milk was in a jug and not a bottle, the jam in little pots and not the jam jar. The kitchen had fitted cupboards and a shiny electric cooker and a fridge.

This was indeed a different world for those of us who lived in back-to-back houses with the lavatory in the back yard and a stone sink in the back kitchen. The kitchen proper was where we ate and lived and there was one more room downstairs, the parlour. We used it at Christmas when a fire was lit in its small grate and we used it to do our homework. Otherwise the parlour door stayed shut and the curtains only slightly parted so that passers-by looking through the window would see a tidy room that looked as if it was never lived in. It wasn't.

I talk about being invited into another world for the first time. It's true that we had been transported into other worlds in the cinema, but somehow that wasn't the same. We knew that was make-believe. We knew that the cowboy who was bashed over the head with a chair and got up unbruised and smiling, ready for more, wasn't really hurt because the chair wasn't really solid wood. So when we saw a scene from a middle-class home on the big cinema screen we suspected that that wasn't real either. The difference with television was that it felt real, that what we were watching was not Hollywood but very close to home. This, we understood, was how otherwise ordinary people lived. It was entirely predictable that it would awaken a latent demand, and so it did.

My mother was the least demanding and least avaricious person I have ever met, though I dare say everyone says that about their mothers. Like millions of other working-class women with five children she spent every waking moment caring for us, feeding us, cleaning up after us, washing our clothes and shopping for us. The only time she ever sat down was to eat and to darn holes in socks or pullovers. She was an intelligent woman but I never saw her read a book when I was a child; there simply wasn't time. She made sure her children read books instead. She did not complain because she could not see that there was anything to complain about. She loved her children and it was her job to care for them and that was that. But she was not a saint and she certainly wasn't a martyr, and she was as thrilled as the rest of us when we finally bought a television set; it was something to watch when she was ironing or sewing. One of the things she saw was that impossibly perfect mother on the tiny screen whisking through her housework in a matter of minutes with Hoover and washing machine, the only visible sign of effort the occasional wisp of hair escaping prettily from a spotless Alice band, and finishing all her work in plenty of time to welcome hubby home from the office, perfectly made up, with a kiss and a smile and a small glass of sherry and . . . Well, who wouldn't want a bit of that?

So along came the Hoover (the cat never fully recovered from the shock) and, much later, a washing machine, the delivery carefully arranged when my mother was out shopping and the huge box gift-wrapped.

(Try giving a modern mum a kitchen appliance as though it's a diamond necklace. 'Happy birthday, my dear, I've bought you a vacuum cleaner.' I think not.)

What was happening in our little house was happening all over the country. We were all becoming consumers. And when commercial television arrived the pressures increased. Now, not only could we see what others had, we were being told endlessly that we could (and should) have it for ourselves. Forty years on from the start of commercial television it is impossible to exaggerate the effect of those advertisements. Even now I can remember many of the jingles. We all repeated them the way youngsters would once have repeated nursery rhymes. I still wonder where the yellow went when you brushed your teeth with Pepsodent and why Murray Mint should be the too-good-to-hurry-mint. By today's sophisticated standards they were truly dreadful, but we were fascinated by them. Nowadays companies who spend millions on television advertising worry about the way so many of us record a programme on video so that we can fast forward through the adverts. Then we were riveted by them. They *were* the entertainment, just as much as the programmes that surrounded them.

But what if we could not afford all those wonderful things now being offered to us, even if most people did have jobs? No problem, there was the 'never-never'. Hire purchase. It was this that really unleashed the consumer spending boom, though not in my home. As far as my mother was concerned borrowing was one of the Seven Deadly Sins. The never-never was a temptation devised by Satan to lure the unwary into a life of profligacy and, therefore, sin. Decent people did not buy something until they had saved up for it . . . *earned* it. I remember telling her years later that a friend of mine had borrowed from the bank to take his family on holiday. She reacted as if he had sold the children into slavery.

Christopher Booker has written in *The Neophiliacs* of the speed of change in Britain after the placid conservatism of the early fifties: 'There stood revealed a different England – febrile, on the make, settling into a new and faster tempo of life.' In 1957 Harold Macmillan made his famous speech in which he told us that some of us had never had it so good. That remark has entered history but, as Booker notes, he went on to say something which was scarcely reported at the time or since. 'What is beginning to worry some of us is: "Is it too good to be true?" or perhaps I should say, "Is it too good to last?"'

The new affluence, car ownership, the whole consumer and media revolution brought with it social change that challenged the very essence of the sort of community in which I had been brought up. In one sense television broadened our horizons. Ultimately it was to have the curious effect of shrinking them again as, more and more, we watched people doing things rather than doing them ourselves. The apotheosis of that was to be the television in the children's bedrooms, the microwaved meals eaten at different times and often eaten alone.

I have been trying to give a flavour of what it was like to grow up in a poor, working-class district of one smallish city in a country going through the most profound changes. To much of the change we were oblivious. There were things happening in London – the daring and dangerous new plays in the theatre and the risqué doings of the Chelsea set – that might have been happening on the dark side of the moon as far as we were concerned. To the best of my memory we were neither looking back in anger with John Osborne, nor discovering sexual intercourse with Philip Larkin, though the pill was to have a profound effect on our sexual habits before very much longer and we did eventually discover that pot was something you smoked as well as something you tried to do in dingy snooker halls. We say rather absurdly today that if you can remember the sixties you weren't there. What we should probably say is that if you can't remember the sixties you weren't in London.

But we were all touched – every man, woman and child in the land – by the new affluence, the rise of consumerism, the influence of the media, the downgrading of the old élites and the automatic deference paid to them. We took some lengthy strides in the direction of a classless society too.

As Christopher Booker says, the New Aristocrats were pop singers, clothes designers, actors and actresses, film-makers, photographers, artists, writers and models. (He might have added television performers.) The Old Aristocrats had not, though, gone away. In a moment of breathtaking stupidity the Tories had given the leadership of their party to Sir Alec Douglas-Home and thus handed the next government to Harold Wilson. Sir Alec had once been a belted earl. Hard to imagine a political party ever making such a mistake again. From then on it was all grocers' daughters and grammar school boys. And that was just for the Tories. Nowadays we must turn to the Labour Party for a leader educated at a public school.

As for the rest of us, we have gained a taste for freedom and no longer wish to be deferential. We have had economic opportunities as never before, both as consumers and as workers, provided by an economic system more productive than any in history, and a welfare politics keen to spread the resulting wealth about. Our whole attitude to poverty has been redefined. Poverty is no longer an absolute; it is relative. As the national wealth grows and the majority become more affluent a child is described as officially poor if he has to share a bedroom after the age of eleven or does not have a holiday away from home. We have become mobile, far less attached to the communities we were brought up in, and yet at the same time we have allowed ourselves to become insulated from much that goes on around us. We have become creatures of a media age as well as of the consumer society. If we look for a handy phrase to describe the dominant culture that has resulted from all that then it might be consumer populism.

It can be called populist because it appears to have done away with deference, with any authority that we are supposed to conform to. And that populism is the reason this climate is so difficult to challenge: it has a specious aura of democratic authority about it.

The argument goes something like this: if the public buys it, it must be because the public wants it, whatever 'it' may be, whether a product or a programme or an idea. And if the public wants it, what higher court of appeal could there be? So any mutterings about responsibility, any expressions of unease about the developing moral climate, must imply a wish to deprive people of their new freedom and to return to a world of deference, where our betters tell us what it is we ought to want. But in its own way the climate of consumer populism wants us to defer to it just as much as the old élitist hierarchy wanted us to. It is just that its way is different. Whereas the old élitists tried to get us to defer to their sense of what was right, consumer populism tries to get us to defer to what it tells us we want and ought to think.

Its claim of democratic legitimacy is false. It says it is about giving us what we want, but actually it is about exploiting the fact that most of us are a bit unsure of what we actually do want, a bit baffled by how to sort out the contradictions between the many things we want out of our lives and for the world we live in. So what consumer populism does is persuade us what we *ought* to want, then tell us it's what we wanted all along, and finally accuse those of us who feel a bit uneasy about where it's all heading of being élitists who want to stop the public having what it wants. That is how we end up being told that we merely want to satisfy our appetites: for money, getting it and spending it; for sex; for aggression; for power and for fame; for feeling victimised; and for an easy, thoughtless sentimentality. And that is why the climate seems to have no real moral resonance to it. It is because its strongest message is 'Pursue what you want. Get what you can. Just be a tourist in your own world.'

If that sounds like a case for stopping people getting what they want, it is not. There can be no return to an allegedly golden age when we all read the Bible in a happy little family group every evening, left our front doors unlocked and shiny-faced young boys gave up their seats to ladies on the bus. I know full well that there's no going back, even if we wanted to, and anyway golden ages were never as golden at the time as they are painted after the event. Can you imagine returning to that sort of instant retribution: regular beatings with the cane at school and the clip-round-the-ear from whoever happened to be in authority, whether park keeper or bus conductor or parent?

But I believe that many people are becoming uneasy about living in a culture where almost the *only* measure of happiness and fulfilment is the extent to which we can satisfy our appetites, whatever they may be, and in which other ideas about how to live, other values that we might want to take into account, are being gradually elbowed out. I believe that a great deal of what the current climate of consumer populism expects us to 'buy' is worthless, thoughtless, harmful, dangerous and, most important of all, that it undermines our idea of what responsibility is.

Chapter 7

The commercial persuaders

IT'S ABOUT TIME someone corrected Napoleon. We are no longer a nation of shopkeepers; we are a nation of shoppers. And how good at it we have become. It was hardly our fault that we used to be so terribly inefficient. All we had a few years ago were pathetically antiquated High Streets where people used to go – often on strange machines called buses – to do all sorts of things apart from spend money. Now we've got it licked: no messing about with public transport, just jump into the car, clog up the motorway, sit in a traffic jam, and sooner or later you're there, all ready to worship in what Cardinal Hume called the new cathedrals of our age: the shopping centres.

Before I sound off about them let's recall what the old High Streets were like. It's true that they were dominated by commerce, but not only by shops. Because of the ad hoc way most of the streets had grown up you'd have found a whole load of other things: churches, chapels, cafés and pubs; the hotel where the Rotarians met; cinemas, a theatre if you were lucky, and a Town Hall; a Victorian primary school, the public library, the run-down premises of the Sea Scouts; banks designed in the imposing architecture that implied that money was to be associated with prudence, caution and responsibility;

solicitors' offices with polished brass plaques; maybe a street
market, whose commercial flavour was quite different from the
shops because it was about badinage, humour and haggling
over prices; perhaps a small park and a war memorial, and even
private homes. The people milling about in it on a Saturday
would not all be there just to shop, even if that was the main
business. Given all the different sorts of building in the High
Street they might be about any number of different activities,
including simply talking to each other. People would be
clogging up the pavements because they had just bumped into
each other and wanted a chat. As I say, a hopelessly inefficient
hodgepodge. But what all that diversity in the High Street did
was reflect the fact that life is about lots of things. That public
space, something we all shared, embodied it. It told us we were
citizens, not just addicted consumers.

The new commercialism undermines the sense of belonging
to some public sphere which we share with other people and
which is distinct from our private worlds. It encourages us to
see the world out there as just somewhere our private needs can
be satisfied. Which brings me back to the shopping malls.
Cardinal Hume was not the only sceptical clergyman. When
the Bluewater shopping centre in Kent opened in 1999, Bishop
Michael Marshall said it was guilty of perpetrating 'social and
economic manipulation on a massive scale, skilfully
administering the anaesthetic of a consumer culture to an
already highly addictive society'. Well, fine, you can
understand the churchmen resenting the competition; we are
far more likely to go shopping on Sundays than to plonk our
bums on their pews and that must be at least partly their fault.
It is not easy for them to compete when the devil has stolen
some of their best Sunday clothes.

Not only do the shopping centres often ape cathedrals
architecturally with their domes and their naves but, in a
bizarre way, they now fulfil the role that cathedrals used to fill.
Shopping is what we believe in. The journalist James
Bartholomew did a splendid tongue-in-cheek comparison
between church and mall, in this case Trafford Park in
Manchester. On Sundays the whole family visits; we have

loyalty cards to make us feel we belong; we queue, as for Communion; there are murals as in churches and a dome like St Peter's; the availability of 'free' credit offers you paradise on earth. Here's the big difference: there is only one commandment. Pay the minimum monthly demand on your credit card or face excommunication. He's wrong about that. There is another commandment: thou shalt buy.

Of course there are similarities between a Trafford Park or a Lakeside or a Bluewater and the old High Street. The cafés are still there – dozens of them – and the cinemas. So also are the banks, though in a very different form; the Corinthian columns and the portly bank manager daring you to spend *his* money have given way to generous holes in the wall where you press the right buttons and they throw the stuff at you. And there will be some people talking to each other, though not very many; because people come from so far to get to these shopping malls they are likely to bump into fewer people they know. Pretty well everything else from the High Street is gone except, of course, the shops. There are literally hundreds of them. One big difference between them and the High Street shops is that they usually have no doors, again a great gain for efficient spending. Once you're in the shopping centre you are in the shops; there is no boundary between the shop and where you walk. Walking and shopping, they're the same thing.

To make quite sure we get the message, the shopping mall is not open to the sky, but is enclosed. If you bother to look up what you'll see are CCTV cameras making sure that you're shopping not stealing. And within this enclosed space the hubbub of people just being people will be filtered out by the comforting anaesthesia of muzak, interrupted only by the regularly broadcast ads telling us where today's particular bargains can be had. This space shouts a single message: consume, gratify yourself and do it now. Its message is the exact opposite of the one implicitly expressed by the High Street. It does not say that we are citizens and that life is about many things; it says that we are consumers and life is about shopping. And if there's anyone around who might be conveying a different message – down-and-outs, for example –

they'll have been quickly shifted out of the way by the ubiquitous private security guards. Then when we've had our fill of shopping we get back into our cars, our private bubbles, and take our booty back home through a public space that has been reduced in its diversity to the single exasperating experience of traffic congestion. Shopping and traffic jams, that is what public space is becoming. Instead of citizens – hey presto! – we are now 'consumers'.

The risk of lamenting the death of the old High Street is that you open yourself to the charge of nostalgia. I've never quite understood why nostalgia should be considered such a heinous crime. I expect one day it will become a new offence under the criminal code. 'You are hereby charged that on dates unspecified you did, with malice aforethought, indulge in several hours of nostalgia in the public bar of the Horse and Groom, since renamed the Rat and Ferret. How say you, are you guilty or not guilty?' I should plead guilty. In mitigation I would claim that we sometimes got it right in the past, so why should we not try to hang on to some of it? Why is 'progress' always better?

It is not that we have just discovered commerce but that commercial exploitation has been taken to new heights. Think of Oxford Street in London. For as long as I can remember it has been commercial nirvana. True, it's become tackier as the years have gone by – more and more of those nasty little shops that sell nothing but T-shirts and loudspeakers blaring hideous music – but look what's happened now to the Christmas lights. Their purpose has always been the same: to get more people into Oxford Street so that they would spend lots of money. But at least they used to be about Christmas. Then someone decided they should get a commercial sponsor to pay for them. So when you stood at either end of the street in December 1998 what you saw was an enormous neon sign advertising Bird's Eye. So striking were the signs that you didn't really notice any of the other lights down the street. What you were struck by was the sheer incongruity of it. For one thing, frozen food has precious little to do with shopping in Oxford Street where they scarcely sell food. But what's it got to do with Christmas? The nearest I could get was that people can't be bothered to peel fresh Brussels sprouts any more (alas), and that the frozen sort now symbolise Christmas. The effect was to snuff out the tiny bit of the non-commercial that had been allowed to creep into Oxford Street. The lights ceased to represent Christmas and now represented advertising. The commercial take-over was complete. Keep a look out and you'll see the commercial take-over of public space happening everywhere.

If you'd been a regular commuter travelling through the sleepy Buckinghamshire countryside by train in the summer of 1998, you might have been surprised to see what was going on in one of the fields. A giant 600-foot sculpture was gradually forming itself – gradually, because it was 'sculpted' out of growing wheat, salvias and white stones. It took almost the whole summer to reach its final shape and what was it? An advertisement for Beck's beer. Quite an accomplishment, maybe, but a horrible commercial intrusion. The Council for the Preservation of Rural England said: 'This is another example of clutter in the countryside.' It was more than that. It was a particularly eye-catching example of public space being colonised by commercialism.

Still on a train, you might find yourself pulling up at East Croydon station. You look out of the window to find out where you are and you discover not that you've reached East Croydon, but that you're at 'East Croydon Home of Nestlé UK'. That bit of information isn't stuck on a piece of billboard advertising nailed to the back wall of the platform, it's an integrated part of the station nameboard, at each end of the platform so you can't possibly miss it and in the same typeface. But East Croydon isn't just the home of Nestlé UK, it's also the home of Mr and Mrs Smith of 24 Railway Cuttings. A railway station, like a town hall and public library, is representative of the whole public identity of a place. Compromise that identity with this sort of commercial take-over and, bit by bit, we feel ourselves to belong less to any public sphere shared by everyone.

There's talk of the same thing happening at other stations and on the London Underground. When the Jubilee Line was finally being completed London Transport reckoned it could raise £10million by getting commercial sponsorship for the North Greenwich tube station which will service the Dome. It was prepared, for the first time, to adapt the famous Underground logo to incorporate the name of the highest-bidding sponsor it could find. What next? McDonald's Marble Arch? Probably. No doubt they'll adapt the station announcement: 'Mind the gap ... and why not fill that gap in your stomach with a delicious Big Mac!!!' Pity the poor old passenger.

Did I say passenger? Sadly, no longer. We are customers. You may think it makes no difference what they call us. I think it does. We still do the same thing – we buy a ticket and make the journey – but the change in the word matters because the words mean different things. A 'customer', according to the *Oxford English Dictionary*, is merely someone who buys something. That's it. In spite of all the windy rhetoric about 'Customer Care Departments' that you get from the PR departments of big companies (shouldn't they *all* care about the customer?) that's all it amounts to. Customers have no interest in, or relationship to, other customers. The whole relationship is with the seller. But the idea of a passenger is a much richer notion.

In the first place you're asking for a service and not buying a product. You're putting yourself in the care of someone else, and asking them not only to get you somewhere but to do so in safety. You know it's going to take some time and during that time you have a certain identity – you are the passenger, and that puts some responsibilities on you too. You have to behave in a way that doesn't prevent them from providing that service – you mustn't frivolously pull the communication cord, for instance – and you have to recognise that there are other passengers too. You share a space, a public space, and just as you have every right to expect them to behave in a way that doesn't interfere with your journey, they have the right to expect you to do the same. So as a passenger you have a relationship with them as well as with the train company.

Turning passengers into customers erodes this sense of entering and sharing a common world with its own particular rights and responsibilities. Customers don't think about other customers. They stay insulated in their own world, concerned only that the seller is going to deliver his side of the deal. A customer doesn't think twice about the nuisance he may be causing when he shouts endlessly into his mobile phone. A passenger does. I cherish the cartoon of the man on the train bawling into his mobile: 'Hello, darling, just calling to show everyone else what a prat I am.' Of course this does not mean that as soon as we start being called customers we're all going to start behaving like boorish louts, or that no passenger ever did, but dumping the word 'passenger' means eventually dumping the associations with it. The only association with the word 'customer' is that of being a consumer. And consumers are interested only in consuming.

What's happening, then, is that commercialism is turning us from citizens into consumers and in the process eroding the sense of responsibility that citizens feel. It fosters attitudes of self-absorption and the need to feel good, which are the traits of the pure consumer. Our appetite for consuming has never been greater and we can indulge it as never before. The figures are interesting. In 1968 our gross average weekly income was about £18. Thirty years later it had risen to £420. That is twenty-three times as much. God bless inflation. But the amount we had to spend every week to keep body and soul together went up only twenty times. That meant that the scope for what they call discretionary spending was much greater, an increase of more than 10 per cent So there is more to spend because there is more left over at the end of the week. Over forty years personal consumption has more than doubled. And if we still don't have enough money we borrow. Never in the field of human economics has so much been owed by so many to so few.

Forty years ago, for most working-class people earning a weekly wage, borrowing at reasonable rates was well nigh impossible. There was always the pawnbroker or the tallyman, prepared to lend small sums at criminal rates of interest to tide the spendthrift and the unfortunate over until the next pay packet, but it was mostly white collar workers with salaries who qualified for that ultimate status symbol: a cheque book and the right to borrow at market rates. Even getting a mortgage when the house was the security was difficult enough. I can remember my elation when my local building society manager condescendingly agreed to lend us the £2,500 we needed for our first home (three-bedroomed end of terrace, through lounge and parquet flooring) but to borrow money at a reasonable rate for anything more frivolous was almost impossible. You had to go to ask the bank manager, who was usually a stern old buffer with a military moustache and three-piece suit, who conveyed the impression that he thought you were a profligate degenerate because you wanted to own a car.

Now it is difficult to avoid having a loan. We get bombarded with offers in the papers, on the radio, in junk mail, and even when we receive bills. If you're a customer of Thames Water you will have received a leaflet with your half-yearly bill offering to lend you money. 'With loans from 11.9 per cent these aren't pipedreams for Thames Water customers . . . Why Dream Any Longer? That sportier car, newer kitchen or dream holiday isn't as far away as you think. You're just one step away from something you've been dreaming of.' I can remember the days when what water companies did was sell water. As Bishop Marshall has put it: 'Soliciting for credit fills our letter boxes daily, pushing people into the never-never land of repayment, massively outstretched by high interest rates. Once people are hooked into the system there is little chance that they will be able to break free from it. The captive customers for this credit solicitation grow younger and younger so that school leavers are immediately mailed to see if they are likely fish for the bait.' The day cannot be far away when the midwife will bolster her salary by flogging Kiddie Konsumer Kredit Kards to the new mum so baby need waste no time.

It says a lot about the last half of the twentieth century that advertising has become one of the great growth industries. Not just enormously rich and profitable, but glamorous too. The creative directors of the most successful agencies have come to define the age in which we live. They sell promises, and never mind that those promises are often patently absurd or even downright dishonest. We pretend to laugh at them, to treat them with scorn or derision, but we buy their snake oil as surely as any wide-eyed Victorian bought Dr Carter's Little Liver Pills. At least the Victorians believed the pills actually *worked* when they forked out their one shilling and sixpence. We know that what modern advertising tells us is, for the most part, a load of old tosh, but we buy it anyway. What's even more astounding is that we happily do their job for them and pay through the nose for the privilege. Whoever first cottoned on to the idea that people would buy clothes with the designer's label on the outside and pay twice as much for them deserves a permanent place in the advertisers' hall of fame and a large silver trophy . . . in the shape of a mug.

The difference is that advertisers seldom sell *things* any longer; they sell lifestyle images. There was a time when adverts were used to highlight the quality of a product. If they were trying to sell you a spade they would tell you that the spade was well balanced and durable, that it performed the functions of a spade as well as possible. Now if you buy the spade you are promised, by association, a whole new lifestyle.

The advertisers seem to think they can buy anything and anyone to promote their products. That's probably because they can. They pay fortunes to people we admire and then *they* do the persuading. When a great sportsman achieves some extraordinary feat the only question he has to ask is which products he will sponsor and how much they will pay him. When Michael Jordan announced he was retiring from basketball he wiped tens of millions off the value of shares in the American firm whose trainers he advertised. Fair enough – sports stars have done it for years – but now even figures like Mikhail Gorbachev and Henry Kissinger can be wheeled in to persuade us to want something. From being the man who loosened the grip of the Communist dictatorship on the windpipe of the Soviet Union and put an end to the cold war, Gorbachev became the man who peddled pizza for Pizza Hut. I fully expect to see British prime ministers accepting sponsorship deals in the not too distant future.

'Tony Blair uses "No Sweat" for those tricky moments in the House of Commons. Turn your arm pits into charm pits! The Blair Essential for the sweet smell of success!'

The way things are going we may well find conventional television, poster or even newspaper advertising struggling to hold on to their share of the market, however clever and sophisticated the ads become, so look out for the other tricks up the advertisers' sleeves.

Product placement has always been a favourite weapon of the advertiser – getting a character in your favourite soap to drink ostentatiously from a clearly labelled can, for instance – but the television rules have always been pretty restrictive. What's the betting they will be relaxed as time goes by. The other technique is to get the soap character to rubbish a competitor's product. One swig from the *other* cola, and he falls down dead, foaming at the mouth. It will come, I promise you, it will come.

The broadcasting rules say, broadly, that advertising must be clearly that: advertising. There must be no doubt in the listeners' or viewers' minds that they are being sold to. So subliminal advertising – the message flashing up on the screen for such a short time that the eye scarcely registers it – is banned. I wonder how much longer it will be before some cleverdick finds a way around that. I wonder, too, how many people are aware of the different ways in which advertisers manipulate programme makers and presenters. One fairly innocuous example is the give-away competition.

A radio or television station will tell you that it is giving away wonderful prizes in a competition over the next few days or weeks. You might, perhaps, think that the station has paid for those prizes. Quite the opposite: the company whose product it is will have paid handsomely for the privilege of giving them away. But the deal is that their product will be mentioned a specific number of times during the contract period, and a precise form of words will be used by the presenter at each stage. So if you thought the presenter was doing his usual job, you would be mistaken. His words have been bought and paid for. If that is not deceptive advertising

I'd like to know what is, but without the revenue from that sort of scam some radio stations would be struggling to make ends meet.

Sometimes it goes wonderfully wrong – I heard of one television station that had been staging a big competition in cahoots with a well-known airline. It involved a lot of money and went on day after day. At the end of it the mischievous presenter made a little aeroplane out of a sheet from his script, threw it into the air and it crashed against the wall. The sponsor refused to pay a penny and the presenter was nearly sacked.

The oldest groan in the advertising world used to be that they knew half the advertising worked; the only problem was they didn't know *which* half. That is no longer the case. Nowadays they can measure these things with great precision. If you use one of the absurdly named supermarket 'loyalty' cards they know every time you buy a bag of salt and vinegar crisps so they can direct-mail you with a voucher for your next purchase. Sophisticated direct marketing used to mean sending brochures for expensive cars only to people who lived in posh houses and could, presumably, afford them. Pretty soon they'll know what colour pyjamas you wear to bed and what kind of Christmas presents you send to your maiden aunt in Scarborough. And what colour pyjamas *she* wears to bed.

But the most effective advertising of all is also the oldest. It needs no powerful computer databases, no sharp-suited agency executives or clever young men in colourful braces and no vast budget. It is word of mouth. When Louis de Bernières wrote *Captain Corelli's Mandolin* his publishers spent virtually nothing advertising it, but the first few people who bought it recognised it as a great book. They told their friends and their friends told their friends. Pretty soon it had become a massive bestseller. The reason is obvious: we are much more likely to trust our own friends if they tell us something is good than if the advertisers tell us the same. But even that is in the process of being corrupted.

When Mark Leonard, who used to work for the think tank Demos, spent a few days with a bunch of advertising hotshots at their annual get-together, he discovered 'guerrilla marketing'. You pay people to start a rumour about how good a particular product is. The rumour spreads and, with any luck and enough money, you create a tidal wave of favourable opinion. Is that honest? No. Will it work? Probably.

You can see the advertisers' problems. There was a time when different products really were different. An Austin Allegro was a truly terrible motor car; its Japanese or German equivalent was vastly superior. Now there's almost nothing to choose between one modern family saloon and another. They could engineer differences. Any company could, for instance, make a car that needs virtually no servicing. Not a bad selling point. The technology exists and the buyer would benefit. But they won't do that because we'd never take our cars to the garage and it's in the so-called after-sales and service that the company makes its profits. So instead they rely on hype and image.

That's where the PR people come in: the image manipulators. They know perfectly well that there is less and less difference between one brand and another, so they try to persuade us instead that the company selling Brand X is much nicer than the company selling Brand Y. They are the ones who care about the community and don't destroy the environment, so we should buy their products. The masters of this type of PR – the ones most assiduous at trying to persuade us that all they exist for, really, is the good of humanity – are the supermarkets.

Take a wander around almost any High Street in the land past the usual collection of charity shops and 'closing down' signs. Now do not think for even a moment that the little businesses that once made a modest profit in those empty shops were in any way affected by the new supermarket. I know they haven't been because the supermarkets tell us so all the time.

'What an absurd notion,' one supermarket boss once told me on *Today*. 'We actually *improve* a local area or small town when we open up there and create jobs.' Well of course. How silly of me even to have considered any other possibility. What I had done in my naïve way was to look at the figures. In the ten years from 1986 the number of food 'superstores' rose from 432 to 1,034. In that same period the number of small grocery shops fell by 50,000. There must obviously be another reason for all those little shops closing their doors as the supermarkets opened theirs. The phases of the moon, perhaps? And when the small chemists and dry cleaners and sub post offices go broke too, I dare say that will be because Venus is aligned with Mars or I put my trousers on left leg first. Something like that. As the man says, it is absurd to think that a supermarket with its vast purchasing power and ability to sell more cheaply than anyone else could be driving the small shops out of business. You might think so; I might think so. The government's own figures might tell us that is the case. But surely it is inconceivable that the supermarkets would seek to mislead us.

It may be just that our needs are changing. In the street where I was born we all thought we needed our local chemist, Mr Morgan. He filled our prescriptions (free in those days) and sold us whatever other medicines we wanted. But he did much more than that. If you got something in your eye and you or your mother couldn't get it out you went to Mr Morgan and he got it out for you. No fee. All part of the service. If you cut yourself he'd take a look and either sell you a bandage or tell you to go to the doctor. He was the gateway to the doctor. You didn't 'trouble' the doctor, by and large, unless it seemed pretty important. Mr Morgan (I never heard anyone except the doctor use his first name) was a vital part of the community. There are not many Mr Morgans left today and soon there may be none.

We need not leave the supermarket to find out why; we need only wander over to the pharmaceutical section. They sell everything that the few remaining Mr Morgans sell, and much else besides. And they sell it more cheaply wherever they are allowed to. There are still some laws restraining their cut-price activities, but they're just about gone and the last of the Mr Morgans will soon join them. Gone the same way as all those other little businesses who cannot stand in the path of the supermarket juggernaut.

So what? I could live perfectly well without my local

butcher. True, he cuts my meat exactly as I like it, makes his own wonderful, herb-filled sausages and buys almost all his meat from farmers he knows personally who treat their stock well. But none of that is essential. He has a little bench in his shop so that customers can sit and have a chat, with him or with each other, while they're waiting for the meat to be prepared. Again, we can live without that, but the community will be that little bit poorer without him and so will many others without all their small traders. Independent local butchers are disappearing from the streets of Britain at the rate of one hundred a week and soon we shall all have to buy our meat from the supermarkets. When my butcher first opened his doors a generation ago there were twenty-five others in the area. Now he's the last one.

But surely the great thing about supermarkets is their huge variety. Magnificent, this array of food. How wonderful to buy strawberries in December and all manner of fruit and veg most of us had never even seen forty years ago and had no idea we wanted. Perfectly true, unless you look for variety in, say, the apple section. Whatever happened to all those varieties that were once the glory of an English autumn? Gone, all save a handful. And so have the little orchards that once grew them. Not economic, you see, but the supermarket spinners will not tell that story. You say you liked them? Tough. Far easier for a supermarket to buy in massive bulk from a few super-efficient producers (we used to call them farmers) rejecting, of course, any fruit with a little blemish or an odd shape. But still, it looks nice and it's so fresh. Or is it? Some of those apples have spent the past many months in storage chambers deprived of the oxygen that would naturally rot them. The lack of taste gives the game away. Or perhaps our taste buds are dulled too.

You will see the words 'environmentally friendly' and 'environmentally conscious' scattered hither and yon around the shelves. The marketing men have been anxious to put them there. Perhaps it *is* environmentally friendly to build supermarkets and shopping centres so far from our homes that we must all use cars to get there. Perhaps it *is* environmentally conscious for a store to transport all its food vast distances in big lorries when there are apples or carrots growing in fields a mile away. Perhaps, but the logic somehow escapes me. It is, however, infinitely more efficient and therefore more profitable to do so. Let us all bow the knee to the great god Bulk Purchase, and pray for those suppliers who have to abase themselves before their high priests, the Purchasers. If the suppliers themselves are very big and very powerful they will enjoy the priests' respect; if not, let them be on their guard.

Now turn to the packaging. How nicely everything is wrapped in its protective covering of see-through plastic. And how monumentally wasteful most of it is. They will tell you they are acutely conscious of the need to reduce wasteful packaging; indeed I have chaired many a conference on waste and heard many a pious statement of intent. But do not listen to the pledges; look at the reality. They will say, 'But that is what the customer wants.' Is it? I don't remember being asked, do you? 'Ah, but you buy it, and that is the proof.' Neat eh? Yes, it's that old populist trick again.

The latest wheeze, you may have noticed, is fruit – apples, pears and so on – individually encased in thick plastic moulds 'especially for children'. *Why* 'especially for children'? Are children no longer to be trusted to take an apple to school in their satchels, as children have done for generations, without it being protected from some unseen menace? Clearly not. Anyway, much better for the environment to pollute the planet once by producing the ridiculous mould and then pollute it a second time by throwing it away. It is called 'marketing'. Some bright spark in a marketing director's office spotted what they like to call a 'gap in the market' and bingo! One more gullible mum or spoiled child demanding her 'individually wrapped' apple. The marketing men will call it 'responding to the consumer's needs in a modern environment' or some such twaddle. What that translates into is: 'spotting another wasteful way to squeeze a higher price out of something we once bought reasonably cheaply.' You can be sure it turns a nice profit.

Ah, but we are told the food is so much cheaper. Indeed the supermarkets spend a fortune telling us that and then telling us again. I wonder sometimes how much cheaper the food would really be if they spent a little less telling us. Then there are all those special offers. Odd, isn't it, that so many of the 'two for the price of one' offers apply to perishable goods such as fruit and veg which would go rotten if they were not sold speedily. As I write these words a government inquiry is looking into the subject of supermarket prices so we must wait to see what it concludes, not that there will be much the politicians can do whatever the conclusion. In the meantime we can make our own comparisons with the prices at our local butcher or fishmonger if we are fortunate enough to have one. Already supermarkets swallow up three quarters of food retailing and are eating steadily into so many other trades once carried on by small businesses. The arrival of the American chain Walmart will inevitably drain even more diversity and individuality from the business of shopping.

There is another little myth the supermarket spinners have succeeded in selling us: the notion that we all benefit equally from their service. Not quite. The latest of the new supermarkets near me is a wondrous sight: a temple to fine food, a showcase store that had no less a figure than Sir Terence Conran there on the opening day. This is Kensington, where the rich fill their trolleys with the fanciest and trendiest food money can buy. There is serious money to be made from these customers. In other, less affluent, areas supermarkets have chosen to close their stores even though the local council has begged them to stay open. There is less money to be made from the poor.

Sir Donald Acheson used to be the chief medical officer to the government. He warned that it is now almost impossible for many of the poorest people in this country to get cheap and varied food because local shops are shutting while supermarkets move out of town. This has led to 'food deserts' in the inner cities with growing malnutrition, especially among children. Tim Lang, Professor of Food Policy at Thames Valley University, agrees with that. He talks about the 'hypermarketisation' of superstores that get bigger and bigger, leaving smaller shops unable to compete. In his view the supermarkets 'have abandoned the poor and have deliberately chased the affluent customer'. The supermarkets don't want *all* the trade. Just the best.

So the supermarkets are the villains of the piece? Well, yes and no. You may say I am looking at only the disadvantages of supermarket living. They offer convenience (assuming you have a car); choice (assuming you have the money); and value for money (assuming you ignore comparisons with similar supermarkets in other countries or the nearest market). Anyway, our lives are so pressured now it is simply ludicrous to imagine that we can manage without them, or so everyone seems to believe. It is true that since modern commerce began big companies have swallowed up smaller ones and driven the weakest to the wall. No chief executive would survive for very long if he didn't do his damnedest to corner as much of the market as the law allows and then just a little bit more again. That's what market capitalism is about. What sticks in the craw in these days of public relations smarm is that they treat us like fools, deny the obvious realities, insist that all they're really concerned with is being good citizens protecting and nurturing whatever community they happen to be operating in.

But even if they are the villains, we are hardly innocent victims. On the contrary, we are entirely complicit. It is we who rush to empty their shelves with scarcely a thought for the effect on all those other little traders we once supported. It is we who acquiesce in the idea that mangoes in winter and blemish-free, taste-free apples and twenty different kinds of breakfast cereal all wrapped together in a convenient package are worth more than an active, living community. How can any one of us assess the balance? In consumer populism, responsibility is not so much shared as lost. The supermarkets become masters of the sales pitch because they have to and we all end up buying it, because by the time we've got our wits together it is the only option available.

If it is difficult for adults to escape the snares of consumer populism, how much more so is it for children. Children are a particular target for the marketing people because so much of what we spend is spent on them: more than £250 on average for every child in the land for Christmas presents alone. Over thirty years the spending on toys and clothes for children has more than trebled in real terms. Spending on sweets, ice creams and soft drinks has gone up by a third. A Loughborough University study in 1997 estimated that the cost of bringing up a child for a family was £3,000 a year each. Christina Hardyment, an expert on the history of childhood, says that childhood is now 'an experience of consuming food, clothes and entertainments manufactured outside the home and bought with parents' hard-earned cash'.

Not surprising, perhaps, when you look at the money being spent to prise that hard-earned cash out of the parents' pockets. The average child probably sees 10,000 commercials a year. The Advertising Standards Authority has all sorts of rules and regulations about kiddies' ads. They must not 'exploit their credulity', for instance. 'Products should be advertised only if they can reasonably be afforded.' They should not 'incite pestering of parents'. They should not make children 'feel inferior if they don't get the product'. Ho hum, I wonder what world the regulators are living in.

Picture the scene at the advertising agency when they're sitting around in their elegant board room discussing the campaign for the latest wonder toy that every seven-year-old absolutely *must* have this Christmas.

'Now then,' says Torquil, 'because we must not exploit the children's credulity there will be none of this "exciting, lifelike, thrilling" language. We must explain very carefully that this is a concoction of rather nasty bits of plastic which won't look anything like it does on television when it's sitting on the kitchen floor. We must make it clear that it will probably break within a week or two, assuming it hasn't already been dumped by the bored and frustrated child by then. We shall target only parents who can afford £29.99 for something that's actually worth a couple of quid at most and on no account must we encourage the child to tell his parents that if he isn't given one of these horrible little things he will run away from home and never, ever speak to them again.' Bye, bye Torquil.

The reality is a little different. As the marketing guru James McNeal explains:

> Children under the age of eight believe advertising unconditionally, tend to see it as a logical part of programming, and tend not to perceive the selling intent of it. Advertising to children is virtually all emotion and persuasion. Advertisers put to work all the creativity they can muster to create a fantasy environment . . . with very little regard for useful information expressed in ways children can understand. Advertisers have the ability to convince children to like and desire practically any product, yet this ability is applied mainly to toys and sugared foods.

The same report goes on to say:

> Children's needs, beyond basic food, clothing and heating, are socially defined; kids must now have and do things if they are not to be socially and educationally excluded . . . The concern of parents, especially poor parents, to maintain their children's public standing may make the pressures to conform irresistible . . . Government attempts to tackle child poverty will be doomed if commercial 'needs' are created faster than any rise in family incomes.

He is not optimistic.

> There is no reason to expect a reversal in this commercialisation of childhood. Children are a vast market and one that will expand. Yet the impact of commercialisation on children is not much discussed by politicians, educators or the media.

You may say nothing has really changed, that there has always been peer pressure and children have always wanted the latest fashion. Possibly, but if that is so it is hard to explain this statistic. In 1998 girls under the age of seventeen were eleven times more likely to have committed a crime than they were fifty years ago. Jan Walsh is the head of Consumer Analysis who did the research. She believes the commercial society is the root cause:

There is a much greater emphasis on what we possess today. From the earliest age, through television advertising and peer pressure, children are persuaded that they must possess all kinds of things. It is now a very basic fact of a young person's life. They must have the right trainers on their feet and the right logo on their backs. This did not exist in 1949.

Philip Burley, Chief Barker of the Variety Club, who commissioned the report, said: 'Crime seems to be the new form of illness in children for which we are going to need complex social solutions.'

There are other more insidious ways than advertising for consumer populism to get at children. Sponsorship is one. It strikes many people as very odd indeed that in one of the world's richest and most advanced countries schools have to appeal to parents to fork out for everything from books to building repairs. Some schools now routinely ask parents to make a contribution of, say, £100 a year. Of course they don't *have* to pay – only if they can afford it – but most make the effort. They don't want their children to lose out. This is fertile ground for big corporations. McDonald's, for instance, has been giving schools what they call 'resource packs' for several years. Many teachers welcome them and – the great thing – they don't cost them a penny. So what do McDonald's get in return for their generosity? Well, there's the nice rosy PR glow that comes from doing a good deed in a dark world, but there's a little more to it than that. All those apple-cheeked youngsters desperate to feast at the table of learning are something else, too – customers. Nick Cohen of the *Observer* took a look at what was in some of the packs. 'History, one pack recommended, should be taught by getting children to "explore the changes in use of the McDonald's site".' Music was encouraged by getting kids to think of words for 'Old McDonald's had a store'.

McDonald's are not alone. Flora, Tate & Lyle, Cadbury's and many others have all supplied kits, either at the schools' request or unsolicited. The *London Evening Standard* published a picture of primary school children whose school had gained £2,000 from getting them to say the name of a new cheese brand over and over. KP sent a hot air balloon around various schools, plastered with the advert for Choc Dips. It was meant to illustrate that hot air rises. So it does. So, no doubt, do the sales and profits of companies who combine good deeds with clever – and sometimes insidious – marketing. We have a long way to go before we match the excesses of the United States. There a maths textbook might cast a problem using a branded product: 'If you have $240 how many pairs of XXXX trainers can you buy if the trainers cost $80 a pair?' and so on. In some state schools they are so much in hock to various big businesses that teachers are required to act, effectively, as salesmen for the product. Children are impressionable, and that is the appeal.

Schools are not the only part of our once purely public world that are being infiltrated by the commercial influence of sponsorship.

And now, ladies and gentlemen, Megabucks Inc. is proud to present to you your own ... your very own ... Megabucks Police Force! Please put your hands together and welcome the Megabucks Chief Constable whose extremely smart uniform complete with gold braid has been sponsored by 'Cops R Us', suppliers to the finest forces in the land ...

Well not quite – not yet – but a significant change took place a few years ago in the way we fund our police forces. The Police and Magistrates Court Act allowed, for the first time, police forces to supplement their budgets by up to 1 per cent through sponsorship. One per cent may not seem a lot, but police forces have big budgets. It did not take long for them to stick hold hands out and now most county police forces have

'sponsorship managers' or something similar. In West Yorkshire there is a department called the 'Income Generation and
Marketing Department'. They got British Gas Home Security,
which sells burglar alarms, to sponsor two scene-of-crime
police cars, which have the firm's logo on their doors. Now of
course there are rules: the police officers are not allowed to
endorse particular products, for instance. But if your house
had just been ransacked and the police showed up in a car
bearing the logo of a company that sells burglar alarms might
you not make a connection? The insurance company, General
Accident, gave £60,000 for two cars to Lancashire Con-
stabulary. Once again they got their logos on the cars in return.
Once again, it's a bit unlikely that no potential customer made
the connection. A local insurance firm in Northamptonshire
sponsored a Neighbourhood Watch magazine. And on it goes.

So there are two problems here. The obvious one is that
responsible public institutions such as schools and police
forces are seen to be endorsing a commercial product. That is,
at best, unsavoury. But here's the other one. Imagine a British
Gas Home Security van being driven like the clappers along a
West Yorkshire road. You are driving behind, going just as
fast, and it's you who gets nicked for speeding. Fair enough,
you're guilty. But might you not wonder why the other driver
wasn't nicked as well? A trivial example, perhaps, but just a
little worrying. For any civilised society to work, its police
force must have the confidence and trust of the public. We
must believe that the police are entirely dispassionate and
disinterested when they are dealing with commercial concerns.
The infiltration of commercial interests into public bodies
undermines the sense that they exist solely to serve our
common, public interest.

I recently came across what struck me as a particularly
worrying example. At a reception hosted by a wealthy trade
association in a posh London hotel I met a detective inspector
from a northern police force. The job of his unit is to detect
fraud on behalf of the association, whose business members
suffer from a lot of it. 'It's brilliant,' he enthused. 'They pay the
costs of my police officers and in return they get millions of

pounds worth of fraud cases cleared up. Everyone benefits.'

Just so, I said, but what if another trade association with a similar problem asked your unit to look into one of their frauds? 'Oh, we couldn't do that. After all, the other lot pays the wages.'

In fact, I discovered later, another trade association in a similar line of business had considered paying for their own unit but had to abandon the idea because they couldn't afford it and anyway they figured they were already paying through their taxes for the police to deal with crime. I suggested to the inspector that they might have a genuine grievance and invited him to come on *Today* to talk about it. He declined.

That prominent figures within the public sphere now welcome the commercial Trojan horse through the gates is a measure of how far we have moved in abandoning the idea of a public sphere that is separate from, and immune to, the commercial sphere. No part of the public sphere should be more defended against commercialism than the police, yet here is a policeman speaking: 'The past fifty years have seen an accelerating loss of the police's share of the security market.' That was Ian Blair, the Chief Constable of Surrey. He was not speaking with regret. Indeed he went on to refer to the police's 'indefensible monopoly of street patrols' and said that police should be able to train and license private security officers to become policemen on the beat. Quite aside from any practical objections, the very idea that a chief constable should speak of a security 'market', of the police's 'share' of it, and of the police's monopoly of part of it being 'indefensible' indicates how far the public service ethos has been eroded by the interests and language of commercialism.

I must, here, declare an interest. I loathe private security – not the wretched souls who have to enforce it for starvation wages, but I have a thing about wearing identity tags. The BBC rules say we are supposed to wear them when we are on the premises, presumably so that if some foul villain manages to infiltrate Television Centre he will be instantly spotted and ejected. Fat chance of that. Who's going to do the spotting let alone the ejecting? But that's the rule, and it was enforced so rigorously a few years ago that one morning I almost failed to present *Today*. It was at the time of the Gulf War, and our security advisers had apparently warned the BBC that we were likely to be a target for Saddam Hussein so we were told we should all wear our IDs all the time. I did not and, as usual, rushed into the studio with a couple of minutes to spare. The man with the peaked cap stopped me at the door.

'You can't go in there', he told me sternly.

'Why not?'

'Because you're not wearing your ID around your neck.'

'But you know who I am and I'm on the air in two minutes.'

'Sorry. No ID, no admission.'

'Okay,' I said, '*You* do the bloody programme.' And I turned my back and walked away, praying that he'd give in. Mercifully, he did and I presented the programme with a naked neck. Yes, I know it was childish and the poor man was only doing his job, but you're allowed a bit of petulance at six in the morning and anyway I thought I was striking one small blow against the growing dominance of the private security industry.

Security experts seem to exert an extraordinary influence over otherwise reasonably sane managements. How did our lot *know* Saddam was going to send his crack troops against us, for God's sake? Did they *ask* him? Of course it's possible that some crazy terrorist will have a pop at us, but the so-called experts have no more or better knowledge of what they're likely to get up to than you or I. The security industry has an infinite capacity for scaring managements everywhere with imaginary risks and, once the additional security has been introduced, it is never removed. It is a perfect illustration of the ratchet effect.

In my thirty years with BBC News I can recall only one 'security incident' in a live studio and that added greatly to the sum of national merriment. A little group of women protesting about lesbian rights or some such managed to get into the *Six O'Clock News* studio just as it was going on the air with Sue Lawley and Nicholas Witchell. Nick wrestled the most vocal of the women to the ground and sat on her while Sue did her best to carry on. She did; the lesbians were eventually ejected and Nick became a national hero. It was his finest hour.

These days, inevitably, we have security guards stationed at the entrance to all our live studios. Perhaps that's sensible. I suppose it's possible that a coup will be launched at any moment by a disaffected branch of the Mothers' Union. Jolly upset because the government has refused to remove VAT on knitting needles, dozens of middle-aged ladies, armed to the teeth, will storm the studio, take over the transmission and declare that they are now in charge of the country and if we don't all do as they say we'll be sent to bed early without our supper. I'm not quite sure what our amiable guard would do if that were to happen, but no doubt it reassures somebody to know that he is there.

The BBC is no worse than any other large organisation in this respect, making everybody sign in at the front desk and issuing them with silly passes. In some cases it may well be necessary. I can understand a research organisation with secret documents lying around all over the place wanting to keep strangers out. There is indeed a great deal of industrial espionage going on – there always has been – and it's difficult to stop it. But for the most part this kind of 'security' serves no purpose at all, save to add a little more irritation to our lives and provide profits for the security industry. We managed without them only a few years ago, so what has changed to make them so necessary today?

The turnover of the 300-odd companies involved in private security has grown six-fold since the early eighties and is growing still. Many police officers share these worries. No doubt they have an interest in protecting their jobs but that does not mean their fears are groundless. Some believe that private security forces, such as the one that operates in areas of Bristol, unnecessarily exacerbate people's fears of crime – which, of course, would be in *their* commercial interest. Others worry that too many firms employ guards at miserly rates of pay with dubious backgrounds. The old notion of 'set a thief to catch a thief' is all very well, but not if the thief in question – or even the ex-thief – is guarding, as opposed to catching.

But there is a more fundamental problem. You look at a police officer and, however much the image of the police may have been tarnished by cases of corruption or of racism, you know that in principle that police officer is there to represent us all. Look at the army of private security officers we see in the shopping malls, or patrolling behind the remote-controlled wrought-iron gates of the exclusive new residential estates that are going up everywhere, and you ask: 'Who are they there for?' Their growing presence symbolises the slow dying of public space and of the citizen and the emergence of a world of purely private interests and of the consumer. That is what we are being persuaded to become, and its effects are already being felt for the worse.

Chapter 8

What commercialism is doing to us

WHENEVER I THINK of football I recall the old man who was asked why he never read books. 'Because I read one once and I didn't like it,' he said. That's me and football. I went with my younger brother, Rob, to see Cardiff City play when I was a boy. He was hooked and eventually turned hobby into career and became the finest sports journalist in Wales. I never went again. The last time I can remember watching a football game all the way through was in 1966. You didn't have to be a fan – or even an Englishman – to get caught up in that one. The Welsh adopted the English for the occasion and to beat West Germany in the finals of the World Cup barely a generation after the war had ended was beyond imagining. But you also don't have to be a fan to regret what has happened to the game over the last forty years or so. Football was once a defining feature of a community. For generations father and son stood together on the terraces to watch *their* team. They felt they owned it as well as supported it. It had sprung from their community, often many generations ago. It represented continuity and loyalty and a set of values that has largely been betrayed by the men with the fat cheque books who have bought it from under their noses, not because they love the game but because they love the profits the best clubs can produce. Of course it is easy to romanticise the old times in sport. In the days of baggy shorts and Brylcreem no doubt there was plenty of foul play and bad behaviour and general skulduggery but the big difference between now and then is money.

At the top of the game is a self-perpetuating élite of superclubs whose success is counted in the figures on a balance sheet and whose existence threatens the future of the smaller clubs lower down the pecking order. The game is being hijacked and often corrupted by commercial interests, the fans exploited, their loyalty taken for granted or abused. The men and women who have supported the game all their lives are treated as mere consumers of a product on which those who run the clubs have a monopoly of supply. The more cash they can screw out of the fans the better. And they call it sport. Welcome to the world of commercial football.

The key to the change is the money that television started pumping into the game in the last decade of the century. It had been happening to an extent for many years. The BBC and ITV had always tried to outbid each other for the big competitions and the clubs happily pocketed some pretty fat cheques. The clubs benefited, the networks benefited, and so did the viewers who got to watch top-class football for free. But then satellite television arrived on the scene. It might not have had many viewers in those early days, but its owners knew what they needed to do to get them and they had deep pockets. In 1992 Sky paid £304 million for the rights to Premier League games and nothing has been the same since. At that time they had two million subscribers. Five years later they had more than three times as many. The strategy had worked. In 1996 BSkyB renewed its rights, this time for £647 million.

There is a wretched irony in the effect of all this. In theory the arrival of a new, powerful broadcaster on the scene was meant to increase the viewers' – in particular the sports fans' – choice. In reality it has done the opposite. Those who used to be able to watch the big games for free now have to pay to do so. If they can't afford it, they don't get it. And now it's the television scheduler who can even dictate when the games will be played. A Birmingham vicar was so cross when Aston Villa rescheduled its game to Sunday morning that he rang his church bells throughout. It made no difference. Mammon beat God hands down.

The effect of pumping those vast amounts of money into the top end of the game was as predictable as the reaction of the home supporters to their own striker scoring a hat trick. Football became such big business that the top clubs floated themselves on the stock exchange. The owners made fortunes, but it piled new pressures onto the clubs. Now they had their share price to worry about. The way to keep the shares rising was to win games and, it transpired, to rip off the supporters. You win games by buying the very best players available, and that usually means foreign players. That finally put paid to any last vestige of the idea that football teams were made up of local, or even British, talent. In a global market competition for the best players led to stratospheric signing-on fees, vast salaries and perks that would cause many a film star's eyes to water. It took a cricketer, Mike Atherton, to make one of the sharper comments about the level of football salaries: 'The overhyped being played by the overpaid.'

The accountants Deloitte Touche have a 'football industry team' and its chairman, one Gerry Boon, describes the English Premier League as the commercial envy of the world. In his review of the 1998 season he wrote: 'It doesn't matter, in the real world, whether it is morally or philosophically right for business to have the level of influence it does. It is simple reality. Once football took the media money and the sponsorship, then Pandora's Box was opened. It cannot now, for whatever good or powerful reason, be closed.' The figures produced by his company give us some idea of what you see when you peek beneath the lid of Pandora's Box. Here are some of them from their latest review, for 1997 to 1998.

- Total income: £569m. (Up nearly a quarter on the previous year.)
- Players' salaries: £200m. (Up more than forty per cent.)
- Cost of transfers: £171m.

That last figure is particularly instructive. Nearly half of it went on buying players from abroad and only one fifth on buying players from the Football League. But by the time League clubs bought back players from the Premier League, they were left with a miserly £1.5million. That is one twentieth of what it was only two seasons earlier. The conclusion is obvious: the rich are getting richer and the poor are getting poorer. Much poorer. The turnover of the top five clubs in the Premier League is greater than that of all seventy-two clubs in the first, second and third divisions combined. As Gerry Boon has put it: 'The financial divide between the premiership and the Football League is turning from gap to chasm to abyss.' Because so much of the money they spend ends up subsidising foreign, especially Italian, clubs there is a corresponding drop in spending on home-grown players. That creates a threat to the existence of small clubs who used to be able to scout around for good local talent and later make money by selling them on to the big clubs. The money helped keep them afloat. So super-commercialism at the top is helping to sink the clubs lower down. These days some big clubs not only import the big foreign stars, but even young foreign hopefuls. When that happens yet another link with the local game, the local community, is cut.

It is those communities and the loyal fans within them who are having to pay for all this. You might have thought all that television money coming into the top clubs would have kept the price of tickets down. Quite the opposite. From the late eighties to the late nineties the cost of the cheapest season tickets went up by 300 per cent In 1998 the cheapest Chelsea season ticket cost £360, the dearest £1,025. That's for nineteen home matches. You can watch a play or a musical in a decent seat in the most expensive West End theatre for less. English season tickets are up to four times more expensive than on the Continent. Clubs offer loans to spread the payments, but the supporter would do well to check the rates. Even the greediest bank would blush at some of them.

The top clubs know they can get away with it because they know the fans are trapped by their loyalty. There is only one

Newcastle United, only one Arsenal, only one Manchester United and if you are a fan, you are hooked. For the wealthy there is no problem. For the low paid supporter, who stood on the terraces as a child in rain and shine with his father and helped to make the club what it is today, and now wants to do the same with his sons . . . well, he *might* be able to manage it, but possibly not. I can't imagine he will get much consolation in knowing that the brilliant Italian striker earns twice as much in a week as he does in a year. As I write these words, wages are rising in the Premier League by 40 per cent a year. That's nearly ten times as much as the national average. And even *that* is chickenfeed compared with his earnings from endorsements and advertising. Nor will there be much consolation in staring up at the hospitality boxes and knowing the fat cats are warm and comfortable and getting the game (if they bother to watch it) for free.

You can, of course, watch the game on television but you need increasingly deep pockets to do that. Top football games are a mighty weapon for the television ratings-chasers and increasingly fans are having to pay to watch games that were once free. Digital television will speed up that process. By the closing year of the century if you wanted to watch all football matches available on all channels, you'd have to find almost £1,000. That includes the BBC licence fee. So yes, television has made more games available to more viewers – but at a price.

The fans are being squeezed in other ways. By the mid nineties the big clubs such as Manchester United were making more money from merchandising their products than from ticket sales. In one five-year period Manchester United changed its strip fourteen times just to make sure the fans kept on buying – and at £45 a time that's a lot of profit. By the end of the century the merchandising figures had fallen a little – perhaps on the basis that you can't soak all the fans all the time – but only for some of the clubs.

Everyone knows that Manchester United is the richest club of all, but the comparison with the others still bears repeating. The next richest in the Premier League at the end of the 1999 season, with *less than half* of Man U's earnings, was Newcastle

Devil's Advocate

United. Put it another way: on a single match day, *The Times* has calculated, Manchester United generates more income than twenty-two of the ninety-two League clubs can manage in an entire season. As one analyst put it, whatever the club does the rest of the industry follows because they see its success. The key to it all, we are told, is branding. Manchester United is the only 'indestructible brand' in the game. Remember when the key to it all was the game itself?

You might, perhaps, expect the men who run the game to show their gratitude to the supporters. Then again, maybe not. Manchester United's directors – with one or two honourable exceptions – showed what they thought of the fans when they tried to sell the club off to Rupert Murdoch's BSkyB. In the end the government stopped it happening, but that doesn't alter the fact that they tried. The supporters did not want it to happen, but so what? The supporters did not want their team to pull out of the hallowed FA cup so that they could take part in that latest invention the World Club Championship, but they did it anyway. The Newcastle United owners made clear what they thought of their fans in a drunken conversation with an undercover reporter in a Spanish bar. They were unlucky – initially. The *News of the World* printed the story and they had to resign. But it wasn't long before the reality of their financial power over the club had them back on the board.

Commercialism has not only stolen sport from its fans; it has also helped erode respect for authority in sport. John McEnroe, perhaps the first of the real super-brats, was often able to get away with his outrageous behaviour on the tennis court because he was such a big moneyspinner that some umpires and referees were nervous about throwing him out of the tournament. We are now seeing it even in cricket, with first-class players increasingly willing to challenge the umpire's decision rather than walking the second his finger is raised. On the football field, some observers say, referees are under growing pressure to turn a blind eye if a big star is involved in some dubious play.

The pay and the superstar status has turned some of the

players into precious prima donnas who behave like the worst sort of Hollywood brats. The impression some of them give is that because they are such celebrities they can treat the fans with contempt, conveniently ignoring the fact that it was the fans who made it all possible. There is nothing new in footballers behaving badly on and off the pitch, but at least they used to acknowledge their boorishness. George Best was scarcely a paragon of virtue – indeed, he was a womanising drunk who eventually squandered his genius – but at least the man had the good grace to accept the blame. When he was sober he was clearly ashamed of his behaviour.

Paul Gascoigne was eventually dropped from the England side not for his drunkenness and his penchant for beating up his wife, but because he simply hadn't made the effort to get fit. His reaction was to behave like a spoiled two-year-old who'd been sent to his room and his reward was to sell the tale of his tantrum to a tabloid for another very large cheque. When Everton player Duncan Ferguson was released from jail after serving time for assault he was paraded around the pitch, according to reporters who were there at the time, 'like a returning hero'.

Perhaps the message that adoring youngsters take from it all is that sportsmanship and gamesmanship have become interchangeable. When a top player wants advice it's more likely to be from his PR agent or sponsorship consultant than from his coach. A reputation for 'laddishness' – roughly translated to mean drunken, yobbish, sometimes brutal behaviour – is good for business rather than career-threatening. It gets you in the papers. In the world of showbiz there's no such thing as bad publicity. And top-class football is nothing if not showbiz.

As with football, so with other sports. Amateur athletics was once the supreme example of talented and dedicated men and women giving their best for not much more than passing fame and a few trophies on the sideboard. Now the pickings are rich indeed and at the top level the sport is so corrupted with drugs it is tempting to believe that the most successful will be those who can most effectively fool the officials. I remember watching Roger Bannister break the ultimate record in athletics – the four-minute mile – and I wonder today how that modest man must feel about what has happened to the sport he graced.

It is tempting to cast a rosy glow over the halcyon days of amateur sport – in truth there was often snobbery and some imaginative ways were found to put a few pounds into many back pockets – but the vast amounts of cash swilling around these days has changed things beyond recognition. The International Olympics Committee has estimated that Coca-Cola alone spends more than £300million every year on sports sponsorship and various marketing exercises.

But it is football that has changed perhaps more than any other. A game that sprang from working-class roots in local communities and inspired fierce loyalty in them is being torn away from the very communities whose passion and support created it in the first place, often more than a century ago. The values that were once associated with the game are being replaced by a different set of values: goal margins have been replaced by profit margins. I can imagine one of football's old timers saying: 'We could have done with a bit of that in my day.' And so he could. They played for a pittance and when they were forced, often through injury, to retire after years of kicking a leather ball that weighed half as much as a rhino's backside, all they had to look forward to was a scrapbook of memories and a lifetime of painful knee joints and no pension. The legendary Tommy Lawton, who played for Burnley and Everton from the mid thirties until the fifties and centre forward for England, was totally destitute in his last years. He was so broke he descended into petty crime. It was not that he had once made a lot of money and lost it; he never had it.

When the commercial bear is released from its cage we all have to watch where it will rampage next. In the emotion-free zone of the balance sheet there is no reason on earth why Manchester United should not eventually leave Manchester altogether. When the cold-eyed accountants study the figures they could well calculate that since the club is now clearly an international 'product' it matters not where it is located. If eighteen out of every hundred fans across the land support Manchester United – as they did by 1998 – they might do even better business in, say, London. Sure the Manchester fans would kick up a stink, but who can hear the powerless fans when money talks so much more loudly? It is already happening abroad. The most powerful team in Italy – Juventus – has threatened to move from its home city of Turin unless the city council lets it build a massive leisure complex including cinemas way outside the city. In the United States the Los Angeles Raiders have become the Oakland Raiders and the Houston Oilers the Tennessee Titans. Attendance has dropped like a stone for the Titans since the move, but they'll take comfort from their share of the NFL's $2.2 billion annual TV contract.

Over the years, my sports reporter brother tells me, it seems inevitable that a European superleague will come into being and the handful of superclubs will become even more super, perhaps playing two teams simultaneously. More and more of the smaller clubs will be driven into bankruptcy. At the moment there are ninety-two professional sides in the Football League. Perhaps half will survive. Superclubs are already being spawned in the once amateur world of rugby union, so we shall watch the same thing happening there. Once proud clubs like Bridgend, Neath and Newport will be consigned to second-class status.

As for football, the next step might very well be to change the game itself. Selling soccer in a big way to the United States would produce serious revenues, but American broadcasters like their own football in small bite-size chunks so the commercials can be more easily accommodated. Perhaps, instead of soccer being a game of two halves it might become a game of four quarters? And fans enjoy goals . . . so perhaps the goal mouth should be just a little wider?

My argument has been that the speed and extent of the commercial advance over the past forty years has been so great that we are being converted from citizen to consumer, from people who share a culture with a wide set of values and beliefs and interests into people for whom what makes money is what matters most. Even when, as in the case of football, we show that we want to hang on to what we've always valued, commercial interests tell us we can't. Other values and attitudes of mind beyond the commercial are being elbowed out of the way. In particular the ways in which we relate to each other are being narrowed down so that we see each other in commercial terms where in the past it would not have dawned on us to do so. Many people are still ready and willing to do something for nothing, to give a hand, to do a service, but the underlying attitude is being chipped away. Just consider the following few examples – extreme, maybe, but indicative none the less.

An old man collapsed on the pavement while he was out doing his shopping. It seemed that he was lucky: on the other side of the road was the entrance to the casualty department of a large hospital and some passers-by rushed in to ask the staff to come and help. They refused and the old man died. It was explained later that the hospital's insurance conditions were so structured that any doctor or nurse who treated him would not have been covered against any possible future claim.

The headmistress of a school in Halifax insisted on charging a parent for a school assistant to give a five-year-old child three tablets a day to treat cystic fibrosis. The argument went that it added to the workload and was not part of their normal duties. The parents moved the child to another school in disgust.

A doctor on an aeroplane responded to the 'is there a doctor on board?' plea and helped save the life of one of the passengers. Then he sent a bill to the airline for his services. There's no reason he shouldn't have; he was a professional doing a job for which he normally gets paid. Inevitably there have been other cases like it since, and the effect will probably be that ultimately doctors won't get their black bag out until they've negotiated a fee. By which time the passenger may be plucking his harp and sailing past the plane on his very own fluffy cloud.

Castle Morpeth Council was fined by the Local Government Ombudsman for refusing to pay for the funeral expenses of a poverty-stricken old lady who'd been in its care for fifty-seven years. The bit I found hard to believe was the explanation attributed to the council's chief executive, Peter Wilson. He was reported as saying: 'One could argue that from a commercial viewpoint residents of a home are its income-producing raw material. Ergo, from a purely commercial view, deceased residents may then be regarded as being the waste produced by their business.' When I interviewed Mr Wilson I expected him to deny ever having said such a thing. Had he *really* described the body of an old lady as 'waste material'? Yes, he had, though he did concede that the words were 'probably inappropriate'. On reflection, perhaps he got it right the first time. If we use the language of commerce and think of patients in a home as 'income-producing' then why should Mr Wilson have been shamed into shying away from the logical outcome of that way of thinking? Clearly Mr Wilson thought he was acting perfectly responsibly – and in his own narrow terms he was. If we start to see each other just as the other party to a commercial transaction, then that will define our sense of responsibility to each other.

That's what has worried many people about the changes that have happened to the NHS over the last ten years or so. Speaking on an *Analysis* programme about the com-mercialisation of the NHS, Professor Julian Le Grand of the LSE said that the way the old non-commercial NHS had worked depended not upon cash figures but upon trust. By trust he meant a complex framework of responsibilities, obligations and mutual understanding, much of it unspecified, but which everyone in the NHS understood because they shared the same goal of serving their patients. Le Grand's worry was that 'Trust takes years to build up, it takes seconds to destroy.' The wider world where people relate to each other as citizens, not just as people to have a commercial relationship with, has a similar framework of unspecified trust. That framework of citizenship, of trust, in which we relate to each other with courtesy, with respect, with an understanding of other people's needs and interests, can also be destroyed at great speed by the power of commercialism. It's like the football clubs. Most of the great ones have taken over a hundred years to build up their following of commitment and loyalty. In a very short time, commercialism has been putting that loyalty to a very severe test. Time here is the key. Consumer populism says we do not have time for the non-commercial.

I think it was Ray Bradbury who once told a tale, set well into the next century, in which the only commodity of real value was time. Because of overpopulation and dwindling resources in the world every human being was allocated a certain amount of time at birth. When the clock ran out, you died. You could not buy more time ... except from another human being, whose life would thus be shortened. It was a wonderful, chilling tale and I recalled it when I heard a Church of England bishop describing a conversation he had had with a visitor from one of the poorer regions of India. The visitor told the Bishop: 'You have the clock, but we have time.' We have infinitely more time than the characters in Bradbury's story; it's a question of what we do with it. Increasingly what we are doing with it is working, or worrying about work. That's yet another effect of consumer populism.

A report by Jonathan Gershuny's Economic and Social Research Centre at the University of Essex showed that men with children under the age of twelve are the group most likely to work excessively, and that single people are the group most likely to work a standard week. In a study of 5,000 households of people working more than sixty hours a week, half the men and three quarters of the women had children under twelve. They complained that it meant they talked to their children less, and were less likely to monitor their homework.

When National Opinion Polls carried out a survey on work half the people canvassed said they felt they were 'surviving rather than living'. Two thirds of people with children felt they did not have enough time for their children. The Henley Research Centre showed how the twenty-four-hour lifestyle is destroying the weekend. Half of all working men and a third of women work some or most Sundays. The main pressures are on white-collar workers to put in extra hours and on the lower-paid to do overtime or to do a second, weekend job. In 1984 fewer than 600,000 people had a second job. Fifteen years later there were twice as many. So that is what we do with what used to be our spare time: we work.

Why do we do it? Partly it's because we let ourselves be persuaded that we must have everything that consumer populism tells us we need, so we have to earn the money to pay for it. But there's another reason with which we are all becoming very familiar. In order to keep the commercial engine going those who run it feel the need to be more ruthless. That means piling on more and more pressures. In a *Management Today* survey of 5,500 managers in 1998, two thirds said they were having to get their employees to do more and more and a third admitted that their demands on them were unrealistic. But it also means being ready to fire. It's called flexibility. The result: we feel less secure and work even harder to hold on.

One of the oldest clichés in the corporate phrase book is 'Our people are our greatest asset'. At every business conference I have ever attended – and I have, God help me, attended an awful lot of them – you will hear that said. It's usually pronounced in the most solemn of tones by the managing director even as he and his boardroom colleagues are plotting a new way to cut the work force by another 10 per cent at the same time as they are increasing their own pay packets by twice that much. You will hear many more such clichés. My favourite is 'No business can afford to stand still.' It always depresses me. If a company is relatively small, but making a respectable profit by providing a good service at a reasonable price, it seems sad that they can't just carry on doing it. I know the argument: if you don't keep growing you will get swallowed up.

By 'growing' they mean making an ever larger return on assets employed. That's another way of saying making a bigger profit. In a country that believes in capitalism, it always intrigues me how many company bosses will do anything to avoid using the word 'profit' in public. 'Margin', yes, but profit hardly ever. In business, increasingly, euphemism rules. They never sack people, they downsize the workforce or, if you are in a more senior job, they 'let you go'. It's as if they're doing you a favour. 'Hey, Jo, good to see you. The company's been doing very well, but it's a competitive world out there and we need to increase the margin so we're letting you go. No need to thank me.'

That sort of thing has been happening much more since we discovered the virtues of flexibility. In theory what flexibility means is that everyone benefits if companies can reduce or increase the size of their workforce depending on whether business is good or bad and the workers can move from job to job without being tied for life to one company. In practice it means we worry much more.

Short-term contracts are all very well for the City whiz-kids with wide braces and wider mouths who can speak the language of derivatives and futures. They're fine for the twenty-one-year-olds who not only know what a computer does but how it does it and even how to fix it when it no longer does what it's meant to do. All of them can walk out of one fat salary into another even fatter one. But there are many more – in their mid-forties and fifties – who do not have that luxury. You meet some of them earning a few pounds driving for the more up-market minicab firms in any of the big cities. They were allowed to keep their nice company cars when they were 'let go', but not allowed to keep their dignity or self-respect. Others hang around their homes all day filling in endless job applications that they know will end up in an executive wastepaper bin. All they wanted was a nice secure job with a pension at the end, but the system tells them they have failed and they believe it.

So there are two sets of pressures that have been increasing over the years: the forces of consumer populism combined with those of a much more competitive world. We have to succeed by the standards of the first and, at the same time, cope with the pressures of the second. It's no wonder that our attitudes and our behaviour and, indeed, our character, are being transformed and it is happening at an ever earlier age.

Dr Jacqui Cousins is an adviser to the United Nations who wrote in *Nursery World* about some work she had done with four-year-olds in nursery schools who were under considerable pressures of one kind or another. One of them told her he was worried about not getting a job if he 'didn't work hard'. Many of them were too tired to play, and those who did were reluctant to get involved with long games because, in the words of one tot, they were always being told to 'Hurry up, hurry up!' It seemed the staff at the nurseries thought the children were getting their playtime at home, and their parents – who were too busy themselves – thought they were getting it at nursery. The parents wanted the best for their children and so they pushed them too hard. They sent them to ballet classes and art classes and every other sort of class when, said the sensible Dr Cousins, what they really need is to do less and just 'be'.

The American sociologist Richard Sennett, now at the London School of Economics, has written a book on how changing working conditions are affecting us. You can get an idea of his conclusion from its title: *The Corrosion of Character*. He believes that the ever-increasing demands for flexibility are creating a world in which we stop thinking about the long term. The effect of that is to corrode trust, loyalty and mutual commitment. The short time-frame of modern institutions, he says, limits the 'ripening of informal trust' and affects our ability to give purpose and direction to our lives. 'What we experience is insecurity and uncertainty, and that makes it difficult, if not impossible, for us to conceive of our lives as being a long term narrative.'

You could argue that the opposite of flexibility is a life of endless routine and drudgery. Perhaps, but it depends what you mean by routine.

I remember feeling terribly pleased with myself when I first landed a job with the BBC. I was based in Liverpool, the most exciting British beat for a reporter in those days, what with the Beatles and the Cavern Club and the dock strikes and everything else. They were still building the Anglican cathedral and one of my first assignments was to make a film about the building work. It was a majestic project, started before I was born. I interviewed one of the stonemasons who had been working on it all his life. I pitied the poor chap. There was me, dashing hither and yon, never knowing what I might be doing the next day, master of my own timetable (news editor permitting) and my own destiny. And then there was this poor chap, turning up at the same time five days a week, chipping out more stone blocks to lay on the other stone blocks he'd been chipping out the day before and the day before *ad infinitum*. 'Don't you get bored?' I asked him.

'Why should I?'

'Well, all you're doing is laying one stone on another year after year.'

'No I'm not,' he said, 'I'm building a cathedral. What will you leave behind you when you die?'

We may not all find the same satisfaction and pride in our work as that craftsman but most of us seem to seek some kind of routine, if only because it creates a stable framework within which we can fashion a life for ourselves, our family and indeed our community. George Eliot's phrase for it was 'the beneficent harness of routine'. In Sennett's terms character requires some element of such a harness.

Sennett tells the story of two generations of an American-Italian immigrant family. The father, Enrico, worked as a poorly paid janitor but stuck at it and was able to build a decent life for himself and his family, saving enough over the years to make sure his children got a good education and a good start. His son, Rico, fretted against the narrow constraints of his childhood, wanted a more exciting and rewarding life, and broke away from his roots. When he married his wife worked, too, and their joint earnings put them in the top five per cent of earners in the United States. Nowadays they call it a 'work rich household'. To succeed in his new world he had to move his family four times in fourteen years and his life could scarcely be more different from his father's. Now, says Sennett, young Rico speaks of the 'frequent anarchy' into which his family plunges and, as a father, 'the fear of a lack of ethical discipline' haunts him. His children take material wellbeing and upward mobility for granted in a way that he never could, but he fears that without a clearer ethical grounding, they'll become mall rats. And you don't need to live in America to know what *that* means. We may not yet have shopping malls so big and splendid that people take their holidays in them but we're on our way.

Rico's deepest worry, says Sennett, is that he cannot offer the substance of his work life as an example to his children of how they should conduct themselves ethically. He says that the qualities of good work are no longer the qualities of good character. Sennett contrasts what is necessary for a family – 'formal obligation, trustworthiness, commitment and purpose' – with what now prevails in the world of work. That, he says, is 'short-term behaviour, weakness of loyalty and commitment'; not things my stonemason knew much about.

Ultimately the insecurity of the 'no long term' economy forces people to act ruthlessly and in their narrow self-interest just to survive, and so it is the harsh ethic of survival that comes to dominate. It becomes an everyone-for-himself society. The bosses I meet on the conference circuit and in radio and television studios are making an entirely obvious statement when they say 'our people are our greatest asset', but they should really insert the word 'disposable' somewhere in it.

To use another popular piece of management jargon, business is 're-engineering' itself, and the outcome of that is almost invariably that 'our people' end up feeling less needed. You might say there's nothing terribly new in that. For capitalism to work, business must be efficient, and old-style capitalists didn't exactly run their companies as benevolent institutions. There are some big differences now though. Before the rise of the trade unions the mill bosses and the mine owners were able to treat their workers pretty much as they chose, and there wasn't much they could do about it. The trade unions gave the workers a collective strength and it balanced the scales, sometimes over-balanced them. Their power lay in being able to talk about 'us', where the management represented 'them'. The effect of the latest changes is that we increasingly talk about 'me'. If there is no 'long term' in a career sense and no 'sense of narrative' then the old links are destroyed.

The sociologists say that more primitive societies than our own were bound together by a set of shared beliefs. The coal mining valleys of South Wales were not exactly primitive when I started work in them – no, they did not keep coal in the bath – but there was certainly a powerful glue binding together the people who lived there. By and large the miners and their families believed they had a job for life, had no wish to do anything else and generally looked out for each other. The ultimate expression of that was when an accident happened underground. It was not considered an act of heroism for a man, or a team of men, to risk their lives to rescue a workmate; it was expected, and they did it.

As I've said, It is too easy to romanticise life in a mining village and I never met a miner or his wife who wanted their son to go down the pit, but there was a powerful sense of community. Partly that was because of the sense of shared danger, but mostly it was shared interest. That is an increasingly rare experience, whether we're talking about a pit village or an assembly line or the smart offices of a big financial institution. The background to our modern shoulder-shrugging society, according to Sennett, is a world of work which 'radiates indifference'. Most of his research has been carried out in the United States, where the flexibility of the labour market is more advanced than it is here but, as in so many other ways, we are catching up. The statistics tell us that most British children will have moved home four times by the age of sixteen, just as Rico's did.

A growing number of sociologists believe, with Sennett, that the end of the 'long term' is damaging to society. Now, not only have we lost our shared beliefs, we have also lost the glue of what they call economic obligations, often enshrined in law. There is a growing subculture of men who feel impotent in the face of all these economic and social upheavals, according to Angus Bancroft of Cardiff University. He blames that for the ghastly phenomenon we call 'new laddism', though he says there is 'increased infantilism at all levels . . . a search for instant satisfaction and the rejection of responsibility, social or personal'.

If the pressures of consumer populism are undermining our character it seems they are also making us depressed. The clinical psychologist Oliver James, author of *Britain on the Couch*, blames this directly on the pressures of consumer populism. Let's look at the figures first. James quotes estimates that women born after 1955 are some five times more likely to suffer depression than those born before 1925 and that a third of the poorest mothers of small children are depressed at any one time. The government's annual report on the state of public health for 1997 seemed to lend him some support, revealing an increase of fifteen per cent for women and nineteen per cent for men of those on anti-depressants. In 1999 a survey carried out by *Men's Health* magazine of 1,500 men with an average age of thirty-three showed that nearly half felt under stress. More than two thirds said they had suffered from depression. James argues that the official drug-taking statistics hugely underestimate the scale of the problem of depression because, in his view, we are 'pharmacological Calvinists': we are reluctant, believe it or not, to take pills. Even so, the amount of money the NHS spends on anti-depressants has shot up over the past few years. Between 1991 and 1997 the number of prescriptions for them almost doubled.

Not everyone in the medical world agrees on what causes depression, but many support a theory about the level of serotonin in our brains. If there's lots of it you'll be whistling on your way to work, even on a wet Monday morning; if there's not you'll want to pull the duvet over your head and stay put. Medical opinion used to think that serotonin levels depended on our genes. If Mum and Dad were happy little bunnies, then you'd be more likely to be one too. But then they did some experiments with vervet monkeys, says James, and discovered that that is only part of it. What matters is something else. It seems that if a monkey is being given a hard time in his group for one reason or another, and he thinks he doesn't have any real social status any longer, then the level of serotonin in his brain falls and you have one miserable monkey. So how do we get from them to us?

Well, James believes that what I have called the world of consumer populism is largely responsible for generating depression in two ways. It helps undermine the strength of emotional attachments, which itself affects levels of serotonin, and it undermines many people's sense of status, which has in turn lowered their serotonin levels and caused depression. In other words if we are endlessly being told through one medium or another that everyone else is doing so much better than we are, then our own sense of status falls and so does our serotonin level. We become depressed. Who can argue that expectations have risen dramatically for personal and professional fulfilment, especially among young women, since 1950.

Another big change since then is that we seem almost to be looking for ways in which we can find ourselves lacking. Television is the biggest culprit here because increasingly we can't tell the difference between real life and what's on the box. That is fatal, James says, because we begin to compare ourselves to a fictional, unrealistic world. This affects men and women in different ways. Men are, apparently, so impressed with those sexy women on television that we find our own partners wanting. So, since women are far more preoccupied with their appearance than men, they are more likely to suffer from eating disorders and twice as likely to report feeling depressed. Women, on the other hand, rate men less in terms of looks and more in terms of where they come on the dominance/passivity scale. This puts pressure on men to succeed and dominate. Television cranks up both expectations and comparisons by disproportionately showing the beautiful and successful. On American television, three quarters of the characters in drama are prosperous whites in their twenties and thirties. And, from my own observations, they all have perfect teeth.

There's something else that television does. Anyone who's ever read the old Superman or Captain Marvel comics as a youngster will remember that heart-stopping moment when our hero is definitely, but definitely, about to come to a sticky end. Superman has been tied to a lump of Kryptonite and his strength is ebbing away fast, or Captain Marvel can't utter the magic word 'Shazzam!' All is lost. And then, with one bound, he is free. Oliver James puts the modern equivalent rather more formally: 'Very often, television drama offers magical connections between desired wishes and outcomes without the intervening means.' I think we're both getting at the same thing: we are encouraged to believe that we can sort out our problems without any real effort and get pretty fed up when it becomes obvious that we can't.

Then there is the advertising. You don't need to be a clinical psychologist to be familiar with the way it operates today. They don't just tell us what we ought to have; they tell us everyone else already has it so we should have it *now*. The effect is interesting. In reality we are vastly better off than we were in 1950. If you had shown a fifties mother a modern kitchen she would probably have fallen into a faint. And if you had shown a fifties motorist what a modern car can do he simply wouldn't have believed it. And yet, not only do we want more – much more – we feel deprived.

According to James, we feel more deprived now than we did in 1950 even though we have so much more:

> An unhappy person is more likely to consume, to 'shop till you drop' or to purchase drugs of solace (illegal ones, alcohol, cigarettes) or to spend money on modern compulsions (lotteries, consumer fetishism, over-working). This may help to explain the usefulness and popularity of the concept of an 'addictive personality' in which a propensity to interchangeable addictions is posited . . . if the addictive personality exists it is probably a by-product of advanced capitalism.

That's the beauty of it from an advertiser's viewpoint. The market research organisation Mintel did a survey in 1998 and twenty-nine per cent of the women interviewed said they were shopaholics. You don't have to believe that figure, but it's interesting that so many people now see shopping as something to which they are helplessly and hopelessly addicted.

So we have been encouraged by consumerism and the media to choose criteria by which to compare ourselves which are likely to cause us to fail, and then we end up blaming ourselves for our predicament. In the past we might have said: 'Well, that geezer's got his Roller 'cos he's a toff and toffs have Rollers don't they?' Now we compare ourselves with a supposedly ordinary bloke on television and worry about not being so successful.

Michael Titze is a German psychotherapist who has reached much the same conclusion: 'We seem to have created today a society which puts such a high premium on performance and success that when people fail to reach these levels they are possessed with a sense of shame and depression.'

There is something else we expect because we are endlessly told we should have it, and that is a successful personal relationship, fulfilled and fulfilling. All the statistics tell us we are increasingly less likely to have one but that doesn't stop us expecting it. After all, popular culture tells us everyone can meet the person of their dreams and live happily ever after. It may be *because* of the message delivered by the media that we are less likely to get what we want: we expect too much. Oliver James says that since the fifties there has been a wholly new valuation placed on personal relationships as a source of happiness.

Whatever the sociological arguments for and against easier divorce, there's not much doubt that it makes us miserable. Which brings us back to serotonin. The levels are much lower amongst those who've divorced compared to those who haven't. The children suffer, too. They don't do so well in school, they become more aggressive and more depressed. An analysis of thirty-nine studies of the effects of being cared for by someone other than a parent concluded that about half the children of divorce suffered from 'anxious attachment'. That's two thirds more than for children who are still with their parents.

So let's look at the effects of depression. The big effect, it seems, is that it makes men more violent. There has been an enormous increase in the amount of recorded violence since the fifties: 6,000 crimes of violence against the person recorded in 1950 and 239,000 in 1996. Oliver James says that since three quarters of convicted violent men are depressed, and since impulsively violent men have low serotonin levels, this represents a large increase in low serotonin men. Dr Theodore Dalrymple agrees. He works in prisons and hospitals and sees a lot of it. He says that 'morbid jealousy' is the most frequent motive for serious domestic violence. 'The perpetrator of the violence, usually unfaithful himself, expects his partner to be unfaithful, even if there's no direct evidence of it, because the climate suggests everybody is.'

Dalrymple has an interesting theory which takes us back to the notion that so many of us feel inadequate in an age when the cult of celebrity dominates the media. The solution increasingly adopted by many men is utterly to dominate one other person. Dalrymple writes: 'Compared with the jealous man at home, Genghis Khan was a constitutional monarch . . . To be fêted, though a monster, is an egotist's dream . . . The combination of loosening sexual restraint and radical individualism may have given pleasure to many; but for many also it has brought misery and violence on a scale that I should not have believed possible and which continues to shock me.'

However you look at it there is no doubt that depression is causing enormous damage, not just to ourselves but to society as a whole.

Commercial pressures within consumer populism are eroding the way we relate to each other. They are undermining trust. They are making us work harder so that we have less time for what used to be called life. They are making it difficult for us to think long term and so build a life in which anything more than the short term matters. And they are making us depressed. In Richard Sennett's terms they are undermining our very character.

Increased commercialism has hugely influenced the climate of Britain over the past forty years but it could not have done so without a powerful ally. It has had one: the media, itself more commercially driven than ever before. It is there I want to turn now.

Chapter 9

Chasing the ratings

LEAVING SCHOOL AT fifteen, as I did, was pretty silly. The sensible thing would have been to go to university. I suppose I was bright enough and the headmaster said I should. But there wasn't much money at home and nobody from my family had ever gone to university and I really couldn't see myself wearing one of those terrible striped scarves around my neck that marked you out as one of the privileged few. And anyway I wasn't really *sure* I was bright enough. The second most sensible thing would have been to join a bank. A job for life, a gold watch and pension at the end of it *and* a cheap mortgage. Even more sensible (according to my father) would be to become a french polisher. He'd made a living from it and it was a highly respected trade. All very sensible, I've no doubt, but I wanted to be a reporter and that was that.

As it turned out I was right, though for all the wrong reasons.

When I became a reporter in 1958, I did not know, and neither did most other people, that I was entering what was to become the great growth industry of the second half of the century: the media. We didn't use that rather nasty word until relatively recently. When I was starting out we had newspapers and radio and television, but we hadn't started to talk about 'the media'. Nowadays every other graduate in the land seems to want to be a part of it. I had some proof of that when I addressed a conference of sixth-formers in that grand old building Methodist Central Hall, a few yards from Big Ben. These were the brightest and best of our young men and women, all of them interested in politics, all come to London to hear from the likes of Tony Blair and William Hague, with one or two of the lower orders like me thrown in to pad out the programme. I asked how many of them thought they might eventually look for a career in politics. A few dozen of the two thousand raised their hands. Then I asked who wanted a career in the media. Half the hands in the hall went up and most of their owners wanted to move into television.

Television is the most powerful cultural force since Gutenberg ran off the first printed copy of the Bible. Those who appear on it have become the icons of our age. Those who watch it are influenced in ways it would have been impossible to imagine only two generations ago. Those who choose not to watch it are influenced whether they like it or not. It is true that television has not brought about the death of newspapers as many predicted; instead they feed off each other. Nor has it killed reading . . . yet. But picture a world without television and then try to deny its force.

Not, as I say, that I foresaw all of that when I took my first trembling steps as a novice newspaper reporter on the *Penarth Times*. I did, however, have the sense to realise that it was not possible to build the New Jerusalem of journalism if I stayed in Penarth so, after two years, I moved to another weekly newspaper, the *Merthyr Express*. That was an altogether more impressive publication. It wasn't just *what* it was – a much bigger newspaper with a grumpy old sod of an editor who scarcely spoke to his staff and wore a real green eye shade, just as editors were meant to do – it was *where* it was. Merthyr Tydfil, unlike sleepy old Penarth, was where real news happened.

Penarth was rather smug and genteel. Not Merthyr. It had real, knee-in-the-groin politics and it had industry. Merthyr is at the head of one of a dozen narrow valleys that run north to south across what was once the most productive coalfield the world had ever seen. But it was iron that had made the town great. If it hadn't been for a few enterprising Welshmen in wode we might never have had the industrial revolution. They were the first to discover what you could do with a load of iron ore, limestone and water. They had plenty of that and plenty of fuel (wood before coal) and pretty soon they were smelting iron. Merthyr was to become the iron capital of the world and the most prosperous town in Wales, but coal had taken over when I arrived. It took me one day to discover that however badly I failed as a reporter I would never be tempted to turn to mining to earn a living.

To drop thousands of feet in a cage through pitch blackness at a terrifying speed, little bits of coal stinging your face and getting into your eyes, is bad enough. To spend the next eight hours bent low on your knees at the coal face as a massive machine grinds its way through the rock, breathing in the dust it creates, is pure hell. To do that day after day for the rest of your working life is unimaginable. How the men managed to work at the same time God only knew. It was all I could do to stay on my feet – or my knees. If ever I have been tempted to feel sorry for myself after a hard day at the word processor or in front of a microphone I have tried to think of digging coal for a living instead. It concentrates the mind wonderfully.

When I went to the pub with the miners at the end of a shift many would drink a pint of water before the real stuff; the first pint washed the dust from the lungs and you couldn't taste it anyway. No point in wasting good beer after all. It didn't really wash the dust away, of course. It gathered in the lungs over the years and worked its destructive ways. A lifetime in the mines so often meant an early and painful death from 'the dust', but there were many who died even more premature deaths, crushed when a tunnel roof fell in or blown apart by an explosion roaring down a tunnel. I often had to knock on the doors of miners' wives who'd been widowed hours earlier, the sound of the pithead siren still echoing in the valley.

'Hello Mrs Jones, I'm from the *Merthyr Express*, can I please have a picture of your husband for the paper?' Almost always they would give you one, and a cup of tea.

People with a romanticised notion of miners – the noble, blackened faces of proud men marching back from the pit head and singing 'Cwm Rhondda' in perfect unison – say how sad it is that there are no deep mines left in the Welsh valleys. Perhaps. But 'Cwm Rhondda' is the myth and clogged lungs is the reality and I shed no tears for the end of that.

Most of a reporter's working hours are spent not on the great tragedies – thank God – but on the banalities of everyday life. I dozed gently for many an hour in the Victorian debating chamber of Merthyr Tydfil Borough Council learning how politics operates on a local level when every member belongs to the same party. Merthyr was the birthplace of that great Labour leader Keir Hardie, and you were as likely to win a seat if you weren't Labour as you were to catch a fat salmon in the black waters of the Taff.

To say that the council was corrupt would not be fair. There were many who gave their time to local politics because they wanted to serve as best they could. Let's just say that if you wanted planning permission for a slightly dodgy enterprise, it did no harm at all to know the right people on the right committee.

Even I, a very junior and unimportant reporter in his seventeenth year, was a target.

I owned a car; I use the term loosely. It cost £37 and you had to wear a plastic bag on your right foot when it rained because the water came up through a hole in the floor. The other thing that happened when it rained was that the wipers stopped. They were fine, more or less, when the car was standing still but because they operated by suction, the faster the car went the slower they went. So if you managed to reach the maximum cruising speed of about forty miles an hour they'd simply give up.

I was delighted, therefore, when a local businessman who'd just won a seat on the council offered to swap cars with me if ever I had to go anywhere. His car was a magnificent Humber Super Snipe and had cost rather more than £37. To my unending shame I said yes please. Several times. And then it occurred to my naïve young brain that the good councillor might expect rather a lot of coverage for his council activities in the *Merthyr Express*. I bought a better car of my own. Not a Humber Super Snipe, exactly, but at least the wipers worked and the phone calls from the councillor eased off.

From Merthyr I went to Cardiff, to the *Western Mail*. This was a real daily newspaper and I felt I had arrived. My news editor was less impressed with me than I was with my new status. His name was John Humphries, different spelling but that didn't stop him; the first thing he made me do was change my name. For a year I was John Desmond. It did nothing for my ego, which was probably the point. Then I got married and the news editor put me on night shifts. My wife was a nurse on early shifts, so as I got home she left for work. It did nothing for my sex life. That was probably the point, too. I never did get on with news editors.

After a year on the *Mail* I was offered two jobs more or less at the same time: one by the *Sunday Times* in London and the other by TWW in Cardiff. I went up to London to have lunch with the news editor (I didn't like that one, either) at Simpson's in the Strand. I had never eaten anywhere quite so grand in my life and, thoroughly impressed and intimidated, accepted the job. Back in Cardiff that night I had several pints with some of the lads who told me I was crazy not to move into the exciting new world of television journalism so I changed my mind and went to TWW instead. I had a letter from the *Sunday Times* telling me what a big mistake I was making . . .

And that was that. At the age of twenty-one my career in newspapers had come to an end and I was about to start working for the medium in which I would stay for the rest of my working life. I wish I could say that I had been showing enormous intelligence and foresight for one so young, anticipating the effect television was to have over all our lives. The truth is, I thought it would be more fun – and the news editor was an old friend of mine.

Apart from sleeping, watching television is what we do most of. True, it has been declining since 1992 but the fall has been small. We used to spend just over four hours a day in front of the box; now we spend just under. We have yet to see what digital television and many more channels will do. The advertising industry thinks it will reverse the decline, or at least slow it down. If we don't like what the schedules are offering us, we will be able to create our own schedules. If you have any doubt about our continuing love affair with the box, just remember the billions that are being poured by investors into all this new technology. Some very smart people indeed think we're going to go on watching, and that we will be happy to pay more for the pleasure of doing so.

But the influence of television is not to be measured just by the number of hours we have our set on. It is also about what happens to us when it is on. Some people, certainly, treat it as background while they carry on having a meal, reading the paper or even listening to a CD. Or even, according to a survey conducted with set-top cameras activated by the on-off switch, making love. Wouldn't you think that the volunteers who took part in the survey would have draped a modest cloth over the camera lens before they moved into action? Perhaps they just got carried away with the heat of the moment . . . or perhaps there are more exhibitionists and budding porn stars out there than we might have thought. But most of the time we turn it on to watch, and we give it our full attention. Nobody with small children needs persuading of the power of the box to seize our attention. Language tells the story. We are 'glued' to the television. We are 'couch potatoes'.

We watch a lot of television; we pay attention to it when it's on; and most of us rely on it as the main source of information for what is happening out there in the world. That goes way beyond news and other factual television. We gain our impressions of what Australia or America are like from their soap operas. If the BBC or ITV dramatise a Jane Austen novel, the bookshops stock up for the extra sales that will surely follow. Television can determine what we buy, what we talk about and what our children play with. If a programme introduces to us four tubby little characters with aerials sticking out of their heads all other toys are swept aside and the person who thought them up goes away £55million richer. As for the grown-ups, if a popular series is set in a specific area of the countryside, that is where the tourists will go. If a politician makes a serious fool of himself on television, he's had it.

Television has become, for most of us, as much a part of our lives as the electricity that comes into our homes or the air we breathe. It is now a central part of what makes us who we are.

There is a particular facet of television which sets it apart from almost all other influences on our lives, with real implications for whether it ends up a good or a bad influence. It is not yet truly interactive. It speaks to us, but we do not speak back, except on a few phone-in programmes. This is a striking feature of something that has such a big influence on our lives. When I was a child the influences were not only more varied, but they tended to be influences you engaged with, talked back to, pushed to see how far you could go with or against them, got your come-uppance if you went too far. That was how you learned what reality was all about, and how you fitted into it. But the reality we get from television is not like that. We are not participants in the making of that reality, we are voyeurs. Sometimes we may be just passive voyeurs, sometimes aroused or indignant, but we're voyeurs none the less. It means we share no responsibility in the fashioning of that reality. It means we don't have to do any learning for ourselves. We just get reality given to us by those who make the programmes. That's why it matters so much what they decide to show us.

They can present us with a picture of the world as it really is – rich, diverse, ambiguous and morally complex – that can stimulate us into being affected by it and thinking about it. The best television today does all of that. But equally they can pander to the worst sides of our nature, or turn everything into something we respond to as if it were all a form of light entertainment. If they do that, then that's how we will start to respond to the world too. My worry is that the trend is clearly in the wrong direction.

Perhaps the greatest of all American television reporters was Ed Murrow of CBS. His wartime dispatches have never been bettered. Nor has what he said about television back in 1958:

'This instrument can teach; it can illuminate; yes it can even inspire. But it can only do so to the extent that humans (that means you) are determined to use it to those ends. Otherwise it is merely wires and lights in a box.'

If that seems, forty years later, a somewhat grandiloquent statement, I suspect it says more about these cynical times than it does about Mr Murrow. Wires and lights which, none the less, can coarsen our view of the world we live in.

When the BBC first started television it was in the hands of paternalists, notably Lord Reith, who wanted to create a service for citizens. They wanted to inform and educate as well as entertain. Those were the days of innocence for television. You could watch any channel you liked, so long as it was the BBC. The Labour Party warned that commercial television would be a 'national disaster' and the Archbishop of York solemnly proclaimed: 'For the sake of our children, we should resist it.'

So the BBC had things all its own way and in the early years of the fifties it reflected life in Britain accurately enough: well mannered, class-ridden, deferential and exceedingly dull. If the excitement of *The Grove Family*, the closest thing we had to a soap opera, proved too much for us there was always the 'interlude' to calm us down. Heaven help us, but we really did sit for what seemed like hours between programmes watching a pair of hands moulding a chunk of wet clay on the potter's wheel. He must have been a hopeless potter; he never did finish the damn thing. Or there was the cute little kitten playing with a ball of wool. Cute for the first dozen or so screenings, at any rate. Then you wanted to strangle it with its own wool and stuff it into the unfinished pot.

When ITV came to Britain, the doomsayers were proved wrong. For twenty-five years it set out to be at least as serious as the BBC – partly because the regulators of ITV demanded it, but also because the big figures in the ITV companies, such as Sidney Bernstein of Granada, wanted to demonstrate that they were not just money men, but were genuinely anxious to contribute to the cultural life of the nation. Bernstein realised that television was here to stay, that it would exercise a profound influence on all our lives, and he wanted it to be good. These were the golden years of the 'duopoly', when British television earned its reputation as being the best in the world.

Lord Reith's 'service for citizens' is more commonly called public service broadcasting, and Rupert Murdoch, arch consumer populist and the most powerful media mogul of the present age, does not believe in it. He told the Television Festival in Edinburgh that he had never heard a convincing definition of what public service television is. He is suspicious of 'élites' who argue for special privileges and favours: 'Much of what is claimed to be quality television here is no more than the parading of the prejudices and interests of the like-minded people who currently control British television.'

So what does Murdoch believe in? He believes in the market. No more, no less. So, incidentally, did Margaret Thatcher. She once said to a BBC executive: 'You take public money, you spend public money. Where is your profit?' The Murdoch view is that anyone who provides a service that the public wants at a price it can afford is providing a public service.

A few years after the Murdoch speech in Edinburgh the same audience heard from someone on the other side of the debate: Ray Fitzwalter. For years Fitzwalter edited *World in Action*, an example of television journalism at its best. He now runs an organisation called the Campaign for Quality Television and points out that a purely market-led system has quite different characteristics from public service television.

The market makes no pretence to universal appeal or universal availability, nor does it necessarily seek to educate or inform, nor does it recognise citizens. Only consumers. The market seeks – quite properly – to make a profit where it may. When driven by global corporations it will seek to produce to the lowest – not the highest – common denominator acceptable to the maximum number of markets.

Fitzwalter was one of those editors and producers who thrived under the rule of men such as Sidney Bernstein. Under a 'purely market-led system' they are a vanishing breed. When Gerry Robinson took control of Granada Television he called the staff together and told them, in so many words, that anyone who did not put profit first, second and third had no place in the organisation. But Robinson operates in a different world to the one occupied by Bernstein and his contemporaries. Back in the sixties all they had to worry about was holding on to their licences. They knew they could do that if they produced good, challenging television and served their regions with local programming. My old company TWW had lost its licence because it was more concerned with reaping the vast profits than putting them to good use in making television programmes. What the old ITV companies did not have to worry about was where the profits were going to come from. Selling advertising time was about as difficult as persuading a Page Three model to take her top off. They were in commercial heaven: no competition. That is no longer the case.

Margaret Thatcher dealt a massive blow to the industry when she insisted on pushing through Parliament the ludicrous Broadcasting Act of 1990, which forced most of the commercial companies to become infinitely more worried about money. It achieved the extraordinary effect of allowing some companies to buy their licences for a pittance (a couple of thousand pounds for Central, the second most populous region in the nation) while others paid a fortune. Yorkshire TV coughed up more than £37million and then another £15million for Tyne Tees. Carlton paid a mighty £43million. That's an awful lot of cash even if the advertising money is rolling in, and it has not been rolling in as it once did. With all the competition from the likes of Channel Four and Channel 5, BSkyB and the cable operators, there is only one way to persuade the advertisers to buy your slots for large sums of money, and that is to deliver big audiences. Most serious programmes do not deliver big audiences. It really is as simple as that.

The response to this commercial pressure has been to regard television as simply a commercial product. Indeed the word 'product' is now routinely used by the new breed of television managers to refer to what programme-makers still call programmes, and the audience is made up of 'consumers'. If programmes are no longer to be differentiated from chocolate biscuits, then 'product' is the right word. The whole commercial apparatus of marketing, product-testing and so on is rapidly being introduced so that the product can be designed, manufactured and marketed in the most efficient way. Whereas one half of television – the half that actually makes the stuff – still talks about news and comedy and drama and all the other sorts of programmes they make, the product managers see things in terms of the available market and have started to divide the schedule up in terms of the niches they want to capture, with names like 'armchair viewing'. The emphasis increasingly is on 'no risk' television. Find out who is likely to be watching at a given time and schedule for them. But what if you have, say, seventy-five per cent of seventy-year-olds watching at the same time as seventy-five per cent of seventeen-year-olds? Well then you find something that upsets neither group. Of course, it will almost certainly offer no great stimulation to either group but, hey, so long as no one reaches for the 'off' switch . . .

The old sense of responsibility is being watered down, the responsibility not just to stimulate viewers, but to do so in a way that recognises the power television has to mould our view of reality. Anthony Smith, one of the most eminent producers from the heyday of the duopoly and one of the founders of Channel Four, is clear how he thinks things are going. 'The old view that broadcasters had wider responsibilities is rapidly fading. Principle comes a poor second to profit.'

I recognise the commercial pressures, and I accept that there are still many very good programmes indeed, but Smith has a point. And anyway there is always the BBC to 'keep us honest', as Michael Grade once famously put it. But the BBC is no longer competing only with the old terrestrial broadcasters. Sky is steadily eating into the audience figures, the cable companies are nibbling away and digital television is here. The government is very anxious to get us all digitalised as quickly as possible so that it can sell off the analogue channels to telephone companies and the like. They are worth several billions of pounds and it will happen sooner rather than later. When it does we shall have many, many more channels and many, many digital TV production companies. The first of them was an operation called Illumina. Andrew Chitty, the man who set it up, was perfectly frank: 'With low subscriptions, little additional advertising and a huge amount of airtime to fill, the budgets for any new programming commissioned by the media giants will be very small.'

Cheap programmes with small audiences, then, but there will be so many of them that the BBC may feel it has to take notice. These are early days in the history of the true commercialisation of television, and the dangers are obvious. If the overwhelming aim now is to maximise the sale of the 'product', other aims are going to have to go by the board or, at least, end up being marginalised. In the future we won't be able to watch a serious current affairs programme anywhere near peak viewing time. Instead it will be shown when we're just about ready to go to bed.

The BBC argues that there can be no questioning its dedication to public service broadcasting. That is its remit and that is its commitment. But the BBC also has to worry about ratings and a problem arises when the two objectives collide. Without the licence fee the BBC as we know it ceases to exist. Yet how can the BBC justify a compulsory tax on almost every household in the land if its ratings fall so low that it is perceived as a minority broadcaster? At what stage do the politicians, who have to approve the granting of the new charter and the licence fee, start getting twitchy because we are asking their constituents to fork out a hundred pounds or so to pay for something they rarely watch? At what stage do you, love the BBC though you may, share that unease?

There was a time when we were told the licence fee would be at risk if BBC1's share of the audience were to fall regularly below forty per cent. In retrospect those were halcyon days indeed. Today's controllers would sell their grannies for that sort of share. As I write these words it has fallen to below thirty per cent. Time to panic? Absolutely not. We should hold our nerve and argue that the BBC is one of the great civilising influences in the nation and the value it brings cannot be measured by how many people are watching or listening at any given point in time. That is the answer to Margaret Thatcher's question: 'Where's the profit?' But we must not only argue it; we must prove it. If we lose our nerve and play the commercial operators at their own game of ratings-chasing then we forfeit our right to the licence fee. Yet that, I fear, is where the BBC may be heading. I have three main worries.

1. The problem with chasing ratings is that there is an overwhelming temptation to produce the sort of attention-gripping, sensationalist television that gives a coarsened view of what life is like. Because television is so powerful it is quite capable of having that effect and can ultimately influence what it seeks to reflect. It can end up making life even coarser.
2. Winning the 'ratings war' necessarily means appealing to as wide an audience as possible. So entertainment becomes the highest goal and we abandon or marginalise programmes that appeal to minority audiences or involve anything too challenging or unexpected.
3. The pressures to be both sensational and entertaining are making themselves felt in the part of broadcasting that's supposed to be dedicated to telling us what the real world is actually like: news and current affairs.

I want to look at each of these.

Michael Grade is one of the more colourful and talented characters the television business has thrown up over the past years. With his showbiz background and his cigar-chomping Uncle Lou, he could hardly have avoided going into television. As Controller of BBC1 from 1984 to 1986 he was so successful that colleagues almost forgave him his terrible taste in bright red socks and wide braces. Grade was a genius in the dark art of scheduling. To viewers scheduling might seem a pretty simple business: bung on a soap before the news, an old movie afterwards, a bit of somebody doing silly things on a Saturday night and loads of sport, and the audience will follow. Well all the evidence suggests that it's not quite that simple. Some of the cleverest people in the business have tried it and come a terrible cropper. But Grade waved his magic cigar over the schedules and the audiences responded. Then he went off to run Channel Four. There was much weeping and wailing at Television Centre – except for those below him who wanted his job and those above him who were worried that he might get promoted to the one *they* wanted – and we all said things would never be quite the same again. We usually do on such occasions.

Some years later, while he was still running Channel Four, I interviewed him for my Radio 4 series *On the Ropes*. He'd been getting a lot of stick from the more right-wing newspapers because of some of the programmes he was scheduling – not least an extraordinary series late in the evening called the *Red Light Zone* which seemed to consist mostly of foreign ladies taking their clothes off for various reasons and an awful lot of very bad language. I asked Mr Grade if all the criticism – the *Mail* was to dub him Britain's 'pornographer in chief' – worried him.

Not a bit, he said, it was the responsibility of television to push out the boundaries. We had a most enjoyable argument but I thought then, and I think now, that he was profoundly wrong. Pushing out the boundaries for its own sake merely creates a ratchet of sensationalism in which what once would have shocked becomes the norm that has to be surpassed. The effect of that, whether it is about sex or violence or language, is to normalise excess and give us a coarsened, harsher view of what the world is like. That is not to say you should never push out the boundaries, but you should do so only if it serves a real dramatic or creative purpose.

I remember as though it were last night a play on BBC1. It was a brilliant satire set some years in the future. All that mattered in that twenty-first-century Britain was money, making it and spending it. The streets were knee-deep in leaflets from companies trying to sell you things; helicopters dropped them from the skies; salesmen rang the door bell endlessly throughout the evening; the only subject of importance in the schools was business and commerce. The pursuit of profit had pushed every other value into the dustbin; the worship of money was the only religion. Even in the hospitals making a bit extra was all that counted, for doctors and nurses too. The wife of the main character was a nurse, an attractive but desperately sad figure weighed down by the worries of her unsuccessful husband who did not make much money, and a loathsome small son who did. He was still at school but busily running something like a loan shark operation and doing very well from it. Naturally he treated his parents with contempt; he was the main breadwinner.

We saw the woman saying goodbye to a patient leaving her hospital after his operation and handing him a card with her home address.

'Do call if you need any help later,' she told him.

The next evening he did. While her husband sat reading the paper she took her patient upstairs. He lay on the bed and she bent over him, apparently about to examine his chest, but instead undid her dress, exposing her breast. Then we understood what kind of service she and the other nurses were selling. By today's standards that is tame stuff indeed. One bare breast and the merest glimpse of a nipple for no more than a second or two but the dramatic effect was electrifying.

Compare that with the opening scenes of a serial thirty years later on the life of Oswald Mosley. The woman who opened the door to Mosley was stark naked and stayed that way while she wandered around the room or draped herself over the sofa. Dramatic effect? Nil. We'd seen it all before, so many times. But the papers wrote about the sex and that, no doubt, achieved the object of getting a few more people to watch. It's all about sensationalism – the main weapon in the ratings war.

In 1998 we had the first 'three-in-a-bed' romp on prime-time television, complete with lots of grunting and groaning and bare breasts and backsides. Dramatic effect? Again nil, though it was quite funny, if unintentionally so. What it did achieve, because it was billed as a 'first', was yet more lovely coverage in the papers before it was shown, and that was exactly the point. Good for the ratings.

But what do they do for an encore? How do they get in the papers next time? Jackie Lawrence has some thoughts on what comes next or, rather, what *should* come next. She was in charge of *Queer Street* – the frightfully witty name for programmes with a gay theme shown late at night on Channel Four. She doesn't much care for the lesbian sex scenes that are now being shown on the box. Far too tame for her tastes. Unrealistic and stilted is what she called them at a recent Edinburgh Festival. The solution? Make them more explicit. 'You only ever see one woman. The other one is so far off camera she might as well be down at the paper shop. I feel we should go the whole hog and show gay and lesbian sex for what it really is,' says Miss Lawrence.

And then there is the burning question of consultants. Ah yes, always consultants. 'For cookery programmes we have cookery consultants, for crime programmes we have police consultants and for programmes containing sex scenes we should have sex consultants,' says Miss Lawrence. Now that one puzzles me a bit, because I thought the idea of hiring a consultant was to receive the benefit of their great wisdom and then decide what needs to be done. Miss Lawrence, it seems, has already decided. Sex scenes with lesbians need pepping up with sex toys. Sadly, she reflects, there is a problem here. Taste and decency guidelines prevent all this sort of thing. Never fear, she will fight these absurd guidelines in the pursuit of her sacred mission. After all, there is a great deal at stake, as she observes, and 'We've got to get to grips with what lesbians do in bed.' How true. The very future of civilisation hangs in the balance. She summed up the crisis thus: 'Watching most lesbian sex scenes you would not know what lesbians do in bed.'

She's quite right, of course. I commissioned my own market research and discovered that 18.7 per cent of the population believes that lesbians spend most of their time in bed playing 'I Spy'; 24.9 per cent trying to remember the names of all four Tellytubbies and 48.2 per cent think they are mostly preoccupied with trying to find an alternative solution to Fermat's Last Theorem. The rest thought they do what men and women (or men and men) do, only a bit differently. A statistically insignificant minority thought they mostly went to bed to sleep.

Forgive the ridicule, but I wonder if it has even occurred to Miss Lawrence that instead of wanting her actors to use sex tools, she might recognise that we in the audience are capable of using a tool that you can't buy in a Soho sex shop and every great writer and dramatist has recognised we all possess to a greater or lesser degree. It's called our imagination. But I forget: leaving us to use our imagination won't cause rows in newspapers, won't make a splash for the programme, won't raise the ratings. So we must push out the boundaries, must we not. But where do we go from here, once we have all got to grips with what lesbians do in bed? *Four* in a bed? Four in a bed all wearing funny hats and wellington boots and nothing else? Four in a bed with a sheep?

Channel 5 makes Michael Grade's Channel Four look pretty tame with its low-budget erotic films late in the evenings and endless factual programmes on sexual themes. The Independent Television Commission attacked it for its 'tackiness' but the channel needs to build an audience and that's the way they intend to do it – whatever the ITC may say. Peter Stuart, who has himself been responsible for pushing out a few boundaries in his time with programmes such as *Eurotrash*, had this to say: 'What I see on Channel 5 is soft-core porn at its very worst and sex journalism at its most irresponsible.'

If pushing out the boundaries is necessary for getting your programme talked about and then watched, at what point do you stop and say the boundaries have now been pushed far enough? By definition the answer is never and Michael Grade's successors have proved it. Sensationalism is the way to attract audiences, so give the heavy publicity to the programmes that will shock. Billboards, newspaper ads, even inserts that fall out of your newspaper when you pick it up, draw our attention to the sensational. 'Scared to go home to your wife tonight?'

screamed the big type headline of one such flier, telling us to watch a *Dispatches* about battered men. Better still, create the row in the press. So the gay soap *Queer as Folk* has an explicit sex scene with a fifteen-year-old boy in its first episode. You just leave it to the newspapers to do the rest of your publicity for you.

The Michael Grades of this world will say that it's silly to worry about whether the boundaries will get pushed too far because something called 'public taste' or even the law will step in if it becomes offensive enough. Really? The 'public taste' argument holds only if you believe that it is you, the viewer, who determines the next stage, and it is not. Again, Grade would have said nonsense. If you don't want it you won't watch it and we won't broadcast it. Well, not on prime time BBC1 or ITV perhaps . . . but late at night on Channel Four maybe? And then a bit earlier. Oh, and if something has been shown and tolerated on one channel, might there not ultimately be a bit of cross-fertilisation? You bet there might. So then they say: 'Look at the figures which deal with the level of complaints. Haven't you seen how the number of complaints we get about bad language/sex/violence/vulgarity are falling rather than increasing?' Well yes, some of them very well may be, but so what?

If we brought back public flogging and hanging next Thursday week there would, I suspect, be a fair number of complaints, particularly if we showed nice juicy close-ups on the evening news (*after* the nine o'clock watershed, of course, and with a suitably worded, sombre warning about how 'some people might be upset by what we are about to show you'). But if we carried on regardless and showed yet more hangings and floggings every Thursday evening, what would happen to the complaints? At first they would keep pouring in, and we journalists would give loads of air time to the objections. But what would happen after three months . . . six months . . . five years? Wouldn't there be a falling-off in the number of complaints? What, after all, is the point of writing the same old letter or making the same old phone calls week in, week out, when it's not having the slightest effect? And anyway, as I write this the latest figures for complaints about sex on the box have shown a sharp rise over the previous lot.

As for the law, that changes all the time too. Remember that pornography is not against the law, only obscenity, and that is defined as something which might 'deprave or corrupt'. It leaves a lot of scope, does it not.

It is argued that all television has done is reflect our greater openness about sex, but that is to ignore the influence and responsibility of television. I believe the increasingly explicit nature and ubiquity of sex on television is a product of the need to sensationalise. And sensationalism requires the ratchet to keep ratcheting on up. We should learn from the experience of those who said fifteen years ago it was impossible that television would ever show the sort of sexual material which we now take for granted, and realise that what we now think of as out of the question will almost certainly soon appear on our screens. Intercourse that is now simulated will be for real. Paedophilia, which is now both beyond the pale and a topic of the most intense prurient interest, seems bound to be 'reconstructed'. Extreme sado-masochism, bestiality . . . what's going to stop the ratchet?

But the main problem with sensationalism is not the ratchet effect, insidious though that can be; it is the effect of sensationalism on the way the material is treated. Aspects of our lives, such as sex, that need treating with a sensitive awareness of the frailty and complexity of human beings, become coarsened and brutalised when they are treated as a spectator sport. The risk is obvious: if television represents aspects of our lives in such terms we are more likely ultimately to see them in those terms. That is the power that television has to influence the climate.

Much of what is said here about sex could equally well be said about violence and aggression on television. Now this is something that really worries the broadcasters. They are extremely sensitive, for the most obvious reasons, to charges that violence on the little screen leads to violence on the streets. Anyway, they say, there are fewer scenes of direct physical violence on television these days than there used to be. That may be true but it misses the point. For a start, there is the question of context. Violence – even murder – is relatively common in soap operas where it was once rare or even absent altogether. And even if there are fewer acts of explicit violence on television across the board there has been a ratcheting up of aggression.

With weary predictability producers claim that academic studies have failed to prove there is any direct causal connection between watching violence on television and then committing acts of violence. Common sense tells us there is very likely to be. If we are to be persuaded that our common sense is wrong – as it may sometimes be – we are justified in asking for pretty powerful evidence. That evidence does not exist. A child who is behaving aggressively may well mutter something about what he saw on television but that is not proof – he might have done it anyway. But we are entitled to draw our own conclusions about the way children and the rest of us behave.

And there is evidence, even if it may not be conclusive, to support the common sense view. Certainly the Americans – weary of children imitating their video anti-heroes and blasting their school mates – are beginning to think so. Barry Gunter, Professor of Journalism at Sheffield University, has made a study of what children watch and how they behave. He says children learn to read and watch television at the same time, as distinct from concentrating on learning alone. He is satisfied that there *is* a direct link between watching violence on the box and aggressive behaviour. A great deal of the violence is in the cartoons, and since that sort of stuff has become so popular there has been a noticeable increase in the way smaller children play. They copy the cartoon characters and there is far more kicking and kung-fuing than there ever was before. At least when we fired six-shooters at each other as children the bullets were imaginary.

The likelihood is that increased aggression on television is making us feel that it is normal, that it is acceptable, and that perhaps we don't need to try as hard as we once might have done to restrain it. One interesting observation here is that broadcasters – even in the United States where every big city TV station has its own cop-chasing cameraman – are reluctant to show *real* violence. When a deluded soul who was shown live being chased on a freeway by the police, stopped his car, pulled out a gun and blew half his head off there was a great fuss. My word, guns can kill. Tut tut. Did it stop the cop-chasing cameramen? Well, what do *you* think?

It is not fashionable in my industry to argue as I have just been doing. The usual sneer is that anyone who expresses a little unease about the direction we're going in wants to return to what a BBC producer has called 'the Pollyanna school of film-making'. You'll remember the sort of thing: there were twin beds in all the television sitcoms, even in Mum and Dad's; if Hollywood had a couple on a double bed (*always* a man and woman in those days) one of them had to keep one foot on the floor. As for the dread act itself, instead of a naked bottom bouncing up and down you would cut away to the shot of a train roaring into a tunnel.

Well actually, no, I don't want to return to that – although I wouldn't mind a few more films such as *Casablanca* or *Brief Encounter* – and nor am I saying that television has become a cesspit of pornography and violence, a Sodom and Gomorrah from which our sensitive souls should be protected lest we be dragged down into some abyss of depravity. But I am saying that this ratchet of sensationalism is coarsening our view of the world. If you want evidence of that, look at what's actually appearing on the box.

Chapter 10

That's entertainment!

IT HARDLY NEEDS stating that the most successful programme in the history of British television is *Coronation Street*. From the moment Ena Sharples sipped her first stout in the Rover's Return the nation was drawn into her world. The Street was populated by characters we could believe in with story lines that reflected our lives. It was funny, moving, absorbing entertainment, television at its best. Quality soap opera had arrived and television was the better for it. Like the rest of the nation, I seldom missed an episode. Then I went abroad to live and tried watching the occasional American soap.

They are called soaps because they were usually broadcast in the afternoons and aimed at housewives and therefore the perfect vehicle for lots of soap powder sponsorship and advertising. American soaps were everything that *Coronation Street* was not: melodramatic tosh, abysmally acted, shoddily produced and entirely unbelievable. Television at its worst. So I lost the daily soap habit and never properly regained it except for the last couple of minutes every evening of *Neighbours*. I may, indeed, be the world's leading expert on those few seconds before the end titles appear because I always switch on just a little bit too early to catch the start of the *Six O'Clock*

News so all *Neighbours* ever consists of for me is that moment of crisis when one impossibly pretty young girl with a big chest and tiny skirt discovers that her boyfriend is having an affair with ... with ... and then the signature tune comes up and I have to wait until the next day to discover the answer. But I never do, because again I get only the last few minutes and then there's another crisis and I never discover how the one the day before was resolved. Come to think of it, maybe *Neighbours* is just one never-ending never-resolved crisis. *Coronation Street* it ain't.

The question is whether *Coronation Street* is *Coronation Street* any longer. The whole point was that it should reflect ordinary life, hold a mirror up to our own lives to see how others might act in situations we might find ourselves in and do it all with a gentle undercurrent of comedy. In the early days they sometimes employed real people taken off Salford market to add to the realism. Clearly, over forty years, the reality which the soaps were supposed to reflect was going to change and there was always going to be a tension to be resolved between the comic, rather cosy element in the soaps and the need to face up to new, difficult issues.

There has never been a controller in the BBC who has not dreamed of knocking the *Street* off its pedestal. How do you challenge a programme that has not only attracted bigger audiences than any other since ITV was in nappies, but is actually loved by that audience? Many a formula was tried. Some were laughed off the stage. All were found wanting. Then along came *Eastenders*. At last, a worthy contender. But this was to be no *Coronation Street* translated from the gritty north to the effete south. Right from the beginning its brief was specifically to break out of what was regarded as the too comfortable worlds that the other soaps had settled into, and reflect what was thought to be the rather harsher world out there.

Now this was something the tabloids could really get their teeth into, a worthy challenger to the champion. Step aside Ena Sharples ... here comes Dirty Den. For a while the *Street* didn't know what had hit it. Every other day there was a story in one or all of the tabloids detailing the sordid goings-on in that small square in East London. And sordid they certainly were compared with anything that had ever happened in the *Street.* All human life really was here and quite a bit more besides. And it worked. The ratings don't always respond to the column inches – nothing can rescue a real turkey; the public isn't barmy – but if the programme is good *and* you get the publicity, you're on to a winner. For a while back there in the eighties it seemed that the cocky Cockneys might knock the nicer Northerners clear out of the ring. In the end it hasn't worked out like that, but that's because the *Street* has itself become a much tougher place.

As a result of the ratings war, virtually all soaps have sensationalised their storylines by concentrating more and more on the seamier side of life, on anything to do with sex, infidelity, domestic violence, abduction, aggression of all sorts, and the more bizarre corners of human behaviour. Even children's soaps are not immune. The BBC's *Byker Grove* ran a storyline about a foster brother and sister who were considering a sexual relationship. The fact that such things happen and are part of reality is not in question. But programmes that aim to reflect reality have to reflect the *balance* of everything in reality. That was the soaps' original brief, but it has gone out of the window.

I recall having to interview the producer of *Brookside* after a particular episode in which a woman with incurable cancer had been put to death by her children holding a pillow over her face. She had told them she did not want to suffer, so they killed her. I may have been a bit more savage with my interviewee that morning than normal. My former wife was dying of cancer at the time, and was receiving the most wonderful, loving care imaginable from my daughter, from MacMillan nurses and ultimately from a Marie Curie hospice in her home town of Penarth.

I do not suggest that cancer sufferers never ask to be put out of their misery. But I wonder how often a woman asks her children to hold a pillow over her face, and I wonder how that episode affected viewers who may have been going through the same agony. The MacMillan people told me later it caused a great deal of anguish. I can believe it.

The point here is not that soaps should shy away from reflecting the darker side of life – no one wants to return to the anodyne pap of *The Grove Family* – but they do have a responsibility. If they are meant to reflect the balance of life that responsibility includes recognising when sensationalism is used purely for the sake of the ratings. A pillow on the face guarantees column inches in the papers or even a slot on the *Today* programme; a long, slow, peaceful sliding towards death does not. More sensitive treatment of this difficult subject may show others suffering from cancer that it can be possible to control the pain and even come to terms with this terrible illness if they are surrounded by people who love and care unselfishly, but it would do little for the ratings. Yes, I know that *Eastenders* and *Brookside* and the rest are not meant to preach or deliver propaganda, however worthy, and the days when *The Archers* existed mainly to give sound advice to farmers have long since gone, but if the soaps are meant to reflect reality in the broadest sense then that is what they should be doing.

Anthony Smith was right when he wrote that 'they portray a fantasy world involving the wildest extremes of human behaviour. That isn't realism; it's another kind of illusion.' Sally Whittaker, who's played *Coronation Street*'s Sally Webster for twelve years, decided to stop her young daughter watching the programme because she thinks it's no longer the programme it was. 'I know the programme goes out before the so-called nine pm watershed, but I really do feel it has become too adult for her.' The Independent Television Commission has warned the ITV soaps for their increasingly aggressive and confrontational approach and for concentrating too much on sex, infidelity and the bizarre.

'These people are so frightened of viewers switching off that if you don't open with two people in bed, they think no one will come back after the break.'

That was not a soaps scriptwriter talking but Andrea

Newman, one of our foremost television dramatists, the creator among other things of *A Bouquet of Barbed Wire*. 'These people' were television bosses who, believe Newman and many like her, are increasingly meddling in the production of television dramas because of their concern about ratings. And they meddle by demanding what they think is sensational. 'All thoughts of tension and any creative development are sacrificed to instant gratification.' But in her view the result is the opposite of exciting. The ceaseless interventions of television executives, desperate to try and make sure they are going to have a ratings hit, constantly contradicting each other, inevitably ends up in them advocating conventional formulas that have worked before.

'I think they are trying to second-guess the public. There's a tendency to give people what executives think they want and the result is that we have too many dramas about the police, hospitals, pathologists, coroners, people in uniform. We're getting closer to the American pattern, where television wants a formula rather than the individual voice.'

So anxious are the men in suits – and a few more women these days – to keep the ratings high that the process now starts with the audience. Large sums are spent on market research to find out what the audience likes and how to give it to them. Seems reasonable, you might say. After all, what's the point of producing programmes nobody wants to watch? The tough businessmen out there in the real world wouldn't dream of producing a new chocolate bar or breakfast cereal if they weren't pretty damn sure that the punters would like it. The Americans started all this, as you might have guessed, when someone first asked: 'But will it play in Peoria?'

I went to Peoria once to do some research of my own – to see if the good folk of this uniquely average town wanted President Nixon to resign at the time of Watergate – and found that it was just like any other town in the midwest which, of course, was precisely the point. Now here's the interesting thing about market research. Creative television producers will tell you that you can't possibly compare a television programme with a chocolate bar or a box of cereal and you can't possibly use the same method to find out what people like. But the marketing men, who really run the world, will tell you that you can. And I can tell you here and now what the people of Peoria liked and, I have to assume, still like. Familiarity.

If their all-time favourite candy bar was a Snickeroo with creamy caramel, crunchy golden flakes, chopped roasted peanuts and a topping of smooooth milk chocolate and you forced them at gunpoint to choose another one, you know what they'd choose? 'Why son,' said my man in deeply boring Peoria, 'they'd go right out there and choose Candy Bar 'X'. And guess what would be in Candy Bar 'X'? Yup, creamy caramel, crunchy ... etc. etc. Goddammit, son, these folk just *know* what they like.' And so they did. And that's why pretty well every candy bar in the good old USof A, or anywhere else for that matter, tastes pretty much the same. Disgusting.

As goes Peoria, so goes the world ... more or less.

So now let's get back to television programmes. If they really are different from chocolate bars it is strange that we carry out research as though they are not. Television drama is the area of programming that ought to depend more than any other on the creative abilities of those producing it. Now here I *am* going to indulge in a little 'golden ageism'. I loved the *Wednesday Play* on BBC1. It was sometimes awful, sometimes brilliant. I freely admit that if some brave scheduler broadcast them all over again next year the ratings would probably be dreadful, partly because many (though not all) would look distinctly old-fashioned, but also because of their very unpredictability. You were never sure what you'd get. And we can't have that today, can we? We do get some one-off plays, but the number is falling all the time and they'll probably die off altogether before long.

There is a piece of jargon to describe this sort of thing: non-genre drama. In real English that means something that's new and innovative and doesn't conform to any of the established formulas such as adaptations of classic fiction or police dramas.

The playwright David Edgar has written about why there are so few one-off plays these days. He says it's because, instead of simply going to good writers and asking them to write something, television executives have gone to focus groups to find out from them what sort of drama they would like to see. But here's where my candy bar conformity theory comes in, and Edgar supports it. Focus groups are made up, quite properly, of ordinary viewers, not of television professionals. Ask them what they want, and their ideas are likely to be confined to what they've already seen. 'Something like that' is Edgar's version of what their reply is going to be. So what has already been shown becomes a formula, a new genre, and gets rehashed again and again because focus groups come to know no different. 'If foregrounding the customer is the end, genre is the means.' I'll forgive him that piece of hideous jargon because he's right; relying on the safe world of genre drama undermines the whole point of drama which, to use another of his phrases, is to 'keep the audience's muscles working' by being 'a balance of expectation and surprise'.

This is not the way television programmes got made in the era of the duopoly. Then it was for producers to come up with ideas, persuade the men in suits to take the risk of turning them into programmes, and then wait to see how well they went down with the viewers. You gauged that by the simple expedient of looking at the viewing figures. If the programme turned out to be a hit, well and good, cheap champagne all round. If it proved as popular as a jellyfish in a swimming pool, the producer might find it a bit more difficult to sell his idea the next time around. If he kept getting it wrong . . . well, he ended up with the job of trying to roll up the ball of wool again after that bloody kitten had spent fifteen years unravelling it. But it was not the end of the world. It just meant that it was up to someone else to come up with a better idea next time around. The point is that it was the people with ideas who drove the process. These days, increasingly, television producers with ideas tend to be very frustrated souls because the process works quite differently. And again it is because of commercial pressure.

Populism is all about trying to give people what you think they want, which may sound entirely laudable but carries real dangers. If you ask us, as I have said, we tend to say we want more of what we are familiar with. Give us something we don't know about and we might like it better. But then again we might not and if you're worried about ratings, best not take the risk. Instead, stick with the formulas you know and try and spice it up with a bit of sensationalism. So we arrive at the dull conformity of sensationalist television.

The scandal of what has happened to television documentaries over the last few years is part of this much bigger story of chasing ratings and making different sorts of programme conform to formulas that entertain enough to get decent audiences. Television executives have obligingly supplied us with new words to help us follow what they're up to. Most ITV companies used to have departments called something like 'Features and Current Affairs'. In the early nineties many dumped them for something called 'Factual'. This was a cover for marginalising or elbowing out altogether analytic programmes that explained how the world works and investigative programmes that found out things we didn't know, or which someone, somewhere, did not want us to know, in favour of shows about crime or lifestyle or missing people or the paranormal. They could claim they were 'factual' because they featured real people as opposed to actors, but their appeal was as entertainment. They were a million miles from current affairs. But that's the whole point: blur the difference, and so long as it's entertaining and gets ratings, who cares?

There is an even more revealing word: 'infotainment'. It's what you get when you cross-breed entertainment with information. The motive behind this is the now familiar one: in the increasingly frantic quest for higher ratings, go for entertainment. In the words of Roger Graef, one of Britain's leading documentary makers, infotainment is 'the Dutch elm disease of quality television'.

In the first place it has pushed out proper documentaries, especially on ITV. The Campaign for Quality Television is supported by independent production companies – the people who make many of the programmes. It has done a great deal of research into serious documentaries on ITV and has concluded that the way things are going their very existence is under threat. The Independent Television Commission shares the worry. In an overview of ITV's performance it concluded: 'The strength of ITV's continuing commitment to regular, serious documentary and arts coverage, clearly set out in the licence applications, now appears to be in question.' That was in March 1997. By 1999 things had got no better. Indeed they said that without *We Can Work It Out*, ITV over the previous year would have had the lowest output of current affairs programmes on record. The CQT too believes things are getting worse. For more than twenty years, as it points out, ITV earned a world-wide reputation for producing major documentary films on matters of public interest in a format which also interested viewers. Now that tradition – which simultaneously served viewers, advertisers, the network of ITV companies *and* the wider public interest – is under threat. In 1994 the main slot for serious documentaries (10.40pm on Tuesday evenings) transmitted thirty-four hours of documentary programming. In 1997 the figure had dropped to eighteen.

What the ITC describes as 'serious documentary coverage' has been cut back to the point where it is barely viable to produce. And having been allowed to wither by ITV itself, serious documentaries are now sown so thinly – so randomly – throughout the network schedules that it is all but impossible for the audience which used to watch them to know when they might appear.

Let's be clear what we mean by serious documentaries. They are at least thirty minutes long and often forty or fifty, well researched original journalism offering, in the old phrase, 'a window on the world'. Some of the best are investigative, revealing corruption in high places or dangers to our health or way of life. They are also the most expensive to make — anything from £200,000 to £500,000 a time. In the first year of Network First on ITV thirty-four were transmitted, some of them drama-docs such as *Date Rape*, others international investigations such as *Death of a Nation*. Most of them were first-rate, and they attracted very respectable audiences of almost four million, not at all bad for 10.40 in the evening. But that did not last long. Gradually the budgets for the programmes were reduced, there were fewer of them and the audiences started to fall.

From the middle of 1997 ITV stopped commissioning new Network First documentaries. The man who was in charge of factual programmes at the time told production companies that he was interested only in films or series that could successfully run at 9.00 pm. What did he mean by 'successfully'? No prizes for guessing the answer to that one: audience figures approaching ten million. Welcome back to the ratings war, and allow me to wheel up the big weapon that was to blow half the other combatants off the screen. If you cross-breed documentary from the old world of serious television with soaps from the new ratings-generating world of entertainment you end up with the docusoap.

Remember *Neighbours From Hell*? It was, as Blofeld might have told James Bond as he stroked his white cat, 'brilliant in its simplicity . . . and deadly, too'. It was based on one of the oldest themes in the book: neighbours who can't stand each other and make each others' lives hell. The first one got an audience of eleven million. When programmes other than the big soaps or interviews with Diana produce figures like that, the men in suits who commission them bow their knee and offer humble thanks to the Great God of Ratings – or, rather, they get one of their assistants to bow their knee; Armani suits do have a tendency to crease rather. But you get the picture: *Neighbours From Hell* was a sensation. So they did what you would expect them to do: they made more like it. And more.

Over at the BBC the penny had already dropped. They were starting to kick great holes in the ITV ratings with such docusoaps as *Airport, Driving School, Hotel, Lavatory Cleaner*. I made that last one up as I was writing this chapter, trying to make a point by being a little silly. Then, a few months later, guess what appeared on television? *Life of Grime*, proving once and for all that there are some things which are beyond parody. One of the appealing aspects of these docusoaps was that they cost peanuts to make because of modern technology.

Old-fashioned documentary-making was horrendously expensive. The unions had a stranglehold on the industry and called the shots when you went filming. You not only had to have a director, cameraman, sound recordist, lighting man and production assistant but some of them even had their own assistants and most of them travelled first class. Each man (again, all men except for the PA) had his designated task, and that was what he did. Nothing else.

I remember once going to Washington to do a very modest bit of filming, nothing much more than a few interviews and a piece-to-camera outside the White House. We fought long and hard to persuade the union that we didn't need to take a man whose job it was to shift things around. They agreed, very reluctantly. When we got there the director wanted me to sit on a bench in Lafayette Park, opposite the White House, to deliver a few lines. But the bench wasn't in quite the right position and the director wanted it moved. No chance. It would have been easier to ask the President to move the White House.

Mercifully, most of the worst restrictive practices have gone now. Indeed, in some ways it has moved too far in the opposite direction. The unions have lost their power, by and large, and too much is being filmed with only a cameraman and, if you're lucky, a sound recordist. Frequently there is no lighting man and it shows. Increasingly in news filming there is no sound recordist, and that can show too. Inevitably we shall follow the trend of some cash-strapped cable stations and have the reporter do the filming as well. It saves money, but there is a price to pay in quality. There might even be a price to pay in equipment. A friend of mine on a small cable station tells of the reporter who set up the camera on a tripod in a rough area of south-east London to do a piece-to-camera, switched it on, walked a few paces away . . . and when he turned around the camera had been pinched.

The other problem with documentary filming in the old days

was the equipment that had to be carted around. There were so many silver boxes you needed half the aircraft hold and a fleet of station wagons to shift it. The eyes of the British Airways staff would light up as you arrived at the check-in. The bills for excess baggage could have sent half the population of Yorkshire around the world for free.

All that has changed, too. Nowadays most films aren't film at all; they are shot on video and the cameras are not much different from what you buy in Dixons. Indeed, the problem nowadays is *adding* a bit of bulk to the most modern cameras so that it gives the cameraman something to hold steady if he's shooting from the shoulder. But what makes it easier and much cheaper still is that instead of having to buy thousands of feet of very expensive film and getting it processed at great cost, the video tape costs next to nothing. You no longer have to worry about leaving the camera running all day if you so choose.

So all the ingredients were there for fly-on-the-wall television to be exploited as never before. It had existed for many years and its pedigree was respectable. A brilliant example was *The House,* which took us behind the scenes at Covent Garden and allowed us to watch one of the greatest cultural institutions in Britain scratching its own eyes out and then slitting its wrists. It informed, educated and entertained. Now where have I heard those words before? The original purpose of fly-on-the-wall was, as far as possible, to allow the camera to tell its own story. A subject was chosen and the activity filmed over a long period by a camera crew almost constantly in attendance, like a fly on a wall, but not intervening in what was going on. The film would then be put together by those making it without the involvement of those being filmed. There would be a minimum of commentary, and viewers would make of it what they would.

Of course it could never be a pure, untouched presentation of reality. It was a journalistic enterprise. Somebody had to select the subject and somebody had to edit the endless hours of footage, to boil them down into a coherent programme. Paul Watson was the pioneer of fly-on-the-wall documentaries in Britain with *The Family* in 1974. His aim was to say, 'This is

how families are, or how some of them can be.' Beyond that he
wanted to leave it to the camera to tell the story. In his view,
however, most docusoap fly-on-the walls today 'say nothing
to us. It is TV at its cheapest and laziest.'

The problem is that docusoaps do not want to leave it to the
camera to tell the story. What they do is use the characteristics
of soap operas – colourful characters, conflict, narrative – to
turn material gathered by fly-on-the-wall cameras from real
life into an entertaining soap opera. But this marrying of fact
and fiction (there's another wonderful piece of jargon:
'faction') can have unhealthy consequences. In the first place,
by presenting real life as if it were a soap opera it encourages us
to think that real life *is* a soap opera. In other words it has
precisely the opposite purpose of journalism.

Life can be looked at in an infinite number of ways, and one
of the points of good journalism is to help us see it in a new
way. That was certainly the purpose of the original fly-on-the-
walls: it was to help us to see aspects of life as undistorted as
possible by any intervening interpretation. But docusoaps, far
from opening up ways of seeing life, close them down. The
people we see in them may be real people, but docusoaps are
not interested in getting across their individuality; the
programme makers want to mould them into the conventional
figures of a soap opera. If all the hotel manager ever did was
smile sweetly at the customer and gently upbraid the staff
when they got it wrong she would be pretty boring and who
would want to watch that? We might as well bring back the
potter's wheel. So the producers have to find 'characters' for
the soap aspect of the programme. And since one soap opera is
much like another, real life, refracted through docusoaps,
becomes all much of a muchness. We're back to populist
conformity, all just entertainment. Or as Allison Pearson, the
Daily Telegraph's perceptive television critic, wrote: 'In the
hands of its most serious and stealthy practitioners,
documentary aspires to tell us something about the human
condition. The docusoap, by contrast, tells us only about the
condition of human beings who know they're on television.'

That is the next stage in the corruption of the original

purpose of fly-on-the-walls. Instead of the subjects being chosen by journalists who think they can shed light on a part of life that's largely remained hidden, the subjects can now virtually choose themselves. What television executive is going to turn down the opportunity to make cheap and entertaining programmes when a police force or a hotel chain or a leading politician comes along and says they're prepared to open their lives and world to the cameras for no charge and with maximum co-operation? So long as such worlds can be made to look entertaining they are sure fire winners. But why should a police force or a hotel chain or a leading politician want to have a camera crew intruding on their lives? It may be because they feel they have a sacred duty to help the public understand the world better but I somehow doubt it. It's more likely that they want the publicity and will take the risk about what image of them the programme will end up conveying. In truth the risk is not great.

If you were one of the millions who watched *The Hotel,* for instance, you were probably hugely entertained by the chaos behind the scenes, the manager eviscerating half her staff, the chef threatening to boil the other half in the mushroom soup, the lager louts trashing the joint and all the rest of it. So you might think that the Adelphi, which is where it was shot and of which I have very fond memories when it was the grandest hotel in Liverpool, would have been gnashing its teeth. You could see the manager watching it and holding her head in her hands. 'Oh God! We're finished! No one will ever come here again!' The opposite happened. Everyone wanted to have a look at the most famous hotel in the country and for a while the tills rang merrily.

In any case the risks can be minimised. Those who agree to be the subjects of such fly-on-the-walls are not usually so green as to relinquish all control over what is shot and what is ultimately shown. Some producers can become a little vague when you ask them what powers of veto the subjects have been allowed over the final product, for the obvious reason that to give them any powers of interference compromises the supposed journalistic integrity of the programme. When

Gordon Brown allowed Scottish Television to make him the subject of a fly-on-the-wall documentary, shot in the period immediately before and after the last election, his then press secretary, Charlie Whelan, took a close interest in what was going on. Some viewers may have been mildly surprised by Charlie and his chums telling us how clever they were but there's little doubt that the overall effect was to convey a sense of Gordon Brown's political operation as smart and professional.

What all this has done is turn at least one aspect of television journalism into a promotional exercise. However entertaining and even informative such programmes may be, journalistic integrity has been compromised and someone is getting wonderful free publicity. Viewers who think they are getting one thing may actually be getting something else altogether. And there is an endless supply of material. Us.

In this culture, hooked on fame and publicity, it seems we will do anything to grab a piece of the action – even get married to someone we have never met. The commercial radio station who set up that particular tawdry stunt got what they were after – lots of publicity. The young couple got that, too, plus a free wedding, free holiday, rent-free flat and, ultimately, a broken marriage. It is for others to judge who had the best of the deal. What is clear is that the couple were chosen because they looked good in the papers and on the box. Appearance in this strange world is all. The script called for an attractive young couple. In the world of docusoaps it invariably calls for 'characters'. The temptation to bend reality can be over-whelming.

In *The Clampers,* the star clamper, Ray Brown, wasn't properly a clamper at all. The press made a great fuss when they found out and the BBC denied that they had been cheating. In the end it turned out that he had been one, but was now a supervisor who spent most of his time in the office. But he was too good a character to miss so he found himself back on the streets with the camera crew. At least Ray did well out of it. He was such a star that he was able to give up his supervisor's job and become a presenter of *Gaytime TV*. Who says life does not imitate art. Other programmes show scenes purporting to be filmed for real when they have clearly been staged for the camera. As one executive put it to me: 'It's not *exactly* like it seems, but it's *pretty* like it.' Precisely.

In the world of docusoaps it is not just the programme makers who can engage in a bit of surreptitious fakery. One couple claiming to be father and daughter conned Channel Four into making a documentary about their near-incestuous relationship. The trouble was that they weren't father and daughter at all, just boyfriend and girlfriend. They got rumbled only after the production company had spent £40,000 in making the programme when the girl's real father saw the pre-publicity and blew the whistle. The programme was junked and stern words were spoken. Michael Jackson, the boss of Channel Four, said that the whole episode was a new public abuse of the trust that once existed between film-makers and their subjects. So then they all hung their heads in shame and disappeared quietly from the scene? Not quite. A few months later Channel Four showed a film about the hoaxers themselves along with chunks of the original faked film. So the hoaxers got two dollops of fame: all that coverage in the papers and then their very own film. The channel's commissioning editor, Peter Moore, got it right when he said, 'Perhaps sometimes we believe the story presented to us because we so want it to be true.'

The only thing surprising about all this is that anyone should be surprised. The substitution of entertainment values for journalistic values makes it inevitable. Documentaries must have big audiences to satisfy the controllers and com-missioning editors and the easiest way of delivering big audiences is to produce sensational material. If the sensational material does not exist, you fake it. Channel Four again did so with a documentary about rent boys – the drivers shown picking up the boys turned out to be members of the production team – and were fined £150,000. The most blatant fake of them all was exposed by the *Guardian*. Just about everything was faked in *The Connection*, Carlton's hugely

publicised documentary about drug-trafficking. The man
shown as a drug cartel boss was no more than a retired bank
clerk with low level drug connections. The courier shown
swallowing heroin and then described as a 'walking timebomb'
had in fact swallowed nothing more harmful than a mint. The
programme pretended to show a continuous journey from
Colombia to London, but it didn't. In all, sixteen cases of
faking were discovered in the one programme. Carlton were
fined £2million.

The point is not that faking is new. What's new is the
conscious and deliberate fusing of journalism and
entertainment in the pursuit of ratings, and that makes faking
much more prevalent. As John Willis, former deputy director
of Channel Four, put it: 'The line between fact and drama in
documentary has grown increasingly blurred and, in the
struggle between journalistic truth and dramatic excitement,
drama is winning.' He is not alone in that view. The British
Film Institute commissioned a survey of more than 500
television executives, producers, researchers and camera crews
to find out what they thought of the way television is going.
Half of those working in documentaries and current affairs
said they felt they had been pressured to distort the truth and
misrepresent the views of those interviewed to create 'exciting,
controversial or entertaining programming'. Richard
Patterson, who wrote the reports for the BFI, said: 'It is
worrying that both new entrants and established workers in
the industry see a diminution in quality standards.'

Fakery has, inevitably perhaps, spread beyond documentaries.
It was difficult to know whether to laugh or cry at the uproar
over *The Vanessa Show*. Actors had been hired to masquerade
as real people and Vanessa herself went on air to say she was
'absolutely horrified' and to apologise to her viewers. The
BBC itself was horrified. Some junior – very junior – heads
rolled. Soon afterwards one of the BBC's most senior figures,
Mark Thompson, gave a lecture about broadcasting. His main
concern was accuracy and fakery, but he confessed that he was
worried about what he described as 'trash TV', particularly

shows like Jerry Springer's which had acquired a kind of chic. 'This really is television as freak show,' said Thompson, 'preposterous and ugly. A public taste for a kind of Grand Guignol parody of human folly is growing. It will require a considerable effort of will by commissioners and producers to resist it.'

Indeed it will. It is hard to think of a better illustration of the schizophrenic nature of the BBC: an organisation committed to public service broadcasting but striving to fight a ratings war at the same time. It sometimes seems that one half of the BBC has no idea what the other half is all about. Eventually *The Vanessa Show* was dumped but, as Vanessa Feltz herself said later, not because of the spot of bother over fake guests. The fact was, it had failed in its remit: to pull in the viewers.

There is a problem with programmes such as the loathsome *Jerry Springer Show* which make you feel like a good bath after you've watched them: they are good for the ratings. It was inevitable that when victim TV took off in the United States British broadcasters would grab on to its coat-tails. Some of our home-grown products run *Springer* a close second in both mawkishness and malice. Channel 5 has a shabby little offering called *My Secret*. I watched one evening when a young woman told her 'secret', which was that she had been sexually involved with her brother's girlfriend. Both brother and girlfriend sat on stage alongside the woman while she betrayed them. The show's presenter then did her impressive best, with the help of a whooping audience, to embarrass the couple to the maximum extent possible and finally goad the cuckolded boyfriend into announcing that he wanted to have nothing more to do with either his sister or his girlfriend. Mission accomplished. Two relationships destroyed in pursuit of better ratings. Ecstatic cheers from the moronic audience. This sort of thing is not just trash; it is exploitative and even vicious and it demeans everyone involved.

Compared with that sort of thing *Vanessa* was altogether more restrained but it was still surprising that the BBC should have snapped her up from ITV when the commercial channel decided it was not prepared to meet her demands. The justification is that everybody should be able to get something of what they want from the BBC and that anyway it is possible to deal with serious issues in a populist, but responsible, way.

Imagine the following scene. The serious young producer, clean shaven, wearing a nice smart blazer and neatly ironed flannels, highly polished brogues, crisp white shirt and discreetly striped tie (okay, you'll need a *lot* of imagination for all of this) knocks on the door of the Controller.

'Good morning, Sir, I have an idea for a television programme. It will be presented by a highly respected figure who has a great deal of experience of dealing with marital and personal problems. He's rather quietly spoken and not very charismatic, but he does know what he's talking about. He will have a sensible and constructive conversation with people who have been happily married for years and get on well with their children and try to understand why. He will also talk to people who have had some problems in their lives and have managed to overcome them in a quiet, calm way and end up getting on with their lives and living happily ever after. There will be a studio audience but they will not be encouraged to applaud or make those ghastly whooping noises. I know it won't get exactly *huge* ratings, but it would mean that people would be able to see complex human relationships being discussed in a way that might prove very helpful to them.'

There follows a long silence.

'So what do you think, Sir?'

When the Controller's secretary pops in later that morning with the coffee, she sees the window open, looks out and there is the body of the young producer, six floors below, the white shirt now a bright crimson colour. She turns back to the Controller to see him hanging by a discreetly patterned tie from the light fitting, a note pinned to his chest. It reads: 'Where did I go wrong? Forgive me.'

The only unlikely part of that little scenario is the Controller doing himself in. In real life, after he'd thrown the producer out of the window he'd have hung his deputy.

Of course *Vanessa* was never meant to be another *Jerry Springer*, which has the words fake and phoney running through it like a stick of Blackpool rock. But to compete in the aggressive arena of daytime television it had to be talked about and written about and that meant it had to be sensational. The guests had to have extraordinary tales to tell and be prepared to tell them with as much verve and colour as possible. They also had to be 'real' people. The problem for production teams who put such programmes together is how to find tomorrow real people who are at least as sensational as the ones you found today – and preferably more so.

In this business one thing to do is ring up Kizzi Nkwocha, who runs 15 Minutes, an agency helping people who think they've got something extraordinary to tell about themselves to get on television or into the press. He told the *Guardian* that he is inundated with calls from researchers on confessional talk shows desperate to find new people, new angles. 'This crazy, topsy-turvy business, the pressure, the panic, the last-minute changes of direction, all comes down to one thing – ratings . . . Satellite TV and now the digital revolution have more or less ensured that the winners in the TV ratings war are the shows that can consistently up the ante – produce something that we haven't seen before, delve into areas previously left unexplored.'

But what if Kizzi Nkwocha can't produce real people who can 'up the ante', what can the researcher do then? Nkwocha knows: 'Researchers only have a certain amount of time to get things sorted and rather than working hard and using genuine people, they want to use the easy option and find people who will lie.' Or they might ring Tony Papotto whose Café Absolute Entertainers Agency has provided actors and actresses to fill many difficult gaps on such programmes – people such as Angelina Candler, a former actress and dancer, who posed as a tearful battered wife even though she'd never been married, or Amanda Cairney and Jill Holt, who posed as sisters in a feud, though in fact they were stripagram girls and unrelated.

All very shocking, but who's to know? If a member of the public wishes to lie, how can they be found out? Alan, a disc-jockey in south London, used a different agency to get on talk shows and told the *Sunday Telegraph* how easy it is. 'You talk to the production staff on the telephone before the show and they tell you what they expect you to say on the programme. If you want to be paid to be a guest again, or paid to go on another show, it's better to sensationalise and exaggerate.'

So there is little point in expressing outrage and sacking researchers trying to do an impossible job. Fakery is inevitable if you put journalism and entertainment in a marriage in which entertainment wears the trousers. You end up with what Matthew Parris calls 'entertaining tosh'. That's where infotainment is taking us. Mark Thompson made another telling point in his lecture: 'When I see an ad nestling in the *Guardian* asking anyone who thinks they may be suffering from sex addiction to get in touch at once with a BBC programme, it gives me pause. Maybe it's a serious programme, maybe I'm being stuffy, but I can't help thinking: is this really what the licence fee is for?'

I suspect he is not alone in thinking that. Another question might be why, if people as senior as Mark Thompson have such serious reservations, it is still allowed to happen.

What we have going on in television, then, is a toxic mix of sensationalism, conformity and fakery, a mix brewed in pursuit of ratings in an increasingly commercial world. It carries with it the populist badge of legitimacy: if people watch it it must be because they want it. Some people certainly do. But the truth is that it's watched because it is now offered in increasing amounts. And the hundreds of channels that digital television is going to give us will not change a thing, because those channels simply will not have the money to produce anything decent. To make money they will go the same route: find a cheap, lowest common denominator formula, and try and spice it up with sensation. That will continue and probably speed up the process of coarsening our view of life and the world in which we live.

Chapter 11

News

IT WAS NOT until the start of the eighties that the BBC screwed up its courage and decided that perhaps, after all, it did make sense to have people who had been reporting the news read the stuff as well. So I was chosen to present the *Nine O'Clock News* and then, a few weeks later, John Simpson. There were serious misgivings at all levels in the BBC about this dubious departure from tradition. After all, people like Richard Baker and Kenneth Kendall had been doing it perfectly well since the dawn of television time and had huge personal followings and who the hell were Humphrys and Simpson? Mere grubby hacks who popped up occasionally for a few minutes from strange parts of the world and who wouldn't be recognised in the High Street even if they wore a big sign hanging around their necks with their names printed on it. Now I would hate anyone to think that the bosses did not give John and me the utmost encouragement. A week before the big experiment was to start we were called into the editor's office and with him was the great man himself, the Controller of BBC1. He did not seem to be a happy man; in my experience Controllers seldom do. 'I just want you fellahs to know,' he told us, 'that if the audience for the *Nine* drops by a million or two . . . you're out!'

'Gosh, thanks Boss,' we said sarcastically, 'you really know how to boost a guy's confidence. You just stick to playing with your schedules and leave us to worry about our news programmes. Okay?' Actually we didn't say anything of the sort. We just backed humbly out of his presence, sweating lightly, with our fingers crossed.

We were not, it is fair to say, an immediate critical success. Jeffrey Archer has found more favour with the Booker judges. I remember being compared to the Mr Humphreys from *Are You Being Served?* Unfavourably. The general conclusion of the review was that as a news presenter I might possibly make a reasonably competent shop assistant, but probably not. It was not the happiest of months for either John or me. Most old troupers say you should never read your own reviews and, if you do, you should take no notice of them. John and I read them and we would sit around for hours plotting our revenge against our critics. We never did avenge ourselves. A few months later John moved out of the studio back to doing what he has done so brilliantly for so long – foreign reporting – and I clung on. I suppose I must have got the hang of it or – more probably – the critics found something more interesting to write about, because eventually they left me alone. But there are two interesting things about that episode.

The first is that the audiences did not drop when John and I took over. Not by two millions, nor even one million. They stayed just where they were. As they had always done, they rose when there was a lot of news about – astronomically so during the Falklands War – and fell when things were dull. Perhaps naïvely, I have always believed that people who watch the news are far more concerned with what is in it than who is reading it, assuming it is presented reasonably competently and with a degree of authority.

The other thing is that the decision to plonk John and me in front of the cameras at nine o'clock every evening was taken by our then editor purely and simply because he wanted experienced journalists presenting his most important news programmes. ITN had been doing it from the beginning and he thought it made sense. The only concession he made to the style gurus was telling me to buy a new suit. Not unreasonably, he thought the wide lapels on my best suit rather gave its age away. I was mildly hurt; it had, after all, been good enough for my wedding and that was only fifteen years or so ago. The Controller of BBC1 did not want us to present the news – with or without new suits – because he thought we would not be good box office. We were neither famous nor glamorous. But in the end he had to lump it. Successive Controllers have kept up the pressure on news over the years with varying degrees of success.

After I had been presenting the *Nine* for about five years the editor – there was a new one by now – decided it was time to give the programme a facelift. He had a point. The old backing behind the desk at which we sat was made of plywood and cardboard and was apparently held together by will power and sticky back plastic borrowed from *Blue Peter*. If you made a sudden movement the whole thing would tremble and shake like the set in an amateur theatrical production when someone slams the door too hard. On one occasion a correspondent sitting alongside me collapsed while I was addressing the nation, fell to the floor and almost brought the whole lot crashing down. Mercifully the camera was not on him at the time but I had to carry on, smiling my way through stories about the radiant young Princess of Wales, while the poor chap was being loaded on to a stretcher and given the kiss of life at my feet and somebody else was trying to stop the whole set falling on my head. So there was no argument about the need to change the furniture.

But eventually the bosses wanted to change the presenters too. For a start, they wanted two instead of one. Predictably enough I thought that was barmy – you really need two presenters to read a few minutes from an auto-script? The boss took me for lunch to tell me who my fellow presenter was to be: Julia Somerville. That was the good news – she's a lovely person – but the bad news for me, though probably not for the audience, was that she was to be the main presenter and I would be number two, Santa's little helper. I was not happy. I said I would resign rather than suffer the indignity – we broadcasters have delicate little egos – but then I remembered my mortgage and decided to grin and bear it until something better came along.

Only a few months earlier I had been told by the very same boss that he wanted me to present the *Nine* five nights a week instead of only three because he thought I was good at it. So what, I wanted to know, had changed? They think she'll be better box office, I was eventually told. You're not blonde and beautiful and female and sexy. True, sadly, all true. As it happens Julia did the job brilliantly – she is a first-rate journalist and presenter as well as being blonde and beautiful etc. etc. – but it was the first time in my long career that I had been made so personally aware of the steely grip of the ratings chasers on the windpipe. Since then the obsession with presentation throughout the television news business has grown.

When I was still finding my way around the mysterious corridors of Television Centre the journalist in charge of the *Nine* one evening decided that his lead story was so important he would get the newsreader to stand in front of the desk in the studio to deliver it. You'd have thought he had made him take off all his clothes and present the news wearing his Y-fronts on his head. The hapless journalist was frogmarched to the boss's office the moment he arrived in the building the following morning. 'Don't ever do that again!' the boss screamed at him. 'Even if World War Three coincides with the abdication of the Queen and the Second Coming the news will be delivered sitting down! That is the way it has always been and that is the way it will continue to be. Got it?'

Thirty years later Kirsty Young – then a largely unknown broadcaster – delivered the news for Channel 5 not only standing up, but walking around the studio. Once again all hell broke loose in bosses' offices throughout the industry. This time it was a different kind of hysteria.

'Brilliant!' ... 'That's it!' ... 'Why didn't we think of that?' ... 'When can we do the same?'

Within a matter of months we had presenters of such

eminence as Jon Snow and Jeremy Paxman and Trevor McDonald striding or strolling or sidling onto sets, posing awkwardly in front of great big screens, doing everything but making their entrance sliding down a fireman's pole. Vast amounts of money were spent on a new set by Channel Four so that Snow could emerge from behind his formidable desk and show us his socks; it was bad enough being able to see his ties.

Back in the days of my cardboard set we had also had cardboard graphics. The letters were stencils which were cut out and stuck on a piece of cardboard for the camera to focus on. It was a pretty dodgy system at the best of times, especially when the caption fell off the board altogether just as the director was about to cut to it. The main problem was that we were always running out of certain letters; it was not easy to caption Harold Wilson when there were no more 'W's or 'n's left and we cursed the system night after night.

Now, as with fancy sets, we have gone to the opposite extreme. Channel 5 were, I think, the first to decide that the viewer was incapable of following a one-minute chat between presenter and reporter unless the points the reporter was making were simultaneously produced electronically on the screen alongside him. It is unnecessary, patronising and even deceitful. We are invited to believe that the two journalists are having a spontaneous conversation and yet, miraculously, his words are being summarised and appear magically even as he speaks them. Good simple graphics used intelligently can help the viewer. Technology for the sake of it – doing something because it can be done – has the opposite effect.

Television news does too many things because they are possible rather than because they are necessary. I have never understood why we must 'go live' to a reporter on the scene two seconds after we have seen the report. You know the sort of thing.

'Over now to Kate for the very latest. Kate, what's happening?'

'I've just told you what's happening in my report, cloth ears, and if you weren't listening properly I'm buggered if I'm going to tell you again.'

Sadly they never do say that, but I live in hope.

I have two worries about the obsession with presentational gimmicks. One is that they can take up too much time, effort and money that would be better spent on other things: perhaps more reporters in the field, for instance. The other is that they can confuse rather than clarify. If we all spent half as much time worrying about writing good, simple English free of linguistic pomposities and jargon and journalese as we do messing about with the latest electronic wizardry the viewer would be better served.

But, once again, commercial pressures are to blame. Every editor is terrified that his or her programme or news bulletin will be deemed to be old-fashioned and 'look tired' compared with the competition. It is a moot point whether we change things for the sake of the viewer or the sake of the competition. Or maybe just fashion. The designers tell us what to do and, by and large, we do it. They say it is what the viewers want, but I suspect that viewers give the answers the designers want to hear. How many people do you know who feel passionately that a news set needs to be changed because it is the 'wrong colour'. I suspect we get used to things the way they are and are broadly resistant to change. Even so, when the designers speak, we listen. Blue is the 'in' colour this year; OK, let's have blue sets. Blue is 'cold'. Right, we'll make them yellow or pink instead . . . anything but blue. And so it goes. The television news industry reacted as it did to Channel 5 because it was different, not because it was better. As for the audience for Channel 5, it has managed to contain its enthusiasm. The viewing figures for its news are dismal.

Many at the BBC feared the worst when the *Six O'Clock News* was re-launched in the spring of 1999. Might we have the new presenter, Huw Edwards, cartwheeling onto the set, scripts clenched in manly jaw? The reality was a mild anti-climax. Huw, a well-respected journalist, stayed rooted behind his shiny desk, looking almost exactly like the old Huw in spite of his trimmer figure and very serious haircut. We were assured before the new *Six* began that it would be 'more adventurous' in the way it used correspondents. Perhaps standing them in front of big screens and lecturing the audience is more adventurous and perhaps having them in the field 'topping and tailing' film reports is a 'refreshing and original' approach to television news. Or perhaps it is just change for the sake of change. The set itself was surprisingly sober, even a little dull. The production people told us, with perfectly straight faces, that it 'preserved the traditional BBC values of honesty, authority and restraint'. Quite how a few bits of chrome and plastic, however artfully arranged, can do all that is lost on me, so I suppose it's just as well nobody has ever asked me to design one. I was more interested in the stories and the way they were reported.

On the basis of the first few months it seems clear to me that the *Six* has, in the jargon of my business, gone softer and opted for an agenda dominated by social issues with a consumerist angle. There's nothing wrong with that if it is what the viewers want, so long as the harder-edged stuff is there, too, and so long as we retain our critical approach to the stories. The first of the new programmes reported on Kosovan refugees in Scotland. The reporter had decided that the local people had taken them to their heart and would give them a warm welcome and everyone was really happy. Possibly, but it would have been difficult for her to have reached that conclusion in such a short time. It seemed for all the world as though we were being fed a cosy little story to make us all feel good about ourselves and that impression has persisted. One series of so-called 'special reports' (beware of that word 'special', it usually means simply longer or more expensive) included an account of what the RAF were getting up to in the Balkans. It was topped off with the obligatory live interview – this time with an RAF officer rather than a reporter – that would not have been out of place in an RAF recruitment film. It asked none of the awkward questions that were being raised at the time about the conduct of the air war.

I will be accused of selective criticism, of ignoring all the other stories that pull no punches, but that is not the point. As I have said, time and again, there is a vast amount of first-rate journalism in television news. But the temptation to chase the ratings by offering undemanding fare to an early evening audience has to be resisted. Of course there is room for lighter stories, for a smile at some of the sillier things that life has to offer, but when we deal with serious subjects we must do so in a serious manner. And when there is a choice between an important, though possibly dull, story and something a little frothier but with more 'punter appeal' we must err on the side of the serious. On that there should be no compromise, but I fear there has been. The forward march of entertainment values against news values has begun to encroach.

It has been a long road from the days when the news announcer – always a middle-aged, middle-class man with a plummy voice but no name – read the news on the wireless without a hint of personality or attitude. It took Adolf Hitler and his propagandist William Joyce – better known as 'Lord Haw-Haw' – for the announcer to own up to his name and it was to be many more years before his successors were allowed a personality. Not for those old-timers the pitfalls that lay in wait for their descendants when the days finally dawned that women were allowed in news studios.

A painful memory for me is the Saturday evening, some years ago, when I presented the news review for deaf people with Moira Stuart. As the credits rolled at the end there was a lot of time to chat.

'Righto, Moira,' I said, in the sexiest voice I could manage, 'now that's done how d'you fancy a bit of the old nonsense back in the dressing room?'

Well, you have to say something and Moira is an old friend and would normally have joined in such silliness; after all, the microphones were switched off. She did not. She sat stony-faced and stared into the camera and said not a word.

'Why?' I asked when we were off the air.

'Because,' she said very slowly, 'this programme is meant for deaf people, remember? And remember what deaf people are very good at doing?' Yes indeed.

We still value at least one quality that those old announcers unquestionably had: authority. Unhappily the authority they conveyed invited not only respect for the truth but also a kind of deference towards those providing it. In the more iconoclastic world of the late sixties and seventies the vital but subtle distinction between respect for what had legitimate authority and unquestioning deference towards those who happened to be in charge was never going to cut much ice. Anything that hinted at deference was suspect. Formality had to be loosened up. Newsreaders had to unbutton, show they were human beings underneath, start appealing to us as people.

That they have done – in spades – and it is hard now even to remember those fruity-voiced, anonymous announcers of yesterday without a slightly condescending smile.

One of the more depressing things about working for the *Nine* when I presented it regularly – apart from cardboard sets – was that most of the time *News at Ten* was a better programme. We would not have dreamed of admitting it, even to ourselves, but secretly we knew that to be so. It was technically superior, better produced, had the advantage of being on the air an hour later and, even though we occasionally sneered at it for being too tabloid with its 'And finally . . .', the truth is it covered the important stories with authority. In his prime Alastair Burnett was the best news presenter in the business. For much of the eighties *News at Ten* was, quite simply, the gold standard. And then, ten years later, they threw it away.

Whatever ITN said about it at the time there was one reason and one reason only for their decision – the network companies wanted to sell more advertising. It was that simple. All the guff about 'making the news even better' was just that: guff. Having the main news at ten o'clock in the evening got in the way of scheduling more popular programmes, such as films, so ultimately it had to go.

The effect in the months that followed was entirely predictable. Audiences for news on ITV fell sharply. It was yet another blow to ITV's once proud record of producing serious news and current affairs for the biggest audience possible. They did, however, throw a bone to the dogs – a very expensive bone – in the shape of *Tonight with Trevor McDonald*. I have always been a shade suspicious of news programmes that attach their title to the name of a popular presenter. Are we meant to infer that the presenter is the key to the programme and if so why does he usually do little more than read a few short links into the reports? It's another example of copying the Americans: 'The CBS Evening News with Dan Rather!' That may be reasonable, just about, if it's Rather reading it, but when he's off on holiday it becomes The CBS Evening News with Dan Rather . . . Percy Scroggings Reading It!' Bizarre.

More important, again, is the content. Within a few weeks of *Tonight* going on the air it was clear that entertainment values were fighting news values and often winning. The first programme was a genuine scoop – the first interviews with the suspects in the Stephen Lawrence murder – but then it settled down. In the first month we had a report which made the extraordinary revelation that if you drink lots of alcohol you get drunk and if you drink it on an aeroplane you get drunk even more quickly and might behave badly. There was a group of volunteer students sitting and drinking – in a scientifically controlled experiment, just in case we did not believe that drinking a lot gets you drunk. And, of course, we had the intrepid reporter joining in and telling us that she was feeling pretty squiffy too. The whole idea was to show what lies behind 'air rage'. I feel they missed a trick. They should, surely, have had the students beating each other up, with the reporter swinging a punch or two herself. Next time, perhaps.

None of this would matter if it were not presented as serious journalism. If the presenter said, 'Look, we know you folks at home have the attention span of a goldfish and can't be bothered trying to understand something that requires a bit of effort, so just sit back, pour yourself a beer and enjoy!' Instead we are shown the bloodied blouse of an air stewardess who has been badly hurt in an attack by a drunken passenger and invited to believe that what we are about to see will offer some real insight into a serious matter. Then we watch a giggling reporter getting drunk on camera.

The problem for the programme makers, with the ratings-chasers on their backs, is that they dare not risk offering any fare that may be too challenging. They must keep the audience watching and that means making programmes that are 'accessible'. What is meant by 'accessible' is anything that we can relate to from experience in our own lives, the patronising assumption being that anything outside our experience will be a turn-off. So out goes much of the difficult stuff and in comes the story to which we can 'relate'. Or the private lives of the famous. Or crime. Or consumer affairs. Or something funny or whimsical. Anything to do with sex, jealousy, conflict, money, power, suffering, anything from which you can elicit an emotional response, is deemed to be 'accessible'. The pressure is on for more human interest stories, or more stories told from the point of view of human interest in mainstream news programmes. This is where populist television news takes us.

You look for drama. You make events part of a never-ending narrative and you make it absolutely clear where you stand in relation to it: everybody in it is either a good guy or a bad guy. That, after all, is the stuff of crude drama and of soaps. Reality is a bit more complicated. If you need a twist you turn everything on its head and make the good guys bad guys and the bad guys good, but you always hold on to the formula that this is a story about heroes and villains.

Famous people – mostly pop stars and sportsmen – are always complaining that the media build 'em up and then knock 'em down. There's a lot in that; it has always been a standard tabloid technique. And why not, you might say. Showbiz needs the tabloids – and increasingly the posh papers – just as much as the tabloids need them. Freddie Starr did very well indeed out of not eating somebody's hamster. Those techniques have been a little more questionable as far as the Royal Family is concerned, but it has been conventional wisdom for many years that the House of Windsor is the longest soap going, and that could not have continued without a great deal of connivance on the Royals' part. Perhaps it is inevitable that the Royal Family is turned into a form of entertainment for us. Perhaps that's why we have them. But the converting of news into soap is starting to go beyond all that.

The case of Louise Woodward, the English au pair convicted of killing an American baby, was a good example. It got the full soap treatment. The strictly journalistic – and, I admit, possibly rather dull – approach to such a story would concentrate on the facts. What was the evidence that she had killed the child? How strong was it? What other factors needed taking into account? And so on. Some of this material was dealt with in odd corners of the media, but what gave the story flight was its potential as a classic soap.

Here was a young British girl, far away from home, charged with a most terrible crime and facing the prospect of long years in prison. The soap writer is not interested in the facts, but in the angle: is she to be villain or victim? She was, at least initially, to be the victim; so the story got told in terms of her ordeal, with the baby's parents and the American legal system cast as the villains. That made it dramatic. It allowed us a storyline to follow in terms of tension, not fact.

First she was convicted of murder, but what would happen at appeal? Then it was reduced to manslaughter, but would she have to stay in gaol? Then she was let out, but would she be able to come back home? And all the while we could watch the reactions of the committed soap audience, in its pub in Elton, now devastated, now elated, as the story went through its twists and turns. And once it was clear she was safe, the story had to find another angle to keep it going, with everyone suddenly cast in a new light. Had her mother been fiddling expenses? Or her father having an affair? Were those we'd taken to be good guys really bad guys? And what about Louise herself? Wasn't there something rather chilling and sinister about the self-control she'd shown? Might there be a whole new plotline here for her? Meanwhile, in the midst of all this soap opera, the journalists' question – how did Matthew Eappen die? – might as well not get asked. Objectivity is far less entertaining than drama.

This story culminated in what may become a standard feature of soaps manufactured from real life: the big interview with Martin Bashir or his equivalent. Bashir's interview with Diana was a brilliant scoop, whatever sniping there may have been later about how he got it and the extent to which she had rehearsed her lines. I can scarcely recall a more riveting hour of television. Giving the star treatment to Louise Woodward was another matter altogether.

There was no legal doubt of her guilt. She had been effectively convicted not once, not twice, but three times. And even if there had been serious doubt about the verdict and we had been setting out to establish the truth, how could a single forty-minute interview, however well researched and competently conducted, do it? A programme such as *Rough Justice* might spend months, sometimes years, conducting painstaking research before it presents its case. So if we accept that there had been no appalling miscarriage in the case of Woodward, what was the point of the interview? Would Bashir have been called in had the killer been a middle-aged, unattractive woman convicted by a British court? I doubt it. This was pure soap presented as serious journalism.

You may ask: but wouldn't *you* have interviewed Louise Woodward on the *Today* programme if you'd had the chance? You bet I would. But a few minutes on a daily programme in the midst of another dozen interviews carries nothing like the prestige of an entire *Panorama*, the most prestigious slot on British television. The placing, the billing, the time allotted, all combine to give it a significance of its own. It invites the audience to say: this is truly important, a real journalistic exercise. It was not.

Allison Pearson summed up the risk in all this sort of thing in the *Daily Telegraph*. 'The commercial imperative to deliver clear-cut fables starring creepy Iagos and ravished Desdemonas has smothered any lingering loyalty to journalism. All the world's a soap-set now and men and women merely players on short-term contracts. Soap opera offers a crisis-crammed vision of life, with precious little breathing space for the unportentous or mundane.' And then she made clear what was worrying her: 'The danger is that, in some weird way, we are starting to apply that template to real lives – our own as well as others.'

The essential ingredient in a good soap is emotion. We had to care whether the otherwise deeply boring Shula Archer would ever find the man of her dreams or we would not have kept listening. We have to be moved by the maundering and the mishaps and the misbehaviour of the *Eastenders* mob or, ultimately, we will switch off. It does not have to be profound or even realistic; it just has to move us. We don't have to believe it is happening (though an alarming number of people seem to) and the more effective the scriptwriters and the actors are at conveying that synthetic emotion, the more they deserve their fees.

In reporting news on television it should be quite the opposite. The only imperative is that we get the facts right. Nothing else matters as much. A good reporter should certainly be able to convey the atmosphere, a sense of occasion. The best reporters will be able to make you feel you have been there, seen it for yourself. But they will not tell you what you should be thinking or, even worse, how you should be feeling.

Dunblane was, by any normal human standards, an immense tragedy: so many small children shot dead by a madman. I doubt there were many people watching the news that night who did not shed a tear. One of the BBC reporters sent to Dunblane was Kate Adie. She told us what had happened. She allowed people who were there to tell us what they saw and what they thought. That seems to me to be a reporter's job and, experienced reporter that she is, she did it competently. She did not tell us how the people of Dunblane were feeling. Could we not work that out for ourselves? And if we could not, how could she? A reporter is no more capable of seeing into the souls of others than anyone else. And yet Kate was attacked by a BBC executive in Scotland for her reporting. He said it had been 'cold' and it was possibly a mistake to have sent her.

She did not reply at the time. Two years later she said: 'Reporters are not told off for wearing their hearts on their sleeves these days; people are demanding that you should care as a journalist about the story you are reporting.'

Now that may seem an odd thing to say if you are not a journalist. Why would reporters not care about the story they are reporting, not care about the murder of children? The answer is that they do, just as anyone would. But the point she was making is that it is not a journalist's job to show it. It is a self-indulgence. Would the reports from Michael Buerk on the terrible famine in Ethiopia a generation ago have been more effective if he had been holding back the tears as he delivered his commentary? Should he have told the audience what effect those appalling scenes were having on him? No and no. He wrote a spare and powerful commentary and left it to us to form our own judgement. I happened to be presenting the news that night, thought we might get phone calls from people wanting to make donations, and volunteered to stay behind and deal with some of them. Hours later I staggered away, my telephone ear aching and the phones still ringing. The response was extraordinary and ultimately tens of millions of pounds were raised.

But that was a long time ago and things are changing. When Fergal Keane reported on the famine in Sudan fifteen or so years later he used his considerable talent to produce a series of reports that were much more emotional. He told us how he felt, what the terrible suffering was doing to him. That is what we have now come to expect. The old, cool, dispassionate style, now so out of fashion, not only allowed people to respond in their own way but, paradoxically, made real emotional responses more likely. Emotive reporting can be self-defeating; you do not have to be too cynical to suspect that a reporter may be milking a situation for what it's worth, and that you are being manipulated. The response of some people to that is to turn off.

I must also take issue with my old colleague Martin Bell, now a much respected MP and once my journalistic hero. When I moved to London from Manchester in the late sixties Martin was already a star in the television news firmament. We used to say that if you ripped open his chest you would find, instead of a beating heart, a Reuters wire machine tapping out foreign news. His professionalism, dedication and bravery were awesome. Over more than thirty years he reported with accuracy, economy and impartiality almost every big story on the globe. His last war was Bosnia and that's when, in my view, he took the wrong turning. His reporting was, as ever, superb but off the screen he began to argue for what he called the journalism of attachment.

He was, understandably, profoundly moved by the suffering and savagery of that godforsaken little country. In the face of such evils, he said, reporters could not and should not remain neutral and detached. He wants a 'journalism that cares as well as knows; that is aware of its responsibilities and will not stand neutrally between good and evil, right and wrong, the victim and the oppressor'. It is a seductive argument and an increasing number of journalists agree with him. I believe it is dangerous and based on a false analysis of what good journalists have been doing for generations. They have not been neutral between good and evil. They have sought out the worst excesses of man's inhumanity to man and exposed them. They have not merely shown pictures of the horrors of a mass grave or mutilated bodies but have tried to investigate the causes, to put the terrible actions into context. Then they have left their readers or their viewers to decide what to do about it and, if they care enough, to force the politicians to take action.

There are, and always have been, campaigning journalists who see themselves as propagandists for a cause, who are confident enough in their own judgement to know who is in the right and who is in the wrong. They do not claim to be objective but seek evidence to prove their case. It is right that newspapers should give them space, and that broadcasters such as the BBC should do the same, but not in mainstream news programmes such as the *Nine O'Clock News*. When we watch a report from John Simpson we believe that he is telling us the facts as he sees them, and not following any agenda of his own. It is vital that that should remain the case.

I was in Istanbul when Diana was killed in a Paris tunnel and, like any normal human being, shocked at the untimely deaths of three young people. I was also sorry not to be in London to report the story myself; we reporters define our journalistic lives by the stories we have reported. When I returned to

London the first news I saw was the *Nine O'Clock*, and it led me to believe that the entire nation was grieving as one, still stunned and shocked by the death of Diana. The final several minutes showed flowers being laid in London with the voices of grieving people over the pictures and poems being read. All very moving, but this was four days after the death. I assumed that some great transformation had overtaken the nation in those four days and that every inhabitant of these shores had been traumatised as never before. The next day I discovered it was not so.

I went to Parliament Square where people were camped out to get a decent view of the funeral. The atmosphere was not one of mourning; many were there because it was clearly going to be a great event and they were curious spectators. The vast majority of people I spoke to in the days before and immediately after the funeral seemed baffled. Of course anecdotal evidence proves little and I did not speak to millions of people. But, as I have written earlier, all the evidence since suggests strongly that my impressions were not too wide of the mark.

Two questions arise. First, did the media create rather than reflect the so-called 'outpouring of grief'?

It's worth remembering that the audience for the BBC1 special programme on the Sunday night, after a whole day of unrelenting coverage, had been surprisingly small. Interest built as the week wore on. I have no problem with newspapers creating a mood if they think that's what their readers want; we don't have to buy the paper if we choose not to. I have a real problem with the BBC doing the same and that is what happened. Our responsibility is to everyone, and it is not for us to make assumptions about what 'the nation' may or may not be feeling. At the risk of being sued for plagiarism by Margaret Thatcher I might suggest that there is no such thing as a nation; there are only men and women, each with their own feelings and views.

To invoke a national mood is to create an almost threatening notion of belonging. There are echoes of totalitarianism about it if you yourself do not share that mood. In the midst of the Diana funeral hysteria there were people who said that the experience made them feel that they no longer belonged. On the day of the funeral itself the BBC was wrong to blanket almost every outlet. We justify our two television channels and five radio networks on the basis of the choice we offer. On that occasion we denied viewers and listeners the choice. It was arrogant, patronising and mistaken.

The second question is more serious. Did we – and our competitors – do an accurate reporting job?

I believe we did not. I accept it would have been enormously difficult to report the other side of the story because many of those who were genuinely grieving would have been offended. So be it. Our job is to tell the whole story and let the chips fall where they may. During a war in which the survival of the nation is at stake and national morale is crucially important, the BBC may permit itself to tell only part of the story. The death of Diana was not a national crisis.

Tony Hall, the chief executive of BBC News, commented on our coverage in an article in *The Times* entitled 'The people led, we followed.'

'Journalists like facts,' he wrote. 'Who, what, when, and where; that's the mantra for every fresh-faced recruit to our profession. Our job is to gather those facts, form them into a coherent report and get them on air. Audiences are supposed to be listening to us, not the other way round. But last week we learned a tough lesson. We learnt that emotion has its political dimension, that by giving voice on our airwaves to "ordinary" individuals' thoughts and feelings, we could get at some kind of truth, which would otherwise elude us no matter how many facts we assembled.'

He was absolutely right about journalists liking facts, but it seems to me that that is the beginning, the middle and the end of it. If we assemble the facts as best we can they will speak for themselves, and the audience must make of them what they will. To move beyond that is dangerous. Emotion does not have a political dimension; it is ephemeral, transient. It is more or less powerful for each individual, but it is not for journalists to try to measure its intensity or its reality. A football crowd will get carried away with a goal in the last minute that means its team wins the cup but the emotion will pass. And how can we get at 'some kind of truth' if we are selective as to where we point our cameras?

Of course it is perfectly proper to give a voice on our airwaves to 'ordinary' individuals; we do it all the time. But we usually strive for some balance and I heard no dissenting voices from our vox pops, though I know from my own experience then and since that there were many dissenters. There were many who were shocked at Diana's death but not unbearably moved by it, who thought it was the utmost nonsense to talk of the nation having undergone some great catharsis such that things would never be quite the same again. The point is that we must always treat vox pops with an unspoken health warning, just as pollsters do when they question only a selective section of the population or interview people only on the telephone.

On Channel 5 the new attitudes to both presentation and emotional reporting come together in a wholly new idea of what journalism is about. Their aim is to appeal to a younger adult audience which they believe is largely alienated from mainstream news programmes. The most obvious change is stylistic, but it is in the content of the news that the real change has taken place.

Chris Shaw, its first editor, believed that the first responsibility of news is to make it relevant to the people who are watching it, to be more 'inclusive', that great buzz word of the late nineties. He told Brendan O'Neill of *LM* magazine that 'many people want news which feels relevant to them. They don't want us to rely on the language of authority, but on language that feels more "on side" and more in tune with their interests.' The result is reporting that concentrates on what might be thought to appeal to the audience rather than matter in any wider sense. O'Neill gave as an example an interview with Don King which spent as much time asking how he keeps his hair standing on end as about his legal battles as a boxing promoter. A victory of style over content? Not according to Shaw.

'I vigorously refute the notion that we are all style and no content. *5 News* is not a format, it's an approach; more than that, it's an attitude.' It's an attitude that says journalism is primarily about identifying with an audience, not reporting authoritatively what is going on in the world. 'What we are arguing is that credibility can be achieved through empathy as much as it can through authority.'

I think that is an extraordinary thing to say. Credibility through empathy means no more than reflecting the world back to an audience as they already see it. It also means talking down to them as if they were children, because it assumes they can't take anything that does not square with the outlook and attitudes they already have. It is patronising but, from a journalistic point of view, worse than that. Getting 'on side' with your audience is just as much a distortion as getting on side with any interest group or powerful lobby. Serious journalism is about not being on side with anything except the facts. Once you let anything have priority over that, you have sold the pass.

Shaw's approach to 'authority' is revealing. He contrasts the language of authority with the language that feels on side. He seems to think authority is in itself bad, presumably because he equates it with the old world of deference. Hence, in his eyes, the antidote to authority is chummy populism. But authority is not the same as unthinking deference. In journalism authority does not flow from someone's position, but from building a reputation for dispassionate reporting of the facts as far as that is possible. The new journalism does not want to build a new authority for us to respect, but to chuck it away in favour of allowing us all to cling together feeling good.

We have come a long way from an anonymous Alvar Liddell intoning the news from his Olympian heights. Of course broadcast news had to become less stilted and pompous, more immediate and lively, more challenging and enquiring, more comprehensive and comprehensible. And so it has. Technology made some of it possible and changing tastes made the rest of it inevitable. But, for the next stage of the journey, growing commercial pressures threaten to send us off in the wrong direction. Populism is the easy route and the wrong one. Accessibility should be about dealing with important, often difficult, subjects in mainstream news programmes and serious documentaries in language that is free of jargon and journalese and in concepts that can be grasped by anyone with an enquiring and interested mind. A journalism that is more concerned with being on side with its audience than reporting what's going on in the world is ultimately worthless, but that is what happens when the need to boost audiences makes entertainment the priority. No one wants to go back to the stiff formality of early news-reading. As with everything in life, it is about balance.

Some people see in this new journalistic language that 'feels more on side' a new, shared vernacular, to replace the class-divided languages of the toffs and the mob. But quite aside from the objections to this particular language, and how it corrupts journalism, why should we want a shared vernacular? Society is richer and stronger when there are a lot of divergent voices having their say, opening our eyes to their view of the world. And if there has to be a new, shared vernacular, do we really want it to be this one? Do we really want to live in a world dominated by a media in which the battle for ratings pushes it into ever more extreme sensationalism and in which journalism and entertainment converge around the easy, comfortable, unchallenging values of infotainment?

I don't, because sensationalism coarsens us, and infotainment lulls us into the view that the world is really no more than an entertainment, for us to watch as disengaged voyeurs. And in such a lulled state we are prey to the manipulation of the public relations industry and the spin doctors of politics.

It will be difficult for ITV to escape from the commercial juggernaut as it bears down upon it at an ever increasing speed. It has clearly calculated that it can escape being crushed by the growing competition only by taking the routes sign-posted 'sensationalism' and 'populism'. It will continue to produce many worthwhile programmes but when the big choice is faced between populism and public service it has to travel in the direction of the biggest audience figures. The BBC, self-evidently, must travel in the opposite direction.

It is not good enough for the BBC to defend itself by trumpeting the excellence of a great costume drama or wildlife programme or the quality of its news service. It is the totality that matters. It cannot defend a piece of meretricious tosh on daytime television by pointing to a serious debate late at night on BBC2. Nor can it hide behind the argument that the licence fee means the BBC must provide something for everyone. If 'something for everyone' means defending the bland or banal, the sensationalist or the scurrilous, the derivative or the downmarket, then the BBC must have the courage to disappoint a proportion of the audience. They can find it elsewhere. Cater for minority tastes as well as the mass market by all means – that is part of our remit – but quality and integrity must be the hallmark of everything we do.

The BBC must have the confidence to believe that if it is doing its job properly it is providing a civilising influence from which every single one of us ultimately benefits, however much or however little we watch or listen. The argument has long been accepted by most thinking people that a nation without great theatre or music is the poorer for it, so we should subsidise the Royal Shakespeare Company or our finest orchestras or even the Royal Opera House, even if only a tiny proportion of the public will ever sit in its plush seats. If that is true for them, how much more true is it of the most important cultural institution in the country, the BBC.

For too long the BBC has subscribed to the theory that big is better, that we must fight on every front at the same time if we are to survive in this hugely competitive world. I believe the opposite is true. To survive we must retain the licence fee. To retain the licence fee we must do those things that our commercial competitors cannot or will not do because they cannot guarantee the ratings. If the ratings for one programme are 'disappointing', then so be it; perhaps the next one will fare better. It must resist the temptation to push serious programmes to later and later slots in the schedules. *Panorama* was once on BBC1 before the *Nine O'Clock News*, then immediately after it; now it is on at 10 pm. *Question Time* has been moved to 11 pm. and *Omnibus* to 10.40 pm. *Newsnight* has lost a chunk of air time as a sop to the Scots. My own *On the Record* has been moved twice, testing the patience of even the most enthusiastic viewer. If the schedules can be cleared for sporting events, they should also be cleared for big debates on some of the great political issues affecting the nation.

In the long term the BBC's ratings will fall. It cannot be otherwise. The rate at which they fall will be determined by how well everyone in the BBC performs, but fall they will. And the more they fall, the more the BBC must defend its intrinsic values: good, honest and accurate information, education and entertainment. If it chases the ratings at the expense of those values it does not deserve to exist. The proliferation of new channels is a threat only if the BBC regards ratings as its justification. Put simply, it is about offering the public a real choice.

The BBC can, in spite of everything, build bridges between all people and all classes and bring us together in moments of crisis or celebration. It is the nation's most valuable cultural and journalistic asset and we must fight to keep it that way.

I have tried to show how the two great engines of consumer populism, commercialism and the media, have influenced the whole climate in which we live, and have helped make us the people we are. For some people it's all fine, nothing to worry about; let's just turn on the telly and order a take-away pizza. But for those who are less sanguine the question arises: what can be done about it? Commercialism and the media are big and powerful forces. Perhaps we should put our faith in the politicians. It is them I want to look at next.

Section Three

What's to be done about it all?

Chapter 12

Politics

OKAY, CONFESSION TIME. I like politicians. Naturally I shall deny it if it is ever held against me. You may think that would be difficult since those are my own words and my name is on the cover of this book, but I shall say the quote has been taken out of context, distorted, misinterpreted, exaggerated. That's what a politician would do and over the years I have learned a lot from them, and about them. I have learned that politicians lie routinely. They cheat and steal and are unfaithful to their wives and husbands and mistresses and lovers. They engage in bizarre sexual practices in secret and claim purity in public. They are hypocrites and poseurs, masters of deception. They are drunkards and gluttons, bullies and cowards. They desperately want to be loved but frequently treat others with contempt. They gossip like fishwives and demand the utmost discretion in others. They are pompous and patronising. They have massive egos and bogus humility. They are consumed with ambition, which they disguise as a wish only to serve humanity.

They are also good company, amusing and entertaining. They are intelligent, articulate and well informed and the best of them work very hard for little reward. They do what can often be a rotten job with relatively little complaint and often great dedication. Some of them even have principles which they are prepared to defend at great cost to their careers. In short, they are almost exactly like the rest of us and we need them. *Almost* like the rest of us. The big difference is that they believe they are better equipped to run the world than the rest of us. Well, someone has to do it, but there is an overwhelming reason why we should not put much faith in politicians if we are worried about the effects of consumer populism.

Far from being a cure, politics is itself infected with the consumer populist virus. One of the reasons for that is the dominant role that the media, especially broadcasting, now plays in the way we do our politics. J. K. Galbraith said: 'The reduction of politics to a spectator sport . . . has been one of the more malign accomplishments of television. Television newsmen are breathless on how the game is being played and largely silent on what the game is all about.' When he wrote that he had the United States in mind, but we cannot be complacent in this country. The best of our political coverage is serving democracy well but there is a growing danger of television turning politics into a populist business and, in the process, helping to turn us all from citizens into political consumers.

There was a time, before politics came to us through the box in the corner of the living-room, when we used to go to it. Many of us would leave the warmth of our coal fires and trudge off to the town hall to see what the local candidate had to say for himself. Thousands of people would stand for hours and listen to Mr Gladstone when he appeared in their towns and cities. We might even join in with a spot of heckling, a fine art sadly disappearing in these orchestrated times. It was at a big public meeting back in the early sixties that I first had a tiny glimpse at first hand of the power that television was beginning to have. Harold Wilson had come to Cardiff for an election rally at which his supporters cheered and his opponents heckled. In those days anyone was allowed in – no careful vetting of credentials as tends to happen nowadays when the leader moves among the people – and Wilson enjoyed the heckling because it allowed him, with his sharp wit, to get the better of the hecklers and cheer up his supporters even more.

Halfway through his speech, in the middle of some fairly mild observations about the state of the Welsh economy or some such, he suddenly did something very odd indeed. He leaned forward, banged the podium and delivered a fierce attack on his political opponents. Then he stopped that as suddenly as he'd begun and returned to his theme as if he had never deviated. It had lasted no more than a minute. A television friend told me later what had happened. The national news wanted a clip from his speech and they were not able, in those technically primitive days, to record the best bit, rush out to a van and satellite it to London. So, since the news was on the air at the time, they planned to cut live to his speech. Wilson's camp had arranged for a producer to warn them when they were about to switch to Cardiff and they had positioned a party hack in his line of sight with a big white handkerchief. When he got the word that they were switching to Cardiff he dropped his handkerchief like a race marshal with a flag and Wilson was off.

Quite what the audience in the hall made of it all I can't imagine. But it was not the audience in the hall that mattered; it was the audience sitting in front of their television screens at home. They mattered then and they matter now, only much more so.

The sociologist Manuel Castells has described the media as having become 'the space of politics' – a good phrase because it captures the idea of where politics now really happens, rather than in those draughty Victorian halls with their mass public meetings. The halls are still used from time to time, but mostly for ticket-only affairs for the party faithful, and only then as a location that will look good on the box. Nor is Parliament the central space of politics any more so far as the public is concerned.

In the past anyone interested could read much of what was said in Parliament in newspaper reports the following day. Not any more they can't. The Labour minister Jack Straw analysed the coverage of debates in the Commons. According to his research, 'gallery' reporting of debates in the Chamber stayed pretty constant in the fifty-five years from 1933 to 1988. *The Times* would average between 400 and 800 lines, the *Guardian* between 300 and 700. Within five years the coverage had dropped dramatically: down to fewer than 100 lines in each newspaper. The *Daily Telegraph* halved its coverage and the *Financial Times* abandoned its parliamentary page altogether.

Five years on Mr Straw did another survey and had his researcher laboriously measure the column inches of parliamentary coverage. He concluded: 'The near-absence of systematic coverage is palpable.' Simon Jenkins was the editor of *The Times* who took the decision to stop parliamentary reporting. 'I couldn't find anyone who read it except MPs,' he told the Nolan Committee when he gave evidence some years later.

It's perfectly clear what is happening. Most people now get most of their politics from television and radio. Ask any politician where they think the space of politics is these days and they will say the same.

It is a space they have to share with people like me, and we are occasionally asked why we give them such a hard time in front of the cameras and microphones. It's hard to answer that question without sounding pompous and self-important. But the truth is that in a world in which people no longer go along to public meetings to give politicians a hard time and no longer check on whether Parliament is doing it for them – some of the select committees do a good job – it is largely on television and radio that real probing of what politicians are up to has to happen.

When I started in this business the BBC was just beginning to emerge from the forelock-tugging school of political journalism. We would approach the Prime Minister returning from an important trip abroad, for instance, and ask tentatively if he had anything to say. If he snapped 'No' we would thank him humbly and back away. Happily all that has gone. The danger now is that instead of using our fingers to knuckle our foreheads we use them to give the V-sign to the politicians. Neither is appropriate. Once we grovelled: 'Have you anything else to say to a grateful nation, Minister?' Now we bark: 'And what have you got to say for yourself you jumped-up little freeloading slimeball who wouldn't recognise the word duty unless it was printed in large letters on the menu of a three-star restaurant!' Of course I exaggerate, but the difficulty is finding the balance between the two.

I said that occasionally people like me gave politicians a hard time and I *meant* occasionally. The punch-ups are remembered; the calmer discussions are not. The vast majority of political interviews are conducted with reason and good humour on both sides and most are straightforward attempts to find out what a particular policy or political development is all about. Sometimes the minister does not want to say, and then the interviewer will persist or, at least, should persist. Sometimes the minister will mislead, or deny the blindingly obvious. Then the interviewer will argue and it may become a little heated. Sometimes the interviewer will stray into an area the politician would prefer not to discuss. When that happens the politician will invariably use some dismissive phrase such as 'tittle tattle'. You know the sort of thing.

'It really is a great shame, John, that all you people in the media seem interested in is the entirely unproven allegation that sixteen government ministers were involved in a wife swapping orgy on board Concorde when what really matters to the ordinary voter – to real people – is the disgraceful way the other party behaved when it was in power.'

'Well yes, minister, but there is the small matter of Concorde being chartered at the taxpayers' expense and . . .'

'You see! There you go again. Tittle tattle! That's all you're interested in. Now let me tell you what this government has achieved since we came to power . . .'

It is a useful rule of thumb that when a politician says the public will not be interested in a particular issue, that will be the only issue being discussed over every dinner table and bar in the land that night. What they mean is they will fight like tigers to make the 'interesting' stuff go away. They may flatly refuse to discuss it on the airwaves in the hope that the papers will lose interest. That tactic invariably fails because there is always someone, somewhere, who will whisper a few words behind his hand to a political correspondent. The first rule of politics is that all politicians have enemies, and the most savage are always in their own party. Another tactic is to distract attention. You will notice how many brand new policy initiatives are suddenly announced on the day an embarrassing report is due to be published. That sometimes works, depending on the size of the embarrassment. When all else seems doomed to fail there is yet another tactic, the last ditch nuclear option that would normally be avoided at all costs: full and frank disclosure of the truth. Or rather, full and frank disclosure of as much of the truth as they can be absolutely sure will emerge whether they go on the air or not. This last option is relatively rare.

When Peter Mandelson suddenly found himself in the papers over the little matter of a £373,000 loan from Geoffrey Robinson we expected him to go to ground. That's what Robinson himself had done throughout the series of embarrassing disclosures about his own financial affairs that had dogged his time as a minister. Requests for interviews were routinely brushed aside. So little hope was there of ever getting an interview with him that when he did suddenly turn up for an interview at Television Centre one Sunday morning a producer sent him away. Apparently there had been some mix-up over names. So no interview . . . and no career prospects for said producer. Nor, ultimately, for Geoffrey Robinson. He lost his job a few months later.

Mr Mandelson's tactics were different. To our surprise and delight he popped up on *Today* to do an interview with me at ten past eight on the morning the story broke, and then popped up on just about every other programme on radio and television for the rest of the day, occasionally shooting himself in the foot. I fully expected to see him on *Blue Peter* that evening. But it didn't work. Mr Mandelson had to resign and that, no doubt, will be the end of that particular tactic.

When I talk about ministers 'refusing to discuss' this or that, let me make it clear what the rules are. I frequently get letters from suspicious listeners wondering why I did not ask a particular question during a particular interview. It is sometimes because I have asked that same question of that same minister at least sixteen times and know that I'm no more likely to get a reply the seventeenth. It may be because neither I nor my editor thought it worth asking. It may be that I should have asked it but was half asleep at the time. It will not be – as the cynical listener often assumes – because we have done a deal with the politician. Here's how it works.

We phone the minister's office or Party headquarters and ask for an interview. They say, 'What about?' and we tell them. Sometimes it is a general political interview but sometimes it will be on a specific subject. If they agree on the basis of that subject, then that is what you would expect to stick to and that is the extent of the 'deal'. That seems entirely reasonable. You wouldn't expect some poor soul who has just managed to get a toehold in the Ministry of Agriculture to answer questions about some arcane aspect of economic policy. It sometimes happens, though, that a story will break between the bid being accepted and the programme being broadcast and we will want to include that development in the interview. Then we'll go back to the minister and say so. If he says no, then we have to make a judgement: to go ahead with the interview as agreed or to drop it altogether. Only in the most exceptional cases, I believe, should we bounce a politician into talking about one thing when we had clearly agreed to talk about another.

Many years ago we had set up an interview with Denis Healey, the politician with the bushiest eyebrows and one of the sharpest brains and hottest tempers the Labour Party has ever had. We were supposed to talk about some European defence matter. An hour before my interview was due to happen he had appeared on television and the question of private medicine – a hot topic at the time – was raised. It turned out that Healey's wife Edna was in hospital and in a private bed. He was furious and stormed out of the studio. He was still furious when he arrived in the doorway of the *Today* green-room an hour later. By then the story was running on all the agency news wires.

'You planning to ask me about Edna?' he demanded.

'Well, yes, I'll have to. It would look very odd if I didn't.'

'Right! Well, I'm buggering off then!' And with that he set off down the corridor towards the exit.

I held my breath, thought about the great hole opening up in the programme in about four minutes' time and prayed. God must have been listening. Thirty seconds later Healey was back in the doorway.

'How much d'you want to ask about Edna?'

So that was that. The interview went ahead; the questions were asked and everybody was satisfied. On reflection, strike that last thought from the record. I doubt that there has ever, in the entire history of broadcasting, been an interview with which everybody was satisfied. If you inflict serious injury on a politician from one party and expose him as a thoroughly bad lot, his supporters will want your head. If you fail to do so his opponents will be just as angry. If you can't get a question answered and give up you will be called a coward. If you persist you will be called a bully. If you get a hundred letters heaping praise on you there will usually be another hundred demanding your resignation. Usually, but not always. There are some things the audience will not tolerate. One of them is bullying and another is downright rudeness. And there are some individual politicians who will always arouse the sympathy of the audience. One of those is John Hume.

Mr Hume is a brave man who has fought tenaciously and at great risk to himself to bring about peace in Northern Ireland. His reward was the Nobel Peace Prize. Mr Hume is also a very canny politician who knows precisely how to win the sympathy of the audience, as I first discovered to my cost one morning several years ago. I was conducting what should have been a pretty routine interview with him about the latest political development in Northern Ireland. Mr Hume was delivering his lecture about the need for understanding and tolerance and, I thought, not dealing with the issue at hand. I told him so.

'I've answered the question,' he snapped back. 'You've not been listening.'

I lost my temper and told him, even more sharply, that I had been and he had not answered the question and would he kindly do so. It is always a big mistake to lose your temper. It is fatal to do so when you're interviewing someone who has the sympathy of the audience. By the time the tenth bag of angry mail had arrived I had learned a painful lesson.

The audience has a pretty chivalrous streak, too. It is usually a mistake to play too rough with women politicians even in these days of what is meant to be sexual equality, though the chivalry starts to wear thin if the audience thinks the politician is not delivering the goods. At one stage in her career it was impossible to ask tough questions of Harriet Harman without getting a barrage of abuse from the listener or viewer. All that changed one December morning in 1997 when she was the Secretary of State for Social Security and I was interviewing her about cuts the government were proposing to make in allowances to single mothers.

I thought she was not answering the questions, pressed her quite hard, and it became a little heated. Nothing unusual in that. The interview would have passed off with no more than a few quotes in the next day's papers and a handful of letters if the Labour Party had not done something the audience will not tolerate: it tried to put pressure on an interviewer (me) through the BBC. David Hill, the Labour Party's chief media spokesman, fired off a letter to my boss. 'The John Humphrys problem,' he wrote, 'has assumed new proportions after this morning's interview with Harriet Harman. In response we have had a council of war and are now seriously considering whether, as a Party, we will suspend co-operation when you make bids through us for Government Ministers.' I was mildly surprised. This, after all, was the party that had defended me against attacks from the Conservatives when they were in power. It was shocking, they used to say, the way the Tories attacked poor defenceless interviewers when they were only doing their job. Is it not amazing what changes six months at the sharp end can produce in a political party?

Hill's letter was, predictably, leaked to the newspapers and the balloon went up. The *Guardian* led its front page with a picture of me and the headline 'THE MAN LABOUR WANTS TO GAG'. It described the letter as 'an unprecedented attack'. The row rumbled on for a couple of weeks and Alastair Campbell, Tony Blair's extremely powerful press spokesman, weighed in. He pointed out for the benefit of *Guardian* readers that 'John Humphrys is not the Queen Mother'. Damn! I knew I'd never get away with wearing flowery hats and waving to the crowds at Ascot. Curse you, Campbell, for blowing my cover!

The listeners were outraged. Their letters, faxes, phone calls and e-mails arrived by the thousand and all but a few dozen made the same point: we *want* interviewers to ask difficult questions and, if they don't get answers, to keep asking them. We do *not* want the politicians trying to tell the BBC how to do its job. The phrase used most often in the letters was: 'Don't let the bastards grind you down!'

The reaction had been exactly the same a few years earlier when I was publicly attacked by a senior Conservative minister. His name was Jonathan Aitken – you can't say I don't choose my enemies carefully – and he accused me of 'poisoning the well of democratic debate' through my style of interviewing. The example he chose, foolish man, was an interview I had done with his boss, Kenneth Clarke. Aitken claimed I had interrupted the Chancellor thirty-two times during a five-minute interview on *Today*. Clarke found the idea that he needed someone like Aitken to defend him against someone like me hugely amusing. The next time I interviewed him I handed him a small calculator as we were about to go into the studio.

'What's this for?' he asked.

'So that you can count up the number of times I interrupt you during this interview and report back,' I told the Chancellor.

He looked at the calculator for a few seconds and then said ruefully: 'You know, I never did figure out how to make one of these things work.'

I think he was joking.

In truth the grown-up politicians scarcely ever complain about interviews. Many of them prefer a rigorous session with robust exchanges and even the occasional interruption because they believe they perform more effectively when they're under a bit of pressure, as indeed they do. The idea that experienced old hands like Kenneth Clarke cannot defend themselves and get their message across is frankly laughable. If they have something to say they will say it. If it is a convincing performance, the audience will be convinced.

In the ideal world the typical listener would like nothing better than endless deeply serious discussions on complex policy issues; they would disdain the more entertaining punch-ups. However, this is not an ideal world. We are endlessly told by our lords and masters that people become bored with party infighting and would prefer a much more reasoned approach where we calmly debate the details of policies in reasoned tones. The evidence suggests otherwise.

As far as most people are concerned it's more fun listening to a politician savagely attacking his leader or his own party's policies and getting angrier by the minute than having to concentrate on a dispassionate analysis of Clause 3b of the Maastricht Treaty and its effect on the sheep meat regime. Consider what happened to *Today*'s listening figures during the final years of the last Conservative government.

Every other day senior Tory politicians would come on the programme to batter their colleagues senseless. I sometimes wondered whether we shouldn't have strung a rope around the studio table with stools in opposite corners for their seconds to sit on and buckets for them to spit in. This wasn't just party infighting; this was a world heavyweight title contest every morning, bare-knuckle politics at its most brutal, the most successful political party this country has ever seen tearing itself to pieces in public. The effect? Our listening figures had never been healthier. We may have put bear-baiting and cock-fighting behind us as a nation, but most people still enjoy watching a good knock-'em-down, drag-'em-out fight between politicians of roughly equal weight. Robust, argumentative politics involving policies and personalities is great spectator sport for anyone with even the most passing interest in the way we are governed.

It is simply wrong to claim, as Tony Benn does, that 'the folk at home aren't interested in personalities'. So they weren't interested in the personality of Margaret Thatcher? Really? And they're not interested in knowing what makes Tony Blair tick? Well, I am and I know they are. I'll bet Tony Benn is too. A prime minister's personality may not matter too much when it comes to deciding who gets to be the junior minister in the Department of Transport, but it sure does if you're fighting a war or struggling to reform the welfare state.

So I believe we must report on the personalities in politics and I believe the audience thoroughly enjoys a good punch-up, assuming that there is a genuine difference at issue. I also believe in reporting what politicians – once they get into power – call the tittle tattle. I want to know if they are using Concorde routinely or throwing too many big bashes at Number Ten at the taxpayers' expense or buying very expensive wallpaper for their grace and favour apartments. Then I can hear the arguments and judge for myself as a taxpayer whether the spending is justified or not. I also believe we have a right to know what politicians – especially ministers – get up to in their private lives if there is the slightest suggestion that it might affect what they do in their public lives or if they lecture us on what we should do in ours. In short I want to know more, rather than less. Then I can discard the stuff I think is unimportant and decide for myself what is tittle tattle.

But I should not leave the impression that in the current state of political interviewing the broadcasters' hands are entirely clean and it is only the politicians who are fouling things up. At the risk of sounding like a revivalist preacher, we are all guilty. Take the issue of soundbites, the glib prepared phrases that politicians routinely churn out. They are the bane of modern political interviewing yet it would be wrong wholly to blame the politicians for them.

It is only relatively recently that the word 'soundbite' has entered the language and we have the Americans to thank for it. When I first started reporting from the United States in the early seventies the typical 'interview' on the main network news programmes lasted for about fifteen seconds. By the time I left, six years later, it was about half that. They now last for about five seconds. That is fifteen words, hardly more than a single line on this page. Not so much a bite as a nibble. It's not so different here. If that is the maximum length of time we are going to allow politicians in a peaktime news programme they are not going to have room for anything more than the simplest of thoughts. Subtlety doesn't stand a chance. And the trouble is that if the politician tries anything a bit more complicated, it's going to get cut back to something simple or dropped altogether.

Then there is the question of distortion and context. I have yet to meet a news reporter or producer who deliberately sets out to distort, but there will inevitably be occasions when we get carried away with our enthusiasm or the time allotted has been reduced because of something important happening somewhere else in the world. A qualifying phrase may be ignored, or another sentence might be dumped because it would weaken the point. That is when politicians cry foul because they are being quoted 'out of context'.

The mother of them all was Margaret Thatcher's observation that 'there is no such thing as society'. Her opponents were overjoyed at what they saw as a terrible gaffe. What a heartless, selfish thing to say! Typical of a woman who cared only about greedy individuals! She was pilloried for it at the time, and has been pilloried endlessly since. But read the whole of that answer: 'There is no such thing as society. There are individual men and women, and there are families. And no government can do anything except through people, and people must look to themselves first. It's our duty to look after ourselves and then to look after our neighbour.' Put like that it sounds rather different, especially when you add in the bit about our neighbour.

Of course politicians cry foul even when they have not been taken out of context. You have heard it many times: 'When I said my government would never put up taxes it was perfectly obvious that what I meant was that we would never put up taxes unless things started to go wrong.'

'But that's not what you said, Minister.'

'That's not the point. You have deliberately distorted my words . . .'

Politicians affect to despise the soundbite culture. That's a bit of a cheek since, as I have said, they help feed it. They have come to realise that their best defence against the chopping of their golden words is to get their retaliation in first. They labour long and hard to find the few words that will survive the savage editor and make it onto the *Nine O'Clock News*. The phrase 'the people's princess', used by Tony Blair to such good effect after the death of Diana, was not something that suddenly came to him as he faced the cameras and appeared to be struggling for the right words. If it had not been dreamed up by Alastair Campbell several hours earlier and carefully worked into the 'spontaneous' reaction, then I will eat my word processor.

I remember a lunch with a certain senior politician a few hours before he was planning to ask a question at Prime Minister's Questions in the Commons. We talked about his question and I made what I thought was a rather witty comment. Four hours later I heard it again: from the politician's lips in a report on the *Six O'Clock News*. I toyed with sending an invoice for services rendered, but there were no witnesses and who ever heard of a politician admitting plagiarism?

Politicians' soundbites are not just a response to shrinking slots on news bulletins. I suspect they would still be churning out those ghastly, pre-digested slogans even if we allocated them twice the time. That's because of their new-found fascination with marketing, to which I shall return. But for the moment I'm still in confessional mode.

The other big problem for politicians is that they dare not say what they think if there is even a minuscule possibility that it may seem to contradict the party line. We in the media do not help. We complain incessantly about how politicians have become speak-your-weight machines, but the moment they say something remotely interesting we leap on them from a great height. We are much too ready to present perfectly sensible and thoughtful comments as 'gaffes' or 'splits'. An MP or – better still – a minister says there just might be an argument for taking a look at the way we criminalise people who smoke the odd joint of marijuana and we pounce on it as though they have called for free heroin for nine-year-olds.

There is an enormous temptation for interviewers like me to see some of these encounters as a game – 'Trap the politician and watch him wriggle', available from all good toy stores price £19.99. We sometimes even use the word 'game'. My more pompous colleagues may deny it, but one of the reasons we play the game is that it's fun. I'm not a fox-hunting man myself, but I imagine that the buzz those characters get when they've finally run the exhausted and terrified beast to ground after a thrilling chase is not entirely different from that moment after some good studio sport when you say, 'Secretary of State, thank you,' and he says 'Thank you' back through gritted teeth and tries to smile. What he really wants to do is what the hounds do to the fox. If he's away somewhere in a radio car you occasionally get reports later from the radio car's engineer about repairs needed because the minister slammed the car door so hard all the microphone jacks fell out of their sockets.

Not that the interviewer always wins: a wily politician knows precisely what you're after and he knows that you know he knows. If he's worth his salary he will be at least two steps ahead of you. That's one of the things that makes it fun: pitching your skill and technique against his skill and his greater knowledge of the subject.

We all play it, to a greater or lesser degree, and there is no harm in a little fun. Not all politics is a matter of life and death, and I like to think that some of the exchanges I had with Michael Heseltine when he was Deputy Prime Minister might even have added a little to the gaiety of the nation. The *Guardian* once suggested we should form a double-act on the end of the pier: Top of the Bill Tonight! The Hezza 'n' Humph Show. I doubt we'd have been a great threat to Les Dawson, but the *Today* audience seemed to enjoy it.

It can also be useful if, for instance, you trap the minister into admitting something that he had always denied in the past and everyone has a right to know. Equally it can be pretty pointless if the exchange is clearly getting nowhere and the interviewer keeps snapping away because he doesn't want to admit defeat. I would like to say that has never happened to me, but I would be lying if I did. What must not happen is that gaffe-hunting becomes a substitute for serious interviewing.

The trouble is, the prizes in this game are so alluring. A big enough gaffe might mean a fat headline in the papers the following morning. What all of us want is to see our programme's name (and, better still, our own as well) being constantly quoted in the press. It is called raising the programme's profile and the higher the profile, or so we are led to believe, the healthier the audience figures. Ultimately the programme will be judged – as ever – by its figures and almost always they will determine whether it lives or dies. It's more or less the same for the interviewer. I imagine that the overworked producers on *Today*, bone weary after a long hard night trying to put the programme together, enjoy that moment before dawn when the presenters start to stagger in.

'You're in the papers,' they tell you.

'Oh really?' you say, affecting weary indifference, trying to pretend that you're such a seasoned old hand that it really doesn't matter one way or another but on balance it's a bit of a bore. In truth you're desperate to get at the first editions. You tear through them, trying not to show your disappointment when, instead of a six-column headline with your picture on all the front pages and leading articles praising your brilliant journalism, there's a paragraph or two tucked away at the bottom of page five of just one of the broadsheets. And even that spells your name wrong.

The biggest problem with both gaffe-hunting and the soundbite culture is not that they may be exploited by the politician or the journalist, but that they inhibit real argument and open, spontaneous discussion. As one Cabinet Minister put it to me: 'It's got to the stage where you won't let us think aloud.' He wasn't whining – he is one of those politicians who can hold his own with the best of us and thoroughly enjoys a robust exchange – and he had a point. We are making it difficult and that is bad for the democratic argument. But however confessional my mood for these past few pages, I am not about to take all the blame. New politics must bear the responsibility, too, for making thinking aloud such a hazardous enterprise.

Nowadays politicians must all be 'on message', to use that hideous expression that came into its own at the 1997 election. They must carry pagers which tell them what the party line is at any moment, day or night. So if party headquarters has the slightest worry that the precise party line has not been understood by the candidates on an aspect of nuclear defence policy or what colour socks candidates should wear, a little message will flash up on their pager screens. Woe betide any careless or maverick candidate who fails to deliver the word as it has been handed down. There were times during the campaign when many of us thought we were interviewing robots. They may have looked like real flesh-and-blood human beings, but clearly their brains had been replaced with microchips.

'You say that you will not put up taxes but you will spend billions more on health and education and public transport. How?'

'The answer to that is perfectly simple. All non-productive citizens will be transported to an uninhabited island in the South Atlantic and ... whirr ... click ... buzz ... *Incorrect reply! Incorrect reply! Programming fault. Programming fault! Report to headquarters for reprogramming immediately. I say again report to ...'*

I swear that by the end of the campaign most interviewers could write down the answer to almost any question before the question had been asked. Robin Day used to joke that when he interviewed Margaret Thatcher he always wanted to begin by saying: 'So what is the answer to my first question, Prime Minister?'

What all this crazy discipline is part of is the much bigger business of politicians keeping control of message and image. They have always tried to lean on editors and newspaper proprietors to provide sympathetic reporting and obliging commentary. But now that broadcasting is the space of politics the whole business has become far more serious. That is why they need the spin doctors.

Most of the spin doctors I know are perfectly delightful people. Indeed, some of them are old friends and colleagues, even Alastair Campbell. Now there's a thing to admit. I have wasted a forest of newsprint defending myself and the BBC against the outrageous and usually inaccurate attacks launched upon us by Campbell ever since he took over in Number Ten, but there is some essential weakness in my character that makes me warm to him none the less. Technically I suppose he is not a gentleman because he plays the bagpipes; Oscar Wilde, I think, said the definition of a gentleman is someone who can play the bagpipes and doesn't. He also has a short fuse and has been known to swing the odd punch in the odd newsroom, but he is funny, very bright, immensely likeable (except when he's banging on about the BBC) and loyal to a fault. He is also very good at his job . . . most of the time.

He has the one essential attribute: a sensitive nose. He can almost always sniff out a story that's turning bad for the government long before putrefaction sets in, and that means there is at least a chance of wrapping it up in cling film and burying it somewhere out of harm's way before the pong reaches the noses of the voters. He knows how the media operates and he knows that what we want most of all is an endless stream of new stories. However good a story, it has a limited shelf life. I can recall only one story in my whole career that has stayed on the front pages and at the top of all the main television and radio bulletins week in, week out, from beginning to end and that was the Falklands War. Even the death of Diana began to move down the running orders after the funeral had taken place, massive though the coverage was for that first week.

So a good new story will always trump a slightly better old story, and Campbell and his team are masters at feeding us with something new either to push a troubling old story out of the headlines or to get two bites at the publicity cherry. The first is when the announcement is leaked to one or two sympathetic Sunday papers, perhaps, and the second is when the announcement is actually made in the House of Commons.

A word of warning: never believe politicians when they protest about leaking. They all do it. When it is done against them by their political opponents it is a serious attack on the very existence of our parliamentary democracy. When they do it to their opponents it is always entirely justified to alert the public to a serious attack on – yes, you've got it – the very existence of our parliamentary democracy. When they do it themselves to get more publicity it is a service to public accountability.

One essential attribute for the successful spin doctor is a willingness to bully. The best technique for dealing with bullies is to tell them to get lost. Not that it's always easy for a young political correspondent whose job depends on providing his hungry newspaper with fresh and tasty morsels of political news every day. There he is, sitting alone and defenceless at his computer keyboard in some sordid, overcrowded Westminster press room wondering where his next story is coming from when a rather shabbily dressed character with a broken nose and aggressive attitude comes sidling up.

'Just a little word in your shell-like,' whispers the spin doctor, 'abaht that story in your first editions wot seemed to say our glorious government is less than kosher in every respect. The Big Man is not pleased. Not pleased at all. Now we wouldn't want to see your nice little kiddies going hungry next month if somefing nasty was to 'appen to your job, would we? Nah, course we wouldn't. So just a bit of friendly advice ... watch it next time! Stay lucky ... eh?' And with that he picks up the baseball bat that he left casually lying across the desk, accidentally knocking a cup of coffee into the reporter's lap, scratches his bent nose and ambles off, his large knuckles trailing along the ground.

The reporter would like to say, 'Sod off!' but it takes a little courage. It is easier for people like me. The spin doctors might occasionally suggest a line of questioning or even – on rare occasions – tell us what we ought to be saying in our introductions. It is not unknown for them to phone up afterwards to complain. Sometimes they have a point. The correct response is usually to listen politely and take careful note. Sometimes the correct response is 'Sod off!' But then, we do not rely on the spin doctors to the same extent as our colleagues in the lobby, except in one important respect and that is access. If we do not have the politician to interview we cannot do our job.

Every political interviewer, without exception, wants the big interview. I can still recall the buzz when the phone rang to say that John Major had chosen *On the Record* for his big interview at a moment of his greatest crisis or when Alastair Campbell invited us to Chequers to interview Tony Blair at the height of the Formula One affair.

Because there are now so many different programmes on a Sunday, each with its different style of interviewing, the spin doctors – sometimes under orders from their ministerial masters – can punish and reward as they see fit. In more than two years Robin Cook, for instance, never once found the time to be interviewed by me for *On the Record*. Too busy perhaps? Possibly, but he managed to fit in fourteen appearances for *Breakfast with Frost* during that same period. David Frost has had a brilliant career in television and we owe him a debt of gratitude for his irreverent approach to politicians in the sixties and, later, some superb, tough interviewing. But I disagree profoundly with what he told Lynda Lee-Potter in an interview for the *Daily Mail*. He said people 'have a right to come well out of a programme, whatever the private thoughts of the interlocutor'.

Of course it is true that the 'interlocutor's' private thoughts should not count for a row of beans, but why on earth do people 'have a right' to come well out of it? Surely that depends on how well they have acquitted themselves, whether they have answered the questions convincingly or, at least, made an honest stab at it. To suggest otherwise is to regard the interview as an opportunity for the interviewee to burnish his or her image.

I dare say that many politicians would agree with Frost, though. Too many politicians – by no means all – regard a television interview purely as a PR opportunity, rather than a chance to have their policies tested in vigorous discussion. If, as I have argued, broadcasting is now the space of politics, that is regrettable. The more the broadcasters offer the politicians the chance to sit on a comfy sofa instead of a hard chair, the more the politicians and their media managers will take it. And the more we move from a politics of argument to a politics of image manipulation.

Campbell seemed to be taking another step in that direction when he threatened to bypass the national press altogether because, he said, it is obsessed with 'trivia, travel expenses, comment and soap opera'. There is nothing new in party leaders trying to deliver their message direct to the voters without the newspapers getting in the way. American presidents have had their 'fireside chats' for decades and Harold Macmillan tried it here at the end of the fifties. Most prime ministers have had their favourite programmes; Jimmy Young was Margaret Thatcher's. What Campbell wants us to do is make more use of unedited live broadcasts and House of Commons statements. He has sometimes favoured gentle chat shows that don't normally deal with politics, where the Prime Minister would be interviewed by people who may be less inclined to press them hard.

Most of the time the cosier interview suits the politicians well. They can make controversial claims and statements without being pressed too hard and generally come across as pretty genial coves making the best of a difficult brief. They will frequently play up the risks of soft interviewing – easy, they say, to get lulled into a sense of false security and let something slip – but then they would, wouldn't they? For the broadcaster it is tempting to collude with the politicians and their spin doctors but, since television is now the space where political argument should happen, it is short-changing the audience. The risk is that the space of politics becomes drained of substance.

But they don't get it all their own way. I cannot tell you the joy that suffused every political correspondent in Westminster after Tony Blair appeared on the Richard and Judy show on ITV. This was meant to show us cynical hacks that the government could get its message across perfectly well without us chipping away in our sneering fashion. So what happened? Mr Blair was asked some deeply embarrassing questions about his wife's thighs (as displayed on holiday) and put his foot in it by saying Glen Hoddle ought to resign as England's football coach if he had made the comments attributed to him in a *Times* interview. He had. The interview proved to be a total PR disaster, not least when Downing Street was accused of doctoring the transcript to remove one word in reply to the Hoddle question. The word was 'Yes'.

The dangers of populist political journalism were spotted some time ago by a man who was to become the most famous political correspondent in the country but who, on the face of it, was totally unsuited to television. When John Cole, the first political editor of the BBC to become a household name, finally retired and took his truly awful overcoat with him there was not an impressionist in the land who did not reach for the bottle to drown his sorrows. Rory Bremner, the master, was distraught.

It had fallen to me as the presenter of the *Nine O'Clock News* at the time, to introduce John, fresh from Fleet Street, to some of the mysteries of television. My editor waylaid me one afternoon after a reasonable lunch and said, 'You'll never guess who they've appointed political editor. Take him into the studio and see if he can read from an autocue.' Two hours later the boss was shaking his head and muttering: 'It'll never work, it'll never work. They won't understand a bloody word he says. He'll be a sodding disaster.'

How wrong can you be. The audience may indeed have had some difficulty with John's impenetrable accent – I once edited an interview he'd done with me in which he kept having the tape replayed because even he had a problem making out one particular phrase – but it did not stop him becoming a great communicator. He might have been wont to say 'bock-buncher' instead of backbencher, but his meaning was always crystal clear and he had a passion for politics and a depth of knowledge that shone through everything he did. Far from being a sodding disaster, John Cole was a huge success. But this is what he wrote about political coverage in his autobiography after his retirement:

> What worries me is that collectively we may all . . . have spoiled the public appetite for serious politics, delivered comparatively straight . . . if you produce cream cakes at the beginning of a meal, children are unlikely to take much interest in their bread-and-butter or meat and vegetables. Have we tried so hard to make public affairs appetising that we have destroyed the palate of adults for more nourishing fare?

Ever since television started becoming important in politics, sharp-witted politicians have realised its power to create the right image. Way back in 1964, Harold Wilson was kicking a football around with a few cheerful kids on a housing estate for the television cameras while his opponent, Sir Alec Douglas-Home, was shooting grouse on a Scottish moor. Wilson was adjusting his own image to suit what he thought the voters wanted. We all remember how, rather than smoke a cigar in public, which he much preferred, he would light up a pipe. It served two purposes: it made him look like a typical down-to-earth Yorkshire lad and it was a valuable prop in live interviews. When he got a particularly nasty question and needed thinking time he'd pull the smelly old thing out of his pocket and start tamping away, for all the world as if he were enjoying a diverting chat in his local, when in fact he was thinking: 'Oh, bugger, how do I get out of this one?'

That seems pretty basic stuff today. Now image is deemed to be so important in politics that almost everything else is geared towards its manipulation. Margaret Thatcher listened very carefully when she became leader of her party to men like Sir Gordon Reece who told her she had to change her image for television. Reece – a dapper little man who smoked large cigars and appeared to eat nothing but steak and drink nothing but champagne – recognised immediately that she'd have to do something about the way she looked and, much more importantly, the way she sounded. Margaret Thatcher at full blast was perfectly capable of stopping a charging bull in its tracks, which was all very well for the hustings or the House of Commons but wouldn't do at all in the intimacy of a television studio. So they went to work on her and produced a softer, gentler Thatcher. Not that soft, and not that gentle, though.

I caught the sharp edge of the old Thatcher when I interviewed her after a European summit meeting in Maastricht – the first of the summits in that delightful little town. It was getting perilously close to my satellite feed time and when she arrived in the room where we'd set up our cameras I was beginning to panic a little. The great lady, flushed with the effort (enjoyable, no doubt) of hand-bagging other prime ministers and presidents and demanding they give her back her money, settled herself in the chair in front of the camera. She fished in her handbag and produced a powder compact. I wriggled impatiently – as impatiently as I dared – and muttered something about being terribly tight for time.

'Yes, yes,' she said, 'but I really must do my face. It's very hot in here and I must look simply awful.'

Then I made a very silly mistake. I forgot, for a fraction of a moment, that she was not just the Prime Minister but that she was a woman too.

'Oh no, Prime Minister,' I protested. 'You don't look too bad.'

Bernard Ingham, her formidable press secretary, was standing behind her and, even as I said it, I saw his eyes go up to the ceiling and his lips move in a little prayer. A prayer for me, innocent fool that I was.

'Oh!' she said, her voice rising and her eyes flashing and her handbag wrist twitching, 'Not too bad! Not too bad! How *very* gallant!'

You had to be there to appreciate the horror of it. I don't

remember what she said in the interview. I don't believe I heard a word of it.

I heard from the good lady again a few years later when I was presenting *Today*. It was about 6.45 in the morning and I had just finished doing an interview with the Soviet spokesman Gennadi Gerasimov when the producer spoke into my headphones.

'It's Thatcher on the phone!' he bawled. Oh sure, I thought, and I suppose the Queen is waiting on the other line and President Reagan has been told to ring back later because we're busy. I considered the matter carefully and, because the microphone was live and I couldn't speak, I gave him a little sign to show I'd heard him: I raised two fingers in the time-honoured salute when somebody is trying to wind you up.

'She bloody well is!' he screamed again and, a few seconds later, there she was and I heard myself saying, 'Good morning, Prime Minister.'

I learned later that she'd been making a cuppa in the kitchen of Number Ten when she heard the Gerasimov interview, didn't like what he had to say, and phoned the programme to put it right. Lucky for her, I thought, that the producer who picked up the phone and heard a familiar voice saying, 'This is the Prime Minister. Please put me through to Mr Humphrys,' did not assume that it was a hoax. I can think of many (myself included, I dare say) who'd have answered, 'Sure, and I'm the Shah of Iran,' told her to clear off and gone back to reading the paper. Sir Bernard Ingham was as surprised as we were. He told me years later that he'd been driving in to work listening to the programme, heard Gerasimov and was thinking 'I suppose we'd better put out a line on that', when his boss came on live.

'I nearly drove off the bloody road,' he said.

It is hard to imagine a modern leader doing what Thatcher did without consulting their spin doctor. She was primarily a politician of the old school – the school of Powell, Foot, Benn – who were in politics to have the argument, to persuade by making a case even if they failed, as so many did. What is alarming about the trend of politics in our television-dominated era is that increasingly politicians are abandoning the notion of politics being a battle of ideas and arguments within a debating context and seeing it primarily as a competition about image. Marketing replaces debate. As Manuel Castells puts it, the domination of the media 'means that the entire political debate has been transformed from a debate on issues to one of credibility and personality. Media politics have to be personalised because the simplest message is an image, and the simplest image is a person.'

The effect of marketing replacing debate is that voters come to be treated less as citizens and more as consumers; political parties become like companies with a product to sell rather than forums within which arguments can be had and interests represented. In short, politics becomes another part of the consumer populist world. For evidence of that, look no further than Philip Gould's book *The Unfinished Revolution: How the Modernisers Saved the Labour Party*. As Dennis Kavanagh, the Professor of Politics at Liverpool University, says, 'It should be read by anyone who wants to understand British politics today.' Gould and his views on how to do politics in the media age were instrumental in winning Tony Blair a majority of 179 in the 1997 election.

Philip Gould describes himself as a political strategist and he has been a supporter of the Labour Party since he was in short trousers. But his first real job was in advertising, his interest in marketing, and his whole approach is from the point of view of selling a product. He learned how to sell a political party by helping with the Clinton campaign in 1992. Now he's in business with two big cheeses from that campaign, the strategist James Carville, who ran Clinton's campaign, and Stan Greenberg, Clinton's pollster. Their firm works for big corporations, which suggests that similar selling techniques can now be transferred between politics and business. His book sets out the steps in the strategy. It's worth looking at what he says to see how extensively the techniques of commercial marketing are now synonymous with political strategy.

First, Labour needed a new product. In 1992 Labour was, in Gould's view, 'unelectable'. The public simply did not want to buy what it was selling. So the memos with which he bombarded Tony Blair and Peter Mandelson were about the need to offer a new product. The result they all arrived at was 'New Labour'. But what should it be? The answer came from targeting the part of the market that needed to be persuaded to buy the new product – voters who had voted Tory in 1992 but might be tempted to switch to Labour – and market-testing the new product on them before it went public. This was done through opinion polling and through the famous focus groups – lots of different groups of eight voters picked by market research teams, but all of them men and women who had voted Tory in 1992 but who were now 'floating'. Hundreds of those focus groups were held between 1994 and the election three years later. During the campaign itself they were conducted every night. What the focus group did was talk, and what they had to say affected what the new product should be and how it should be marketed.

They did not design it themselves, but they provided the market information about what would sell and what would not. So the product was shaped to suit the most important key potential purchasers. The cynical interpretation is that policies and positions were dumped not because they were thought to be wrong but because they were thought to be unsaleable. The strategists' view is that if you are not offering the public what it wants you might as well pack up and go home. If they don't like you and your policies they won't vote for you, so you must find out what they like and give it to them.

It's not just what they like but *who* they like. Remember that Castells comment: 'The simplest message is an image and the simplest image is a person.' Philip Gould and his marketing men knew that very well. That's why 'people metering' was invented in the United States. If the party did not have the right leader you'd have a much more difficult job selling the rest of the product. So the 'people meter' is a useful tool. Groups of people sit around watching a television set and use dials to respond instantly to whatever politician is speaking. The meter shows how 'warmly or coolly' they respond to what's being said and who's saying it. Gould describes how all the Shadow

Cabinet were tested back in 1990 'and the person who scored highest was Tony Blair. Even when he was faltering or not at his best, the line would shoot up when he started to speak.' During the leadership election in 1994 Gould conducted focus groups in which television clips of Blair were played to the group on video. 'Before television exposure Tony Blair was "liked and considered a different sort of politician", although some – particularly men – thought he was too young. However, exposure to Blair on television transformed perceptions. They like him, "his charisma, his message of pulling together, and the sense of a new kind of politics. And a new politician."'

So, once you've developed your product you have to set about selling it. At this point you and I might talk about advertising slogans. Gould talks of 'message development', the rationale that underpins your campaign. It is your 'central argument, the reason you believe the electorate should vote for you and not your opponents'. So what was that message? Gould reminds us: 'Enough is enough; Britain deserves better; people not privilege; future not the past; leadership not drift; the many not the few.'

Again, you might think those are pretty simple points, the sort of thing you might dream up over a few pints of decent beer in the local and then, in the morning, wince a little at the banality of some of it. Have you ever heard a politician say, 'past not future'? But you and I would be wrong. They took, says Gould, years to develop and they were 'compelling to the electorate'. Well you can't argue with that. Labour won by a massive majority. Nor can you deny the impressive attention to detail. Gould recounts the launch of a new document 'New Life for Britain' in July 1996, and how he and Mandelson sat up all night proof-checking it. 'The most difficult decision was whether or not to include stakeholding as a section heading. 'Stakeholding had fallen out of fashion somewhat, but for reasons of continuity we felt it better to keep it in.' That phrase 'fallen out of fashion' speaks volumes.

So you have the product and you have the message. Now you have to 'make an offer'. You know the sort of thing. A car manufacturer builds the car and advertises it and then, when you go into the showroom, they make you an offer. 'Tell you what, sir, you won't get a better deal than this anywhere in London and if you sign up now you'll be getting a three-year guarantee and free air conditioning.' Gould pays tribute to a colleague, Peter Hyman.

'We needed to give people an offer. We needed to get people to say, "I want that; I will go out and vote for that." ... Hyman's relentless pursuit of populist communications paid off.' The result was the five 'early pledges'. They had, of course, been fully market-tested through the focus groups and they were printed on little cards the size of a credit card. Every supporter and candidate was supposed to have one on his person at all times and the promise was simple: if we don't deliver, chuck us out.

Matthew Parris, *The Times* columnist and former Tory MP, captured the flavour of this approach: 'Manifestos begin to resemble those miracle cures for baldness: money back if we fail to please, letters from satisfied customers available for inspection.'

Now the candidates, the politicians themselves, come onto the scene. They have the product to sell and they must set about selling it. The problem with politicians – whatever evidence you may think there is to the contrary – is that they are people. And people are all different, with different likes and dislikes, different views and opinions, even if they agree broadly with a particular philosophy. New politics does not allow for those differences. Hence the bleepers, the pagers, the autospeak, and the impossibility at times of conducting an intelligent interview. Were there still independent minds there to interview?

So, the turning of politics into a marketing process is a seam-less operation. You fashion a new product according to your own values but also, essentially, according to market research about which product will generate the biggest profit (votes); you create an advertising campaign (message) based on market testing, heavily dependent on image (the leader) and emotional triggers. Then you make an offer (a bargain) with a sort of money-back guarantee. Then you manipulate the media to deliver the message supported by commercials based (as with conventional ads) on the belief that attention spans are short.

But in the process of all this the political party may begin to change its nature too. Instead of being a democratic forum of argument as well as of campaigning, it becomes more like a commercial company, driven from the top. Companies have mission statements, a structure to make sure the staff are obedient to the company's commands, systems to keep them all on message, an emphasis on corporate identity. A successful modern political party operates in much the same way. The Conservatives even created a 'Chief Executive' – a title first held, appropriately enough, by a businessman turned politician.

When a company holds a conference for its senior staff it expects them to behave. If the big boss agrees to take questions he will allow his subordinates to show a little independence of mind – but only a very, very little. Democracy is not allowed. So it is now at the conferences of the two big parties. The Tories have always preferred a rally to show the party faithful cheering their leaders, rather than a genuine, policy-making forum. The Labour Party has moved the same way. Their conference is, in theory, the supreme policy-making body. That has never been true in reality. The delegates were allowed to ban as many bombs and soak as many rich as they wanted, just so long as everyone knew the leadership wouldn't take a blind bit of notice. Now there's scarcely even the pretence of policy making.

Philip Gould himself argued for a party structure more like that of a company in a memo written in the early days. He wrote: 'Within the context of a new unitary command structure, the organisation must become flexible, responsive and innovative. It needs fewer people but better people; it needs flatter management structures; it needs a new culture of rewarding risk and excellence.'

All of this is much more than a new way of fighting and winning elections. It is changing the relationship between us – the voters – and them. To use Gouldspeak: 'In a media age, new forms of dialogue must be created.' He does not see focus groups and market research as mere campaigning tools. Increasingly he sees them 'as an important part of the democratic process: part of a necessary dialogue between politicians and people, part of a new approach to politics'. You may note that his book is called *The Unfinished Revolution*. Peter Mandelson went further in a speech in Germany in 1998. He said that 'the era of representative democracy may be coming to an end', and spoke approvingly of it being superseded by a politics of referendums, focus groups, lobbies, the Internet etc. He went on to say that people 'have no time for a style of government that talks down to them and takes them for granted . . . Today people want to be more involved.' But that raises the question of what involvement really means.

Certainly it is right that politicians should pay close attention to what we think, but who are 'we'? Which of us should they listen to, since we don't all think the same thing? The political technicians and strategists are now adept at identifying the relatively small number of people who can swing an election and put their clients in power, and they are the people they will listen to most carefully. All of Gould's focus groups consisted only of people who had voted Tory in 1992 and had become 'floaters'. So no one else gets a look in. The influence of relatively small groups of 'swing' voters may be disproportionate to their size. That's why representative democracy matters. It allows people who think something else to elect representatives who can voice what they think. It allows politicians who think the focus groups may have got it wrong to say so. That's why the German politician Wolfgang Schauble rejected Mandelson's line, saying that a politics of focus groups and referendums amounted to an 'abdication of responsibility'.

When Kenneth Clarke gave the Brian Redhead Memorial Lecture in 1999 he lamented the way things are going. He recounted a conversation with an extremely senior American statesman who told him that politicians still sought his advice. 'But,' he said, 'they don't any longer ask me what I think they ought to do; all they appear to want to know is what they ought to say.' Clarke said that told us a lot about what is happening to the parties in Britain and he went on:

> Good government does not depend on image: good government depends on a rather simple thing – taking the right decisions as often as you can. After you have taken a decision, decide how you are going to present and explain it. Do not put it the other way round. Do not begin with 'what shall we say?' and allow that to dictate what you should do to get the right headlines. Your press officer cannot govern the country and get away with it for more than a few months.

The notion of a press officer governing the country is a typically colourful one from a politician like Clarke, who is not himself entirely oblivious to his own public image, but who has a healthy contempt for the new political technicians.

> I do not wear a bleeper with a little screen on which the line of the centre is communicated to all. I refuse to repeat slogans, though all the experts say it is the key to political success. I hate focus groups. I absolutely hate image consultants: anybody looking at me can see that. And of course I hate spin doctors. I resist all these techniques, not because I have become a crusty old fool but because I think they are useless – indeed, worse than useless. I think they are dangerous – and suffocating our politics.

I suspect Clarke is engaging in wishful thinking when he says these techniques are useless. He would like to believe that because he prefers the older politics that is more about argument and less about competition between image manipulators. He is not alone. None of us likes to think we are being manipulated, treated as mass consumers of politics who can be sold a product by the image men, rather than as individual citizens. It may be that much of what we end up buying is what we would have chosen anyway, but that is not the point. The democratic process is at its healthiest when the argument is at its liveliest.

But it is surely mistaken to say the techniques are useless. Any party leader who looks at the size of the Labour majority in 1997 and the sheer coherence of Gould's analysis of politics in the television age is unlikely to come to that view.

Clarke is right, though, about them suffocating our politics. The danger is that the new politics is not so much democracy as populism. Gould himself speaks of 'a new populism'. In crude terms the difference is that in representative democracy politicians stand for what they believe in and try to persuade people to vote for them through the force of their arguments. In populism, it's the other way about: politicians stand ready to offer people whatever they might want so long as those are the people who can put them into power. It takes us away from a politics of argument to what Matthew Parris calls 'windsock politics'. If the wind is blowing too fiercely in the wrong direction politicians do not have the argument – they just watch which way the wind is blowing.

A good example of the retreat from argument might be whether Britain joins the Euro. It is, by any standards, a profoundly important issue; many believe it to be *the* most important since the war. But at the time of writing there is relatively little national debate about it. In the summer of 1999 I chaired a conference on behalf of a large national organisation who wanted to stage a debate with the pros and the antis arguing the toss, but none of the leading lights in the pro lobby would come. The government says we will not join the Euro without having a referendum and then there will be plenty of time to have the debate. But if the referendum were to be delayed until the government were sure that entry was inevitable, the debate might become meaningless and the suspicion might arise that we were being taken in by stealth. Potential Labour voters may have been sending the government a message about the non-debate when so many of them abstained at the 1999 elections to the European Parliament.

In any democracy there is always a balance for politicians to strike between pushing an argument and trying to win votes. But everything – the way politicians are behaving and the way the media is treating them – is tilting that balance. It is tilting it away from argument and towards marketing and PR; away from democracy towards populism; away from treating us as citizens towards regarding us as consumers. In that world our votes become the equivalent of the cash we pour into the shopkeeper's till.

The French philosopher de Tocqueville said in the last century that if despotism were ever to establish itself in modern, democratic societies, it would be 'more extensive and more mild; it would degrade men without tormenting them'. In almost every respect our democracy is infinitely more healthy than it was when de Tocqueville wrote that, but we are degraded if we are manipulated as consumers in a market. Real citizenship is about being participants in an argument. If all the politicians are interested in doing is offering us reassuring images of the leader and seducing us with facile slogans, then political argument will be pushed aside to the margins. Sooner or later, we will no longer have a choice between parties and principles but merely between managers. If we are not careful the media, responding to the tug of commercialism on its leash, will simply aid that process. What has been fought for over generations may slip slowly away.

Those who have no great interest in Party politics – and that is most of us – may lose no sleep over this, at least not unless things start going wrong. Neither will those who are broadly happy with the way things are at the moment. But for many others it's bad news, especially for those who are unhappy with the culture of consumer populism. If politicians set their compasses according to the pull of that culture there is little point in looking to them to do anything about it. So where do we look?

Chapter 13

The dissident citizen

WE TAKE SOME terrible liberties with our long-suffering interviewees on programmes like *Today*. There they are, poor souls, having done their damnedest to get their argument across in the face of various provocations, battered and bleeding and begging to be allowed out of the studio to go home to their loved ones to recuperate and be assured that they have not totally destroyed their careers and reputations, when we ask the last question.

'Finally, and very briefly, could you please explain the reasons for the outbreak of the First and Second World Wars and what the nations of the world must do if future generations are to live in peace and prosperity. In just fifteen seconds if you would please . . .'

It takes them at least ten seconds to recover from the question and by the time they're beginning to stammer out a tentative sentence or two we're at it again. 'Sorry, we've run out of time.'

I dream of a special chair for presenters. The seat would be fitted with an audio sensor and a pair of electrodes. Every time the presenter spoke the words 'Finally and briefly' the electrodes would deliver a powerful electric shock to the most sensitive part of the anatomy. Occasionally it would also deliver a shock to the chair of the producer or editor who decided that two minutes was enough time to do the interview in the first place. But mostly the presenter is to blame for the crass question. The day after the elections for the Scottish Parliament I heard an interviewer *begin* by asking the politician to explain his position 'very briefly please'. It's not as if it works. There are probably only half a dozen interviewees who even register that the 'and briefly' demand has been made and if they do they probably say to themselves, 'I've come here to give my views and I'm going to bloody well give them and if you've run out of time that's your problem.' They're right about that. It is. But anyway, what is 'brief'? To a professional broadcaster it's probably a couple of sentences; to an academic who is expert in his field it's more likely to be a chapter of closely argued text and to a politician it's a party political broadcast that lasts as long as he reckons he can get away with. So we shouldn't do it.

But I wish I could do it now. I wish I could say: 'Well, that's my book almost written and I'm afraid I've run out of time. Until the next one . . . good morning.' But you can't do it with a book, can you? It must have a beginning, a middle and an end. I've tried to explain why I decided to write this book in the first place. I've tried to explain my worries about the direction we've been taking over the past forty years, and I've tried to say what I think has been pushing us down that route. Now I have to bring it to an end by saying what I think should be done about it if we do not like it, my Grand Solution to Everything. There's a slight problem here. I don't have one. My excuse is that it does not exist.

There are societies in which it might, in which orders would be issued and prohibitions would be enforced, making life very nasty for those who didn't want to toe the line. For some people that is the appeal of fundamentalism today: get yourself a tough, hard-line force to impose a moral code and everything will be all right again. But for most of us the Taleban, or even the version of fundamental Christianity that is now so fashionable in many states below the Mason–Dixon line in the United States, are not an attractive option. Whatever the problems of today's world, being able to think for yourself and say what you like are benefits too great and too hard fought for to throw away just because we've hit the problem of a responsibility-lite society.

So what we have in place of the Grand Solution is a continuing, unresolved argument in which the old authorities and former élites are now just voices among many who find it increasingly difficult to get a hearing. See how today we smile indulgently at the dear old Church of England. It is trying so desperately to convince us it still has a job to do while, at the same time, turning to focus groups to find out what its 'customers' want and glancing nervously at the breakaway cliques who manage to fill their pews with happy clappers and strange people who speak in tongues. That does not mean that the church no longer has anything worthwhile to say; it means that it is now just part of the general conversation. That is all any of us can be.

What has happened to the Church of England is evidence of the evaporation of old, relatively benign, authority. The new authority is more insidious, more intangible. Its name, as I have been suggesting throughout this book, is consumer populism. What else has such a great influence in shaping our outlook on the world, in affecting our behaviour, and in determining what we value? You might think consumer populism is value-free, morally neutral, or bankrupt even, but it has its values all right. There is only one measure of success: does it sell?

In the art world Damien Hirst became the great British figure of the last decade of the twentieth century for that very reason: he sold. His most famous works may have been idiotic, exploitative, nihilistic nonsense, but some powerful people with much more money than sense or taste paid a fortune to buy them. Thus they were talked about. Thus they sold for even more money. Thus Hirst became an even greater artist. If any small boy dares shout that the emperor has no clothes he is condemned as a philistine. Who is he to argue with the market? Artists have always had their patrons but it used to work differently. A rich man might have chosen to support a Michelangelo or a Beethoven because he saw some intrinsic value in his work and his support enabled the genius to flower. There is all the difference in the world between that and an artist such as Hirst achieving greatness largely by virtue of a wealthy speculator investing in his work.

By the end of the century we are being asked to believe that shopping centres are no longer shopping centres. 'You get one chance in your life to build a great city,' says the architect Eric Kuhne, 'and I have done it.' His 'great city' is the Bluewater shopping centre in Kent, a massive monument to consumption. The managing director sometimes refers to himself as 'Mayor'. Where you or I might talk about shopping Mr Kuhne talks about 'the beginning of a new era ... the restoration of the robust vitality of civic life'. And, again, nobody laughs at him or says the emperor has no clothes. How could they, because Bluewater is all about consumption on the grandest scale imaginable, beyond ridicule. The idea that spending money in the sterile setting of a modern shopping centre somehow restores the vitality of civic life is simply breathtaking. Yet as a symbol of our new values it cannot be faulted.

For a little more evidence of the authority that consumer populism casts over us, return with me for a moment to my local supermarket. There you will find the long queue waiting to buy its Lottery tickets. I do not like the strip club that now graces my neighbourhood, nor the empty shops which are boarded-up victims of the mighty supermarket. I do not like the queue for the Lottery either. For every person in this queue who looks as if he or she is going to spend a pound or two for a bit of fun, there are several more for whom it is demonstrably no fun at all. There are many drawn faces here, poorly dressed women with a couple of fidgety kids at heel who want desperately to win. More than that, they need to win. This is their way out of whatever miserable penny-pinched life they may inhabit. Millions of us may throw our useless ticket away at nine o'clock on a Saturday or Wednesday night with a curse and a laugh; these people will curse but will not laugh. And they will try again and again with money they can ill afford. The Lottery queue is a depressing sight.

There are few things that illustrate better than the Lottery

how our attitudes to life in Britain have changed. Forty years
ago there was trouble enough introducing premium bonds.
Many an indignant bishop denounced them as a moral
outrage: disgraceful that the state should encourage gambling.
But it was only just gambling; you could always get your stake
back again if you lost and not many bookies make that offer.
The Lottery could scarcely be more different. This is a pure
gamble: vast prizes, but odds outrageous enough to make a
bookie blush. And what did the bishops of today say about
this? Not a lot. A few clerics, mostly of the Nonconformist
variety, muttered uneasily on *Today*, but most rushed to their
desks to get their application forms in so that they might grab
a piece of the action when the booty was handed out. Some
defended it on the grounds that good causes would benefit.
Did they raise the roof when politicians started seizing the
cash to pay for things our taxes would once have financed?
They did not. Jesus was said to have thrown the money
changers out of the temple. When *Today* staged an
ecclesiastical lottery in a church most listeners failed to spot
the date: it was April 1st. A tiny handful were indignant that
the Church should have apparently embraced Mammon to
quite such an extent; most seemed unmoved.

Just as the great shopping centres have become the new
cathedrals of our age, so the Lottery is a variant on a religious
theme. The form of redemption offered by the Lottery is
utterly consistent with the underlying creed of consumer
populism: redemption through money, through getting
something for nothing. Redemption is also available through
celebrity, if that is what the winners choose. The dark side of
it, too, is consistent with the ethos of consumer populism. Loss
is so much more likely than gain. The image polishers talk up
the good causes and ignore the huge sums that go to the
organisers and back to the exchequer for general government
spending. There is an inequality: the poor become that little bit
poorer. And the final parallel is that it is an opiate: we have
become addicted to it, even though it is doing us no good.

In so many ways the Lottery perfectly reflects our emerging
values: instant gratification, reward without effort, the appeal

of living in a fantasy world. The operators of Camelot – the biggest winners of all – will say we have always been a nation of gamblers, have always enjoyed a flutter. No doubt. But this is different. Have you noticed how angry some people get because they have spent so much money and never won more than an occasional paltry tenner? It's not as if they did not know perfectly well how high were the odds stacked against them, but there is somehow a sense that it is their right to win. Others have so why shouldn't I?

It is easy to overlook the malign authority that consumer populism exerts over us – partly because it has been bred out of the most successful economic system the world has ever known, and which has given us much of what we genuinely do want, but also because we seem so ready to go along with it. That is the populism at work. Rory Bremner hides a sharp political brain behind his brilliant mimicry and he has written about the great cop-out of consumer populism. 'The People Have Spoken – and therefore there is no argument.' Richard Hoggart put it another way in his book *The Way We Live Now*. He wrote: 'The only standard is the echo back. If the roar of the crowd comes back, that is success, and so unanswerably right and good. This is the numbers game, a substitute for judgement, and the refusal to tangle with "better" or with "worse".'

If we want to tangle with better and worse, we are going to have to do the work ourselves. There is no possibility any more of looking outside ourselves for an authority to do the work for us, because the only authority there is not interested. We have to make the choices ourselves.

I had a lesson in choices a few years ago from what may seem an unlikely source and it happened, as it so often does, on *Today*. The question that *Today* presenters are asked more than any other (apart from 'What time d'you get up in the morning?' Answer: 'Too bloody early') is 'Who is the most difficult politician you have ever interviewed?' Enoch Powell is near the top of my list. I was scarcely out of short trousers when he made his infamous 'Rivers of blood' speech and it fell to me to interview him when he came to Liverpool a day or two later. I tried to expose his argument for the racist claptrap I then believed it to be. Let me offer a word of advice to all young reporters who are tempted to make a reputation for themselves by trying to be clever with an experienced politician who happens to possess one of the most brilliant minds of his generation and a ruthless debating skill to go with it: Don't.

I can still feel those unnaturally pale eyes boring through my skull as he took my pathetic attempt at an argument and, his flat monotone delivering one perfectly formed sentence after another, tossed it aside with contempt. It was like putting Mike Tyson in the same ring as Andy Pandy. I crawled away from the studio with my youthful dignity in tatters, a lot more humble and possibly a little wiser. But not enough; I forgot my own lesson and, many years later, tried something similar with another politician – the one at the top of my 'most difficult' list. Her name was Margaret Thatcher.

She was at the height of her powers, worshipped by her followers, feared by her opponents and she routinely ate interviewers for breakfast. She had come into the *Today* studio (prime ministers don't do that any more; we have to go to them) for what was to be one of her last interviews before a general election. I cannot tell you how soul-destroying it can be to interview a party leader at the end of the campaign. There is no question they have not been asked during the campaign, no answer they have not honed to repetitive perfection. So I thought I would be clever.

I had heard her being asked, some days earlier, about her faith; she is a church-going Christian. So I wondered how a tough, cynical, battle-hardened politician defined Christianity. Instead of asking her a routine question about how she could defend policies that had contributed to unemployment of more than three million, would it not be very clever to start the interview by asking her to define her own version of Christianity. I hoped, and believed, that she would be greatly surprised and mumble something about morality or love. Then I could pounce. 'Ah! You talk of love and you condemn millions to a life on the dole!' or something similar. You can see how naïve I was. In my dreams she would sob and beg forgiveness and I would be hailed as the great interviewer who had brought the iron lady to her knees. It did not work out quite like that. I confess I was nervous – she had that effect on all of us – but I knew that I was on to a winner here and I delivered my brilliant sucker punch with great panache.

'Prime Minister, what is the essence of Christianity?'

She did not miss a beat. Her eyes, hooded at the best of times, may have narrowed a fraction of a millimetre but the answer came out like a bullet.

'Choice!'

There are occasions as an interviewer when you pray that a great thunderbolt will strike the power supply that serves your studio and you will be wiped off the air . . . possibly even off the face of the earth. Or at the very least that something will happen to give you a few seconds to regroup your devastated forces and launch a counter-attack. This was one of those occasions but, sadly, there was no divine intervention. I gulped, tried to imagine what on earth she was getting at, and failed. The interview was indeed a triumph . . . for her. Thirty seconds too late I realised exactly what she meant and, dammit, she was right. The whole point of Christianity is that you have a choice between doing good and doing evil. If you end up in Heaven, that's because you made the right choice; if you end up in Hell, it's your own damn fault. So it was sound theologically and, from her point of view, just as sound politically. I resolved not to try to be too clever next time.

The problem with the way we live now is that we are discouraged by the culture of consumer populism from making responsible choices. We live in the blame society where it is usually someone else's fault. If we see ourselves as victims – which we do – we remain passive or we claim compensation because it simply cannot be our fault. Even when there is no one else to blame we find reasons to dodge our responsibility for our own actions: it's because of our environment, our background, our genes that we are as we are. Or we invent some sort of syndrome. The thuggish motorist who loses his temper and punches another driver in the face is the victim of 'road rage'. In a way we do not understand we persuade ourselves that perhaps it is not really his fault. With the lout who gets drunk on an aeroplane and assaults the young stewardess it is now 'air rage', possibly caused by the thinner oxygen he's been breathing. Or maybe because he was denied his right to smoke. Or maybe the meal was not to his liking. Anything but the obvious: he is a drunken lout who's probably been using his fists or a broken bottle to get his way all his misbegotten life.

We cannot be trusted to take responsibility for the things we do and we must be guided every inch of the way. In the end it all comes down to responsibility and making our own choices. A pretty obvious thing to say, I know, but the whole point of consumer populism is that it fights against the notion of individual responsibility.

To make profits, boost ratings, get our votes off us, it needs to turn us into zombies. It's not doing a bad job of it at the moment, and we have been going down this road for a relatively short time. A couple of generations is scarcely more than a blink of the eye in a nation's history. It could be that we are all perfectly happy with this direction, but the evidence of my own eyes and ears suggests otherwise. The old lady averting her eyes in my street from the offensive T-shirt has a right not to be ignored, as do the worried mothers and despairing teachers and many thousands of people who have written to me over the years, each with their own anxieties. We might say to them all, 'Look, things change. What do you want to do? Go back to the fifties with all its smug conformity and hypocrisy and intolerance?' But that is a pathetic response. They are entitled to say, 'No, but why must we accept that this is the only way to change?'

The answer is that we don't have to accept that. But the only way to do anything about it lies in our own hands. We have to dissent. We have to become dissidents.

It is in the nature of things, I suppose, that all societies ridicule those who are not afraid to be different. The early suffragettes were a fine music hall joke; today they are heroic figures. Their feminist descendants who wanted equality as well as the vote got the same treatment at the start of their campaign; it is a brave and foolish man who would argue against equality today. In the United States Ralph Nader was dismissed as an obsessive eccentric when he took on the might of the most powerful automobile company in the world because he said one of their cars was not safe. He won. Remember how we all chuckled away at the 'beards and sandals' weirdos, those sad characters who kept banging on about the need to get a bit closer to nature and worried about what the factory farmers were getting up to? They don't look quite so silly today as we prowl the supermarkets trying to find something to buy that hasn't been genetically modified or saturated with chemicals. As for Mary Whitehouse, she was the ultimate figure of fun, with her carefully permed hair and middle-class suburban values trying to tell us what we should and shouldn't be able to see on the sacred box. I wonder how many of us watch some of the meretricious, ratings-chasing rubbish that masquerades as adult entertainment today and suspect that perhaps – just perhaps – some of her worries might not have been entirely groundless.

You cannot, I accept, compare the fight for democracy with a campaign against smut on television but the factor that unites all those people is dissent. My own favourite dissenters are a small group of middle-aged men and women who happened, by chance, to find themselves living in the same corner of West Wales in the seventies. There was quite a little pilgrimage to West Wales in the late sixties and early seventies. Most went there, in the jargon of the day, to drop out. The magic mushrooms helped. They reasoned: why spend a fortune and risk PC Plod's hand on your shoulder buying wacky baccy when you could wander off into a field and pick your own happy potions. Not so Peter Seggar and Patrick Holden and one or two other immigrants. They bought farms – or shares in farms – and started growing organic food. It was a crazy thing to do. When I first met them I assumed they must have been sampling the odd magic mushroom themselves.

Seggar had worked for a large company in London, packed it all in because he tired of the rat race, and borrowed the cash for a few acres of stony ground with a tumble-down old house near Lampeter. Then he put up some polythene tunnels and started growing organic lettuces. Wiser heads pointed out that there was no market for organic lettuce or any of his other organic veg. They cost a fortune to grow because of all the labour involved and what was he going to do with them? That's assuming he ever managed to produce enough after all the bugs and the insects had spread the word that they could enjoy a fine feast without having to worry about life-threatening pesticides.

A few hilltops away Patrick Holden was trying to make a living from a dairy farm without using any chemicals. His neighbours told him it could not be done – especially on top of a Welsh hill where the soil was as thin as the hair on a prelate's pate and the wind was so strong the trees grew horizontally – and they shook their heads sadly when he took no notice. You needed to spread chemicals on the fields to grow enough grass to feed a herd of cows, they pointed out. You also needed to feed them concentrated protein, made from whatever the manufacturers fancied, to increase the yield to operate profitably. And when the cows got sick you needed chemicals to make them better. Cows get sick a lot when they're put under pressure to produce much more milk than their bodies were designed to deliver. Holden ignored all that. He figured that if forcing cows to produce too much milk made them sick, then the solution was not to force them and they wouldn't get sick so often. You'd get less milk, but it would be less costly to produce because you wouldn't have to keep sending fat cheques to the chemical companies, and the milk would be a lot more wholesome. The cows would be happier too. He took the same view of his land. If you did not force it to grow lots of grass by spreading chemicals it would eventually become healthier soil and healthier soil will eventually grow all the grass you need.

In another valley on another tiny farm a young Scot called Dougal Campbell was producing cheese from his own few cows without any chemicals. It was hellishly hard work, seven days a week – tending the fields, milking the cows, making the cheese – but Campbell used to climb difficult mountains for pleasure and he relished it.

They all relished it – even the crazy souls who tried growing vegetables in their unsuitable fields when they knew that if the insects didn't eat the young plants the weeds would end up choking them. I tried growing a field of carrots myself. It looked promising at first – millions of healthy little green shoots against the brown earth, holding out the promise of fine organic carrots in a few months' time. Then the weeds came and, because I was not allowed to spray them, I tried pulling them out by hand. The field was twelve acres. Picture a very large beach. Imagine that you have to clear the sand from the beach by crawling along and picking up one grain at a time. After half of one row I gave up, ploughed the whole lot in, and called myself a fool for ever trying in the first place.

The others didn't. They found better ways of getting rid of the weeds and scaring off the insects. They formed a co-operative to sell the carrots and anything else they could grow. It started with a few part-time workers in a muddy shed on a steep hillside and then Peter Seggar took it over. Now it is the biggest distributor of organic food in Europe with enormous, computerised packing warehouses all over the country. Seggar travels the world persuading farmers everywhere to grow organic produce.

You are able to buy organic food in every supermarket in the land today because of what people like Seggar and Holden and Campbell started in West Wales in the seventies. Holden himself took over the sleepy old Soil Association and transformed it into one of the most dynamic lobbying organisations in the land, which spreads the message and polices the organic system. When other small farmers are struggling to survive, his organic farm is prospering. His farming neighbours who laughed at him are now lining up to do the same as he did. Dougal Campbell was killed in an accident on his farm on a summer morning as he was about to set off to his beloved Swiss mountains for his first holiday in many years. He would have been proud of what has happened.

I tell their story at some length partly because I have great admiration for what they have achieved, but mostly because they bucked the system. They did what they did, in the face of the most appalling difficulties, because they thought it was right. The system told them they would never make it work, and they said to hell with the system. They dissented. That seems to me to be the responsible thing to do, especially when society is in thrall to consumer populism. For some people, either because of their temperament or their beliefs, dissidence has always seemed the responsible thing to do. For most people, though, responsibility has seemed largely synonymous with conforming to how society is. Try to make things better by all means, they say, but let us not risk too much by kicking against conformity. Such is the moral vacuum created by consumer populism that the opposite is true. To conform is to be irresponsible, and to be the responsible citizen is to be the dissident citizen.

Imagine this country today without the great dissidents of the past. No democracy, no workers' rights, no state education or state health care. No freedom. You may say, then, that most of the great battles have been won and perhaps that is true, but in a culture dominated by consumer populism there will always be a need for the dissident citizen. My own definition of what it is to be dissident is a broad one. It might just mean complaining when it is customary to keep your mouth shut. It might mean taking on the agro-chemical industry, one of the most powerful in the world, proving that it is possible to feed a growing population without polluting the environment, destroying the remaining natural habitats, and treating animals as you would a piece of machinery. It might mean a hundred and one other things. It always means arguing for the values that you think matter.

It may be that most of us are perfectly happy with the value-free state of consumer populism. There is an argument that says we have struggled for thousands of years precisely to achieve the state that people in the world's richest countries now find themselves in. We needed powerful moral and ethical codes to arrive at this; the great religions thrived because life was so hard. But now there is plenty to go around and the battle to survive in comfort and relative security has been won, so we can all relax and enjoy our prosperity. Let's polish our credit cards, switch on the latest docusoap and feel good about things. I believe that is not only defeatist but also dangerous. A state of complacent contentment produces apathy. If we take democracy for granted and cannot even be bothered to vote, then our leaders take us for granted.

A truly rich society is not concerned only with material prosperity but with what is now called 'social capital'. Society builds up its social capital when people become involved, when they take part in voluntary or civic activities, when they socialise with each other and learn to trust each other. One study, in Italy, showed that you could get a rough idea of how many people would vote in an election by counting the number of choral societies in that region. If there were a lot, the turnout would be high. If there were not, it would be low. Professor Paul Whiteley of Sheffield University has studied the impact of social capital on a country's economic performance and concluded that it appears to be quite strong.

Mine is not an argument for turning back the clock, returning to a mythical golden age, but nor do I accept the politicians' insistence that we must always embrace the 'modern'. Why is 'modern' always good? Why, when politicians seek to persuade us to vote for them, do they promise to create a 'modern' Britain, whatever that may mean? The truth is, it means nothing. Give me a choice between a 'modern' television set with its digital sound and brilliant picture and an ancient box with its flickering black and white images and I will choose the modern version. Give me a choice between some of the modern television programmes whose purpose is solely to shock in order to increase the ratings and serve only to coarsen life still further, and I will choose old-fashioned programmes in which producers had to rely on their creativity and imagination.

The past is not the only alternative to the modern. Suffragettes were not wanting to hark back to the past; they wanted to create something new. The opponents of dissent try to colonise the future. They claim that it is theirs, so that no one else is allowed to choose a different future.

The great lie of consumerism is that we are all entitled to our share of happiness and if it does not come to us naturally we can go right out there and buy it. The philosopher John Stuart Mill was brought up by his father on the principle that 'the greatest happiness of the greatest numbers' should govern human affairs and legislation. Mill was not persuaded by that and produced a different notion. He said, 'It is better to be a human being dissatisfied than a pig satisfied. And better to be Socrates dissatisfied than a fool satisfied.' They might not have invented consumerism when Mill scratched out those wonderful words a century and a half ago but they do – if you will forgive me for using the phrase – fit perfectly into a modern context. They should be inscribed on a plaque above the desk of every politician and populist in the land.

I began this forty-year trek on a tiny weekly newspaper in the seaside town of Penarth and I shall end it there, in the Holm Tower cancer hospice overlooking the grey waters of the Bristol Channel. My former wife had gone there to die and I went back to Penarth to be with her at the end. Her doctor was a young woman, not yet thirty, fiercely bright, articulate and attractive with a smile that lifted your spirits and the gravity of a woman twice her age. I can imagine nothing more soul-destroying than working in a hospice. Every patient has gone there to die and you know that, barring a miracle, nothing you can do will alter that. You will never have the joy of helping a baby to be born or a sick person get well again, let alone the glamour of so-called cutting-edge medicine and the prospect of a lucrative Harley Street practice in years to come. I asked the young doctor why she had chosen to work in a hospice and she seemed surprised by the question. 'It's a privilege,' she said. 'I know we can't cure the people who come here, but we can do so much to make the last stages of their life mean something. We can help people die at peace, without suffering more than they have to, and with some dignity.'

She paused and then said again, 'It means so much. It's a wonderful job.'

When you write the words down like that they look a little corny. They did not sound corny at the time. This was a patently good person who wanted to help, and that was that. A few weeks later I was back in the hospice again for the death that was inevitable.

She had only a few hours left and I sat in a corner of her large room as the sun went down. I have seen a great deal of violent death in my years as a foreign correspondent but this was peaceful death and I had never seen it before. In war the dying is surrounded by hate; here there was love. When the room was almost dark a nurse slipped in through the half-open door. She did not see me and stood for a few moments looking down at the dying woman. Then she leaned down and gently stroked her hair. And then she went out again. It was the most tender gesture I have ever seen, not least because it was a gesture of love for a woman she scarcely knew, who could not respond, in a place where death is the most regular of callers.

You may ask what any of this has to do with the theme of this book, apart from the entirely obvious point that there is a great deal of good as well as bad in any society. As I returned to the town where I began my story, so I return to the question I asked right at the beginning: are we happy with the direction we have taken as a society in the past forty years? You will know my answer if you have struggled this far: I am not, and I believe many people share my misgivings. But I do not want that to be the last word. Society is changing. Consumer populism cheapens, coarsens, makes false promises and offers phoney solutions and I think we should make a fuss about it. We should make dissent a habit. That hostel is able to do its wonderful work in part because a young doctor dissented and rejected the obvious career path.

We cannot – nor should we – rely on the old élites, nor seek a rigid new moral framework. We should certainly kick the backsides of the new élite, who cynically go along with consumer populism because they see it in their own interests to do so – not least those of us in my own trade of journalism who have an exalted notion of our own status. We need to be reminded that we are mirrors to reflect society as accurately as we can. We should not measure our worth in audience ratings.

We hacks are meant to ask the questions and not answer them, which is probably just as well. If the great philosophers have such problems defining what the 'good life' is we should certainly aim at more modest goals. One of them says the three major questions confronting every thinking person are: 'What can we know? What ought we to do? What can we hope for?'

This old hack dares to suggest a small part of the answer to the first question: each of us should know more than the system wants us to know. Then we can decide for ourselves whether we like it or not and whether we want to do something about it. One of the many illusions peddled by consumer populism is that there are guaranteed outcomes to everything, and that we need not bother ourselves thinking about the risks of failure. But there are no guaranteed outcomes in life. There were none for Patrick Holden or Peter Seggar or Dougal Campbell but they took the risk. For all the dissidents who have succeeded there have been plenty who have failed. The only thing we can choose is the route we take.

I can see no alternative to the dissident route and sooner or later we will find out whether it gets us where we might prefer to be. As a Welshman I am naturally pessimistic about outcomes, though not about people. So when it comes to hoping I am with the Italian Marxist Antonio Gramsci: pessimism of the intellect, optimism of the will. Or to put it in Welsh terms: just because the odds are against us it doesn't mean we shouldn't bloody well try.

Bibliography

John Cole, *As It Seemed to Me*, Weidenfeld & Nicolson, 1995
Nick Davies, *Dark Heart*, Chatto & Windus, 1997
Future Foundation, 'The Millennial Family', 1998
Oliver James, *Britain on the Couch*, Century, 1997
Christopher Lasch, *The Revolt of the Elites*, Norton, 1995
Sonia Livingstone and Moira Bovill, 'Young People, New
   Media', LSE, March 1998
Mental Health Foundation, 'The Big Picture', 1999
Bryan Rodgers and Jan Pryor, 'Divorce and separation: the
   outcomes for children', Joseph Rowntree Foundation, 1998
Michael Rutter and David Smith, *Psychosocial Disorders in
   Young People*, John Wiley, 1995
Richard Sennett, *The Corrosion of Character*, Norton, 1998

Acknowledgements

IT MAY BE the oldest cliché in the business, but I could not have written this book without the help of John Wakefield. He encouraged a semblance of order from the chaos that passes for my mental processes and made it possible for me to say what I wanted to say with more coherence than I would otherwise have managed.

Victoria Wakely convinced me that the Internet really does have a lot of useful material if you know where to look – and she did the looking.

Kathleen McGoldrick helped enormously to keep it all in order. My thanks to all of them.

My thanks also to Brian Appleyard, Angus Bancroft, Martin Bell, Mark Boleat, Kenneth Clarke, Theodore Dalrymple, Roy Porter, Polly Toynbee, George Walden and many others for writing and saying things that stimulated or infuriated me.